W9-BNK-342

"FIRST-RATE . . . IF JOSEPH WAMBAUGH HAD BEEN A DISTRICT ATTORNEY HE WOULD BE WRITING BOOKS LIKE *IMMORAL CERTAINTY*."
—*The Flint Journal*

"MEMORABLE . . . STOMACH-CHURNING . . . INTENSE." —*Kirkus Reviews*

"CRIME AND PUNISHMENT WITH A SAVAGE TWIST . . . A special treat for those who love police and murder-mystery stories mixed with high and shivery drama."
—*The Neshoba Democrat*

"BRILLIANT PERSPECTIVE!"
—*The San Diego Tribune*

"QUICK, COMPETENT WRITING THAT CAPTIVATES . . . conveys a sense of realism that places this book above others of its genre." —*The West Coast Review of Books*

# IMMORAL CERTAINTY

Robert K. Tanenbaum

A SIGNET BOOK

SIGNET
Published by the Penguin Group
Penguin Books USA Inc., 375 Hudson Street,
New York, New York 10014, U.S.A.
Penguin Books Ltd, 27 Wrights Lane,
London W8 5TZ, England
Penguin Books Australia Ltd, Ringwood,
Victoria, Australia
Penguin Books Canada Ltd, 10 Alcorn Avenue,
Toronto, Ontario, Canada M4V 3B2
Penguin Books (N.Z.) Ltd, 182-190 Wairau Road,
Auckland 10, New Zealand

Penguin Books Ltd, Registered Offices:
Harmondsworth, Middlesex, England

Published by Signet, an imprint of New American Library, a division of
Penguin Books USA Inc. Previously published in a Dutton edition.

First Signet Printing, April, 1992
10  9  8  7  6  5  4  3  2  1

*As always, for those most special,
Patti, Rachael, Roger, and Billy*

# CHAPTER
# 1

On a damp spring night in New York City in 197-, Patrolman Russell Slayton and his partner Jim Finney of the 114th Precinct, Queens, observed a man carrying a large plastic trash bag climbing out of a second-story window. They believed that they had probable cause to stop and question the man they suspected was in process of committing a burglary.

Slayton, the senior of the two men, told Finney to pull the patrol car over and stay put, get on the radio and tell the precinct what was going on. He then got out of the car, unbuttoning the retaining strap on his pistol and fixing it so that the butt protruded from the slit in his tunic. He left his nightstick in the car and took instead a six-cell flashlight. This was not the kind of flashlight you buy in the hardware store. It was the kind policemen buy in the special little shops that cater to the law enforcement trade. It was made out of the same quality aluminum alloy used in the skin of an airliner, with a double thickness at the head and an acrylic lens thicker than the bottom of a Coke bottle. Except that it lit up, Slayton's flashlight would not have been out of place at the battle of Agincourt.

Swinging this flashlight, Slayton walked toward the man, who had by this time descended the fire escape to the street. Ten years on the force and the butterflies were still flapping around in Slayton's belly.

The man looked around and spotted Slayton and the patrol car. Slayton tensed, but to his amazement, the guy waved cordially, shouldered his trash bag and started to walk away. He even smiled; Slayton could see the flash of his white teeth.

"Hey, you!" Slayton shouted. The guy kept walking. Slayton clicked on his flash and caught the man in its sharp beam.

"Stop right there, fella!" The man turned and pointed inquiringly at his chest, a look of surprise on his face. Slayton thought later that this was the time he should have pulled his gun out, but something about the man's appearance made him hesitate. He was well-built, fairly tall, good looking, and expensively dressed in a short leather jacket and tailored slacks. His dark hair was carefully barbered, and he appeared relaxed and confident, almost jaunty. And he was white. Slayton, who was black, didn't actually think of what would happen to him if he were to shoot some rich white dude involved in some suspicious-looking but actually innocent business in this quiet middle-class neighborhood, but he was aware of the consequences at some level of his consciousness.

He therefore did not pull his gun, nor did he shout "Yeah *you*, asshole, you see anybody else on the damn street?," which was what came first to his mind. Instead he said, "Ah, sir, if you could step over here, I need to ask you a couple of questions." The guy shrugged and approached Slayton.

"Sure, Officer, what's the problem?"

"Could I see some identification, please."

The guy put the trash bag down carefully, reached into his back pocket and brought out a wallet. He handed Slayton a Visa card and a Social Security card made out to James P. Otto.

Slayton examined the cards and handed them back.

"Mr. Otto, could you tell me what you were doing climbing out of that window just now?"

The guy smiled. "Yeah, well, it's a little embarrassing, Officer. That's my girlfriend's place. Ah, she's married to a guy who's on the road a lot. Actually, they're in the middle of breaking up. Well, tonight we were together and he buzzes up from downstairs. He just decided to come home. A panic—unbelievable! She's got to buzz him in, right? I mean, what else could she do? So, needless to say, I get dressed and go out the window."

"And what's in the bag?"

"Oh, that's my stuff—some shaving stuff, cologne, some clothes. Like I couldn't leave it there, you know?" He laughed. "Christ, I hope to hell I didn't forget anything."

"Mind if I take a look?"

"Sure, go right ahead."

Slayton knelt down, opened the bag and shined his light in. He saw several bulky objects wrapped in towels. He pulled on the material, which came away, revealing the dull sheen of an expensive stereo tuner. He reached further into the bag, felt something cold and hauled out a silver sugar bowl. He stood up quickly then, and as he did he saw the knife, glistening, impossibly huge, rushing towards his throat.

Slayton screamed a curse and brought up his left hand to protect himself. He still held the big flashlight and this is what saved his life as the keen blade chopped through the middle joints of his first two fingers, gouged the steel case of the flashlight, and buried itself in the meat of his left shoulder. He went down on one knee bellowing for Finney. The pain from his hand was staggering; it made him sick and weak. He fought the sickness and jammed his injured hand into his armpit to staunch the gush of blood. Everything was slowing down. He heard a car door open and a shout and running feet. He felt a blow against his back and a flood of warmth on his skin there. He went down on his face as he struggled to pull his gun from its holster. Breathing hurt. His cheek touched the damp pavement and he fainted.

Finney was out of the car the instant he saw Slayton go down, without pausing to call for backup. The man was ten yards ahead of him when he passed Slayton's prostrate form, but by the end of the block he had narrowed it to five. Finney held his own six-cell flashlight in his right hand as he ran, like the baton of a relay racer, which, a scant four years ago he had in fact been at Richmond Hill High School, and on a citywide championship squad at that. He was still in pretty good shape.

The two of them crossed the deserted intersection about six feet apart. The fleeing man snapped a look over his shoulder. Finney saw his eyes widen in surprise. The man put on a burst of speed and cut sharply right, as if he were a running back shaking a tackler. This proved to be a serious error, as the cop cut inside, reached out, and clocked the man across the base of the skull with his flashlight.

It was not a heavy blow, but Finney's flashlight was the same model as Slayton's and even a tap was enough to throw the man off balance. He caromed into a street sign, stumbled, and then Finney had a hunk of leather jacket in his left hand. The big flashlight came down on the man's head once, twice. After that, Finney had no trouble handcuffing the man's wrists together around a lamppost. Then he ran back to see about his partner.

After Slayton was rushed off by ambulance, and after the seven police cars that had responded to the "officer down" call had dispersed, they took the burglar back to the precinct and found, unsurprisingly, that he was not James Otto. His name was Felix M. Tighe, of Jackson Heights, in Queens. A local boy. They checked his name for criminal history, and were mildly surprised to find that he had no record. They booked him for burglary, felonious assault, resisting arrest, and attempted murder. Then they patched his head and put him in a cell.

Patrolman Finney stayed at Queens County Hospital until the surgeon came out and assured him that Slayton would see the dawn. Then he drove back to the 114th to make his report. He filled in his UF 8, the summary arrest card, turned it in, and then looked up the detective who had caught the case.

The detective, a slight, tired-looking man named Howie Frie, was filling out his own form, this one a DD5 situation report. He had already tagged the two major pieces of evidence—the big bloodstained knife and the bag of swag—and sent them to the lab for routine fingerprint and blood-type analysis.

Finney introduced himself as the arresting officer. Frie scowled. "Oh, yeah. How's your partner?"

"He'll live. His flash took some of the knife or the fucker would have sliced his head off. I never saw a blade like that before."

"Yeah, it's a real, what they call a bowie knife. A reproduction—not cheap either. By the way, he looked like shit when they dragged him in. What'd you do, slap him around a little?"

"Fuck, no! It's just like it says in the report, man. I pursued the perp and subdued him using necessary force."

"You hit him a couple with the flash, huh?"

"Nightstick," answered Finney, unconvincingly.

Frie smiled, "Yeah, stick to that, kid. You don't want any of that police brutality screwing up the case. Not that it'll ever get to a jury."

"It won't? Why the hell won't it?"

"Oh, yeah, it could. But probably, his lawyer'll try to cop, probably to B and E and the assault. Three years max. He'll be out in a year and a half, he keeps his nose clean. I figure the D.A.'ll take it."

"What! Why the fuck should he? He practically killed a cop. I'm an eyewitness. We got shitloads of physical evidence. Why should the D.A. give anything away?"

Frie shrugged and finished filling out his form. He scrawled a signature and tossed the report into a wire basket on top of a dozen others.

"Why?" said Finney again. "Slayton could've bought it tonight."

Frie looked at the young patrolman and tried to

recall what it felt like to get pissed off because the system stank on ice.

"Yeah, but he didn't, so your case, instead of being one of half a dozen cop killings, is one of ten thousand burglary and fifty thousand assaults. Ok, it's a cop, it gets a little more juice, but not much. The main thing is, the mutt got no sheet on him."

"No?"

"I wouldn't lie to you, Finney. He's a clean motherfucker. Now, that's not saying he don't have a juvie sheet twelve feet long, maybe he's Charles Manson Junior, but age eighteen they wipe it, and he gets a clean start. So figure, all's he got to do is stay out of trouble for—how old is he? —twenty-eight, there, figure ten years. Our clearance rate on burglaries is about right to catch a professional burglar about once every ten years. But I doubt he's a real pro."

"No? How come?"

"No tools. Pulling a boner like coming down a street ladder instead of going out through the building. Knifing a cop. All kid stunts, junkie bullshit, and he ain't no junkie. No, I figure he's a square, got a little behind on the car payments, maybe he's into the books on some sports action, could use a couple hundred on the side. So he goes into the den, takes the bowie knife down from the collection on the wall, there. Shit, he figures every shine in town is getting rich, why shouldn't a nice white boy? Something like that. Good thing he don't collect Lugers. And you know what proves it?"

"What?"

"He gets in trouble, who does he use his one dime to call? A Queens Boulevard shyster who specializes in springing small-time mutts? Not him. He was a pro he'd have Terry Sullivan's or Morrie Roth's number fuckin' memorized."

"So who'd he call?" asked Finney.

"His momma," Frie answered, and laughed.

Detective Frie's and Patrolman Finney's handiwork was delivered to the Complaint Room at Queens County courthouse, where an Assistant District Attorney transmuted the simple facts of the case into a criminal complaint, which was duly laid before a Criminal Court judge in the presence of the accused the next morning.

The arraignment of Felix Tighe lasted approximately as long as Felix's attack on Patrolman Slayton. The jails were crowded in the City that year, and their precious spaces had become more exclusive than suites at the Carlton. Jail was reserved first for the most ferocious, the most untrustworthy and implacable enemies of society and second, for those too stupid to avoid it. Thus when the judge heard that Felix had a job, and roots in the community (was that not his own mother in the courtroom, dabbing at her flowing eyes?) and—most important—no prior record, he had no trouble in walking Felix on five thousand dollars bail. His mother wrote a check for five hundred dollars to a bondsman and took her son home.

Felix had not liked jail, not even one night of it. He was sure he would not like prison either. And he hadn't liked the way the cops treated him, as if it were his fault that stupid nigger had attacked him. Well, as good as attacked him. You could see it in his eyes, he was going for his gun. A man has a right to defend himself. And then he was beaten almost to death by that other asshole, just as he was about to surrender peacefully.

Thoughts like these continued throughout the day, as Felix recuperated from his ordeal at his mother's brownstone on 78th Street, near Riverside Park. By the end of the day, Felix had made up his mind and come to the decision: he was not going to stay in Queens, where the cops obviously had it in for him. He would move to Manhattan.

# CHAPTER
# 2

The same morning that Felix Tighe walked out of the Queens County Courthouse, a very tall man and a woman of moderate size walked into the New York County Court House, at 100 Centre Street on the Island of Manhattan. They walked hand in hand until they reached the main doorway, at which point the woman pulled away. From this you could tell that they were not going into the courthouse to be married; if they had been, the woman would have held on tighter. In fact, both of them worked in the courthouse, as assistant district attorneys. Although they were not going to be married today, they were more or less in love, and had been for nearly four years.

The very tall man—he stood just over six-five— was obviously a familiar figure in these halls. A number of people called out greetings as the two of them moved through the lobby crowd. He acknowledged these with a nod or a grin or a wisecrack. The man had an aggressive walk, a City walk: head forward and casting from side to side like a rifleman on point, shoulders slightly hunched. You had to look closely to see that his left leg was

18

a little lame. The hands were big in proportion, the wrists thick and strong.

He had an aggressive face too—a heavy, broad brow, a big bony jaw, a long nose that had been broken and then straightened out, leaving a bump just north of center. The lines and other accessories were what you might expect from thirty-four years of this life, lived mostly in the City.

Except for the eyes, it was an ordinary face, in New York at least, although it might have drawn a second glance in Marietta, Georgia. The eyes were long, narrow, slightly slanted, gray with yellow lights: wolf eyes, perhaps a souvenir of a Cossack raid on some eastern *shtetl*. It was not a peaceful face.

The man was Roger Karp, Butch to his friends, who were few, but good ones. He was at this time Chief of the Criminal Courts Bureau of the New York District Attorney's office. The woman was Marlene Ciampi, an assistant district attorney, his employee and intermittent main squeeze.

It was Marlene's fantasy that their affair was a private matter, and one that, if public, would expose her to disdain—the bimbo who screws the boss. The fact that the newest secretary was filled in on the details of her involvement with Karp soon after being shown where they kept the typewriter ribbons did not matter to Marlene. If she did not acknowledge it publicly, it did not really exist. Karp had been irritated by this obsession at first, but now regarded it with something like fond amusement, another of his sweetie's infinite skein of eccentricities.

Over one side of the marble entranceway to this building were inscribed the words, "Why should there not be a patient confidence in the ultimate justice of the People?" As they passed through the security checks and entered the swirl of the main lobby, they received, as every morning, the answer why not. This area of 100 Centre Street is to the City's justice what the pit of the stock exchange is to its finance—a confused interzone full of worried, nervous people making deals—with the difference that the ethnic mix of the participants is spicier and the deals are about time, not money.

Even at this early hour, the lobby was crowded with people: the law's servants—bored cops expecting hours of tedium sitting on hard benches, scurrying clerks and messengers, technical experts with bulging briefcases, lawyers in sharp suits, smiling hard, public defenders gearing up for another day of saving ingrates—and its more numerous subjects—the criminals, their victims, witnesses, and their families and attendants.

Besides these, the lobby also included a population that had, since the repeal of the vagrancy laws and the closing of the mental hospitals, used the courthouse as its dayroom, having nowhere else to go. And why not? It was dry, warm in winter, cool in summer; it had water and bathrooms in reasonable repair; and it was safe. No one got mugged in the Courthouse, except after due process of law. If you were homeless, the courthouse was shelter; if you couldn't afford the movies or TV, here was a never-ending source of entertainment.

The scene that greeted Karp and Marlene this, and every, working morning was like a throwback to an earlier period in the evolution of justice, when the king laid down the law in the course of a royal progress through his domains, surrounded by nobles, clergy, and retainers in a kind of moving fair, attended also by mountebanks, jugglers, clowns, humble petitioners, cutpurses, rogues, freaks and the kind of miscellaneous idlers attracted to any show.

In the marble halls, whole families clustered in corners, eating spicy food out of paper bags. Ragged children played on and under the worn wooden benches and lumbering men made of dank clothes, hair and grease shouted at each other or at no one, until the tired security forces tossed them out. But they came back. This area was known to every denizen of the courthouse as the Streets of Calcutta.

Marlene checked her wristwatch. "Court in ten. I got to go prep. So long," she said, giving him the favor of a smile. She had a beautiful smile still, in a face that was not quite beautiful any longer. Stunning, rather. Arresting. Marlene Ciampi had started out with a face from a fashion magazine —flawless bisque skin, long, tilted black eyes, a wide, luscious mouth, million-dollar cheekbones, and the usual accessories—had lost it all when a bomb went off in her face four years ago, and then got a lot of it back through the most advanced and expensive surgery a hugely successful lawsuit could buy.

The disaster had burned out her left eye and everything extra from her face and body. She had become tough, wiry, and graceful with contained energy, like a flyweight boxer or a jaguar. She wore a glass eye at work and a pirate patch off duty. Either way Karp still thought she was a being marvelous and heartbreaking at the same time. She made him suffer, also—an added attraction.

"Aren't you going to give me a big hug and a kiss good-bye?" asked Karp. "God knows when I'll see you again."

Her smile twisted into a wry grimace. "It could be tonight, if you play your cards right, and no, I'm not, not in the middle of the Streets of Calcutta as you know, so stop asking."

Karp tugged gently at the sleeve of her raincoat. "I'll never stop," he said. She rolled her eyes to heaven and began to pull away again, when another hand landed on her sleeve.

This belonged to a small, bald, sweaty man wearing a three-piece dark suit, with dandruff, thick glasses, and a pervasive cologne. This was one of the fraternity of petty lawyers who derived their living from representing defendants prosperous enough to pay cash for their day in court.

"Ah, Miss Ciampi, am I glad to see you!" the man said breathlessly. Marlene stared at where he had grabbed her sleeve until his hand fluttered away. "Why is that, Mr. Velden?" she asked coolly.

"Oh, I just thought we could save some time, come to some workable agreement on De Carlo."

"Save some time? You've decided to plead your client guilty to felony assault and robbery?"

Velden smiled and held up his hands in protest. "Please, lady, be serious. Larceny I'll give on, but don't bust my hump with the felony assault. It's a ten-dollar purse snatch and the kid's never been convicted."

"Yeah, this'll be a first. Also, counselor, my witness informs me she received a phone call the other night suggesting that she'd get worse than a bang on the head if she testified. You wouldn't know anything about that, would you?"

A look of pained innocence appeared on Velden's

face. "What are you implying? Me? Arthur Velden? Threatening witnesses?"

"Have a chat with your client, Mr. Velden. Explain the rules. See you in court."

She turned and elbowed her way into the crowd.

Velden chuckled as he watched her go. "What a little pisser, heh?" he remarked to Karp. "She'll learn."

"I doubt that, Arthur," said Karp, walking away. "She's a slow learner. And I wouldn't play games with her, if I were you. She's not one of the boys."

Karp rode up on the elevator to his office on the ninth floor, and walked into the Bureau offices, a large room about the size of a squash court and about as elegant. Karp was not in favor with the administrative powers of the district attorney's office, a fact reflected in his office furniture, much of which ran to green and gray steel and sprung vinyl in reptilian colors.

The Bureau secretary, a middle-aged, tough-minded black woman named Connie Trask, greeted him as he entered.

"I'm glad you're here," said Trask. "His Excellency has been on the phone twice."

"Don't tell me—his mother's coming over and he wants to borrow my law-school diploma."

She giggled. "You're late on the budget."

"Yeah. That's what he wants to talk about, right?"

"I guess. He don't talk to *me*, sugar. Should I put it through?"

Karp nodded glumly and Connie dialed the D.A.'s number. He went into his private office and sat down in a squeaky wooden chair purchased new during the senior Roosevelt administration. He picked up his phone. After the obligatory two-minute wait on hold, the District Attorney came on the line. There followed a minute or two of the inane and insincere small talk without which politicians cannot conduct the most trivial business, delivered in Sanford Bloom's marvelously deep and mellow voice, beloved of the networks, but fingernails on the blackboard to Karp.

"Ah, Butch, it's the fifteenth. I don't have your draft budget submittal."

"I'm working on it. I just got off a trial yesterday."

This reference to trials was calculated to annoy. Bloom was not, and never had been a trial lawyer, unlike Bloom's predecessor, the illustrious, almost legendary, Francis P. Garrahy, deceased. After a brief, pointed silence, Bloom ignored the remark and went on. "Yes. Remember I want you to include resources for community relations and affirmative action."

That meant, Karp thought, lawyers sitting in meetings and writing plans instead of trying cases, so that Bloom could flash a few meaningless sheets of paper at other meetings. He uttered a few noncommittal phrases in the flat voice he always used with Bloom and the conversation trickled to an end. As usual, after any conversation with his boss, Karp felt hollow and vaguely ill. The previous year Karp had caught Bloom in a piece of nasty malfeasance, since which time Bloom had stayed out of Karp's way on big issues, allowing him to run his bureau as an independant fief.

On the surface. Beneath lay a rich vein of deathless hatred, hatching pitfalls, traps, petty harassments. Karp looked at the budget sheets on his desk with distaste. He was at least ten lawyers short of where he should be, but he was extremely reluctant to ask for new people. Any transfers into Karp's bureau were liable to be either spies, or more probably, turkeys that Bloom had hired to do a favor for someone and who were too dreadful even for Bloom's cronies in the other bureaus to stomach. It would be a double score for Bloom if he could stick a couple of losers in Karp's shop.

Karp never asked directly for new troops. Instead, he overworked the small team of decent lawyers he had gathered around him over the years, and himself worst of all, and occasionally allowed disgruntled people from other parts of the D.A.'s office to get some serious trial experience under his direction.

There were few other places for them to get it under the Bloom regime. Garrahy had been a trial lawyer, and Karp was a trial lawyer in the old man's image, he hoped. Bloom was not a trial lawyer. He was a bureaucrat and a politician, and good at it, too. He could weasel and delay and obfuscate like a sonofabitch, and trade favors and get elected.

But not try cases. If you went to trial a lot, unless you were prepared, and understood the law, and made sure that the cops didn't screw around with the evidence, you might lose, and let some bad guy get loose, and what was worse, get loose *publicly*. It was much safer to bargain, and do the people's business in whispers beneath the bench, and if some monster got out on the street in eighteen months, well, that surely was the business of the courts, or the prisons, or the parole board, and couldn't be blamed on the D.A.

Karp didn't think about this stuff anymore. He

did as many trials as he could and he made sure
his people understood that the trial was the foundation of the whole system. That this was peculiar, even bizarre, that this was like the Air Force
having to belabor to its pilots the importance of
airplanes, was a fact that no longer occupied the
center of Karp's thoughts. It just made him tired.
With a sigh, he switched off Bloom and turned to
the endless and unsympathetic columns of figures.

Felix Tighe slept nearly eight straight hours at
his mother's house, in his old bed in the room he
had occupied as a boy. His mom kept it just the
way he had left it—the weight set, the Jim Morri-
son poster, even his high school books still lined
up neatly on a shelf. He awoke around five in the
afternoon, feeling peaceful and secure, and after
limbering up, performed three repetitions of the
*Ten-no kata* of the *shotokan* school of karate. Felix
had recently been awarded a *shodan*, the first degree black belt in this school, one of the few
projects he had ever completed, and an accom-
plishment of which he was inordinately proud.

Sweating slightly now, he stripped, showered,
and dressed in the clothes his mother had laid
out: tan whipcord pants, a green plaid sportshirt,
a gray cashmere sweater, gray socks, and shiny
penny loafers. His mother always seemed to have
a supply of clothes in Felix's size; a good thing
too, since he had thrown away the clothes he had
been wearing the night of his arrest.

His mother was in the kitchen cutting up pota-
toes on a butcher's chopping block. She looked up
and her face brightened when he came in. "My,
don't you look nice. Does that shirt fit?" She put
her knife down, walked over to him and adjusted

his collar. Felix hugged her and kissed her loudly on the cheek. "How's my best girl?" he said. She giggled and kissed him back, and smoothed her hair when he released her. She was a small woman of about fifty, with the same dark handsomeness as Felix. Her hair was thick and dark, showing no gray, swept back in a large bun at the nape of her neck. She was wearing a cotton shirtwaist dress in some neutral color and a white apron around her waist.

"You're still the prettiest mom in the world," said Felix, going over to the refrigerator. He poked around and pulled out a can of Schlitz and a bag of Fritos.

His mother said, "You'll ruin your appetite. I'm making fried chicken and french fries."

"Ma, I got to go back to Queens tonight. I thought I told you."

"Felix, it's your favorite! And it's all prepared—"

"I'm sorry as hell, Ma, but it's business. They've got me writing this big report, and it's got to be at the front office day after tomorrow. I thought I could finish it last night, but those crazy cops locked me up. I can't tell the boss I was in jail, can I? I mean they wouldn't understand and all . . ."

Her face softened. "Well then, if it's business. Oh, but I do wish you'd take it easier. I want you to be a success, dear, but you should relax more."

"Yeah, well I'll try, Ma. But you know how it is, the executive rat race." He shrugged and showed a wry smile.

"Yes, I do, and I don't forget what it did to your poor father."

"And how's your business, Ma?" said Felix quickly. He disliked talking about his father. "Doing good?"

"Oh, fair. It's a lot of work, and I do it all. You can't get help today. Doesn't matter what the pay is, they'd rather go on welfare. And your brother . . . if you're not watching him every minute, he makes a mess of everything." She came toward him and touched his cheek. "Now if I had *you* here, it'd be different."

"Yeah I know, Ma. We talked about that a million times. I appreciate it, but I got to follow my talent. My own star, like you used to tell me. I got lots of deals now, one of them has got to pay off. I'm real close, I know it." He grinned sheepishly. "Speaking of which, I'm a little short this week. And they cleaned out my wallet in jail."

"They did? Did you report it?"

"Sure, but don't count on anything happening there. The cops are just as bad as the crooks. They probably take a cut."

"You poor thing! I'll write you a check."

"Thanks a million, Ma," said Felix warmly. "Hey, you know, I've been thinking about moving to Manhattan. It's closer to work and, you know, I'd get to see you more."

"Felix, that's wonderful! Have you found a place?"

"Not yet. But rent is sky high in the good neighborhoods. And they want first and last month security, and sometimes you got to tip the super to get you in."

Felix's mother went to a drawer in one of the kitchen cabinets and took out her checkbook. "I know," she said. "Soon decent people won't be able to afford the city at all. Will five hundred do it?"

"That'll be great, Ma. But, uh, if you could, I could use a couple hundred in cash."

She looked at him, and something odd seemed to come over her face, as if there was another person sitting behind her eyes. "That's fine," she said pleasantly. "I have some stuff I need to drop off in the safe deposit. You can take that along when you get your cash."

At about four-thirty that afternoon, Karp left his office and began the daily inspection of his empire. This was comprised of his own Bureau Chief's office, a secretarial bullpen, two large partitioned bays where the rank and file worked, and a set of tiny colonies—little offices, alcoves, and closets that the Criminal Courts Bureau had accumulated in various deals and trade-offs over the years, every square inch of which was sacred soil to be defended to the last memo.

People called out to him or waved good-naturedly as he threaded his way through the warren of neck-high glass and steel barricades that choked the work space. Karp liked this part of his day. Although he accepted that his temper and impatience made him an indifferent bureaucrat, he liked to think that he was a good manager. Managing was like coaching a team, he thought: You develop your players, you teach them how to work together, give them some tricks, and send them out to win.

In fact, the Criminal Courts Bureau was and had always been a jocky sort of place. Most of the young attorneys who came to work as prosecutors had played some ball in school. The squad bays were busy with energetic young men, their hair cut unfashionably short, making loud wisecracks. Nobody ever just threw a piece of yellow legal paper into the can; it was always a graceful hook or jumper and an exhalation of "Yessss!" or "Two points!"

In general, Karp was pleased with the quality of the kids who came to work for him; what was wrong was what became of them after a zillion cases and no trials. It was like training a team to a high pitch and never letting them play. It wore them out and made them dull and cynical before their time.

He walked into the cubicle occupied by Tony Harris. Stacks of large-format computer paper, books, brown accordion folders, and sheaves of various sorts of paper covered the small metal desk and flowed down over the straight wooden visitor's chair to the floor. More paper, some of it in dusty cartons, was stacked precariously against two walls. It looked less like an office than something geological, a cave or the results of a retreating glacier. Harris had made the mistake of admitting that he knew something about computers and had been tagged with piles of administrative work on top of his court schedule. Harris was a skinny young man with bright blue eyes and a bush of brown hair that sprouted like marsh grass from either side of his face and down his collar. A scraggly mustache floated over a wide mouth, which, when he saw Karp, expanded into a wide crooked-toothed grin.

"What are you so happy about?" asked Karp.

"I think we stole about ten more trial slots than we're entitled to this week—all homicides, by the way. Our clearance rate is piss-poor, but, ah, I made some adjustments on the computer. Of course, if the chief administrative judge or the D.A. ever find out about it, I'll probably get disbarred or something."

Karp chuckled. "Don't worry, kid, they'll never catch us. His Honor the chief administrative judge has other fish to fry, like running for the Court of Appeals, God help us. He's not going to make any waves. As long as the numbers balance he'll never notice we jacked up the intake figures. Same thing with Bloom. Wharton might catch on, but I can handle him. Worse comes to worst, they'll charge us with falsifying records. We'll plead insanity and walk. But the main thing is . . ."

"Yeah, trials. More trials."

"That's right. Keep the mutts honest. The only way. Incidentally, how many homicides do we have this year so far?"

Harris shuffled through some papers and pulled out a chart.

"Six-hundred twenty-one. Up seven from this time last year."

"Great. We must be doing something right," Karp said. "I'll tell that to Mr. District Attorney next time he wants to clean out the whores from Times Square or some other goddamn project. Hey, have you see Freddie Kirsch around recently?"

"Yeah, I think he's in his cell. I heard suspenders snapping. Speaking of cells, there any chance of me getting a bigger place? You got me doing all this administrative and computer crap, and I got green stripers coming up around my ears. There's no place to fucking sit down."

Harris gestured toward his cubicle, which was about the size and shape of an apartment bathroom or a walk-in closet.

Karp spread his hands in helplessness. "Tony, I got nothing to offer. And I need you to handle the admin because nobody else I got knows how to fuck with the data." He looked sad. "This was a great place to work in forty years ago when the crime rate was about ten per cent what it is now. You know, this bay we're in now was a reception area, back when the D.A. had about thirty attorneys in all. Joe Lerner told me when I started here. Can you believe it? A *reception* area?"

"A long time ago," agreed Harris. "Still," he added, taking in his office with a sour glance, "it's a definite statement by the people of New York. You're garbage. Every day in every way you're getting worser and worser."

"Come on, Tony, what's an office? You're getting a great legal education. Couple of years, keep your nose clean, you'll be defending pimps and making a fortune and this'll all seem like a bad dream."

Harris laughed and Karp walked off toward the cubicle of Freddy Kirsch, his mood darkening. Harris was one of the best, a decent funny kid with terrific courtroom instincts, but Karp could read the signs of wear and tear that meant he was not going to last. In general, Karp had found, only three kinds of lawyers stuck with the D.A.'s office in these corrupt times—one, slobs: those who had no other option, who, however talented legally, were too sloppy for a white-shoe firm and too disorganized to set up a practice, like Ray Guma; two, hobbyists, who had private income, and got a kick out of being hard-asses, like Roland Hrcany; and, finally, fanatics. Karp himself was a fanatic. Freddy Kirsch was another hobbyist. Harris was neither.

Karp found Kirsch at his desk, reading a tabloid. On the front page was a picture of a couple of cops standing next to a dumpster in an alley looking glumly at a small bundle at their feet. The headline read "GRAB MOM IN GARBAGE BAG KILLING." Karp tapped his knuckles on the glass and the young lawyer looked up and grinned. He had hired Kirsch nearly a year ago on the recommendation of one of his law school professors. Kirsch was a Californian, a Berkeley graduate, smart and rich, hence a good prospect. Also he was tan, he had razor cut dark hair, he wore sharp, tailored dark suits, all of which endeared him to Karp, who was always having to lecture the scruffy polyestered St. John's graduates who made up much of his staff on the importance of appearances in the legal game.

"What's going on, boss?" asked Kirsch genially, leaning back in his swivel chair and hooking his thumbs behind his canary yellow suspenders. Karp perched on the edge of the desk, which was suspiciously clean. "Not much, Freddie. I thought I'd drop by and check out the Stahlmann trial. How's it look?"

Kirsch kept his grin. "Looks like we won't need a trial. He's going to plead."

"What? To murder two?"

"No, man one. I just talked to his lawyer this morning. We'll go with it in Part 34 tomorrow."

"Wait a second, Freddie. How come we're accepting manslaughter as a plea on this one? This is the trunk murder, right? The guy bashed in the girlfriend's head with a tire iron and stashed her in the trunk of her car."

"Yeah, that's the one. Stahlmann's a religious nut with a thing about pure women. He thought he'd found the last virgin in New York until some guy in his church told him one of his buddies had porked her a couple of years back. He went batshit."

"So? What has that got to do with it? On a man one he could be walking in two years, out looking for more virgins."

Kirsch's smooth brow furrowed. "Extreme emotional disturbance is what. They're arguing he lost his marbles from disappointment. They got a psychiatric examination confirms it." He shrugged. "It's an affirmative defense under the law. I figured it cast enough reasonable doubt on the case so that trial wasn't worth it. So I took the man one. I'll try to push for years on the sentencing."

"Shit, Freddie!" Karp propelled himself violently off the desk and slammed his hand down on his thigh, making a sound like a gunshot. Kirsch jerked and sat up.

"What're you talking 'reasonable doubt'?" asked Karp contemptuously. "It's an affirmative defense. The burden's on *them* to show extreme emotional. *They've* got to have a preponderance of evidence. Do they? They've got crap. The guy laid for the girl in her apartment, wasted her, and hid the body. That doesn't sound like he was out of his mind to me."

"But they got a shrink—"

"Fuck the shrink, Freddie! The trier of fact can reject testimony as to extreme emotional disturbance, even if the prosecution presents no testimony to rebut. *People v. Shelton.* Come *on*, Freddie. You *know* this stuff."

Kirsch looked so genuinely miserable that Karp's ire receded. He perched again on the desk. "Look, Freddie, I'm sorry I have to be a hard-ass with you, but there's no way around it. You want to be a trial lawyer, you got to worship perfection. That's the goal. You can't tell what a jury will do, maybe you'll lose, but you have the obligation to walk in there with a perfect case, which includes knowing the relevant law."

Freddie bit his lip and stared at his desk. "Yeah, I guess I fucked it up royally."

"Come on, kid, you got a basically good case. Just call them up and tell them you reconsidered."

"I can do that?"

"Shit, yes. It ain't over 'til it's over. Tell them you were suffering from extreme emotional disturbance."

Kirsch laughed and the flush left his face. "OK, will do, boss. Say, speaking of emotional disturbance, you seen this yet?" He tapped his finger on the front page of the tabloid, which splashed the news of a murdered child found in a trash bag.

"Yeah, they picked up the mother. Who's handling it?"

"Ciampi."

"She is, huh? I better go over and talk to her about it. Let me know when you fix that Stahlmann thing."

"Yeah, Christ, these homicides take a lot of time don't they? How come they don't have a separate bunch of people that just does homicides? I mean, we spend most of our time just running people through the Criminal Courts on petty shit, and then one of these comes along and it throws everything off kilter. Breaks the rhythm." Freddie moved his shoulders rhythmically, to illustrate this perception.

Karp sighed and said, "Well, you got a point there, Fred, but as it happens there did used to be a homicide bureau."

"Yeah? What happened to it?"

"Our D.A. shitcanned it the first year he was here."

"No kidding! How come?"

"The homicide guys were all trial lawyers. Bloom doesn't have much use for trial lawyers, and they didn't have much use for him. Also, everything runs on clearances now—a murder's just another case, nothing special about it, and so if you're going to plea bargain away everything anyway, why bother having a bureau that specializes in prosecuting and trying murder cases? So he broke it up, and now most homicides come here, to Criminal Courts."

"Uh-huh, I always wonder about that, why they didn't go over to felony bureau."

"Oh, that. That's because of me."

"Yeah? What do you mean, because of you?"

"Well, I guess I'm the closest thing the office has to a homicide expert now, so that's one reason; and the other reason is, sometimes homicides get a lot of publicity and if I were to lose or otherwise screw up a big important case, then Bloom would have the excuse he needs to get rid of me. I think that's the real reason."

"So how come you're still here?"

"Because I haven't blown one yet."

"You won *all* your cases?"

"Yeah. So far so good."

"Holy shit! How do you *do* that?"

"By being perfect, Freddie," said Karp with a tight smile.

"And how do you achieve this perfection?" Kirsch asked. Karp shot him a look, suspecting Freddie's usual light sarcasm, but for once Kirsch appeared to be in the throes of a genuine admiration. Winning, Karp thought, the unimpeachable argument.

"Like I said, know the law. Know the witnesses. You have to have a mental picture of every one of your witnesses. You have to *know* what they'll answer in your direct case, where they're vulnerable on cross, and how you're going to compensate for however they screwed up when you get them again on redirect."

Kirsch looked dismayed. "I got to do this on what—thirty to fifty cases?"

"Yeah, you do, and not only that—you have to orchestrate the presentation of each witness so the whole show has the maximum impact on a jury. Like for instance, you have two eyewitnesses. One of them remembers a lot of detail—the day, the car, what the defendant was doing before, after—he's a whole newsreel. The other guy just remembers the mutt had a red jacket and scar. Who you going to put on first?"

Freddie looked blank. "Does it matter?"

"Of course it matters! Everything matters! You put the guy with the details last. If you put him first the defense will question the lightweight on the very same details, and he won't remember and that'll leave the jury thinking maybe the first guy was making it up.

"Then there's the evidence. You have to keep straight what documentary or physical evidence you're going to present along with each witness and work that into the orchestration. And the Q. and A.'s: They have to be perfect too. Hammer them with the evidence. Make sure they identify the knife or the gun in detail, the bloodstains, whatever. . . ."

"On *every* witness?"

"Not on every witness, Freddie. You don't take Q. and A. on *your* witnesses. The less the defense knows about what your witnesses saw and did the better. You do it on witnesses friendly to the defense or on hostile witnesses. And on the ones you know are going to flip."

"Shit, Butch! How the hell do you know which ones are going to flip?" asked Kirsch plaintively, suddenly aware that he was not to be supplied with a secret substitute for work or a simple trick.

"How do you know? It's part of being perfect, Freddie," said Karp casually, on his way out of the cubicle, "just like you're going to be from now on."

As Karp made his way through the maze of tiny passages, he was reflecting simultaneously on two related subjects. The first was that in the old days, somebody like Freddy would not have lasted two weeks in the homicide bureau. He would not have even gotten *in*, but if he had he would have been shredded and flushed after a single confrontation with the rock-hard men who had, under Francis Garrahy's direction, made the New York City Homicide Bureau one of the finest prosecutorial organizations in the world.

The fact was, Freddie was bone lazy, but his intelligence made him worth a salvage effort. Also, he might stay a while. To such expedients had Karp been reduced. Ring in the Age of Brass!

The other subject was Marlene, and the unwelcome news that she had picked up the trash-bag child murder. Karp headed toward her office, which lay at the extreme end of a sixth-floor hallway leading to a pair of fire stairs. The architects had left a tiny alcove in the hallway beyond the stair doors and this alcove had been walled off and given a cheap door. There was just enough room for a desk, two chairs, a filing cabinet, and Marlene.

Karp knocked and, receiving no answer, entered. A bomb had once gone off in this office, but that was four years back, and the place looked to Karp as if it hadn't been straightened since. He moved a stack of files off a chair and sat down to wait among the drifted papers. Sitting alone in Marlene's office was an unnerving experience. Since the office was only seven feet wide and the hallway ceilings were almost fourteen feet high, it was like being at the bottom of a mailbox, an impression that the great rafts of paper scattered around did nothing to dispel.

He studied the dusty cream ceiling moldings. After a while, heels clicked on the marble floor outside. The door opened and Marlene came in, looking smudged and rumpled. She flung her handbag and a brown accordion folder down on her desk and flopped into the other chair. Kicking off her shoes, she put her feet up on her desk and lit a Marlboro.

"Rough day?" asked Karp.

"Rough? I wouldn't say that. The usual. I got a new case today, another murdered child needless to say."

"Oh, yeah, I heard. The trash-bag thing. Why 'needless to say'?"

"Oh, because for some reason, whenever anybody decides to take the clippers, or the red-hot coat hanger, or the baseball bat, or the lit cigarette or the boiling grease to some little kid, which in this city is about forty-three times a day, whenever some asshole decides to do anything like that, in the rare instance where the case attracts the attention of the fucking *law*, then for some strange reason *I* get the case. Even though, my dear boss, I have mentioned this to you from time to time, that I cannot stand any more to—"

"Marlene, you know that's not true. All the cases get assigned off a rotation schedule from the complaint room."

"—stand any more to see little. Punctured. Bodies. Or talk to their mommies and daddies. And, as long as we're being technical about it, do you know how many child homicide, child rape, and child felony assault cases I have had in the past year? You do not? Let me tell you. One hundred and fourteen. This is coincidence? The luck of the draw? Can you recall the last time Ray Guma, let's say, had a case like that? Or Roland? Or any of the male attorneys? I'll tell you, Cindy Pitowski has got 'em, and so does Ruth Kammer, and that's all the ladies you got working for you right now.

"So I put it to you, counselor, on the preponderance of the evidence, is somebody saying, 'who wants to fuck with this messy doo-doo, there's no *challenge*, it's a piece of shit, open and shut, smoking gun, it's not roughie-toughie armed robbery, assault with a deadly, drug-crazed shoot-out, so let's give to the *cunts!*' "

She stared at him so intensely that he dropped his gaze. At moments like these it appeared that she was flashing emotions from both of her black eyes, even though Karp knew that the left one was glass. Marlene lunged furiously toward her bag for another cigarette, and the motion caused a minor landslide of paperwork off her desk.

"You ought to get some of this cleared up," Karp ventured, knowing instantly that it had been exactly the wrong thing to say. He saw her face grow tight and her lovely soft mouth knot into a ridged pale line. "Oh," she said carefully, "is this what I owe the honor of your visit to? The inspector general is making his rounds. I'm sorry my desk isn't all neatsy, sir, but I've been over to Bellevue, to the morgue, to see the child, a little girl named Lucy Segura. What her loving mother did to her body wasn't too bad. She just cut off one of her fingers and shoved something into her little twat, and then strangled her. It wasn't as bad as the one where they baked the little girl in the oven. You remember that one? I do.

"So I didn't have time to clean up! I better do it now or the big man will be mad at me." She sprang to her feet and began to sweep the piled papers off her desk with broad, violent movements of her hands and arms.

"Marlene! Stop!" shouted Karp. He rose from his seat and grabbed her around the shoulders. This was the only thing that really frightened Karp. Like most naturally brave men, he had little imagination, which doth make cowards of us all, and physical pain held no terrors for him, but when the black screamers took charge of Marlene it turned his bones to jelly.

She struggled and turned a stranger's face up to him. "I can't stand it," she said, her jaw rigid. "I can't can't can't can't can't! It's too much. All the little children. . . ."

Wisely, Karp kept his mouth shut for once, didn't give a pep talk or useful advice, just held Marlene, who began to cry. After a while her sobs subsided into loud snuffles and her body relaxed against his.

"Whew, God! Sorry. Where's the Kleenex?"

"Use my tie."

She giggled. "No, I got them here." She broke away and rummaged through her huge bag until she extracted a wad of tissue the size of a cabbage. She blew lustily into it. Then she sat on the edge of her desk and lit a cigarette.

"Sorry about that," she said. "Things are getting hairy again. I used to wait for the dullness to set in, to where I get tough and cynical down deep inside. I don't mean the pose. I got a pose as good as anybody's. I mean deep, so you're really dead. And I guess I can't do that, I don't want that to happen. I'm fighting it."

"Not everybody's dead," said Karp defensively. "I'm not."

She looked at him narrow-eyed through her smoke. "No you're not, that's true," she said at length. "But you are also a lunatic, in your own sweet way." She shook herself and started rooting around in the drift of papers. "Well, the performance is over for this afternoon, folks," she said with a tight smile. "The divine Ms. Ciampi will be signing autographs at the stage door."

Karp felt a familiar flood of relaxation, tinged with exhaustion and not a little resentment. The storm was over and once more his sweetheart had returned from the precipice to the world of the passably sane. He watched her thin body move as she hauled papers up onto the desk. It was clumsy work, but she made it a dance; in everything she was as graceful as a snake.

"What are you digging for, Marlene?"

"The fucking Segura file. Ah, here it is."

"Marlene, are you really all right?"

The concern in his voice made her look up. "Yeah, I'm fine, now. I've been feeling real weird recently, weepy and, I don't know . . . vaporous.

Thanks for putting up with me." A real smile, this time. Karp felt his pupils expand.

"Um, hey, no problem. It's a rough job, but somebody's got to do it. Want to get some deli, later?"

"Yeah, sure. I need to call this social worker and start documenting the history of abuse. Great stuff. If I'm lucky, I can put her away until she's too old to have any more kids. She's twenty, by the way. Had the dead kid at fourteen."

"I guess there's no question she did it? I mean, for a mother to do something like that. . . ."

"A mother? My dear, you would be amazed what mothers do. Mostly they let daddy do it, but sometimes they step right in and wale away. Like last month, we had one, a junkie, she held her daughter's legs apart with her own hands while guys came in off the street and fucked the kid for two, three bucks a shot. Two years old, the kid was. Dislocated both hips as a matter of fact. Kid checked out in the hospital from shock and infection."

"But what does what's-her-name, Segura, the mother, what does she say? Does she admit it?"

"No, she doesn't. She says she was sleeping off a drunk. She's a wino. She says when she woke up the kid was gone. That's all she knows, she says, until the cops came knocking. But there's a history of serious child abuse there. The kid was in Bellevue last year with a busted arm. Fell down the stairs, hah-hah."

Marlene let out a long, sad breath. "No, she probably did it, or there's a boyfriend. Who we'll probably have to dig up. Ask me why I do this work."

"Why do you do this work?"

She fluttered her eyelids and put on a Miss America false smile. "Because I guess I just love people," she said.

Karp leaned over and kissed her, something she normally objected to during office hours, but this time it seemed to be alright. More than alright.

When they surfaced, Karp murmured, "Here's a sweet nothing for you—Tony just told me there were six hundred twenty-one homicides this year so far in New York. If you'd like to accompany me to the fast food restaurant of your choice this evening, we might get lucky and see one."

"Or be one. Gosh, Butch, my eyes are shining. How romantic you are! But if we see a murder, we won't have to get involved, will we?"

"Of course not! Us? Besides, the district attorney is a personal friend of mine."

# CHAPTER
# 3

The 622nd murder actually took place that night, in the section of lower Manhattan known as Little Italy, in a restaurant. The victim was Vincent Ferro, known around town as Vinnie Red because of the unusual color of his hair. Vinnie Red was a gangster, and his murder was appropriately "gangland style" as the tabloids always put it.

The same papers also called him a "Mafia figure," which was untrue, since Vinnie was not a member of one of the five New York crime families. Instead he was an independent, and had recently expanded from loan sharking and numbers into narcotics, using a distribution network based on a cadre of black men he had met while serving eight years in Attica. Vinnie got along well with black criminals, an unusual talent for an Italian gangster, and he was now capitalizing on it.

On the last evening of his life he was taking his two sisters to dinner at Alberto's, a seafood place on the corner of Grand and White Street. He had been doing this once a month for years and did not see any reason for stopping simply because a contract on his life had been taken out by at least two major criminal organizations. Vinnie had a reputation for rubbing the Mob's face in it, and the choice of Alberto's, which is to Mob society what the Stage Delicatessen is to stand-up comics, was typical bravado. Besides the two women, his party included his driver-bodyguard Salvatore Meccano. Sally Mitch was a pretty good driver, but not much of a bodyguard, which everybody knew and which thus added to the luster of Vinnie's rep. And of course tonight, as usual, and burnishing the luster even more, Vinnie was unarmed.

Vinnie and his party swept into Alberto's at about ten, Vinnie dressed to kill in a gray sharkskin suit, white silk shirt, red tie with diamond stickpin, with a fawn leather trenchcoat flung over his shoulders, and his ladies appropriately dolled up. They headed straight for the banquette table in the front room where they always sat. There was nobody sitting there at the moment, but if there had been, Vinnie would have stood in front of the table frowning silently until the people vacated, which they would have done instantly if they recognized him, or if not, then somewhat later, when the waiter had nervously explained the mores of the locale.

Vinnie Red got good service in Alberto's, just as the Czar probably didn't have to wave a lot to flag a waiter at the Winter Palace. As they started on their clams oreganata, which were served about forty seconds after the order hit the kitchen, a man of about thirty got up from his *zuppa di pesci* and walked rapidly to the door. Although he did not even glance at the Ferro table on his way out, Sally Mitch spotted him and remarked to his boss,

"Vinnie, that was, you know, that Frank Impellatti —Little Noodles."

Ferro shrugged and poured another dollop of Alberto's famous incandescent hot sauce on his clams. "So, it was Little Noodles. So what?"

"So he left pretty fast just now. He's with the Bollanos. I think he drives for Joey Bottles, him or that other hitter they got, Charlie Tonnatti. . . ."

Vinnie didn't like to talk business in front of female members of his family. A faint scowl dropped his perfect curly pompadour a quarter of an inch down his forehead. He said, "Eat your clams, Sally. They could get cold, there, eh?"

Sally Mitch shrugged too. If Vinnie was not concerned that Frank "Little Noodles" Impellatti, who drove for the Bollano crime family's principal assassins, had left his dinner in a hurry shortly after their arrival, he was not going to worry.

Forty minutes later they were having coffee and cannoli. Vinnie had just stuck the end of a cannoli into his mouth when he saw it coming. The man who came through the door was about fifty. He had a face from a Toltec monument: broad nose, thick lips, slit eyes, pocked skin, a head unnaturally round, an unforgettable face that nobody ever remembered. This was Giuseppe Botteglia, Joey Bottles.

Joey Bottles pulled an Army Colt .45 pistol out of the pocket of his gray topcoat and walked calmly toward the Ferro table. The maitre d' did not ask him if he had a reservation. He saw Vinnie see him and paused for a moment, confident that Vinnie would do the right thing.

Which Vinnie did. He flung his table over on its side, grabbed his sisters, each by the nape of her neck and threw them behind this barrier. Sally

Mitch availed himself of the same courtesy, without being asked. Then Vinnie Red leaped over the table and made for the door.

Joey Bottles turned and walked after him, calmly firing shot after shot into the fleeing man's back. At each shot Vinnie jerked like a galvanized frog, yet he kept somehow on his feet through the short lobby and out into the rainy street. There he collapsed at last, face down on the pavement. Overcoming his natural desire to clear out as soon as possible after a job, Joey Bottles bent and turned Vinnie over to make sure he was dead. This was more than a matter of professional pride. Machiavelli said, "When you strike at a prince, you should be sure to kill him." Joey had never read Machiavelli, but like most of his colleagues he was a spiritual inhabitant of the sixteenth century, and the wisdom of vendetta had been bred into his bones.

After assuring himself that Vinnie was indeed dead, Joey looked around. The window and the doorway of Alberto's were crammed with white staring faces. From within he could hear the keening of the sisters. They were being held back by Sally Mitch. He heard one of them yell, "Blood will run in the streets for this!" Joey shrugged, doubt on his face. Ferro's operation would fall apart without him. In any case, it was not his concern. He turned to the restaurant and snarled, "Nobody saw nothing." It was his theme song and always well-received by the crowd. The faces withdrew.

A squeal of tires on the wet pavement announced the arrival of his transportation. Joey got in and the car roared away. He lit a cigarette. Frank Impellatti, at the wheel, glanced over at his companion.

"So?"

"So, nothing. It went OK. We going to Nyack, right?"

"Yeah. So. Vinnie Red. He's been looking for it years, y'know?"

"Yeah, years. Since he whacked out Tony Abrutte."

"He did Abrutte? I never knew that."

"Fuck, yeah. Nineteen, he fuckin' takes out a guy is practically a *capo regime*. Don't clear it with nobody, just pops him. Harry Pick got no fuckin' use for Abrutte, but he can't sit for no little sardine hitting no fish the size of Abrutte, you understand?"

"Yeah, it's the principle of the thing."

"Yeah. So from that day he's a dead man."

"Right. Still you gotta admit the guy had a pair of stones on him. I mean it took, what, twelve years to get him?"

Joey shot him a hard stare through the smoke. Joey Bottles packed a world class hard stare and Frank looked quickly back to the road. Joey said, "Stones got nothing to do with it. He spent ten in the slams, out of that. Then he starts this bullshit with the jigs uptown. He was way out of line."

"Right. Hey, you want to stop for something? Coffee or something to eat? I didn't get to finish my dinner."

"Nah, we'll eat by Nyack. Or we could send out. I wanna get off the road." Joey smiled, then grinned, then chuckled far back in his throat.

This was so startling that Frank swerved out of lane.

"Hey, Joey, what's so funny?"

"What you said, it reminded me. Vinnie didn't

49

finish his dinner neither. When he went out, he still had a cannoli stuck in his mouth."

"No shit? A cannoli?"

"Yeah. A fuckin' cannoli, right in his mouth, like a cigar."

"Yeah, well they do a good cannoli at Alberto's," said Little Noodles.

The morning after the Ferro killing shone through the windows of a condo in Nyack, New York, and sent a beam of sunlight into Frank Impellatti's eyes. He cursed the light and rolled over in bed. Then he sat up and looked at the clock-radio on the side table, which read seven forty-five. He remembered that his boss was coming over this morning, at eight-thirty. This was something of a ritual in the Bollano family. When somebody whacked somebody out, or did something equally calculated to arouse the interest of the authorities, he and his accomplices would stay in this condo in Nyack, or in one of a number of similar accommodations, until the heat died down, or until other arrangements could be made for their futures.

Into such a safe house on the morning after the event would come the *consiglere* of the Bollanos, Umberto Piaccere, and a small entourage. If Piaccere was pleased with the event, he would bring with him a small white box of pastries. There would be civilized discussion. If he was not pleased, there would be no pastries. There would be no civilized discussion. In either case, Piaccere expected an alert crew and strong coffee on these visits. Little Noodles rolled out of bed and headed for the bathroom.

As he shaved, he considered the events of the previous evening. The Bollanos had nothing to complain about: It was a clean hit, easy, no big thing. He expected pastries.

Little Noodles got dressed. He wore beltless tailored black slacks, with suspenders, a pale green silk dress shirt, with french cuffs, open at the neck, and white Gucci loafers. The sliding doors to the closet in his room were full-length mirrors. He checked himself out, turning from side to side. He put on a beige linen-silk weave sport jacket, adjusted his collar, and checked himself out again.

Despite the care he took, Impellatti was not by nature a vain man; he understood that he was not much to look at. He was short and slight, swarthy and dark-jowled, with thinning black hair. He had a little round bulb at the end of his nose, a small cleft chin, and a wide thin mouth with not much lip. His teeth were capped. Nevertheless, in his world, where there were no examinations or résumés or quarterly reports, impressions counted a great deal more than they did in the civil service. They paid you enough, you weren't supposed to look like some kind of bum.

Walking down the hallway from his bedroom, Impellatti could hear the heavy snores of his colleague, Joey Bottles, coming from behind the shut door of the apartment's other bedroom. Standing well to the side of the doorway, he knocked twice.

Instantly the snores shut down, like the sound shuts off when you mash the button on a TV. Impellatti knew that if he walked through the door right now, he would be looking into the barrel of Joey's Colt pistol. He had no intention of doing this. Instead he said clearly and slowly, "Joey. It's eight o'clock. The boss'll be here in half an hour." He heard the answering grunt from behind the door and then went to make the coffee.

As it brewed, Frank looked out the kitchen window. The condo building was built high on a hill facing the river, with woods at the back. The river was a far silvery line beyond the powder green of the spring trees. Closer, the window gave a good view of the building's winding driveway and its parking lot. You could see if you had visitors, which was one of the main selling points of the building to Little Noodles's employers. A sliding glass door led from the kitchen to a narrow covered balcony, from which fire stairs led down to the ground. That made two ways out—another selling point.

The coffee started to brew in the electric pot, and Frank pulled six cups and saucers out of the cabinet above the sink. These domestic arrangements were part of his job. He also cleaned cars, picked up laundry, and ran various errands. Occasionally he drove. He did not mind the menial tasks; he had no great ambition beyond being a soldier for the Bollanos. For this he made about seventy-five thousand dollars annually, all of it in untaxable cash. Once he had to go to jail for eleven years. It was still a good deal.

Five minutes after the coffee maker dripped its final drop, the front door of the apartment was opened without knock or ring by a broad shouldered, thin-faced man with small eyes. This was Tommy Vecchio, the *consiglere*'s driver and bodyguard. He nodded to Impellatti and looked around the apartment's living room and dining nook.

A few seconds later a man in his mid-forties, wearing a snap brim loden hat with a feather in it, walked into the apartment. He was a medium sized, compact man, with a round head and deeply pouched dark eyes, after the manner of the late

Eddie Cantor. "Charlie," said Little Noodles. Carlo Tonnatti, also called Charlie Tuna by his many acquaintances, said, "Noodles, how you been?" He was Piaccere's personal leg breaker and shooter.

Charlie Tuna turned on the television set, loud, and flopped down on the long white couch that occupied the center of the living room. Tonnatti was not interested in the programs available at eight-thirty in the morning. Although the condo was routinely examined for listening devices, Piaccere liked loud TV in the background when he discussed business.

Then two men came in together. One was in his mid-fifties, beautifully dressed in a double-breasted navy chalkstripe, Sulka tie, and mirror-bright wingtips. The other was younger, in his twenties. He wore slacks and gold-mounted loafers and a dark silk shirt open at the neck, displaying gold chains.

The older man's face was broad, heavy-lidded, thick-lipped. His nose was large, with prominent pores, and he bore a deep comma-shaped scar to the right of it. The younger man was less distinguished in appearance, a forgettable face with large ears and a scant chin. Each of these dissimilar faces had two things in common: a good tan and the expression of brutal self-confidence often worn by people who can have anybody who annoys them beaten up or killed. The younger man was Salvatore Bollano, known as Little Sallie. He was nephew to the don, learning the family business. The older man, his tutor, was Umberto Piaccere. Or Harry Pick.

Piaccere looked around the living room. His eyes fell on Frank Impellatti. For a long instant it seemed as if he was trying to remember who

53

Frank was. Then he nodded, the slightest down-
ward motion of the big head. Frank noted with
some relief that Piaccere was carrying a white
bakery box wrapped with string.

Joey Bottles now entered the living room, casually dressed and with his thin hair still damp from
the shower. Piaccere greeted him warmly and held
up the bakery box. Frank moved in unobtrusively
and took the box. He went into the kitchen, where
he had already set up the coffee things on a tray.
He opened the box and put the pastries on a
plate. There were two zabaione, two zeppole, a
millefoglie and a cannoli.

The five men arranged themselves around the
large glass coffee table in the living room. Captain
Kangaroo was blaring from the TV. Frank served
the coffee and pastries. The men selected the pastries in order of their precedence in the family,
first Piaccere and Sallie, then the others, with
Impellatti last.

Piaccere said, "Looks like Little Noodles got the
cannoli."

Sallie said, "Yeah, right, looks like cannoli ain't
too popular today."

Charlie Tuna said, "You eat cannoli, it could be
bad for your health." Everybody had a big laugh.
Even Frank laughed, although he didn't think it
was very funny. Harry Pick laughed loudest of
all, and as he did his eyes met Frank's and he
winked, and raised his hand and pointed his finger at Frank and let his thumb fall on the base of
his index finger, in the bang-bang gesture familiar
to children the world over.

Frank felt a shock of cold fear stab through his
middle and the chill of sweat on his forehead. He
looked at the cannoli on his saucer. Of course, he

would be the one to get the single cannoli—they had set it up.

The men began talking business. Frank couldn't concentrate on what they were saying. He was trying to recall something he had done or failed to do that would warrant being killed. He couldn't think of anything, but he realized this hardly mattered. It could be that somewhere in the high politics of the Honorable Society a deal had been struck, some codicil of which required that Frank Impellatti take the fall. He was under no illusions about his value to the organization.

And he had taken the fall once before. Frank, at nineteen, had driven the car for the two guys (one of them Charlie Tonnatti) who had whacked out Alfredo Baggia in the barber shop of the Park Terrace Hotel. The cops had picked him up, slammed him around, pumped him for the names of the shooters. He had kept his mouth shut. Then a man had come to see him in jail, and gave him the deal: You keep quiet, say you pulled the trigger, we'll take care of you. So he did, and they did. Eleven years in the joint and nobody ever looked at him funny. He got out, he was a made man. But this was different. Dead was dead.

Piaccere said, "Noodles, make some more coffee." Frank got up and took the pot. As he walked away his back tingled and it was all he could do to keep from cutting and racing out the door with the pot in his hands.

He went to the kitchen and washed out the pot, filled it with fresh water, measured out the coffee and plugged it in. After a while, the smell of fresh coffee filled the apartment. Piaccere called out, "Hey, Noodles, you gonna bring that coffee in here?" There was no answer. Then they looked for him, but Little Noodles was gone.

The Ferro killing made the front pages of all the tabloids, which meant that Karp had to look at the photograph of Vinnie in the gutter at every newsstand he passed on the way to work, and his spirits sunk lower at each one.

He knew what to expect when he got to the office and he got it. A message from Bloom was waiting, and on the phone the district attorney made it clear that Karp's job was to leave no stone unturned (his actual phrase) in the prosecution of the killers.

"Look, um," Karp said, "I just got in here and I haven't had time to find out what happened, except a hood got killed last night. After I meet with some people, I'll know more."

"Vinnie Ferro was not just a hood, Butch," Bloom replied, a hint of condescension oozing into his voice. "He was big time. The media are suggesting this could be the start of another major gang war."

And wouldn't you love that, thought Karp. Nothing like a Mafia-organized crime-Cosa Nostra-gang war to put the D.A.'s office in the news. What he said was, "I don't know about big time. They're all mutts when you get right down to it. Mr. Garrahy used to say, whenever there was one of these hits, that if they wanted to shoot each other he'd be glad to make Yankee Stadium available at public expense, and pay for the bullets."

This reference to Garrahy had its usual effect. Bloom's tone stiffened and he broke the connection after a few meaningless rumblings.

"Something wrong?" asked the secretary, Connie Trask. Karp's face was contorted into a rictus of disgust and outrage. He looked at her blankly and then massaged it slowly with a big hand.

"No, just what I expected. Ever since Tom Dewey, every damn prosecutor in the country's been playing gangbusters, figuring they put enough Mafia skells in jail they could get to be president or some damn thing. Especially including our own leader. Which means I'm going to have to pull people off stuff that means real paydirt and chase down shooters who are in Palermo by now and witnesses who didn't see nothing, don't know nothing—aah, shit I wish they'd all kill each other and get it over with."

Trask made sympathetic noises; Karp took a deep breath and collected his thoughts. Even at this late date, any interference in his bureau by Sanford Bloom, the district attorney of New York, got his back up, and made him want to shout obscenities.

"OK, Connie, set up a meeting. Get whoever caught the squeal from Midtown South, the detectives, me, ah, Tony Harris, Roland Hrcany, and let's get Guma in on it too. As soon as they all can. Not that it'll matter."

"So where is this guy anyway, the guy that fingered Ferro?" asked Butch Karp. He was holding, unenthusiastically, but true to his word, the meeting on the shooting of Vinnie Red. Four men were sitting around the battered oak table in the bureau chief's office: Roland Hrcany, Ray Guma, and Tony Harris, all Assistant D.A.'s, and Art Devlin, a police officer. None of them were quick to answer the question. Karp looked at the heavy, sad-faced man sitting at the far end. "Art? Any ideas?"

Art Devlin, the detective lieutenant who had caught the Ferro case out of Midtown South, said, "Could be anywhere, Butch. Out of town, probably." He shrugged. "I mean, wise guys—who knows?" His tone implied that he didn't much care either. This annoyed Karp. If *he* had to participate in this bullshit, everybody else was going to pull their weight. He frowned and replied, "Um, that's not all that helpful, Art. I mean, has anybody seen this guy the last couple of days? You got *any* people working on it, or what?"

Devlin shrugged again and ran his big hand across the bristling blond stubble on his skull. "Yeah, we got people on it, like we got people on the other six hundred and twenty one unsolved homicides on the books. There's just so much we can do. And also, a Mob hit. . . ." A final shrug.

Karp sighed. "Sure, Art, I understand. What about the shooter? Any line on that?"

"Yeah, not that you'd ever get anybody to stand up in public and repeat it, but it looks like it was Botteglia—Joey Bottles, from the Bollanos. He has a distinctive appearance."

"And he's gone too, I bet."

"I don't know about 'gone,' but he's sure as hell not at home."

"So we have no leads?"

"I didn't say that, Butch," Devlin protested, "it just takes time for information to flow in on one of these Mob things."

By which he meant, Karp knew, that the cops intended to put the minimum force into the effort until such time as mob rivalries or happenstance threw up a reliable snitch. This was fine with

Karp; he would have done the same, in fact, *intended* to do the same.

He looked around the table. "Anybody got any ideas?" he asked. "Roland?"

Karp looked at the man sitting to his right. He was ever an interesting and unusual sight. A back-swept mane of white-blond hair almost obscured Hrcany's eighteen-inch neck. His massive shoulders and arms stretched his shirt to drumhead tightness. He had a heavy-browed, hawk-nosed, belligerent face. Karp and Roland Hrcany went back a long way, having begun working for the D.A.'s office the same week, eight years ago.

Hrcany snorted. "Yeah, I got an idea. Watch the river. That's where you're gonna find Little Noodles."

"You think somebody killed him?" asked Karp. "What makes you say that?"

"It figures. He disappears the day after he fingers a hit on Vinnie Ferro—in public, by the way. We checked the planes, the trains, buses, car rental—he didn't leave town any of those ways. His wife knows from nothing and he didn't pull any money out of the bank. Also we got word from the state cops: Umberto Piaccere's got this condo up in Nyack he uses for meetings and to stash people. The state cops and the Feds keep an eye on it, maybe there'll be another Appalachin or something. There was what they call 'unusual activity' up there the morning after Vinnie got it. They spotted Piaccere and a couple of his heavy hitters and also Joey Bottles."

Hrcany paused for effect. "They also saw Impellatti. That also happens to be the last time *anybody* saw Impellatti. The cops didn't see him leave, and he sure as shit ain't there now. So it's got to be they gave him a ride down the river in a Sicilian speedboat."

"I don't understand, Roland," said Karp. "Why would they do that? I thought he just did them a favor by helping them nail Ferro."

"Favor, schmavor—come on, Butch. These are wise guys. Who else can tie Joey and Harry Pick to the Ferro hit? Hey, your nose is dripping, you're grateful you got a piece of Kleenex, but do you keep it around after it's full of snot?"

Karp grinned. That was one of the reasons he liked Roland. Karp's view of the human race had become fairly bleak by this time, but Roland made Karp look like Rebecca of Sunnybrook Farm. "That's a nice image, Roland," he said. "But if you're right, we might as well pack it in."

"He's not right, Butch. In fact, it's total bullshit," said a gravelly voice from the other end of the table. Its source was a chunky, dark-jowled, greasy-locked, pop-eyed figure slouched back in his chair and looking like a heap of dirty laundry. He wore a lavender brocade tie with a knot the size of a jelly donut yanked down to the second button of his shirt. The shirt, a white-on-white silk job, was open at the collar, revealing a mat of dark hair like old Brillo.

"Why is it bullshit, Guma?" asked Hrcany testily.

"Because," said Guma, "there is no fuckin' way Harry Pick would be worried that Noodles would rat him out on this thing. Noodles is a stand-up guy."

Hrcany rolled his eyes. "Christ, Guma! You really believe that *omerta* shit? You really think that if we dragged that little mutt in and hit him with a felony murder rap he wouldn't roll?"

Guma placed his finger beside his nose and

screwed his face into a reasonable likeness of a crafty Sicilian peasant's, which did not, after all, require much screwing. *"Cu'e orbu, bordu e taci campa cent'anni 'n paci,"* he replied.

"What the fuck's that supposed to mean?"

"It means, 'He who is deaf, dumb, and blind will live a hundred years in peace.' It's like a motto, like 'Better Living Through Chemistry.' You better believe these guys take it seriously, especially Noodles."

Hrcany looked away in disgust, but Karp signalled Guma to go on. Guma said, "You know why they call him Little Noodles? He got the name in the joint—this was Sing Sing, so it was maybe twenty years ago, before they closed it down. Impellatti was the wheelman on the Baggia hit. You remember that, Art?" Devlin nodded and Guma continued, warming to his tale. He had been with the D.A. longer than anyone else in the room and had an encyclopedic memory.

"What a mess! It was in the old Park Terrace Hotel at Thirty-fifth and Lex. There was a barbershop in the hotel with a window on the street. Al Baggia used to get shaved there every morning, get a little hot towel. Needless to say, given his line of work, he always had a couple of buttons sitting in the hallway leading to the shop. Anyway, Impellatti, he couldn't of been more than about eighteen, whips this big Caddy up onto the sidewalk right up against the window of the barbershop and the shooter—who was Charlie Tonnatti, by the way—smokes Baggia with a shotgun. And they're gone, boom!

"So the cops pick up Frank and they take him over to the Fourteenth Precinct and they give him the business, and this was before Miranda was fuckin' *born*, so they had no problems with really tearing into him. But no way could they get the name of the shooter out of him. The D.A., same shit—nothing! Then—boom! All of a sudden he confesses to being the gun. So he gets the max, nineteen years they sentence him and he don't even blink. He's in the can eleven years, not a word about the hit to anyone, and believe me they sent ringers in there to listen, too.

"Oh yeah, about the name. There was a guy in the joint at the time, a huge hulk, looked like Primo Carnera, but beefier and not as smart, name of Angie Lasagna. Frank hung out with him a lot, they kind of looked out for each other. So, naturally, because of his name they called Lasagna 'Big Noodles' and Frank was Little Noodles. Angie died a couple a years back, walked in front of a bus—"

Karp broke in, "And the point is, Goom . . . ?"

"The fuckin' *point* is that no way is Harry Pick gonna waste Frank 'cause he's worried he's gonna rat. Not if Frank had to go over for fifty years."

"OK, I see what you mean," Karp admitted. "So where is he, and why'd he skip?"

"Hey, the fuck I know! Am I his brother? But the Pick didn't kill him."

Devlin cleared his throat and said, "Ah, Butch, I got to agree with Guma. Now that we're talking about it, I remember one of my guys telling me that some Bollano people were asking around after Impellatti the weekend after Ferro got hit. They don't seem to know where he is either."

There was silence in the room for a few moments after that, which was broken by Tony Harris. "What about his car?"

Everyone looked at Harris. He was a wiry young

man in his fourth year with the Bureau, a good lawyer and the regular third-baseman on the D.A.'s softball team. "What car, Tony?" asked Karp.

"Impellatti's car. He's got a car, hasn't he? I mean, he doesn't go to work on the subway. Also, he's a driver. He wanted to get away for some reason, he'd probably take the car."

Karp looked at Devlin, whose expression was admissible evidence that no, the cops hadn't thought of looking for Little Noodles's car.

# CHAPTER 4

"So, you goin' a work today, Felix, or what?"

"Yeah, maybe, if I feel like it. You goin'?"

"I guess. But it don't start 'til four."

"You still working that security job?"

"Yeah. Fuck, I get paid for rackin' out, which I would do anyway, so. . . ."

"Yeah, hey, so what do they keep there, that, what is it, a warehouse or somethin'?"

"Yeah, a warehouse. It's all white goods, like fridges, and stoves, washers, like that."

"Any TV or stereos?

"Yeah, sometimes. Hey, Felix, you thinkin' maybe you wanna take the place off?"

"No, Stevie, I'm thinking of goin' into the fuckin' warehouse business, I wanna check out the competition. They know you been in the joint? At the job?"

"Fuck I know. They didn't ask. Shit, fuckin' half the dudes work there been in. If not, they're some kinda gook or some kind of weird nigger, from Pakistan or some damn place. Who the fuck else is gonna work that kinda job?"

The two men were silent for a moment, as if

contemplating the economic reality behind that question.

Felix Tighe was lying on a narrow sofa bed in the living room of his friend's apartment. His friend, Steve Lutz, was leaning in the doorframe that led to the apartment's bedroom, dressed in maroon gym shorts and a cut-off Rolling Stones T-shirt, the first Schlitz of the bright morning in hand.

He was a lean, muscular man in his early twenties, with a narrow, lantern-jawed face and lank, dark, neck-length hair. His arms were tattooed with the usual assortment of hearts, knives, names and snakes. He kept his mouth open, even when not talking, showing uneven yellow teeth.

Lutz took a long swallow and asked, "You wanna work out?"

"Yeah, in a minute."

Lutz disappeared into the bedroom, and shortly afterward Felix heard his grunts and the clank of weights. He rolled over and reached for his first cigarette. He tried to remember if he had exceeded his self-imposed ration of five daily cigarettes the previous evening, and decided he probably had. He had been with Anna, who smoked like a chimney. He'd have to get her to cut down.

He sat up and looked around the living room, wrinkling his nose in disgust. There were dirty clothes strewn in piles on the floor and the remains of a large pizza on the square bridge table in the center of the room. Beer cans, some crushed, some still holding stale dregs, littered the floor and overflowed the large rubber garbage pail in the corner. He could see into the tiny alcove kitchen through a torn curtain made of an Indian bedspread. Filthy dishes were piled in the sink and three squat brown bags of dripping garbage were lined up on its drainboard. The close air stank of old beer and orange peel.

Felix got out of bed, naked except for a pair of bikini underpants printed with a zebra-skin pattern, and picked his way carefully through the litter to the bathroom. He wondered how Lutz could stand to live this way. That junkie bitch he hung out with never lifted a finger around the house, at least she hadn't in the four months Felix had been crashing here. He would have to get Anna to come over and clean the joint up, or better still, get her to let him move in with her. He would ask her tonight.

The shower was tepid and weak, the tub ringed with black grime. Felix thought of his mother's spotless house. He could move back there in a minute. His skin crawled. No, he could hit her up for meals and cash, and stay an occasional night, but no way was he going to move back with Mom. It meant no women for one thing, and for another . . . he could not quite put his finger on it but there was a big reason why not. No, it would have to be Anna, even if he had to marry her, because he sure as hell was not going to spend any more time in this garbage dump, and the only other alternative, even more unattractive, was moving back in with his wife.

"Hey, little girl! Want some candy?"

Marlene Ciampi looked up from the papers on her lap as Karp sidled into the seat next to hers. He dangled a Milky Way in front of her face.

"What do I have to do, show you my undies?"

"For starters." He dropped the candy bar into her hand. She stripped off the wrapper and a full third of it vanished into her mouth. They were sitting in the back of a courtroom, Part Thirty, a calendar Part of the Supreme Court of the State of New York, watching the Honorable Albert A. Albinoli dispense justice.

"Ummpph, God, don't even joke about that stuff!" mumbled Marlene around the Milky Way. "I'm waiting on the Segura case here; we're arraigning on the indictment." She finished the candy bar and sighed contentedly as the chocolate was transformed into incandescent plasma by her remarkable metabolism. Marlene lost weight on six thousand calories a day. She radiated heat. Karp could feel it warming him on the next chair. He wanted more.

"The little girl homicide," said Karp. "Yeah, I remember."

"Look," said Marlene, "Albert's going to do a far-be-it-from-me."

Judge Albinoli was berating a young public defender who had had the temerity to argue a motion to supress evidence, thus taking up time that could be spent in getting through the calendar. Albinoli resembled the late Thomas E. Dewey, but run to fat and with an excruciatingly silly toupee. The calendar was his god.

He sprayed when he spoke. "Young man, far be it from me to make a commentary on the jurisprudence which you have averted to, far be it from me, but I too have passed the bar examination, and I have to tell you that I wouldn't throw out this evidence if you paid me." A mild titter drifted through the courtroom. Albinoli smiled, as if he had delivered a witticism. Although there were many in the purlieus of Centre Street to whom the term might apply, when people around the courts said "The Asshole" the reference was almost always to this particular one.

Marlene rolled her eyes and looked over at Karp, but he seemed lost in thought. After a minute he said, "Speaking of that case, Marlene, do you recall that little spat we had, couple of months ago, about you and the other female person attorneys picking up more than your share of these juvenile rape and murder? You still feel you got a problem?"

"As a matter of fact, now that you mention it, I do sense a slacking off in that department. I also see by the smug expression on your face that you think you had something to do with the fix."

"You could say that. I had a few words with the clerical staff in the complaint room."

"So it *wasn't* a random thing at all. Somebody *was* putting it to the ladies."

"Somebody was, and they ain't any more, so far as I can tell. Anyhow, the boys are pulling their load in the child abuse area, and not too happy about it either."

"My heart bleeds, the scumbags!"

"Yeah, for some reason it's hard to get them to take those cases seriously, except when they're actual homicides. They call them 'spankers'."

"Spankers?" Marlene shook her head. "Oh shit, that's nauseating."

"Yeah, well, they're a hard bunch . . ." His voice trailed off. Marlene's attention had turned to the business of the court. Karp stood up to go. "Gosh, thanks, Butch," said Karp. "You're welcome, Marlene."

She looked up at him sternly. "Thanks. For the candy. I'm not going to thank you for doing your job. Which you should have started doing a year ago." A look of pain and guilt spread like a stain across Karp's face. She saw it and felt an instant and stunning remorse, but kept her face hard. Somebody had to pay for all her misery, and Karp was her favorite target, both handy and vulnerable.

"Fine, Marlene," answered Karp tightly, "as long as we're being so professional, what about this Segura case? She going to plead?"

"As a matter of fact, no. She insists that she's innocent. I offered her a good deal, but she turned me down. Wouldn't even consider it."

"Shit, Marlene, you mean we're going to *try* this thing?"

"Yeah, we're going to try it. Unless you want to say, 'Hey, Mrs. Segura, sorry about the inconvenience, but try to watch it with the other kids, OK?' What the fuck, Butch! I thought you were Mr. Trial."

Karp felt his face grow warm. It was true. He needed trial slots to threaten the professional badmen and their lawyers. Otherwise, why would anybody, even the most patently guilty, take a stiff prison sentence on a plea bargain? After all, didn't they have the right to a speedy trial? So spending a trial slot on what in his true heart he saw as a crummy domestic slaying irked him, and worse, filled him with shame that his situation had led him to regard the brutal murder of a little girl as a professional annoyance. Marlene was still staring at him. The court was hearing a plea of not guilty on a vehicular homicide. Something nagged at his mind.

"Umm, OK, Marlene, you offered manslaughter one?"

"Of course! And negligent homicide. Nothing doing. She says she never touched the kid."

"Are you sure she did?" asked Karp.

Marlene opened her mouth to say something, but at that moment the clerk called out "Segura!" and Marlene had to walk down the aisle to the well of the court to help Albert the Asshole arraign Maria Segura for the intentional murder of her daughter Lucy.

Two burly female guards brought in the accused, who proved to be a small, biscuit-colored woman, barely out of her teens, with a sharp nose, a downcast mouth and dark, soft-looking pads under her eyes. Karp watched as she pleaded not guilty in an accented and almost inaudible voice. Karp thought she looked about as dangerous as a dust mop.

The judge remanded her for trial. The public defender made a perfunctory argument for a reduction in bail. The woman had two small children to look after. The judge said that this woman asking for a bail reduction so she could look after her children was like the man who killed both his parents asking for mercy on the grounds that he was an orphan. The judge got his titter from the onlookers. He beamed horribly. The guards shuffled Maria Segura out the narrow door. Next case.

Marlene came up the aisle tight jawed and frowning. Karp said, "I like the way your eyebrows almost touch when you have that expression on your face. What's wrong? I thought you did OK. The dread Mrs. Segura is not out menacing our citizens."

"Fuck you, Karp! What did you mean, 'Are you sure she did it?' "

"Well, it just struck me that one explanation of Segura's intransigence on the plea is that she is in fact innocent. Also, if you're going to try a homicide against a defendant with no priors who doesn't look up to wasting a cockroach, you better have the case really nailed down. Do you?''

"Yeah! Of course I do. Shit, Butch I got an indictment from the grand jury on this thing—''

"Marlene, don't bullshit me!" said Karp, his voice rising. "The grand jury would indict Mother Theresa if a D.A. told it to, as we both well know. I want to know what we *got*.''

Marlene looked over her shoulder at the judge, who was glowering at them. "Miss Ciampi, far be it from me to interrupt what appears to be a fascinating conversation. . . .''

"Yes, Your Honor," said Marlene. "Sorry, we were just going.''

With that she gathered her brown envelopes under her arm and made for the door, Karp following.

A few minutes later they were in Marlene's office. She lit up and watched the smoke rise up the high, narrow shaft of her office. "All right,'' she said after a while, "I fucked this up. We got garbage for a serious trial. I was figuring the percentages: a parent kills a kid, what they *want* is punishment. Ninety-nine times out of a hundred they'll cop to anything you offer, just to avoid standing up in public while somebody tells all about how they used the knitting needles on little Mary.''

"So what *do* we have?" said Karp unsympathetically. He was angry with Marlene, and angry with himself for not keeping closer tabs on her and the other attorneys. That doing so was plainly impossible, given the caseload of the Criminal Courts Bureau, did not diminish his anger one whit. A case like this would have been laughed out of the old homicide bureau in a New York minute.

"The history of child abuse. Butch, honestly, that's what threw me. This kid has been through Bellevue emergency over forty times—broken wrists, ribs, bruises, cuts, burns, the whole nine yards. It just seemed too *obvious* that the mom had gone a hair too far.

"Then the clothes. The kid was naked when they found her in the dumpster, in the trash bag. The cops found her bloody clothes in another trash bag—the same kind of bag—in the air shaft right under Segura's window. There was a package of the same kind of trash bags in her kitchen.

"The sexual abuse part—the child was raped, repeatedly, but what else is new? The mother had men in, nobody steady, different ones, all the time. Maybe one of them wanted seconds after the mom passed out. Or maybe ten of them. Did the cops interview every one of her known companions? Hah-Hah. So that's fucked up too.

"But . . . the woman doesn't have an alibi for the time of the killing. Says she was sleeping one off, alone. That's it. Pretty thin, huh?"

"Yeah. So where's the finger?"

"The what?"

"The finger, Marlene, the little girl's finger. I seem to remember you telling me it was cut off. Did you find it?"

"No. I figure she got rid of it, down the can or something. I was thinking a crazy punishment that got out of hand, you know? 'Be a good girl or Mama will cut off your finger.' Then afterward, the kid wouldn't stop crying, the mother got scared, tried to shut the kid up, and bingo! Lights out. It's happened before."

72

That was just the problem, Karp thought. It's all happened before: repetition, the boring banality of crime, of seeing what people did to one another. It deadened not only the intellect, as in this case, because Marlene Ciampi was arguably one of the most intelligent lawyers in the bureau, but also extinguished the moral imagination, so that the people of the Courthouse could no longer look at the accused and say, "Could this person have done thus and so? Could *I* have done thus and so, if I were that person?" There were so many, and so alike, that after a while the association between the particular crime and the particular defendant—the essence of justice—didn't matter. And if that didn't matter, nothing mattered: the creeping death of Centre Street.

He wanted to shout at her, to shake her, but instead he sat and looked down at his hands, and said in a low voice, "That's an interesting idea. What does the M.E.'s report say? Does it confirm?" He saw in her face that she didn't know, that if she had read the Medical Examiner's report (among a thousand such reports) its message had failed to penetrate the part of her consciousness that was frozen into horrified routine.

Wordlessly Marlene shuffled through the case file and began to turn pages. Karp looked at the distant ceiling. In a few minutes he heard a gasp, a muffled "Oh, shit!"

"What?"

"It's right here." Marlene wailed, her cheekbones red with embarrassment. She read, " 'Fifth digit of right hand missing. Signs of recent amputation at point one centimeter proximal to the first carpal joint. Crushing of tissues on both lateral and medial surfaces of stump suggest removal

73

instrument was a heavy shears. Lack of circumferential bruising and normal clotting suggest amputation occurred *post-mortem*.' I'm *dying!*"

She slapped the base of her hand hard against her forehead. "God! What an idiot! I can't *believe* I missed that. OK, Marlene, superstar, do you believe that this ratty little woman, who wants a trial, strangled her daughter in a fit of rage, and then calmly cut off her finger with a scissors? Why? And then took her body down to the dumpster, forgetting the finger? And . . . oh, shit, why go on? It's all garbage. We got to check the men . . . no that doesn't make sense either. I can't believe a casual . . . oh, shit!"

She sprang to her feet and started gathering up her bag and raincoat. "What are you going to do now?" asked Karp, surprised by this instant action.

"Do? I'm going to reopen this investigation. Jesus, Butch! If Segura didn't do it, and I don't think she did any more, we got some stranger running around who likes to kill little girls. And takes souvenirs."

After his shower, Felix Tighe put on a black exercise suit and went into Steve Lutz's bedroom to work out. They helped each other with bench presses, whooshing air out of their lungs and groaning at the peak of the effort. Then Lutz did sit-ups with a twenty-pound weight held behind his head while Felix did bicep curls with thirty-pound dumbbells in front of a full-length mirror. He was feeling good, lifting smoothly, in control, just getting into watching his definition ripple, when the phone rang. He dropped the dumbbells with a clang. "I'll get it, man, it's probably for me anyway. Anna's supposed to call me."

He took the phone off its hook on the kitchen wall. It was for him, but it wasn't Anna. The voice on the phone was rich and dark. Whenever he heard it he felt the same odd feeling, a mixture of desire mixed with something close to dread.

"Hello, Denise," he said, his mouth dry.

"How's my big boy today?"

"Fine, Denise. What you up to?"

"Oooh, just lounging. Lounging in my tub, in perfumed water with lots of suds. I'm making my skin silky and clean. And you know why, don't you. Yes you do. I'd like to have your hairy body in this tub right now. I'd like to bathe you and lick you dry, like a momma cat. Lick you everyplace. Would you like that? Yes, you would, you dirty child. But not today. It's not our day yet, is it?"

"No, Denise."

"No, it's next week. Next Friday. I'll just have to wait. I'll just have to wait, and keep myself stimulated until then. Would you like to listen to that, to me stimulating myself?" She giggled. He heard faint splashing, and then other sounds.

He listened. His skin burned and felt thick, as if he were on some drug. He had to listen to the sounds. She called out his name, her voice rising, cracking. There was silence on the line, except for her breathing and the movement of the water.

Felix said, "Good-bye, Denise," and hung up the phone. He slid down the wall and sat on the floor and put his head between his knees, and waited for the strange pleasure sickness to go away.

He tried once again to figure out how he had gotten in with Denise, when it had started. He couldn't remember, which was odd in itself, because Felix kept a meticulous record of all his appointments and accomplishments in a series of small, black notebooks, going back to high school. She had just appeared one week and after that, she was always there once or twice a month, forever.

He stood up, shakily, and at once the telephone rang again. It was his lawyer from Queens, a morose little man named Dudnick.

"Mr. Tighe," said the lawyer in his precise, dry voice, "I've been trying to reach you all week."

"Yeah? Well, I been busy. What do you want?"

"I wanted to remind you that your trial begins in four days. There are a number of things we need to discuss beforehand."

"What things? I'm getting off, right?"

Dudnick cleared his throat. Criminal law at this level was not really his specialty. The white-shoe law firm that Mrs. Tighe used for her business and trust dealings retained him as a convenience for its distinguished clientele. The bulk of his practice consisted of arguing for leniency in cases where wealthy people had gotten drunk behind the wheel or bought marijuana from the wrong person. He had racked up thousands of hours of community service sentences. This was different.

"Well, in fact, Mr. Tighe, I have been in contact with the Queens District Attorney and he appears willing to accept a plea of guilty to breaking and entering and felony assault, which is quite an advance for us. The indictment is for attempted first-degree murder and burglary."

"Does that get me off?"

"Not exactly, Mr. Tighe. We would expect a sentence of from three to five years in—"

"Three to five! You're outta your mind, three to five!"

"Of course, in all probability you would only have to serve eighteen months."

"Fuck me, eighteen months! Listen, asshole—I'm not serving eighteen minutes. I want *off*, understand! I'm not going to goddamn prison on the say-so of some dumb nigger cop. They got nothing on me."

"Well, actually, Mr. Tighe, as I've tried to explain to your mother, they have quite a bit on you. You actually were caught red-handed, so to speak, in that they were able to remove samples of that policeman's blood from your hands and clothing."

"That don't mean shit. They could of made it all up just to frame me."

"Yes, but that's something we can discuss at our meeting. Now when would you like to come by? Mr. Tighe? Hello, Mr. Tighe?"

Felix slammed down the receiver, shaking the phone and making it ring faintly. He went back into the bedroom, fuming. Felix had never been a clever burglar, just a lucky one. And considering the priority given in recent years to low-grade burglaries by the police in New York, he did not even have to be that lucky. He'd been picked up a couple of times as a kid, but his Ma had got him off. Since he'd turned eighteen he'd been pulling a couple of jobs a month and never a breath of trouble. Felix was not into self-criticism, but he had to admit to himself that he'd gotten cocky, coming down the ladder like that, with a cop car right under. He'd have to lie low on the burglary business for a while, maybe figure out another scam.

"So, who was it? You look pissed off," ob-

served Lutz, who was setting up the weights to
do his jerk and press sequence.

"My fuckin' lawyer, the dickhead. He says I'm
going to have to go up for this piece of shit thing
in Queens."

"Hey, man, that's a son-of-a-bitch, ain't it. So
what're you gonna do? I mean split or what?"

Felix didn't bother to answer. He had all he
could do to ride out the waves of fury that were
rolling through him, blackening his vision and
churning his guts. He was furious at the lawyer,
of course, and at his mother for hiring the asshole,
and at Anna for not having been on the phone
instead of Dudnick. He slammed his knotty fist
into his thigh. None of those people was immediately to hand. There was only one person in the
apartment besides himself.

"Hey, Stevie," he said, "get out the mats. We'll
do a little karate."

Lutz dropped his barbell and looked up, an
expression of nervous concern wrinkling his low
brow. "What, you mean *gohon*?"

"Nah, fuck that shit. I feel like some freestyle."

Lutz whined, "Ah, crap, Felix, you're gonna
whip my ass again."

Felix grinned unpleasantly. "I don't know, Stevie.
You might get lucky. Meanwhile it's good training. You don't spar, you'll never make black belt,
hey? So stop being a pussy and get the mats out."

Marlene was in the bullpen of the Criminal
Courts Bureau, perched on the corner of a clerk's
battered desk, making the calls necessary to get
the Segura case started up again. It was a place of
business she often preferred to her own isolated
office. She was trying to get a homicide lieutenant

in Manhattan South to assign people to a case he thought he had wrapped up weeks ago. Since he had about sixty working homicides that were no-where near wrapped up, he was less than excited at the prospect.

"Let me get this straight, Ms. Ciampi," said Lieutenant Shaughnessy, his voice on the phone suspiciously calm. "You're throwing out this case because you just found out the kid's finger got cut off after she was dead and not before."

"Yeah. You understand what that means, don't you?"

"Um . . ."

"Lieutenant, the mother beats up the kid. We know that. She's an abuser. So the theory was that she went too far, killed the kid in a rage, and then tried to get rid of the body. But the fact that the finger was amputated after death doesn't jibe with a typical domestic child murder."

"It don't, huh? What does it jibe with, then?"

"A maniac."

"What are you talking about, lady?"

"A maniac, Lieutenant. Who else kills kids and cuts off their fingers? Jaywalkers? And he did it once, he could do it again."

"Maybe the mother did it and cut off the finger to make us think it was a maniac," said the lieu-tenant, grasping.

"Right. Good idea. You want to take the chance that there won't ever be a repeat?"

There was silence on the line for a long mo-ment. Of all the things that could derail Lieuten-ant Shaughnessy's stately progress toward thirty-and-out with a captain's pension, a serial child murderer was close to the top of the list. There would be reporters. There would be outraged editorials. There would be parents with placards.

The brass would be watching his every move and they would set up a special task force that would take half his men, and naturally, he wouldn't get any relief from his normal clearance quota in the meantime. Of course, if he told this crazy bitch to get stuffed, which was his first impulse, and it turned out there really was a loony cutting up kids, he would spend the rest of his career running a motor pool in the South Bronx. An idea flickered across his mind.

"Uh, well, you sound like you could have a real problem there, Miss Ciampo. Tell you what I'll do. How would it be if I transferred a couple of good detectives over to the D.A. squad?"

"That would be great," replied Marlene cautiously. "But what's the catch, Lieutenant? They stop killing people in your end of the city?"

"Yeah, we stopped crime around here. The thing of it is, Miss Ciampo . . ."

"Ciampi, Lieutenant. Ms."

"Yeah, right, the thing of it is, we'd naturally expect them to carry over their cases for the duration of the detail."

"Naturally," Marlene agreed. She vaguely suspected she was being shafted in some subtle bureaucratic way, but didn't have time to figure it out. And the offer was too good to turn down.

"So, if that's OK with you . . . ah, Ms.?"

"Yeah, deal. What do I have to do?"

"Not a thing. I'll call Fred Spicer and put together the detail papers," said Shaughnessy smoothly, and broke the connection before she could change her mind.

An hour later, having made several dozen telephone calls from the same perch, setting up witnesses, talking to public defenders, and making appointments, Marlene became aware that she was sitting in the workspace of another person, who had for some time been carrying out her tasks minus the advantages of either a phone or a Marlene-bottom-sized section of her desk.

"Uh, sorry, Dana, I'm in your way."

The woman fluttered her hands and grinned, revealing a row of crooked poor-people teeth.

"Garsh, Marlene, that's awright," said Dana Woodley, in an accent infrequently heard in the halls of 100 Centre Street. Woodley was an anomaly on the D.A.'s support staff, which ran more typically to gum-cracking tough kids from Queens with stiletto heels and whore make-up or struggling black single mothers. She hailed from an Appalachian hollow called Daggersville, and had been transplanted to New York by way of a crashed love affair that left her with a kid, a suitcase, and no prospects. She dressed in frilly white blouses tied with little velvet bows, and narrow dark skirts. Her best feature was a mass of glowing auburn hair, which she kept in a long cheerleader's pony tail. Besides that, her face was long and sallow, and devoid of make-up, and her eyes were the color of damp stone, thin and wary.

As she smiled back at this woman, Marlene could not help but be aware of the admiration, nearly the adoration, in the other's look. The notion that a woman could be a lawyer and deal with men on an equal footing had hit Dana Woodley like a shot of benzedrine. For her part, Marlene had not been a role model before this, and was not averse to a little admiration.

Marlene got off the desk, lit a cigarette, and

said, "What a day! Did you ever feel, when you bought something you thought you wanted, that whoever sold it to you knew you were coming?"

"Oh, sure, all the time. 'Course, I am an ol' hillbilly, no reason they shouldn't try to treat me like a sucker. If'n they can get away with it, which they-all'd have to get up purty early in the day t'do."

Marlene laughed. "Whut's s'funny," asked Woodley.

"Sorry, I get a kick out of your rap, is all. No, it's no lie. I could listen to that corn pone talk all day. It's like a cheap tour out of here. Meanwhile, speaking of sucker, I just arranged to get two cops in here on a detail to reopen the Segura case, and I think I got taken, and I can't figure out how."

"Shoot, Marlene, long as they gave you the overhead along with the two bodies I don't see how they—"

"Wait . . . overhead?"

"Uh-huh. That's support staff, paperclips, phones, and like that. See, if'n they come 'n work outa this office, we got to supply all o' that? So they got to agree on a fund transfer cause it's a different budget—the po-lice, 'n all?"

"Oh, shit! You're probably right. That jerk-off! I better go see Karp before Spicer gets to him."

"Yeah. Say, how come y'all reopenin' Segura?"

Marlene quickly explained the reasoning behind the decision, which Dana grasped rather more quickly than had Lieutenant Shaughnessy. Her mouth tightened and her eyes got flat and hard.

"I swear, Marlene, thing like that. . . . 'Vengeance is mine saith the Lord' according to gospel, an' I mostly believe it, but a man'd do a thang like that to a little girl, it's just so purely mean, some'n like that just wants killin'. An' I always think of Carol Anne. Shoot, they make it sorrowful hard on motherin' in this city!"

"They do, all right. How's the kid, by the way. Day care working out?"

The thin face brightened. "Oh, my, yes! We got us a scholarship through the church. It ain't half a purty place, too. Carol Anne cain't wait to go in the mornin's."

"Terrific! It almost restores my faith in anything working out. Speaking of which, I better get right in there."

Karp's day had continued to deteriorate. During the afternoon of the initial meeting on the Ferro killing, Tony Harris had come grinning into his office with what he imagined was good news.

"Hey, Butch, how about this!" Harris was waving a piece of yellow paper, his face creased by a snaggly smile.

"What you got, Tony?"

"I was right. His car's gone. Impellatti's. One of Devlin's guys just called. They talked to the attendant at the garage where he kept it. The guy remembers Impellatti coming in and asking for it, maybe three in the afternoon the day after the Ferro hit. The guy said," here he read from the paper, " 'Impellatti looked dishevelled and nervous, not normal, like he'd been running.' "

"That's real interesting, Tony," said Karp, finding it difficult to enjoy the other man's enthusiasm. "So where did he run to?"

"This I don't know. The other question is why was he running, if Guma's right."

"You mean about Harry Pick having no beef with him? It's a plausible theory, but it doesn't get us anywhere. He could be in Timbuktu by now, and even if he walked in the door tomorrow we still wouldn't have a case against the shooter or Harry Pick."

"You mean because there's no independent corroboration? Yeah, but if we had Impellatti, surely we could get somebody at the scene to come across."

"At the *scene*?" exclaimed Karp, his eyes popping. "That crowd at Alberto's? *Witnesses*? Dream on, child!"

Harris's face fell. "So what do we do with this?" He flapped his paper.

"File it, Tony. File it deep. If Noodles walks in here or if Harry Pick has a crisis of conscience and wants to confess, then you can dig it out. Don't look at me like that! You think I don't sympathize? Everybody wants to fry a don. It beats the shit out of running fucked-up skinny black kids through the mill, hey? But right now, my boy, there's no percentage in putting any more steam into this one."

Then the phone rang and he had a long, unpleasant conversation with the head of the D.A. Investigations Squad. And then Marlene came in, looking belligerent.

"I just got my ass chewed by Fred P. Spicer, our noble D.A. squad chief," said Karp sourly when he saw Marlene. "And as you know, he is one of the people I least like to get chewed by. What did you do?"

"I know, I know, I forgot to nail down the overhead."

"The overhead! Shit, Marl, that's only the half of it. You said they could keep their cases? On a detail? Which means Shaughnessy's going to maintain his clearance quotas on my budget. Plus, you didn't name-request the two officers, which means Shaughnessy could send over a couple of clapped-out boozers he's been trying to get rid of for years."

"He wouldn't dare!"

"I don't know about that, but as it turns out he didn't. We're getting Balducci and Raney, which from his point of view is almost as good."

"Why? Are they duds?"

"No. Balducci's a decent cop, a good detective. Trouble is, he's retiring this year. So, what happens is, Shaughnessy fills the vacant slot with a fresh body. The quotas that go with that body are supposed to be assigned to the refill, but since Balducci'll be checking out from Spicer's shop, the quotas'll hang around here for at least a couple months. Nobody'll really expect us to follow up on them, but Shaughnessy'll get a free ride for the duration of the switch. It's a classic buddy-fuck: cop trick number four-oh-seven-two-b. Spicer's gonna need a quart of Vaseline for his ass."

"And Raney? Tell me he's the famous brain-damage case."

"No, but I could see where Shaughnessy might want to get rid of him. You remember that Clint Eastwood shoot-out in the Schmitkin Bakery last summer? Off-duty cop, four perps, heavily armed, all four ended up dead?"

"Yeah, in Jamaica. That was Raney?"

"That was Raney. Pistol Jim Raney, as I believe he's called. A credit to the force, especially if the Viet Cong ever try to take Manhattan."

"Oh, Christ, that's all I need on Segura!"

"Segura! You're doing this for Segura?"

"Yeah. What's the matter? I told you I was reopening the investigation. We discussed it."

The phone rang. Karp ignored it.

"We didn't discuss anything, Marlene," he said testily. "You made up your mind and ran off, and left me with the mess. As usual."

"As usual! Fuck you, 'as usual!' That's what I love about talking to you, these little zingers you put in there—like I'm nothing but a fuck-up around here."

The phone rang again.

"Aren't you going to answer that?" Marlene asked.

"No! And, first of all, I didn't say you were a fuck-up. I just meant there's a way to do stuff right, procedure—"

"Procedure! Do my ears deceive me? When did you become such a bureaucrat all of a sudden? Look, Butch—you really going to tell me I can't have two lousy cops to look in to what could be a goddamn maniac wandering around out—"

"I didn't say you couldn't have them! Did I say you couldn't have the damn cops? Although, of course after Balducci hands in his potsy, you'll only have Raney, the biggest loose cannon in the N.Y.P.D. And as I recall it, you were going to hang the mother for this one until I stepped in."

"You're never gonna let me forget that, are you? I can't believe you're being this way, just because fucking Spicer . . ."

The door opened, after a perfunctory knock, and Connie Trask's face appeared in the doorway. "That call's for you, Butch," she said, smiling sweetly. "See, the way it works is, when it rings, you're supposed to pick it up and talk in the little holes there."

"Connie, come on, I'm busy. Can't I call them back?"

"Um, guy sounded like he had to talk to you right now. It's long distance. A Mr. Frank Impellatti."

"Holy shit! Little Noodles?"

"He didn't say nothing about noodles," said Trask. "Pick up on three."

Karp was on the phone for about two minutes, during which he said "uh-huh" half a dozen times. Then he said, "Wait a minute, Impellatti, I got a lot more questions. How do I . . . ah, shit!" Karp stared angrily at the receiver and then tossed it back in its cradle.

"What was that?" asked Marlene.

"That was Frank Impellatti, the guy who fingered Vinnie Red. I can't believe this—I was just talking to Tony about this, that we needed this guy to walk in, and now he walks in. This is like the movies."

"Where is he?"

"He's hiding out in California. In Beverly fucking Hills, if you can believe it. He wants to come in and spill his guts on the Ferro hit, maybe some other stuff, too."

"Butch, that's great!"

"Yeah, maybe," Karp said glumly. "He says he won't move unless I go out there and get him. It has to be me, and alone."

"No kidding? Why'd he pick you?"

"The fuck I know. He said, 'I'm a no bullshit guy, and I hear you're a no bullshit guy, so maybe we could do business.' That was it."

"You don't get a tribute like that every day."

"Yeah, my head's still in a whirl. Look, kiddo, about the two cops, I'll figure out some way to fix it. But only until Balducci retires. We don't have a case by then. . . ." He shrugged and made a gesture of helplessness, his hands spread and fluttering.

But Marlene seemed to be thinking about something else.

"So. You're going to California."

"Looks like it."

"You'll be down in L.A. Were you thinking about going up north, checking out your old stamping grounds?"

"I hadn't thought about it, obviously, but it's an idea."

"Like where might you go? For instance."

Karp looked at her. She was staring out the window. When he was silent, she turned to face him, holding her head slightly cocked so she could make full use of her good eye.

Karp said, "This is an interesting line of questioning, counselor, but I'm not sure where you're leading."

"Oh, well, I just thought that since you asked me to marry you lo, these many months, and since we might be considered to be engaged, but we can't really, because you are, after all, still married to a woman who, I seem to recall, lives north of L.A. out there, I just thought that you might take this opportunity to locate this woman and obtain her signature on a petition for divorce. That was my thinking."

"It was, huh?"

"Yes. And since the fact that we are neither married nor engaged has not prevented you from leaping on my body at every possible opportunity to do the dirty, and monopolizing my time in the bargain, thus preventing me from finding an alternative life's companion, and since I have absolutely no desire to be a forty-year-old office girlfriend, which I have recently felt well on the

way to becoming, it strikes me that this would be
an ideal time to take care of that little business."

"It strikes you that way, does it?"

She came toward him then, and leaned over
him as he sat in his chair. She put her face very
close to his, and placed her warm hand on the
back of his neck, above the collar. It burned against
his skin and he felt the sweat start from his
forehead.

"Yes, it does," she said. "And moreover, as we
say in subpoenas, 'therefore, fail not,' because if
you come back from California without said petition, as much as I love you, and as much as I dig
to explore the ultimate frontiers of sexual pleasure
with you, I will fucking cut off your water, and
you will never get to experience the elaborate
erotic treats I have been storing away for my wedding night since the first glimmers of puberty.
What do you say to that, buster?"

"You got a deal," said Karp.

# CHAPTER
# 5

**K**arp was gone the next morning, the Tuesday, flying the friendly skies to Los Angeles and Little Noodles. On the unfriendly earth, meanwhile, Marlene Ciampi trudged through her day, trying not to think about Karp, or where he was going, or whether he was really going to find his wife, and do the necessary thing. Mostly, she succeeded, helped in no small part by the deadening routine of the calendar court at which she was now representing the people of the state in their fight against crime.

"Calendar 104, John Mogle," said the uniformed court officer. Two men got up from a bench at the rear of the courtroom and started up the center aisle. Marlene checked her files and the list of numbers she had prepared and found 104. She stuck her list between her teeth, balanced most of her folders on the hip-high wooden barrier that divided the well of the court from the spectators' benches and thumbed rapidly through the stack of folders that pertained to this court, Part 42.

She pulled the right file, read through it: a hit and run with injuries. The two men, one thin, middle-aged in a gray suit, the other bigger, younger, in a long leather coat—lawyer and defendant—reached the barrier, and the court officer let them through. Marlene piled her stacks on the edge of a table and went to join the two men before the bench, still reading the complaint.

"Are the People ready?" asked the judge.

"Yes, Your Honor," said Marlene, voicing the perpetual lie of the Criminal Courts, as she finished reading the complaint and simultaneously prepared her plea bargain, all thoughts of Karp driven from her mind.

Four cases later, having finished her responsibility at this particular Part, Marlene loaded her files into a ragged brown paper portfolio, waved to the clerks and court officers and headed out for her next courtroom.

Two men stood up as she passed them and followed her out.

"Miss Ciampi?" said one of them, touching her arm.

She could tell they were cops because they had their shields dangling from their breast pockets. But even without the shields, she would have known. They were both cops around the eyes.

The older of the two, the man who had spoken, was a medium-sized man in a cheap gray suit, with a face the color and texture of a used grocery bag left out in the rain, folded, wrinkled, covered with pale brown spots. He had thinning black hair combed straight back and dark pouches under dark eyes that were liquid, sad and wise.

"I'm Detective Balducci," he said in a soft voice. "This is Detective Raney." Raney was the Bad Cop of the team, naturally. He had the classic wiry track-and-field body and was a strawberry blond besides, with thick dollops of hair like red gold framing a flat, pale face. As she shook hands Marlene saw a scattering of freckles, no nose to speak of, a long thin mouth curled in a wise-ass smirk, eyes the color of the shallow end of a swimming pool.

His handshake was slightly harder than necessary. The smirk again, but the eyes didn't join in. The eyes were distant, intelligent, but with something there besides, something a little scary. An odd feeling shot through Marlene, repugnance mixed with curiosity, even attraction. Another crazy Irishman. *Pazz' irlandesi*, her grandmother would have said, rolling her eyes heavenward.

They walked to her little office, where she laid out the case of the murder and violation of Lucy Segura. Balducci took notes. Raney perched on the side of her desk and stared at her, except when she happened to look at him, when he looked quickly down at his long, freckled hands.

When she had finished, Balducci closed his notebook and got to his feet. He gave her an avuncular smile and said, "OK, Miss Ciampi. . . ."

"Please, it's Marlene."

"Yeah? I got a niece Marlene. I'm Pete. He's Jimmy. OK, Marlene, we'll get right on this thing. I'm not saying we're gonna devote like full-time to it or anything, but we will check it out."

"I appreciate that, Pete, but really, what do you think?"

Balducci glanced at his partner before he answered. "Well . . . you know, these things, with kids. It's usually somebody they know. . . ."

"Right!" said Marlene vehemently. "But this doesn't *feel* right for one of those. . . ."

"Intuition?" Raney asked this in a flat voice, almost mocking. Then he added, "Marlene."

Marlene scowled at him. He looked away and joined his partner in the doorway. "No, not intuition. I notice you didn't say woman's intuition. Jimmy."

"Not guilty," said Raney.

"The reason it's not intuition is that somebody chopped the girl's finger off after she was dead. You recall? I can't see the family sex offender doing that, can you?"

"If he was trying to make somebody think he was a weirdo, I could," Raney snapped back, a bar of color starting across his cheekbones.

"We'll check it out, Marlene," said Balducci. "C'mon, Jimmy."

In the car, Balducci fished the butt of a Parodi cigar out of the ashtray and lit it. "So? What do you think?" he asked, puffing vigorously.

"The D.A.? I'm in love, Petey. What a face! What a terrific little ass! In that little knit dress. I had to sit on my hands up there. I was wondering what would happen, all the time she was yapping away, what would happen if I just reached out and gave it just a slow, firm squeeze."

"A ninety-day suspension would happen, asshole. I meant the fuckin' case."

"Oh, that. A piece of shit. Some spic fucked her, then killed her, then he panicked and figured to lay it on some looney. But, you know, Peter, I believe, in the interests of crime-prevention we should leave no stone unturned in this one, and since it's such an involved case, I think we're gonna need a lot of guidance from the D.A. A lot of conferences. A lot of reviewing the evidence. Strategizing. In the evenings."

Balducci glanced sourly at his partner. "Forget

it, Raney. She's definitely out of your league. Besides, you know Karp, the bureau chief?"

"Yeah, the big guy. What about him?"

"She's the girlfriend. They're a serious item, I hear."

"I could care less. I don't want to marry her. I just want to spread that little ass and fuck her brains out a couple three times. Don't look at me that way, Balducci! You're not my goddamn father."

"I wish I was, I'd break your head."

Raney rolled his eyes and assumed his habitual expression of disdainful boredom. He started the car and shot out into traffic.

"One-fourteenth and Lex, the bereaved momma," he said. "Then some strategizing with the D.A. Marlene."

Maria Segura sat up stiff in her chair at her kitchen table, looking at nothing. Balducci sat across from her, his notebook out. Raney paced back and forth behind her. A child, the three-year-old Carmen, played on the dirty floor with some pots, a broken and naked plastic doll, and an old carton. The other child, five, was in school. In the other room, a large color TV blared out *Lust for Life*. Segura shook her head loosely. The etheric stink of active alcoholism filled the apartment, floating lightly over the basic stench of East Harlem tenements: garbage, bad drains, stale urine.

"I tole you. I tole you a million times. I don' know nothin' 'cep what I a'ready tole you. I lay down, she's here watchin' TV. I wake up, she's gone. Then the cops came. I tole them the same exac' thing."

"You remember seeing her with anybody? Did she talk about meeting anybody? A man?"

"Bogeyman!" shouted the little girl from the floor. "Bogey, bogey Man!"

"Shut up, Carmen!" said her mother. "What I know, where she goes, who she sees? She's a wild kid, Lucy."

"Was," said Raney from behind her. "Was. She's dead."

Segura did not respond to this, but looked longingly toward a cupboard, where dwelt her true love.

"How about this one here," asked Balducci gently. "She a wild one, too?"

"What, Carmen? Nah, she's a sweetheart, never gives me no trouble." She turned to the child and cooed, "Ain't you a sweetheart, baby?"

The child looked up, as if startled by this affectionate tone. She scrambled to her feet and toddled over to the table. She wore a Care-Bears T-shirt and underpants. "Dolly," she said, and placed the broken pink carcass on the table, stretching on tip-toe to reach.

"That's a nice dolly," said Balducci affectionately.

"I'm going to look through Lucy's stuff, Maria. That all right?" Raney asked. The woman nodded and he went down the narrow hallway to the children's bedroom.

Carmen was rummaging in her carton. In a moment, she stood up and trotted back to the table. She had a doll in each hand, both of which she gravely handed to Balducci.

"Go play, Carmen!" said the mother. "Don't bother the man, hey!"

"No, that's all right, Missus. I want to see the dollies."

Balducci held one in each hand and smiled at the little girl. Then his scalp prickled and his belly tightened. One of the dolls was a filthy Barbie with one leg and half its hair gone. He put it on the table and held the other one up.

"Mrs. Segura," he asked, "where did this come from?"

Mrs. Segura looked at the doll and shrugged. "I dunno. I think, maybe Lucy brung it home. I think she say she found it inna garbage."

"Uh-huh." He turned to the child. "Carmen," he said, as gently as he could, "where did you get this doll?"

"Lucy's dolly," she said. "I could play wif it," she added, growing worried.

"Sure you can. But do you know where Lucy got it?"

The child was silent for a long time. Balducci waited, smiling hard. Then in a low voice she said, "Bogeyman. It's a secret."

Raney clumped back into the room. "Nothing except this." Raney held up a glittering object, but Balducci gestured him into silence and turned his attention to Carmen.

"Honey, are you saying that a man gave this dolly to Lucy?"

A solemn nod.

"And did you ever see this man?"

Another nod.

"What did he look like? Can you remember?"

"Bogeyman!" said the child, screwing up her face.

"The bogeyman, huh? And what did the bogeyman look like?"

"He have no hair, an' no ears, an' big eyes an' big, big, teef."

"What's going on here, Pete? We doin' some bedtime stories?"

"I think we got something, but I can't figure it yet."

"What is it?"

"Tell you later. What did you find?"

"Just this. It didn't fit with the scene." He held out a small, heart-shaped box covered in gold foil. The name of a Belgian chocolatière was embossed on the top.

Balducci took the box and held it out to Carmen. "Do you know what this is, honey?"

"Lucy candy. She give me *one* piece."

"And where did Lucy get the candy?"

"Bogeyman."

"What is this 'bogeyman' business, Pete?" asked Raney.

Balducci gave him a warning look, stood up, and patted the little girl on the head. He picked up the doll, the one from the Bogeyman. It felt dense and heavy, like a nightstick.

"We're going to have to take this along, Missus. It's evidence," he said.

The woman nodded, glad to see them going, but little Carmen began to sniffle.

As the two policemen left the apartment, she broke out in a wail. "Wan' my dolly," she cried, betrayed by the nice man. They were down at the first landing when the slaps began. They could hear them, sharp and solid, through the door. The slaps went on and on, and the shrieks, but by that time the two men were far enough away that they could pretend that they didn't hear.

Driving downtown, Balducci took the opportunity to study the doll more carefully. He clucked and muttered for a mile or so on the East Side

Drive, until Raney said, "Pete, will you stop it with that doll, for cryin' out loud! What the fuck is goin' on here? Bogeyman?"

"Jimmy, I got four daughters. I put a lot of cash into dolls over the years, you know? I never seen nothing like this one."

"She could have ripped it off."

"Fuck, she could have! Look at this thing, Jimmy!" He propped it up on the dashboard. It was a fourteen inch doll dressed in a royal blue shot-silk traveling dress of the eighteen-seventies, with matching bonnet, the elegant costume only slightly soiled by grubby hands.

"Look—porcelain head, handpainted, same with the arms and feet. The dress is real silk, hand stitched. And this trim, here, is real lace, and not just real lace, but made to scale. The stitches are so fine you can hardly see them. This thing must have cost, shit, a grand easy, maybe more. Places that sell dolls like this, it's by appointment only and they keep the goods locked up until they see your money. You think a seven year old PR kid could have lifted something like this? What, she found it in the garbage, in East Harlem?"

"OK, I get the picture. But now the question is, if we assume that some guy gave her the doll, and the chocolate, why'd he do it? The first-class treatment, I mean. For Lucy Segura, if he'd a wanted to win her over, he could've gone into Macy's and picked up something for fourteen ninety-five that would've knocked her socks off. Same with the ten-dollar imported candy. A Mars bar would've done it. Not to mention, there's probably not that many of those dolls. We could trace it."

Balducci looked at the doll. He closed its blue eyes with his fingertips, gently, and let them pop open again. The hair was done in chestnut ringlets, probably real hair, he thought.

"Yeah, we could trace it. Which we'll start tomorrow. But about why: Christ, Jimmy, we know the guy's crazy. Maybe he's dumb, too. Maybe we'll get lucky."

"I hope so," said Raney. "I'd like to meet the mutt. I bet he packs a knife. Or a gun. In fact, I think I might have his gun in my trunk."

Balducci scowled at his partner. "I didn't hear that, Jimmy. No bullshit like that, OK? I'm too short for any of that stuff. I mean it!"

Jimmy Raney flashed his fallen angel grin. "Hey, Petey, just a joke. You know me. By the book, asses in jail. Besides, I want him for Marlene."

The man and the little girl sat in the park together, not touching, on the broken bench, amid the flat bottles in their bags and the broken shards of glass. It was dusk. Boys were still shooting baskets on the other side of the playground.

The child said, with a giggle, "You not the bogeyman. The bogeyman bad."

The Bogeyman said, "The bogeyman isn't bad. It's the children he comes to get that're bad. Are you bad?"

The girl shrugged. She said, "You got more candy? That gold candy?"

The man smiled and brought out a small heart-shaped box covered in gold foil. He offered it to the girl. She took one of the chocolates and looked at the man. He nodded and she took another. She put one into her mouth and waited for the explosion of sweetness.

The girl's name was Brenda Meigs. She was seven years old, plump in an unhealthy way, frizzle-haired, plain. Her racial make-up was complex and obscure. It had given her a pale ochre skin, which was marred on the arms and the edge of the jaw by bruises, some fresh and livid purple, others aging to dull yellow. The man observed them with a practiced eye. He touched a long bruise on her forearm with a pale forefinger, gently. The child snatched her arm away.

"You hurt yourself," said the man.

"I fell down."

The man smiled. It was the common lie, used by the child as well as the abusing parent, for who can believe at such a tender age that the source of love is also the source of death? He knew a lot about child abuse. He was a connoisseur of damaged children. He knew them in all their guises: the cringing ones, the broken in spirit; the violent ones, who acted out on the playground their harsh domestic dramas. He befriended them, gave them candy, toys and affection, and after a while he carried off a chosen, select group to a place where no one would be able to hurt them again.

He looked happily down at the little girl, who was sucking on her second chocolate, her eyes closed in delight, scuffing her ragged sneakers against the concrete under her bench. It was getting dark, but he knew that no distraught mother would be out on the streets looking for this little one. Brenda's mother, he had learned, was a pillhead, and she had a new boyfriend with a good connection.

Brenda would wander the streets, popping in on friends and a few relations in the mean neighborhood, cadging meals, hoping to be allowed to sleep in a bedroom corner. If not, she would slip into a supermarket and steal something small and sweet, and then try to sneak back to her bed, praying that her mother had scored downers and was nodding off.

He could supply her with food, at least, if not shelter. Not yet. He gave her candies and bought her meals at fast-food joints. He liked the same fast food that she did. In any case, it seemed to him that she was healthier.

And of course, he could not take her to a regular restaurant, because people might remember. That had been drilled into him quite thoroughly, along with the rest of the specifications. The children had to be abandoned and abused. But there was nothing that said he couldn't be kind to them. Or that he couldn't feed their little spirits as well as their bodies.

"Tell me, Brenda," he said. "Do you think you would like a nice doll?"

The bar called Larry's on 48th Street west of Seventh was not the sort of place that Anna Rivas would ever have gone alone. She didn't understand why Felix had brought her here. It was not the kind of place she thought a rising young executive ought to frequent.

It was dark, for one thing, which was sort of romantic, but Anna suspected that the illumination was designed not so much to encourage romance as to conceal the stains on the red-flocked wallpaper and the carpet. The vinyl booth they sat in was cracked in places, and the cracks were roughly patched with masking tape. And the other people, what she could make out of them, were not the kind she thought she would be mixing with when Felix Tighe had asked her out for a "night on the town," as he had put it.

The men were either dirty-looking and dressed in trucker's jackets and baseball hats or sleazy types with shirts open to the breastbone, wearing dangling gold at neck and wrists. One of these was sitting at their table now. Felix had been talking to him for ten minutes, some kind of business deal, something about refrigerators, ignoring her.

The booths were lit with red glass candle lamps and divided above the seat backs by sheets of glass. Anna sipped her rum-and-Coke and studied her reflection. Not bad for nearly thirty. Good eyes, large and black; straight, sharp nose with flaring nostrils. Could have used some more chin, though. It went double the minute she gained a pound over one-ten. Her black hair had been arranged around her small head in a pixie cut, for an outrageous forty-two fifty. The reflection was flattering, she knew. It didn't show the lines.

The other women in Larry's were brassy-looking, hot-panted, heavily made-up, and loud. Anna had worn her best little black dress, the only thing she owned from the better dresses department of Macy's. Now nobody could see it, or the haircut, and if they could, she began to fear, they would think she looked mousy and square.

They all looked like criminals, she thought, but what would a schoolteacher from the Bronx know about how big-time international executives disported themselves. That's how Felix had described himself when she had timidly brought up the subject of his profession. He always seemed to have money, though. She vaguely recalled that in the old days rich people would hang out with gangsters in speakeasies, for the thrill of it. Maybe this was what was happening now. She tried to feel thrilled.

The other man got up and left, gold chains jingling. Felix finished his Chivas and water and gestured to the waitress for another. He reached over, patted Anna's hand, and smiled. Anna got the hot chills when Felix smiled at her like that. She felt herself blushing like a kid.

They talked, or Felix talked and she listened, rapt. He had been everywhere and done everything. College at Yale, then Harvard for an M.B.A. On the fast track at several big companies. Business adventures in Europe and the Far East. Driving race cars and piloting his own plane. His life among the glitter people of New York. Did she see him in *People* two months ago? In the picture with Angie Dickinson and Joe Namath? Yes, she had, she admitted. Maybe she had.

What she did know for certain was that for the past four weeks she had been engaged in the hottest affair of her life, as hot as her dreams, long nights and whole weekends full of pounding, ferocious sex. Anna had been to Hunter and had a reasonably sharp brain. Where Felix was concerned, however, it was disengaged in favor of another set of organs entirely.

Now he was talking about the problems he was having with his condominium. ". . . anyway, then I said to him, 'Mr. MacReady, I don't know what kind of people you're used to dealing with, but I'm not used to being treated this way. My contract specifically guarantees a sauna and a Jacuzzi. I am not satisfied with your excuses. Our dealings are at an end. You will hear from my attorney.' You should've seen the expression on his face.

"So I packed my bags and left. My lawyer, my *attorney*, advised me. He said if I was living there, you know, it would be, like, implied consent."

"Where have you been staying?"

"Oh, in hotels. My club. But, you know, it's apt to be a long wait. I mean, it'll go to court, and all."

"Yeah, maybe you could rent a furnished place, temporarily."

Felix looked mournful and sighed. "Yeah. Yeah, I could do that, but . . . Oh, hell, Anna, I'm tired of living alone! I'm so sick of that golden life I lead. It's so hollow. I need somebody to share with. Somebody real. Somebody like . . . like you."

Anna, a perfect child of the movies and television, took this in without a qualm. A lump filled her throat and tears of joy and gratitude sprang into her eyes.

"Gosh, Felix, I don't know what . . . Oh, God, I'm gonna cry."

"Ah, Baby Doll, don't. You know how I feel about you."

She dabbed at her eyes with a crumpled tissue, hoping that her mascara would not run. She said, "When, ah, what do you want? I mean, you want me to move into your place, or what?"

Felix smiled. Anna saw love-light in his smile, but what Felix was thinking was what a great line that was, a line that never failed. He thought it was a winner the first time he heard it on *As the World Turns* a couple of years back. (Felix watched a good deal of daytime TV.) He had written it down in his notebook and used it often.

He squeezed her hand. "Ah, you're a honey, all right. We can talk about that later. Hey, I'm hungry. Let's go to dinner."

And they did, at a very nice little Mexican restaurant in the Village. Felix took her to a different restaurant every time they went out and always paid with one of his large collection of credit cards. "Corporate cards," Felix called them, and they must have been, because for sure none of them had Felix's name on them.

Although the summer night was fine and warm, they took a cab back to Anna's place. It was a two room third floor walk-up on Avenue A, in what realtors called the East Village. The neighborhood was druggy, but the building was fairly clean, and the rent only took two-thirds of her schoolteacher's take-home. She clerked three nights a week at Macy's to get by.

The street was lively with kids and strollers as they got out of the cab. While Felix paid, Anna was hailed by a woman sitting on the wide stone ledge. It was her neighbor from down the hall. Anna went over to chat with her and when Felix approached she introduced her.

"Felix Tighe, my friend, Stephanie Mullen."

Felix took the woman's hand and shook it, holding it for slightly longer than the woman wanted, as he always did. He smiled to show it was just fun.

"Any friend of Anna's is a friend of mine," he said. Stephanie's smile in return was slight and forced. Anna said, "Stephanie is the building celebrity."

"Come on, Anna," said Stephanie, grimacing.

"No, really, Felix. She was married to Willie Mullen, the bass guitar for The Blue Disease, *and* she was one of the original Jersey Turnpikes." Anna started swaying and singing a song that Felix recognized.

Felix looked at the woman with renewed interest. A hit song they still played meant big money. Why was she living in a dump like this? She wasn't bad looking for an old broad, he thought. Long blond hair, in hippie braids. Nice big tits and she wasn't wearing any bra under that T-shirt. He turned up the voltage on his smile.

Stephanie waved her hand as if shooing away flies.

"Stop it, Anna! That was a million years ago. Christ Almighty, every time that thing comes on the radio I practically break my neck trying to turn it off. The kid keeps moving the dial to the oldie station, the little tramp!"

"Your kid, huh?" asked Felix, his interest in Stephanie Mullen draining a little.

"Yeah," said Stephanie, looking down the street. "That's him there."

She pointed to a sturdy yellow-haired boy of about seven years trotting down the street toward them, blasting the passing cars and lounging people with beams from a plastic ray gun. He wore dusty jeans and a Darth Vader T-shirt and his round face was flushed with play.

Stephanie grabbed him as he passed by and plopped him on her lap. He laughed and struggled in her grip. She hugged him tighter and said, "Hey, you know what time it is? School day tomorrow. Time for a bath and bed."

"Nooo, Ma! It's still light out. All the kids're playing," he complained.

"Don't make no never mind to me. Come on. Say hello good-night to Anna. And Felix."

"G'night Anna," said the boy, squirming out of his mother's grasp.

"Good night, Jordy," said Anna, beaming.

The boy looked at Felix unsmilingly for a moment. Then he played the red beam of his gun slowly up and down Felix's body, from knees to head. Felix's smile grew tight. In the red beam of the gun it looked to Stephanie almost demonic, not a human expression at all.

"Cute," Felix said.

"Yeah, he's my doll, aren't you, Jordy?" said Anna.

"I'm a Jedi!" shouted the boy, and ran up the steps into the apartment house.

"I got to go," said Stephanie, rising. Her jeans were skin-tight, almost white with wear, ragged and covered with patches and embroidery.

Felix followed the roll of her backside as she climbed the stairs. Definite possibilities there, he thought, if it weren't for the kid.

Later, Felix lay in bed, exhausted, watching the smoke from Anna's cigarette curl toward the ceiling. She ran her fingers along his thigh, along the high ridges of muscle.

"What a man!" she said. "I feel like a million bucks."

Felix grunted. He was dying for a cigarette. He said, "You know what? You smoke too much."

"Oh, I'm sorry, baby. Does it bother you?"

"Yeah. Put it out."

As she did so, he sat up abruptly in the bed. He felt antsy. He was thinking about Stephanie Mullen. When he moved in here, Anna would be at work all day and a couple of nights a week. Maybe he could work something out there.

He felt Anna's lips brush his shoulder. Christ, the woman never got enough! But he figured he'd already paid the rent. He climbed out of bed and started poking around for his underwear in the heaps of clothes scattered around the room.

"Felix? What're you doing, honey?"

"Getting dressed."

"Dressed? Aren't you coming back to bed?"

"Can't, babes. You remember, I told you I had a big meeting tomorrow, early. Power breakfast."

"You did? I don't remember. I thought, you know, we could spend the night together."

"Hey, I *told* you. You saying I don't know what I told you?"

"No. No, of course not, but . . . it just seems weird, you running off in the middle of the night. Like you were going back to your wife." She laughed, a sharp titter with little amusement in it.

Felix grunted something about business being business and slipped into his Italian loafers. He kissed her briefly. "I'll call you," he said.

Felix walked to the IND station at Houston Street and took the F train to Jackson Heights. He walked to an apartment house not more than a quarter of a mile from where he had been arrested and rode the elevator to the third floor. He opened the lock on apartment 302, eased the door open a few inches and slid his hand inside, lifting a loop of wire off a nail stuck in the inside of the door. He entered the apartment and switched on the light. The living room was furnished with a cheap new living room set in gold velvet. A couple of flower prints and a karate exhibition poster were tacked to the walls.

The most unusual furnishing was a chrome kitchen chair standing in front of the entrance door, a chair that had a cut-down twelve-gauge two-barrel shotgun affixed to its back with duct tape. The wire that Felix had just removed from the door led through a small pulley taped to the leg of the chair and ended at the triggers of the gun. The weapon was set to blow the belly out of anyone who came through the door without first detaching the wire.

Felix walked to the kitchen and took half a loaf of sliced white bread out of the refrigerator. Leaning next to the refrigerator was a piece of broomstick about ten inches long, with a straightened steel coathanger attached to it with duct tape. Felix picked this up too and went into the hallway outside the kitchen.

There was a door in this hallway, shut with a padlock on a shiny new hasp. Felix opened the padlock and went through. On the other side of the door was a short hall, with doors leading to a bathroom and a bedroom. He heard a metallic sound as he approached the bedroom door, the clinking of a long chain moving.

Felix smiled and swished the coathanger through the air a few times, making it whistle. A whining groan, weak and high-pitched came from the room. The bed creaked. Felix went through the door. "Hi, honey, I'm home," he said.

# CHAPTER
# 6

Los Angeles was as Karp remembered it: compared to the City it was warmer, sported brighter colors, and the crazy people were in cars rather than stumbling down the street. The sun was impossibly high in the sky when he arrived at his hotel, a unit of one of the tackier lodging chains. It was on a gritty side-street off Sepulveda, convenient to the brake job and bodywork district, and was what he could afford on the miserable per diem paid by the New York D.A.'s office, which did not approve of foreign travel for its agents— except, of course, for the D.A. himself, who was out of town being famous half the year.

Karp felt cranky and disoriented and knew he would sleep badly. He didn't like to fly or drive. He liked to walk.

He remembered jet lag from the days of his marriage, when he had made the coast-to-coast trip several times a year to visit his in-laws. They paid. He went to the window of his room and looked out past the tiny balcony to the heat-shimmering parking lot and the freeway beyond. He opened the window and the thick air of L.A.

summer flowed around him, a melange of smog, chile, eucalyptus and eroded mountains.

It jogged his memory again, and he found himself thinking about Susan, and the uncomfortable occasions he had spent as a guest in her parents' house in Bel Air. Four years ago, she had gone back to California. She hadn't actually left him. She was going to get a Masters degree at UCLA. It was a very modern arrangement.

He tried to remember her as she had been in their apartment in New York, and found that he could not, that the image that came to his mind was the nineteen-year-old cheerleader he had married. He remembered a round, open face, a dusting of pale freckles, the red-gold ponytail swaying, the long, tan California legs flashing as she leaped on the sidelines at basketball games. That was before he screwed up his knee.

A perfect girl. A perfect marriage. Right now he should be living here, in Westwood or Beverly Hills, after a successful pro basketball career, probably a partner in her father's law firm, probably a couple of kids. He felt his chest tighten. That had been one of their jokes: He wanted five boys, so he could coach. He'd be wearing white Guccis now, and doing deals for sitcom stars.

Would it have made any difference if he had stayed? Once again Karp experienced the feeling of hopeless confusion, and an embarrassment bordering on hysteria, that came over him when he recalled the breakup of his marriage. It was like a parody of the sixties, something out of a TV soap: husband preoccupied, wife runs away and joins lesbian commune.

He had turned all that off, he thought, put it out of his mind by an act of will, crumpled it up like a sheet of legal bond and sunk it in the trash can. But when he thought of seeing Susan again, his gut knotted. Did he still care, or was it shame? It was shame. He knew in his heart that he would never have thought of seeing his wife again had it not been for Marlene's ultimatum.

Karp closed the window and opened his briefcase. He took out a picture postcard that had arrived at his New York office the previous week. On one side it had a picture of the midway at Santa Monica Pier, full of tourists, and on the other a phone number. He sat down on the bed and dialed it. Two rings and then the phone was picked up at the other end. Nobody said hello.

Karp said, "This is Roger Karp, Mr. Impellatti."

After a pause, a voice said, "You in town?"

"Yes, I am."

"Alone?"

"Right. Where are you?"

"You got the card there?"

"Yes."

"Look at it. You see the guy with the red shirt with the kid? He's got a balloon."

"Yeah, I see it."

"I'll meet you tomorrow at twelve noon where that guy is standing. Be alone." With that the phone went dead.

Karp was impressed. As a connoisseur of paranoia himself, he thought that Little Noodles had come up with a neat method of arranging a meeting so that somebody listening in on the conversation wouldn't know where it was.

This conversation was cordial compared with the next one Karp had, which was with his mother-in-law. She slammed the phone down when he identified himself. When he called again, she informed him that this whole *mishegas* was his fault, as was her husband's recent heart attack, that if he had stayed in California, and had a nice home, and joined a temple like a decent Jewish husband, instead of living in a crummy apartment in that crazy place with God knew what kind of people for neighbors, so he could chase *momsers*, he should be ashamed of himself, and so on and so on.

Karp waited for a pause in the guilt-bath and asked for Susan's address. After some hesitation, and some artful lying on his part, he extracted a rural address in Ladero, California, a small town in the mountains above San Jose.

Karp's third phone call was to an old law-school friend with a practice in L.A., to get the no-fault papers drawn up. He spent the rest of the day by the pool, went to bed early, tossed around for a couple of hours, and then watched movies on TV until four in the morning. He got up at ten, breakfasted in the motel coffee shop and then called V.T. Newbury in New York, the man he had left in charge of the Bureau.

"V.T.? It's me."

"The Incredible Hulk? How's California? Are you snorting cocaine amid the perfect oiled bodies of blonde starlets?"

"Yeah, right. What's happening at the store?"

"Karp, you've been gone a day, what could be happening?"

"So I'm nervous. What's Bloom doing?"

"Not much. He came to work this morning in a silk peignoir and white satin mules. Besides that, nothing new. Did you connect with your guy yet?"

"Yeah, I'm meeting him in a couple of hours. How do you like the agony of command?"

"My respect for you grows hourly. I signed a bunch of leave slips and a purchase order for a new copier. I feel like Erwin Rommel. Speaking of which, you might have a word with Roland when you get back. He seemed a little miffed he didn't get the deputy slot."

"Yeah, I figured he would. It's kind of hard to explain the situation. Roland thinks hard work and kicking ass is the way to get ahead. But you're the only guy I got Bloom won't touch."

"Hey, I work hard."

"When you feel like it. Your family and their friends also control about a trillion dollars in political money, which is why you're golden with the D.A. Meanwhile, I got to go. Is Marlene around?"

"No, I saw her leave with those two cops she's got working for her. Oh, I almost forgot, Guma wanted to talk to you. Let me switch you over. Bye . . . hey, and get some sun, take it easy."

Buzzing and clicking and then Guma's heavy voice was on the line.

"Butch, how ya doin'? Getting any sun?"

"Why does everybody ask me that? Yeah, sun up the ass. What d'you got, Goom?"

"I talked to Tony Bones. He's in town."

"Goom, you ever think that hanging around with wise guys is not a particularly smart move, assuming you're interested in staying in the D.A. business?"

"Butch, I could give a shit it's a smart move or not. What am I, bucking for bureau chief? I'm trying to impress fucking *Bloom*? I was putting goombas in jail when he was in finishing school. You too, come to that, so don't *you* give me any horseshit about Tony Buonofacci. I know him from when we're both snot-nose little guineas in Bath

Beach. We used to hustle chicks together down Cropsey Avenue, for chrissake."

"Goom, stop with this old neighborhood crap! Half the guys he's whacked out got the same story. You think he shoots East Side Presbyterians?"

"Hey, did I say he wasn't a cold-blooded killer? But one, he's based in Miami now, which puts him off our turf. Let him shoot all the sun tans he wants! And two, he knows if I ever get the chance, I'll hang his ass, and no hard feelings on either side. He's a pro—he'll get the best lawyer in town, he'll try to fix the jury, and if he loses he'll go down without a peep. Meanwhile, he's a *paisan*, and it's getting so there's not many of us left."

"Wait, Guma, I got to wring out my hankie," said Karp, laughing. "So tell me, what does Tony Bones have to say that I would find interesting?"

"Just that the word is that Harry Pick went apeshit when Little Noodles disappeared. He started stirring things up, as only Harry can, and among the things he stirs up is a little hood named Carmine Scalliose, who it looks like is the last guy to see Noodles in the City. This is in a spaghetti joint on Grand, two days after Ferro got his. Apparently, Noodles walks up to him, gives him a big smile, and starts schmoozing like crazy, which is weird, because him and Carmine have never been such great friends.

"So after a while he leaks out that Harry Pick's after him. He don't know why, but he saw Harry give him the shot, he says, up at Nyack."

"What's that about, 'the shot?'"

"I don't know, some kind of gesture—you know, like kids going 'bang-bang.' But Noodles thinks it's for real—he's a dead man. So he panics, he splits, he hides—"

"He hides from Harry in *Little Italy*?"

"Yeah, I know, it's like hiding in Harry's Jockey shorts, but here's the thing: He tells Carmine he's going to Puerto Rico—even shows him the ticket. So he gets Carmine to drive him to Kennedy: bon voyage, Noodles."

"Knowing, of course, that Carmine will go straight to Harry."

"Like shit down a chute. So Harry tears up PR, looking for him, for a couple of days. Then he starts thinking it's a scam. Tony thought it was pretty amusing, Harry in PR, and all the time Noodles is in L.A."

"Wait a minute, Guma—Tony knows Noodles is in L.A.?"

"Shit, Butch, *everybody* knows he's in L.A. After he got back to the City, it took Harry twenty-four hours to get wise to the switch. You think he don't have people in the airports? Tony says he's got Jimmy Tona's outfit looking for him out there. Harry's pissed, Butch. Maybe in Nyack he was just dicking around, but now it's serious, you know? I mean, Noodles knows where all the bodies are buried."

"That's probably not a figure of speech, is it?"

Guma chuckled, a sound like marbles running down a bathtub drain. "I doubt it. You're in a bind, son."

"So it seems. It's a shame I'm going through all this to bring Noodles back, and he doesn't even make a case to nail the shooter and Harry."

"What d'you mean, he was driving the . . . Oh, right, no corroboration."

"Right, it's too bad Noodles was an accomplice. Of course, Harry doesn't know we don't have a corroborating witness. We might try to play with that, assuming I can bring Noodles in in one piece. You have any Sicilian wisdom to convey on that?"

"Yeah, stay away from the cops. Noodles goes anywhere near a jail, he won't get much older. Which he knows."

"Uh-huh. He does seem a hair paranoid about me being alone."

"I don't blame him. Look, you got a meet set up yet?"

"Yeah, in about an hour and a half."

"OK, make the contact, then get in a car and drive like a sonofabitch someplace where they won't look for you. Lay low for a couple of days and I'll get something together, bring you both in."

"What are you talking about, Guma? Lay low, my ass! I'm going to pick up Impellatti, drive to LAX, get on a plane, and come home."

"Butch, you're not listening. Listen to me! You think Harry Pick would lose sleep over wasting a planeload of people to get this guy? You remember why they call him Harry Pick? No planes, and stay out of big towns. Hotels ain't such a good idea either. Can you think of any place you can hide out? Like in the country?"

"Yeah," said Karp, after a moment's pause. "I just thought of a place they'll never look."

"What do you mean, the doll's a dead end?" snapped Marlene. Peter Balducci sighed. "Marlene, for *now*, a dead end. I'm not saying something couldn't turn up." He and Raney were in Marlene's office at the end of a long and frustrating day. He looked at his partner for support, but Raney had his chair tipped back against the wall, staring up at the high ceiling, watching the smoke from his cigarette and Marlene's curl and twine up to the high ceiling.

"Like I told you on the phone, I saw this guy, what's-his-name, the doll guy . . ." He checked his notebook. "Schlechter, he's got a place on Madison, a doll expert. He recognized the maker. The doll's Belgian, made about nineteen-ten. He said there's only about fifty of them around."

"Eleven grand a copy," said Raney.

Balducci snorted. "Yeah, can you believe it?"

"Did he know how many of them were in the city?" Marlene asked.

"No, and he didn't sell that particular one, either. But he gave me a list of the kind of collectors who could touch an item like that." He passed a sheet of paper to her across the disordered desk. "Fourteen names. Three were out of the country. I checked out all the others. Nothing."

"What, 'nothing'?"

"Nothing, nothing. None of them got a doll like that missing. None of them got a record with anything more than a parking ticket."

Marlene looked at the list. The addresses were all Silk Stocking East Side or upper West Side. "How do you know none of the dolls was missing?"

Balducci rolled his eyes. "Christ, Marlene! We don't know these folks *had* a doll like that. Just they *could've* had. We had to check them out because we could've got lucky. Like, 'Oh, yeah, officer, that's the one that cousin Reginald the sex fiend ripped off last June.' Besides that, what am I supposed to do? People who can pay eleven grand for a doll, you don't just walk in and toss their place."

"What are you telling me, Pete? Above a certain tax bracket we don't have sex killers?"

Balducci glowered at her and got to his feet. "Marlene, you know damn well I don't think that. Now come on! We're two people, we got a full load besides this crap, we're not gonna follow every citizen that could've had access to an expensive doll. Not until we know something else about who we're looking for."

"He's big, he's white, he wears black clothes, and he's got short, blond hair," said Raney.

The others looked at him, dumbstruck for a moment. "How the hell you know that, Jimmy?" Balducci demanded.

Raney let his chair drop down with a crack like a gunshot. "Because while you were talking to the doll collectors, I went back to Lucy Segura's neighborhood and hung out. There's a playground, a couple of schoolyards. I figured if the little sister saw him, he had to be in some public place where he was hustling her. I mean, he didn't pick her up at her door, right? So I found a couple of kids playing basketball in a schoolyard on One-sixteenth. They remembered seeing a guy with that description talking to a little kid three days before Lucy disappeared. They thought he was a priest."

"Kids!" snorted Balducci. "They'll tell you any damn thing . . ."

"Right, so I cruised the fast-food joints on One-sixteenth and up Lex. The day manager at the MacDonald's also remembered a guy in black and a little girl. They came three, four times. Guy bought a meal for the kid and himself. He wouldn't have recalled it, but the guy was so big. Maybe six-four, three hundred pounds. Black raincoat, black suit, and fedora. He doesn't remember if he had a dog collar on or a regular shirt."

Balducci frowned. "Maybe it *was* a priest, Jimmy. Maybe it was a priest with another little girl."

"It's the guy, Petey."

Balducci looked at Marlene for support, but she was gazing at Raney with admiration, who was gazing back with a similar expression.

Balducci shook his head. "Right. It's the guy. An arrest is imminent. You two figure it out. I'm going home."

After Balducci left, Marlene said, "Your partner seems grumpy."

"Yeah, he can get that way. He's just P.O.'d because he wants to can this case, and I don't. We're gonna get that guy." He smiled at her.

He's got a nice smile, thought Marlene, returning it. "Well, I'm glad you're with me on this," she said. "How are you going to handle it?"

"We'll nose around the buildings where the doll people were, see if anybody's seen a big blond dude."

"What if they haven't?"

"Then Pete's right—it's square one again. Hey, we got lucky. There's no guarantee our luck's gonna hold."

Marlene nodded and sighed. "Yeah, you're right, I guess." She looked at her watch. It was six-ten. "Anyway, time to go home." She stood and started stuffing her briefcase.

"Can I drop you off?"

"Don't you want to get home yourself?"

"Haven't got one. I share a place with a couple of other cops in Jamaica."

"OK. I just have to drop some things off at the Bureau office. I'll meet you on the Leonard Street side in ten minutes."

Marlene expected the Bureau office to be deserted this late in the day, but the lights were on and she heard the sound of typing. She threw some files in an in-basket for filing. At the sound, the typing stopped and Dana Woodley stuck her head up over a partition. She looked startled.

"Dana? Hey, it's quitting time. This is civil service, you know?"

Woodley smiled sheepishly. "Jest finishin' up some briefs."

"Yeah? Who's making you work so hard?" Marlene looked over the partition. On Woodley's desk was an open ream box of 100 percent rag paper, the kind used for dissertations. A few dozen sheets of neat typing were stacked at its side.

"A little moonlighting, Dana?"

Woodley blushed deeply. "Yeah, I, ah, put up these cards? At all the colleges? This 'un here got to be done Friday. I won't get in no trouble, will I?"

"Over this? Hell, no! We had a clerk here once ran a real-estate business on office time for twenty years. Retired a millionaire, I heard." Marlene looked at the other woman closely. Her lip was trembling, and she was obviously close to tears.

"Dana, I meant it. I'm not going to rat you out."

"No, gosh, it ain't that! I'm just goin' crazy with Carol Anne."

"Carol Anne? But I thought you had that great day care. . . ."

"Yeah, I do, but she's started actin' real strange, like, she has these turrible nightmares, like she never done before. And she cries somethin' fierce when I drop her off in the mornin'. And last night, she was playin' with her dolls and shouting, and when I went over to see what she was doin', she had the little Ken and Barbie there with their clothes off, and she was makin' them *do* it.

121

And the language, filthy words, comin' out of that little mouth. It purely broke my heart. And I got to work, to save any money at all, don't I? So I got to, I got to . . ."

Here the woman broke down in sobs. Marlene went around the barrier and placed her arm around Woodley's shoulder. "Dana, it's OK, kids go through stuff like that," said Marlene soothingly, thinking at the same time that she actually had no idea whether that was true.

"I don't believe it," said Woodley through her sniffling. "Somebody at that center been putting evil in that child's head."

"Did you talk to them about it? The center, I mean."

"Oh, no!" Woodley said, shocked. "I jes couldn't, Marlene. I'd be so ashamed. And I *cain't* take her out, not right now when I'm jes startin' to get a little ahaid." More crying. Marlene comforted her, and found herself, to her own surprise, volunteering to ask about the day-care center.

Raney was waiting for her outside the D.A.'s office entrance on Leonard Street, at the wheel of a ten-year-old Karmann-Ghia, bottle green except for the left fender, which was primer red. The passenger seat, she learned as she climbed in, was rotted to the springs and covered with a dirty tan chenille bedspread.

"Gosh, Raney," she said, "I thought you were offering me a ride in a real po-lice car, and now this. Does it go?"

"Better than most cop cars, but of course you don't get the genuine cigar and puke smell. I'll make it up to you some day. Where to?"

She gave him her address and they turned north up Centre Street. The early summer night was warm and Raney had the window open and the stereo playing a tape. Chopin flowed out of expensive speakers. Marlene added up the junker car, the expensive stereo, the classical music, the cop driving: It made an intriguing sum. It made her curious.

Raney drove aggressively and fast, squirting the little car in front of cabs and around trucks, barreling through intersections on yellow lights. While he drove, they talked, the inconsequential chat of strangers—shop, personalities, the damn City. Nothing personal.

In a few minutes they were in front of Marlene's loft building on Crosby Street, a grim looking industrial structure on a narrow road strewn with debris. "You live here?" Raney asked doubtfully.

"Yeah. Why, you think it's unsuitable for a classy broad like me?"

Raney grinned and shrugged. "Hey, what do I know? I'm just a working stiff from Queens."

"Me too. I went to St. Anthony's in Ozone Park."

"No kidding! I went to Curran. You go straight through? We must know a lot of the same people."

"No, I got a scholarship to Sacred Heart."

Raney drew back in mock awe. "Hey, hey! Very fancy. I'm impressed. I never had a Sacred Heart girl in my car before. I guess you don't kiss on the first date."

She tried to summon up an appropriate cold look at this remark, but as she got out of the car she felt her mouth twitching into a copy of Raney's crazy grin. "You think this is a date, Raney," she said through the window, "you spent too much time with the nuns. Let's keep it professional, hey?"

As she unlocked her door, she realized that the vibes in that car had owed nothing to the professional. She recalled that nasty old tingle, no mistaking it. *Why am I a sucker for the bad boys?* she asked herself. And speaking of bad boys, she wished Karp would get home. *Is he divorced yet?* she wondered. *Am I going to be a respectable married lady, married to a rising legal bureaucrat? Is that what Butch has turned into?* She shook her head to straighten out her thoughts. *Don't be crazy, Marlene,* she said to herself, knowing it was advice she rarely took. As she walked up the stairs a tune popped into her head. It was "Bonnie Light Horseman," an Irish ballad about a girl who loved a dashing cavalry man. Who of course has dashed off to the wars, never to return. *Marlene, control yourself,* she thought. But the tune wouldn't go away.

"I brought you some food," said the Bogeyman. He handed the girl a white paper bag. She opened it and started chewing listlessly on a cheeseburger. She was sitting on a bed in a small room on the ground floor of a brownstone. The Bogeyman had one just like it, down the hall. This room had in it a bed, a hooked rug, a small deal table that supported a color TV, and an armchair. The TV was tuned to a cartoon show. There was one door and one window, which was barred with a heavy grille.

The Bogeyman sat in the armchair. "Are you happy here, Brenda?" he asked gently.

"Do you got any ice cream?" she replied.

"Yes, we can get you some ice cream. How do you like your dolly?"

Brenda glanced at the doll, shrugged, then turned

back to watch the cartoons. It was a twenty-four inch French porcelain doll, dressed for winter in green velvet, with a muff of real sable.

"Not every little girl has a nice doll like that," he said. Then, after a pause, "You know I gave a nice doll to another little girl, and I got in trouble."

She looked up at this. "Who? Emilia?"

"No, not Emilia. Is Emilia your friend?"

"Yes, but I hate her. Can she come to our house and play?"

"No, not today. Anyway, I got in bad trouble with my mother, 'cause this little girl lost my doll. My mother yelled at me. And she spanked me. On my heinie. With a strap."

The girl's eyes grew wide. Then she giggled. "Your momma can't spank you. You a big man."

"No, no. Your mother can always spank you, if you're bad. She's always your mother."

"My momma mean," said Brenda. Then, "Do I live here now?"

"Yes."

"Could I see your momma?"

"I don't think so," said the Bogeyman. "Maybe later. After the uncles."

"What's uncles?"

"Men who tickle you. After the uncles tickle you, you can see my mother."

"Is she nice?" asked Brenda, doubtfully.

"Sometimes she's nice," said the Bogeyman. "But sometimes she's a witch."


Anna Rivas awakened to the sound of music and, rolling over, discovered Felix was gone, as usual. Anna was confused about that part of Felix. On the one hand, she wished that he would stay over on nights when they were together, and had hinted shyly to him that it would make her happy, but he was always gone. No note, no farewell, just gone. On the other hand, it was part of the mysterious romance of the relationship—the dark stranger appearing and leaving unpredictably. Anna had read a lot of romantic novels.

She stretched luxuriously and wriggled, remembering the previous night. She sniffed the pillow where his head had rested and retrieved a faint whiff of the heavy cologne he favored. Her body was still tacky with sex. She sighed and began her day.

As she drank her coffee and watched the morning news on the TV, there was a knock on the door. Anna opened it and Stephanie Mullen came in, dressed in a thin bathrobe under which she was obviously wearing nothing. Anna observed that the bathrobe was none too clean.

"Hiya, cutie," said Stephanie. "Look, I hate to bother you, but I'm trying to get the boys off to school and I'm out of milk." She came into the one room that served as the parlor, dining area, and kitchen. "Boyfriend take off?"

"Yeah, he had an early meeting," said Anna. "I'll get the milk."

"Thanks. A meeting, huh? I hope he's up to it. You guys didn't get much sleep last night."

Anna felt a blush rising on her face. Stephanie saw it and laughed. "Hey, I couldn't help noticing. The damn walls are thin, you know? You gonna see that guy much you ought to get the bed bolted down or something. I could sell tickets."

"Please, Stephanie, you're making me embarrassed."

"Sorry—hey, look, nothing to be ashamed of. The guy's a stud, so enjoy!"

Anna said nothing, but busied herself with cleaning up her breakfast. She liked Stephanie, ordinarily, and respected her as someone more experienced in the world, but she did not care for the implication that she was having herself serviced by Felix, like some animal. As she handed Stephanie a quart container of milk, she said, "He's . . . it's not just that, you know. He's just wonderful. Exciting. Romantic. I can't believe it . . . me! It's crazy, but . . ."

Stephanie looked at her closely. "You really fell for this guy, huh? What's he do for a living, by the way?"

"Oh, he's in business. He's some kind of big international executive."

"Is he? Well, I'm glad you're happy, but . . ."

"But what?" Anna was disturbed by the expression on Stephanie's face.

"Nothing. I guess I'm naturally suspicious. You know, you work in clubs, in the record business, you get like a sixth sense about dudes. This guy you got . . . I don't know. Look, I don't want to rain on your parade, but there's like, something *off* about him, dig?"

"I don't know what you mean," said Anna. But, in her heart of hearts, she did.

Felix Tighe was selling a living room set on credit, which was what he did for a living, besides being a burglar. Of course, it was just temporary, until he could put together a really big operation, something that involved flying first class and wearing nice silk suits and having a Mercedes with a car phone. Felix hadn't figured out what those guys who had those things did, or where they kept the really good-looking girls, the ones from the magazines. You sure didn't see any of them around his usual haunts.

While he waited for this better life, his current job was at least adequate. The commission was decent, he got the use of a company car, he got to cheat people, which gave him a kick, and it gave him an excuse for wandering through neighborhoods during the day.

The neighborhoods were not that hot—the one he was in now was the part of Queens known as East New York—but Felix had learned that even fairly poor families had some hockable little item: a gold cross, a set of silver spoons, that he could pick up without much effort. Or pills. He could get rid of any number of prescription sleeping pills or diet pills at Larry's.

Like this woman here, fat as she was, might have an interesting medicine chest. Felix watched with amusement as she pawed through the samples of fabric. Selling didn't take much: just a lot of soulful staring into their eyes, and appreciating their good taste. A coo, a wink, and there it was, $695.95 for a living room set, Spanish Renaissance in crimson velvet, nothing down and thirty-six months to pay, only 21 percent interest, and a contract that said that if they missed even one month, they had to come up with the whole principal or the stuff would be dragged away. But right now all the bitch was thinking about was the nothing down and *having* the furniture, so that maybe her old man or somebody would look at her the way Felix was looking at her, like she was a person.

The woman sat poised with pen in hand over the contract, stretching her little moment out. She was talking about how her little dog had died.

She was thinking about getting another one. Felix smiled and invented a little dog of his own. He didn't mind old ladies, up to a point. It was always amazing to him how people could get through fifty, sixty years of life and stay so dumb, so pluckable.

Suddenly, for no reason he could think of, the image of his own mother flashed into his mind. His mother didn't know what he did for a living. She thought he was a big-time executive, which stopped her from nagging him, but made it difficult to hit her up for money. She had money, that was for sure, and friends with money. Not for the first time, Felix began to think about how he could get his hands on some of it, or maybe use her contacts to set himself up in something with a little more class. But if he did that . . .

The woman signed the contract and held it out to him, smiling, flapping the pages slightly, like a five-year-old back from the first day of school with a finger painting. Felix took it from her, his smile blank, his eyes elsewhere. The woman felt the first stirrings of disappointment.

"When will they deliver, you think?" she asked brightly, trying to recover the mood.

"Soon, a couple of days. I'll call you," he growled, and made his escape. Outside, he paused and shook his head. No, Ma was for emergencies, like this burglary business, or the odd hundred "loan."

Whether she believed his success story or not, he didn't know, or care. He only knew that he couldn't ask her for anything serious or accept anything from her that would give her an edge on him. He stopped, startled. Where did that thought come from? His Ma loved him. He was her favorite boy. But he knew if he ever got dependent on her she would get him involved in that church of hers and he couldn't hack that. That was it. He turned off those thoughts, which were starting to make him nervous. He was good at that, shutting off thoughts.

When he wanted to remember things, he wrote them down. In the car he noted the sale down in the small black diary he always carried. He used a fine-pointed marker pen and wrote in tiny capitals, like the lettering on engineering drawings. He looked over the display of the week's appointments. Each completed task had a tiny check next to it. "Date w. Anna" was checked. "Take care of M. /move out." M. was Mary, his wife. That was checked. He had taken care of her. "Date w. Denise" wasn't checked. It was written in the slot representing this coming evening.

Therefore Felix did not tarry in the neighborhood after making his sale. He drove quickly back to Manhattan, to Steve Lutz's apartment on Tenth Street. There he showered and dressed carefully in his best suit and tie. He had all his stuff at Lutz's now, in suitcases and cardboard boxes. He could tell Lutz was starting to get pissed off, but he didn't care. Lutz was a pussy, one, and two, he would be moving in with Anna soon.

He checked himself in the full-length mirror. The suit was a real Armani and the tie had cost thirty-five dollars. Denise had bought both for him, for his last birthday. She was pretty good to him, all things considered. Although she would never give him any money, she didn't mind buying him stuff. And she didn't want anything from him, anything permanent, except she was loopy about keeping it quiet, which was why when Mary had followed him that time and freaked out he had to put her away, lock her up and pound on her head and scare the shit out of her. He didn't understand that too well, since Denise seemed otherwise to be a pretty sophisticated old broad. Why should she give a shit? Unless she had lied to him and she really was still married. Something else he couldn't understand was why Mary had gone batshit. It wasn't the first time he had played around, so . . .

As he thought about this, and about seeing Denise, Felix became increasingly nervous. His palms began to sweat and his stomach started to spin over. This was a familiar feeling and he knew how to deal with it. From a suitcase he took a large plastic jar and shook from it into his hand two Gelusil and two yellow Valium tablets. He threw them down and swallowed them dry. Before he hit the street both his stomach and his nerves had begun to relax. Felix, of course, had no more interior life than a salamander, so that he never wondered why this liaison affected him this way, and why he continued to make himself available to Denise.

By the time he arrived at the East Side hotel that was their usual rendezvous, he had managed to cast an almost romantic light on what he was about to do, almost Boy Scoutish in a way, the equivalent of helping an old lady across the street. This did not last as long as his trip up to the twelfth floor in the elevator, for by the time he stepped out he was excited and sick at the same time, with his sex throbbing and the sour taste of bile in his mouth.

As always, the door to the room was open; as always the room itself was dim: the lights off, the curtains drawn. The scent of her was heavy in the air. Her face was a white nimbus framed by coils of thick black hair. Pale, soft arms reached out to him and he heard her deep laugh. His breath came in gasps now, as he tore off his expensive clothes and threw them to the floor. He heard a sound, a whining sob, and barely understood that it was coming from his own throat.

She threw the covers aside and he saw her naked body, saw her wide hips roiling and her thighs lolling apart. With a cry he flung himself on her, his eyes tight shut. As his body moved spasmodically, his mind became totally blank, as if he were in a deep sleep fragmented by nightmares. In an hour or so, he would find himself neatly dressed, walking in the street in a state of lassitude and exhaustion, and remember that he had had a date with Denise, and that he could now go to an expensive store and buy something for himself. There would be scratches on his back sometimes, and he would recall someone shouting in his ear a man's name, one that was not his own. But of the thing itself, he retained no memory.

# CHAPTER
# 7

The next day the People of Queens tried Felix Tighe for attempted murder and the other charges in their Courthouse on Queens Boulevard. The trial occupied two and a half days. On the first two of these, the prosecution presented its case: the arresting officer, the injured officer, the huge knife covered with Felix's fingerprints, the forensic evidence, the bag of swag also covered with Felix's prints.

By the end of the second day Felix had gotten the hint and on the third day, which had been reserved for closing arguments, the guest of honor chose not to attend. This did not stop the trial. While the Constitution gives us the right to confront our accusers in open court, it doesn't say we have to hear ourselves convicted, and so Felix was convicted, on all counts, *in absentia*, like an escaped spy.

A warrant was duly issued for his arrest. His folder, with its mug shots and personal information, was thrown into the felony warrant basket and taken to the office where the warrants were converted into arrest cards and sent to the NYPD and to police departments throughout the country and to the FBI's National Crime Information Center. There it rested a while among its thousands of fellows, until a clerk pulled it from a bottomless stack and began to prepare the arrest card.

Then she noticed something peculiar. Most arrest warrants are for people who are avoiding prosecution, but here, right in the folder, was a Disposition of Trial form that said the guy had just been convicted. But if he was convicted, he would already be in jail. Something had to be wrong. The clerk was a fast worker and didn't want to fall behind in her quotas. She stuck Felix Tighe's file in the center drawer of her desk, intending to ask her supervisor about it later. She forgot. Two weeks after this she was promoted and had to move her desk. By that time Felix's file was an embarrassment. She stuck it in a drawer where they kept incomplete records and, after a short interval, expunged it from her mind, and thus from the consciousness of the law. Felix Tighe, fugitive from justice, was now, for practical purposes, a free man.

This made no substantial difference to Felix himself, since he had put out of his own mind long since any possibility of having to pay for his crime. If he was tense and irritable all day that Friday, it was not because he felt the law at his heels. Instead, it was the usual aftermath of a session with Denise. Felix's ordinary relief for tension was violence. He went to a Chinese theatre on Canal Street that showed Bruce Lee films continuously, and watched *Enter the Dragon* for the fifth time. His body twitched in time with the action and he grunted along with Bruce's punches. Thus warmed up, he went to his karate dojo for some of the real thing.

Felix's dojo was a small room above a restaurant on Division Street. He had selected it because it was cheap, and none too selective about whom it let in; because it allowed full-contact karate; and because most of the clientele were Asiatic men, whose typically slight build made them convenient victims. Felix believed, with some justification, that a good big man can beat a good little man any day, and was anxious to demonstrate the principle. "Pounding chinks" was how he put it among his acquaintances.

Although sport karate is supposed to be about using form as a means to physical, moral, and spiritual development, Felix believed, and said so often to his fellow karatekas, that such considerations were a pile of horseshit, and that the whole point of turning your body into a deadly weapon was to use it on other people and make them hurt. The sensei of the dojo, a small, elderly Korean man named Wan, smiled vaguely and shook his head whenever Felix unloaded this line, but made no move to confront him. Felix knew he was frightened of him, which added to the pleasure of the sport.

Today Felix hurried into his outfit and strode confidently out into the dojo mat room. After doing his warm-up and some *katas*, he looked around for a likely victim. All the clientele of the dojo were gathered in a circle watching a sparring match. Felix went over and looked over a small shoulder to see what was going on. Wan was engaged in *ipon-kumite*, a kind of restricted no-contact sparring with a man Felix had never seen in the dojo before. Felix was amazed. He had not realized that there existed Oriental people who were that large. He observed that the enormous Manchurian was also very fast and very good.

When Wan saw Felix, he stopped his exercises at once. He smiled at Felix. The Manchurian smiled. All the other karatekas smiled too, and backed away to form a large circle. The Manchurian bowed and, still smiling, proceeded to pound the living shit out of Felix Tighe for fifteen minutes.

When Felix got to Larry's Place later that afternoon, the first thing he did, after drinking two scotch and waters, with Valium, was to call up a guy he knew who did freelance torch work, to see about burning down Mr. Wan's dojo. After Felix explained the situation, the man said he would do it for five hundred, over the weekend.

"I want the people in there, you understand?" Felix said.

"You want the people . . . ? You mean burn them up?"

"Yeah, that's part of the deal."

The man laughed. "No fuckin' way, man. Hey, let me explain something. Anybody's in a place when I torch it, and they can't get out, that's tough titty, you understand? It's like a bonus—I don't charge for that. But making sure they fry— that's a whole 'nother line of work than what I do, dig. Hey, you talking about frying a dozen people, you talking specialists, you talking the Mob, you understand? Job like that set you back maybe ten, twelve yards easy."

"Yeah, well, I got to think about that."

"Yeah, I guess. So—you want the torch job or not?"

Felix decided against it. He had by this time calmed down enough to realize that he didn't have even five hundred dollars, and he doubted that this guy would take Visa, not even if it was a real card.

He wasn't thinking clearly and he hurt all over. It was worse than when that cop had bopped him. He sat down in a booth and ordered another scotch. Then he opened his attaché case and took out his diary. He wrote, "Anna—move in, tonite." That was critical. He had to get settled, get out of that shithole at Lutz's. That was what was bringing him down. He needed some space, and someone to take care of the daily bullshit, the rent, the cleaning, the meals, so he could do some serious planning. Also, once he was set up there he could try a move on that Stephanie, see if there was any real money involved there. He thought for a moment. There was something missing. It took him a few seconds to think of what it was. Then he wrote, "Get knife."

Which he did. At a shlock joint on Eighth Avenue he purchased a bowie knife with a wide fourteen inch blade and a fake horn handle. It came with a leather sheath. It was just like the one he had stuck Officer Slayton with in Queens. He put it into his attaché case and walked back to Larry's. He felt much better.

When the courts recessed for lunch that Friday, Marlene remembered what she had promised Dana Woodley and, instead of camping in her office with a yogurt and a trashy book, went to visit Suzanne Loesser. Loesser was a social worker assigned to the Criminal Courts building by the New York State Department of Social Services. Her official function was to arrange protective custody for the minor children of convicted felons, but over the years she had taken on a wide selection of other duties occasioned by the blowback of crime.

This was because, unlike virtually every other social worker in the City, Loesser never said no, never said, "It's not my department," always treated her pathetic clientele with some measure of dignity. The existence of Loesser meant that no agent of the criminal justice system needed ever to exercise any compassion or evince any human feeling. As long as they had Loesser's number on a slip of paper they would never have to deal with a messy problem, and could concentrate on their vital and implacable mission of assembling criminals, saying words at one another, moving the criminals around and returning them to the streets.

Throughout the Streets of Calcutta, she was known as Suzie Loser. She weighed well over two hundred pounds, lived on coffee, Danish pastry, and cigarillos, and only God knew more about the intimate problems of the poor folks of New York, although He was often not as sympathetic.

She was on the phone (she was always on the phone) when Marlene walked into her office, a space that made Marlene's office look like an operating theater.

"Hi, Marlene, baby, get me that long green box please," said Loesser. Then, into the phone, "No Audrey, they *are* eligible under section 20. I just *told* you . . ."

Marlene lifted a speckled green card file box off a swivel chair piled with folders and handed it to Loesser across her massively disordered desk. The social worker thumbed through the dingy cards, pulled one out, plucked a chewed pencil from her pepper-and-salt bun and made a notation on a yellow pad. "Audrey, listen to me! I got all the forms filled out. Just get Ben to sign the requisition when I send Rivera up there. I'll cover it with Welfare personally. Thanks, Audrey, you're a doll."

She hung up the phone, which immediately began to ring again. "Suzie, I got a problem . . ." Marlene began.

"Who doesn't? So how's by you? You never come by. Listen, you want to adopt a kid? Seven years old, half Puerto Rican, half Oriental, a sweetheart . . ."

"Not today, Suzie. What it is, a friend of mine has a kid in a day-care center and she's getting weird vibes off it. I thought I'd check it out with you. . . ."

"Uh-huh. Wait a minute, let me get this." Loesser picked up the phone and began a conversation. While the other person talked, she put her hand over the mouthpiece and said, "What's the organization?"

"St. Michael's, up on the Drive."

Loesser said, "Yeah, I'm here, Sullivan. How old are the kids?" Then to Marlene, "St. Michael's? Fancy schmancy. Good works for the poor. This friend of yours on welfare?"

"No, she's a clerk." Marlene related what Dana had told her about Carol Anne. Loesser responded in the interstices of her conversation with Sullivan.

"OK, the center's affiliated with St. Michael Archangel Church—very high tone. The Reverend Andrew Pinder, a lot of social conscience—runs the Crusade for Children. They started this center about three years ago in a big brownstone one of his parishioners contributed. It's supposed to be a model. The board of directors is gold-plated. OK, Sullivan, I get the picture. Send them around, I'll see what I can do."

139

She hung up. "Mom kills Dad, my favorite. Usually, when Dad kills Mom, he takes out the kids too. Anyway, I never heard anything but good about St. Michael's but you never can tell. It's a sick world. If you were a child molestor, where would you get a job? In an old age home? Making boxer shorts?"

"So one of the staff could be a creep?"

"It's possible, but unlikely. This place is first cabin—the staff ratios are right up there. But who knows? It's New York, right? Look, here's the director's name and their phone number. You can go check it out yourself." Loesser pulled out a card and scribbled on a piece of paper, which she handed to Marlene. The phone rang again. Loesser smiled and shrugged helplessly. Marlene smiled and made for the door. As she left, a court officer was delivering two weeping, fatherless little boys to Suzie Loser.

The name of the place was on a black iron plate in raised letters: St. Michael Archangel Child Development Center. The building was a five story brownstone, one of three biscuit-colored aristocrats set in a row in the middle of a Riverside Drive block dominated by towering apartment houses. Marlene didn't even want to think about what such a building might cost. She climbed the front steps and pushed the buzzer on the side of an ornate wrought-iron and glass door.

A fresh-faced young woman opened the door. Marlene said she had an appointment with the director. The woman smiled pleasantly and ushered Marlene into a paneled hallway floored with parquet. The place smelled of furniture polish and leather. As the woman led her down the hall, Marlene asked, "Where are the kids?"

"Oh, they'll be in the back now. It's nice out today and there's a little yard. Actually, the center occupies only the rear of this floor and the basement floor. The rest of the house is the director's residence."

"It sure doesn't look like a day-care center. Where's the pink vinyl couch? Where's the green linoleum?"

The woman laughed. "Oh, we have linoleum. A tasteful beige though, of course."

"Of course. Have you worked here long?"

"No, just six months, and I'm only part time. I'm getting my masters in child development at Hunter."

"Very good. And what do you think of this place?"

"St. Michael's? It's paradise. It's probably the best day-care center in New York, maybe the world."

"That's great," said Marlene uncomfortably. She was starting to think she was on a fool's errand. This had happened before. Marlene's dirty secret was that she was not tough at all, at least not all the way through, a kind of stainless steel Twinkie. Snarling and cursing all day at Centre Street eroded something inside her, and on occasion she would either break down, as she had with Karp, or fling herself thoughtlessly into some kind of Good Deed, as now. She had lent money she didn't have to people who would never pay her back. She did favors for people she hardly knew, like Dana Woodley. Now she started thinking about ways to keep from making a complete ass of herself.

Her guide opened a walnut-paneled door and

let Marlene into a small reception room, furnished in quiet good taste, like the office of an expensive internist. The secretary, a grandmotherly woman, took her name and went through another door. In a moment, she was back. "Please go in," she said. "Mrs. Dean will see you now."

The room beyond was large, high-ceilinged, toast colored, and carpeted in pale green. Tall windows gave on the green trees of Riverside Park. Soft light entered through pale curtains. In front of the windows a woman sat in a high leather chair behind a Sheraton writing desk. She looked up as Marlene approached and held out her hand. "I'm Irma Dean," the woman said. The voice was measured and cultivated, and the hand that Marlene shook was firm and dry. "Please sit down," Mrs. Dean said, indicating a red leather armchair.

Marlene noticed herself being careful to keep her back straight and her knees together. This is just like my interview with the Mesdames, she thought. A Proustian experience, and I never got through *Swann's Way*. It's the furniture polish, the smell, and the dust falling through shafts of sunlight in the still air. She kept her hands folded carefully on her lap, with the bad one, the one with the black kid glove, concealed.

Into her mind came an image of the well-brought-up parochial schoolgirl she had been at thirteen, before sex exploded into her life. She was a sweet kid, Marlene thought. Why did I dump her? What if I went back to the nuns and tried to explain my life, my moral life. What would I say? This lady even looks like Sister Marie Augustine. The heavy eyebrows are what does it. And the sharp nose. And the confidence in those big dark eyes. No habit, but the heavy dark hair did as well. It was impossible to tell the woman's age—it could be anywhere from forty-five to sixty. A no-nonsense lady. And Marlene was here to find out whether they did *sexual abuse*?

"You have a beautiful location . . . the building, Mrs. Dean," Marlene began lamely.

"Thank you, Miss Ciampi. We've been very fortunate. The building was left to me by my late husband. My own boys are grown now and I was about to sell it, when Reverend Pinder suggested that I start a day-care center. And here we are."

The woman paused and looked expectantly at Marlene. Marlene said, "Yes, well, the reason I came down to see you, Mrs. Dean, that I asked for an appointment was, um, I'm interested in your center. I mean, I've heard it's very good. The best."

"Interested? In what way? Are you seeking employment?"

"No, no! I have a job . . . I mean, I'm an assistant district attorney."

The polite smile faded a fraction. "The district attorney? Are we being investigated?" Mrs. Dean asked lightly.

"Oh, no! Of course not. I'm interested for a child, I mean I'd like to put my child in St. Michael's."

"How old is the child?"

"Seven. I think. I mean, actually, I haven't got the child yet, but I'm in the process of adopting one. Thinking of it, actually."

"I see," said Mrs. Dean, her face taking on the expression Marlene imagined she must use with her little charges, especially those who were brain damaged. I have to get out of here, she thought.

This woman is going to start hitting me on the hand with a ruler.

"So, I thought, I could sort of check out the place, look around . . ."

"Of course. Visitors are always welcome. But, you should understand that St. Michael's is a charitable institution. All our children come from lower-income families. So in your case. . . ."

"I see. I'm sorry, I didn't realize. Um, but as long I'm here, could I . . . ?"

Mrs. Dean nodded and pushed a button on her intercom and told her secretary that Miss Ciampi would be touring the center. Marlene scuttled out from under Mrs. Dean's imperturbable gaze, blushing uncontrollably, sweat pouring down from her armpits and dotting her upper lip. She knew I was bullshitting her, she thought. Just like Sister Marie Augustine. I'm such a shitty liar, why the hell did I ever become a lawyer?

The tour was uneventful, conducted with enthusiasm by Penny, the young woman who had let Marlene into the center. The place was spotless, the children were playing what Marlene took to be educational games, the littlest ones were napping peacefully. The caretakers appeared to be like Penny—bright, enthusiastic student-teachers. Nobody was reading pornographic magazines or yanking down tiny cotton panties.

There was a whole room full of athletic equipment suitable for all ages from toddlers to preteens. "We take them to the park every day in the summer," Penny said. "They play ball and jump rope and we roller-skate a lot. They love it."

Marlene nodded absently and spun the wheels on a pair of roller skates. She hadn't skated in years; she wondered if she'd forgotten how. She sensed this was not the time to suggest a romp through the park.

The tour was telling her nothing, since there was obviously nothing to tell. When they returned to the main playroom, Marlene asked her guide to point out Carol Anne Woodley. Penny indicated a thin child in a blue Snoopy T-shirt and red corduroys chatting away with two girlfriends around a large dollhouse. "Is she a friend of yours?" Penny asked.

"Daughter of one. That's how I knew about the place. Is she doing OK?"

"Far as I know, but I only see her for about an hour. I'm with the pre-schoolers on the morning shift. The older kids get bussed over from their elementary schools and the parents pick them up after they get off work. Carol Anne's on half-day kindergarten so she gets here about twelve."

"Uh-huh. And who takes over then? Students, like you?"

Penny frowned. "No, most of the kids I know are on mornings, so we can go to class in the afternoon. The P.M. shift is mostly older. And there's an evening shift, too, because some of the parents can't pick up until eight. I've never met any of them. Why do you ask?"

"No reason, just curious. It seems like a well-run operation." Marlene looked around, trying to interest herself in cute doings. Penny's bright smile was wearing thin. Feeling more a fool than ever, Marlene glanced at her watch, made her excuses, and left.

Once outside, she strode rapidly up the incline of Seventy-ninth Street to the subway station on Broadway, thinking bad thoughts about herself and about Dana Woodley. The rest of the day was no bargain either. She was late for a calendar court at one-thirty and got yelled at by a judge. A witness in the case of an armed robber with about fifty priors failed to appear for the third time and the P.D. got the judge to can the case. The mutt blew Marlene a kiss as he jive-walked out of the courtroom. This can't get worse, she thought as she slumped against the courtroom rail, forgetting for a moment that she was in the New York City criminal justice system, where it always can.

Carol Anne Woodley watched the shadows creep across the day-care center floor. She was arranging plastic blocks, some squares of fabric, and various wooden toys in a special way in order to make her mother pick her up early, before the regular people went away and the witch people came. It had only worked once, but Carol Anne tried it every evening just in case. Nearby, her best friend, Stephanie, and her other best friend Alice were talking to a new kid, a boy named Otis. Otis was dumb. He was only a five-year-old baby.

"You got to take off your pants, if they say, Otis," said Stephanie. "They're uncles!"

"My uncle's in Virginia," said Otis, confused. Both girls broke into a fit of giggles. "Stupid! Stupid!" they both cried. Alice added, "They're not real uncles, they're special uncles. They tickle you and they breathe on you . . ."

"Yeah, like this, 'A-hungh, a-HUNGH, a-HUUU-UNGH!' " said Stephanie.

". . . and then they give you candy."

"What kind of candy?"

"Any kind. Any kind what you like. And money."

"Real?"

"Yeah," said Stephanie, "even dollars."

"You lying," said Otis.

"Am not. They really do. Right, Alice?"

"It's true, Otis," Alice confirmed. "And," she continued, lowering her voice to a whisper, "you not allowed to tell nobody, not even your Mommy. 'Cause, 'cause, if you do, they kill you!"

"Liar, liar, pants on fire," cried Otis, getting to his feet. He wished his Mommy was here right now.

"You better not tell, Otis," said Alice sternly. "They get the Bogeyman to kill you. They showed us. Tell him, Carol Anne!"

Carol Anne looked up from her construction. "It's true. They take you down cellar with no clothes on and all the witch people stand around with no clothes on and the bad kid gets stabbed with blood and then the Bogeyman takes them away. And they sing funny songs. About the devil."

She added a little yellow plastic lion, the last touch, and looked up towards the door of the playroom. Her mother wasn't coming. Instead, the witch people were coming in, and talking to the regular ladies as they left. They were all smiling and laughing. Carol Anne smashed the construction, kicking it with both feet, making the blocks and animals skitter across the floor.

Otis looked up in alarm. Stephanie said, "She always does that." Carol Anne hunched in the corner with her head on her knees. She wished Otis would go away with his dumb questions. In a few minutes, she knew, one of the witch people would come around with glasses of chocolate milk. You had to drink it, or if you were allergic, you could have orange juice, but you had to have a nice drink. After the drink you would sit around and watch television. Then you started to feel sleepy and warm, and your face felt like it was under a blanket. Then the uncles came.

Otis was still asking dumb questions. "But, but," he stammered hopefully, "they just *pretend* kill you. Right, Alice?"

"No, dum-dum, they kill you for *real*," answered Alice with contempt. "Really real. Just like on TV."

Otis started to whimper and one of the witch people came over and led him away. Then they gave out the drinks and it became very quiet in the day-care center. Nobody wanted to play any more. Carol Anne started to feel dreamy, like she did on weekends, lying in bed and thinking about flying around the rainbow with her special pony. After a while, she found herself in a bedroom. She didn't remember how she got there. There was an uncle in the room. She closed her eyes and tried to go back into the dreamy place. The uncle got onto the bed and took her pants and underpants off.

The uncle's face was pressed against hers and she could hear his funny breathing and smell his sweat and his perfume. He was making her hurt down there. She squeezed her eyes shut and didn't cry, like they told her. They told her they would hurt her worse than this if she cried or told. They said her Mommy knew all about it already anyway, and it was OK, and you weren't supposed to talk about it, because it was nasty, like talking about poop at the dinner table.

The uncle finished his business and went out and a witch lady came in and took Carol Anne out. There were some other children in the hallway. Some of them were new and were still crybabies. Carol Anne hoped they would go back to the day room, but no, they were being led downstairs.

Now you weren't supposed to close your eyes. You had to watch or the witch people would pinch you. Down the stairs and across the playground and down the stairs again to the red door.

Carol Anne hated this worse than the uncles. Past the red door all of the witch people and the children were standing around a long black table, built with a thick candlestick at each corner. Jesus Upside-Down was on the wall. Sometimes they took Jesus down and made you spit or pee on him, but they weren't doing that today. That meant something worse. A lighted fat black candle stood in each of the table's holders and the air smelled of perfumed smoke.

There was a screen across the room, with a goat head on it, a black goat head with yellow eyes. All the witch people were humming. You had to be very quiet and keep your eyes open now.

From around the screen came the devils. Three of them were dressed in black robes and masks, with horns and red tongues. One of them was naked, with a black goat head instead of a real head.

Carol Anne heard a child scream and then a slap and a stifled whimper. Carol Anne didn't make a sound. She knew this wasn't the scariest part.

The devils and the witch people were moving around, humming and singing and making smoke come out of a swinging ball. Some of the children began to cough, the smoke was so thick.

Now one of the devils was standing at the head of the black table, singing very loud in a high voice, like she was calling somebody: *Zariatnatmits! Tabots! Membroth! Aorios! Bucon! Minoson!*

A big gong rang and the Monster came out from behind the screen carrying a naked little girl in his arms. The girl was tied up and had something stuffed in her mouth so all she could make were little squeaking sounds. The Monster had an animal head too, like a pig, but hairy and with long fangs. He was naked too, and his skin was white, like Crisco. The little girl's skin was brown.

The Monster tied the little girl to the black table, an arm or a leg to each candle holder. The grown-ups started humming and shaking and singing and the naked devil came around and jumped up on the table on top of the tied-up little girl. Carol Anne could see his butt bouncing up and down. All the grown-ups were shouting now and beating on the gong.

Then the devil got off the little girl. There was blood coming out of her. The other devil, the one who had yelled out the names, took out a small curvy knife and began to cut marks in the little girl's skin. The girl jumped around every time she got cut. The other devils came around and poked at the girl. Carol Anne couldn't see what they were doing, but after they were finished, the little girl didn't jump around any more. You could still hear her breathing, though, a whistling sound, thin and high.

She was dripping with blood. The devil with the knife brought out a silver cup and collected some blood and pulled the mask away from its face and drank it. Then the other devils and the witch people all drank some and sang more and beat the gong.

The Monster went up to the end of the table where the girl's head was and did something to her neck. The whistling breath stopped. Carol Anne was glad, because that meant it was almost over. She felt a little sorry for the girl, but that was what happened when you were really, *really* bad, and told. Besides, that little girl wasn't a friend of hers.

Now the Monster held up the girl's hand by one finger. In the other hand he held a big scissors. He cut off the finger and ate it, putting it into the pig mouth of the mask. The girl's hand flopped down on the table. They beat the gong. The grown-ups hummed and the devils and the Monsters went behind the screen. The witch people took the children out and washed them up and took them to the nap room, all the time telling them that if they said anything about what they had seen the same thing would happen to them as had happened to the little girl behind the red door.

All the children lay on their cots in the nap room. Some of them were eating the candy they had been given, after. Nobody was talking. In a while, parents came by and picked them up. Carol Anne saw her own mother come in. She got off her cot and walked over to her. Her mother gave her a hug and looked in her face. Carol Anne could see she was worried, she had that little wrinkle between her eyes.

"Everything OK, honey?" her mother asked. "You all right?"

"Fine," said Carol Anne.

"Did you have a good day? Anything special happen?"

"No, just regular," said Carol Anne.

Felix had never called Anna at the school before, and the tone of his voice and his frenzied insistence that she meet him immediately were unprecedented as well. After telling the school office she was ill, she hopped a cab and headed for a rendezvous at Larry's. In the cab, she was aware of a feeling of satisfaction beneath her concern: With all his friends and connections, Felix had called *her* when he was in trouble. He needed her.

But she was badly shaken when she saw what Felix in trouble looked like. Even in the dim light of the lounge she could see the dark bruises on his face and hands. He was unshaven and his hair was matted. And he was drunk. He looks like a bum, was Anna's first involuntary thought. In shame she suppressed it and rushed to sit by his side.

"My God! Felix, what happened to you?"

"What does it look like? I got in a fight." This was said so curtly that Anna drew abruptly away. Seeing this, Felix said in what he imagined was a more genial voice, "Yeah, a crazy thing. I was jogging in the park and I saw a bunch of guys hassling this woman. So I went over to talk to them, and they jumped me. I put three of them away, but then one of 'em must have popped me with a rock, because I went down and they started dancing on my head. What a jerk, huh?" He uttered a self-deprecating chuckle.

"No, I don't think that was jerky, Felix. I think that was a wonderful thing."

"Ah, that's nice, baby. I knew you'd under-stand." He stretched and winced. "Damn! I could use a good hot soak. They only have a shower where I'm staying."

Which was Anna's cue to invite Felix back to her place, because she had a big tub, and in short order Felix was soaking away, with Anna sitting on the edge of the bath, admiring her hero, and plying him, on request, with iced beers, cigarettes, and sandwiches.

Eventually, Felix got out of the bath and stood naked and dripping on the bathmat. From where she sat, Anna could see that he was bruised also on the thighs and midsection. She felt a wave of pity and admiration for him. Felix made no move to dry himself off. He just stood in front of her, with his groin at the level of her mouth. "Hey," he said and jerked his hips, so that a drop of bathwater jumped from his stiffening penis to splash on her face. Blissfully, she closed her eyes and took him in.

Anna sat in a chair watching Felix snoring on her bed. It was close to midnight. He had walked in and plopped down immediately after getting sucked off, and had been out ever since. Felix was not one for tender afterglows. He had a brutal streak: no, not brutal, she edited, strong, vigor-ous, masculine. It excited her, she had to admit; he was so different from the male schoolteachers and administrators she mixed with every day, or the floorwalkers at the department store. They were rabbits compared to Felix. Imagine, taking on a gang of thugs singlehanded!

He stirred and rolled over. She hoped he would wake up and make love to her. She had stripped and put on a bathrobe to make it easier. Fuck me, she thought, concentrating hard. Get up and fuck me! She felt herself blushing. What's happening to me, she thought. I'm becoming a sex-crazed schoolteacher. The thought struck her funny. It's true. She didn't know how much she would give up to have a nice warm, hairy man in her bed, but she knew they hadn't got there yet. The thought struck her as so funny that she chortled out loud.

At the sound, Felix popped his eyes open. His body tensed as it always did when he awakened. "What? What're you sitting there for?" he demanded.

"Nothing. Just looking at you."

He scowled and swung out of the bed and walked to the bathroom, saying nothing more. Anna turned the lights low, turned on the radio to a soft music station, lay down on the bed and stretched out in what she thought was a fetching pose. But when he returned he had his pants on and he was buttoning his shirt. Her face fell.

"What's the matter?"

She summoned up a weak smile. "Nothing. I just thought you'd, you know, stay."

He seemed to look at her for the first time, taking in her bathrobe and the way she was lying on the bed. A wolfish look came over his face and he bent over and shoved his hand roughly between her thighs. "Oh, can't wait for it, huh?" he said, his face close. He still smelled of the whiskey. "Hey, baby, I'll be back real soon. I'll jam it in you good. But now I gotta go. My friend Steve's getting off his shift at one and he's gonna lend me his car so I can move my stuff over here."

"Your stuff? What are you talking about, Felix?"

"What do you mean, 'what am I talking about'? I'm gonna move in here, today, like we said."

"We didn't say, Felix. I said you could stay here when you got lonely, but we never talked about you moving in."

"Fuck that!" he cried. "I'm moving in. What is this shit now!"

Anna recoiled at his tone and at the frightening expression on his face. Immediately, all Anna could think about was her last conversation with Stephanie. Her rational doubts about Felix and what he really was came rolling forth, like freeze frames from a movie: the funny credit cards, the sleazy bars he took her to, the vague and grandoise "business" he was in, the fight he got into last night. Anna was skilled at unraveling the lies of naughty fourth-graders and now she began to apply her skills to Felix.

She got off the bed, flicked on the lights and snapped the radio off. "Felix," she said sternly, facing him, "we have to talk. I mean moving in together is serious business. And, you know, we never talk seriously. We go out, we have dinner, we jump into bed, and bang!, you're out of here. Not that it's not great, in bed and all, but I don't really know anything about you. Like, I tried calling you last night, the number you gave me, and this guy was really nasty to me, he said you'd be out all night." She looked at him appealingly and held out her hands, palms up. "Felix, what am I supposed to think? Maybe you're seeing other women . . . ?"

Without warning, Felix hit her across the jaw. She staggered back against the wall and brought the bedside lamp crashing down. He grabbed the front of her robe, pulled her upright and back-handed her again. She screamed, "Felix! Stop! For God's sake . . ."

"Shut up, you lying cunt!" he screamed back. He punched her hard in the stomach, a neatly executed *chudan oi zuki*, and she crumpled to the floor, gasping. He kicked her in the side, still yelling at the top of his voice, "Bitch! Cunt! I'll kill you."

She crawled on her hands and knees toward the kitchen. When she got some breath back, she started crying, and between sobs screaming herself. Somebody started pounding on the other side of the bedroom wall with a solid object. Dimly, Anna heard a woman's voice yelling, "Stop that noise or I'll call the cops!" Anna screamed louder and kept crawling.

He followed her into the kitchen, lashing out with his foot every couple of steps. He might have hurt her more, but he was still stiff from the beating at the dojo. She crawled under the kitchen table, and curled up beneath it, with her head covered by her arms, weeping and listening to Felix smash up her kitchen.

The table was a solid pine job, built into the wall and anchored to the floor at the outboard end. Felix yelled, "Don't hide from me, cunt! Don't hide from me! You're gonna get it, you lying bitch! Bitch! You're gonna wish you never been born," as well as similar statements that quite undermined the image of the suave international executive he had tried so hard to cultivate. He blamed Anna for this loss of face, too, and his inability to get his hands on her flesh at this instant redoubled his fury.

After he had broken everything in the kitchen he could reach, he got down on his side and grappled under the table, hoping to haul her out, but Anna flailed her legs so wildly he couldn't get a good purchase. Besides, his bruises really hurt in that position. He stood up and, good black belt that he was, began to smash the top of the table, accompanied by the traditional grunts and yells.

He had succeeded in breaking through one plank, when there came a loud knock on the door, and a voice: "Police, open up!"

Felix took a deep breath, brushed back his hair, went to the door and opened it. There were two cops standing there.

"We had a report there's been a disturbance here," said the nearest of the two, a square-faced blocky man of about forty-five. His partner was dark, skinny, and much younger. Felix noted that they both carried two-foot-long black flashlights. He said calmly, "No, there's no problem here, Officer. Who sent in the call?"

"You mind if we take a look around?" said the first cop, and before Felix could object they were both in the kitchen. Anna had crawled out from under the table and was sitting on a chair, her head in her hands, sobbing.

"Just a little argument, Officer," said Felix, smiling, the lord of the manor. The older cop made Felix with a two-second glance: a scumbag, he concluded, and probably not the husband. The place is torn up, he observed, and in his experience it was mostly the boyfriends who tore up. The hubbie wasn't going to rip out the shelves and then when he made up with wifey, he has to put them back again. The hubbies take it out on the wives and kids. On meat.

He turned his attention to the woman. "Everything OK, ma'am?" he asked politely. She seemed to have difficulty finding her voice. "Yes," she croaked. "No." Then, "Could you ask him to leave, now?"

"This your apartment, ma'am?"

"Yes, it is."

Felix moved in Anna's direction and she flinched. The cop's arm came up slightly as he moved between them, and Felix could feel the skinny cop move into position behind him. Those fucking flashlights. He had to be cool.

"Anna," he said. "Honey . . . God, I'm sorry . . . I'm sorry."

"Felix, I'd like you to leave now, just go, just leave me alone."

"You heard the lady, Felix," said the older cop. "Let's get dressed, OK?"

Felix went into the bedroom and got his shirt and jacket on, and his shoes and socks. The skinny cop followed him in and watched from the doorway, impassively. Felix ignored him. He went into the bathroom and combed his hair. Then he picked up his attaché case. In his imagination, briefly, he played out for himself a scene where he whipped out his new bowie knife, slashed the skinny cop's throat, ran into the kitchen and gutted the other one, and then got to work on Anna again. He'd have to tie and gag her first, to keep her quiet, so he'd have time for a really good job. He'd start on her tits . . .

"Hey, lover boy! Hey, Felix! Look alive now, we ain't got all night here."

Felix snapped out of his reverie. They were too far apart, and they had those goddamn flashlights right in their hands. He'd never make it, and if he didn't get all three of them, he'd be in deep shit with the cops here in Manhattan, too, and he couldn't afford that.

He allowed the cops to accompany him out of the apartment. He heard Anna double-bolt and chain the lock behind them. She'd calm down, the dumb cunt, but there was no denying that his plans were a shitpile right now. As they entered the hall Felix saw that the door of the apartment opposite was partly open. Felix saw Stephanie Mullen's face for an instant before she slammed the door.

"Is that her?" Felix asked the cops. "Is that who called?"

"Just move along, buddy," said the older cop wearily.

"I'll remember that," said Felix, grinning.

# CHAPTER
# 8

When Karp arrived, at just five minutes to noon, Santa Monica pier was packed with tourists and local office workers in search of a greasy lunch in the open air. The air was thick and hot under a silvery sky, laden with pale vapors from the Pier's line-up of small eateries, every offering of which was either fried or carbonated. It was Karp's kind of place.

He bought a chili dog with onions and a soda and went over to the rail that edged the boardwalk. From there he could observe the spot where the man and the boy with the balloon stood in the postcard picture. Karp had to lean over as he ate his chili dog, so that the grease and bits of chili would drip on the ground and not on his shirt. When he straightened up, Little Noodles Impellatti was standing next to him.

Karp nodded and finished his chili dog. Noodles waited politely, saying nothing. He was dressed in a white silk jacket and a black shirt open at the neck. He had a good tan and wore large sunglasses. He looked like what he was, a gangster on the lam.

"So," said Karp at last, wiping his mouth with a paper napkin. "Any trouble?"

"I'm here," said Noodles. "What's the score?"

"The bad guys are ahead," answered Karp, and he briefly went over what he had learned from Guma.

Noodles took this in without emotion. He leaned on the rail and looked out to sea. "Tona, huh? I did some work for him once. He's good." He looked at Karp, waiting. Karp realized, with something of a shock, that Noodles had placed himself in Karp's hands, as agreed, and considered that this was the end of his contribution to their escape. Karp had assumed that Noodles would be a treasure-trove of clever Mafia-style evasion plans. But having cut himself off from everything that had directed his life, Impellatti was now as passive as a stone at the bottom of a hill. That's why they call them button men, Karp thought.

"We have to hide for a while," Karp said lamely.

"Good idea," Noodles replied. Karp couldn't tell whether the other man was being sarcastic. Probably not, he decided.

"Um, have you got a car?" Karp asked.

At this, Noodles lowered his sunglasses and looked at Karp as if Karp had asked whether he had a nose. "Yeah. I got a car. Where're we going?"

An hour later they were headed north on the San Diego Freeway. Impellatti's scant possessions were in the trunk already, and it had taken only moments to check Karp out of his motel. He still hadn't told Noodles where they were going, and Noodles hadn't asked again. He seemed content enough to be behind the wheel of a fast car, attentive to orders.

There was almost no conversation during the drive. The two men had little enough in common besides business, and Karp was not inclined to bring up business. When he interrogated Impellatti it would be in a formal setting, with a stenographer. Either that or some thug would kill them before they got back to New York, was Karp's thinking, and the thought made for a sort of timeless quality in the journey, a version of what the sages called Living in the Now.

Karp watched the brown California hills flash by, and the pastel cities named for obscure saints. The car was large, cool, and comfortable, and Noodles was one of the best drivers in the country. The afternoon wore on, the shadows lengthened on the hills. Karp dozed against the glass of his window.

He was brought awake by a change in the motion of the car.

"Where are we? Something wrong?" he asked thickly, rubbing the sleep away.

"No. You said the San Jose exit. This is it."

"Yeah, OK. Head for Los Gatos on 17. Then take 546 into Ladero. I'll give you directions from there."

They continued through progressively smaller and dustier towns, the road becoming narrower and rougher, until they were on a mere farm track, high in the Santa Cruz mountains.

"Hold it. This is it," said Karp, consulting a crumpled slip of paper. A white sign nailed to a pine tree read "Alice Farm."

"We're going here?" asked Noodles.

"Yeah. My wife lives here. I mean my ex-, I mean my soon to be ex-wife. I'm in the middle of a divorce." Why did I tell him that, Karp wondered a second later. It's none of his business.

"I don't believe in divorce," said Noodles. "You could always work something out."

*Great*, thought Karp, *I need a morality lecture from a Mafia wise guy*. He said, "You just believe in murder, right, Noodles?"

Noodles looked offended. "That's different. It's business. I was talking personal."

They continued up the farm road in silence. A tractor trundled around a bend and Noodles pulled the car over to let it pass. It was driven by a large tanned woman wearing a red bandanna on her head, but otherwise naked from the waist up. Noodles stared after her until she vanished in her dust cloud. "What is this, some kind of nudist colony?"

"Why? Don't you believe in nudism either?"

"I could give a flying fuck. But if they're flakes . . . you know? Flakes make me nervous."

"No flakes, Noodles. These are all solid citizens. OK, here we are."

They had driven into a dirt yard outside a large gray farmhouse. Children and chickens scratched happily in the dirt. There was the smell of smoke from a wood fire. Karp got out of the car and stretched. The children stopped playing and stared at him. There were six women sitting on the wide porch that ran along the front of the house. They were shelling peas, knitting, lounging, chatting. They also stopped when they saw him, as if he were someone come with a telegram to announce the death of a loved one. One of the women pulled a T-shirt over her bare upper body. Another of the women stood up abruptly, and Karp recognized his wife.

She looked good, he thought. She was wearing tan shorts and a white sleeveless shirt that showed off her taut, tanned limbs. Her hair was sunbleached and shorter than it had been and her face was clear of the nervousness he remembered from their New York apartment days.

They greeted each other warily, while the other women looked on with expressions ranging from hostile to mocking. Susan herself seemed embarrassed. She led him into a small room in the back of the house and served him some iced tea. They sat in chairs at a dusty white enamel table and talked awkwardly about their separate lives. She was at peace. Karp was happy for her. Karp's life was going fine. She was happy for him. Karp didn't mention Marlene, nor did Susan mention her relationship with her lover.

An awkward silence then. Karp looked at her and tried to see her as a no-sexual object, or at least one that was not sexually available to him. He couldn't quite do it. Despite himself he was making comparisons between Susan and Marlene. Susan was basically more good-natured and forgiving than Marlene. There was, or had been, a sweetness, a comfortable yielding quality of body and spirit about Susan that Marlene definitely did not have, that he desired. It meant peace to him with a woman. But then why did he care so much for Marlene? He blanked this out of his mind, but not before Susan had responded to his stare.

"What are you looking at?" asked Susan.

"What?"

"You were staring at me."

"Oh, sorry. Just musing on times gone by. If I had done this, if you had done—et cetera. Like that."

She smiled and said, "Hey, it wasn't like that. It was just something that happened. It's nothing to be sorry about either way."

"So, we could still be friends, and like that."

"Sure," she said. "I'd like that." She really was good-natured.

"Great," he said. "Let's get divorced then."

He brought out the no-fault papers and explained them. He handed her a pen. She smiled thinly and said, "I guess I should use Susan Karp."

"It's your name."

"Funny, I haven't used it for years. We call ourselves with our mother's first names or we make one up. I'm Susan Belles."

"That should make your mom happy. She thinks all this is my fault."

"All this? Oh, my being gay. Yeah, Mother did always think that anything that happened could be traced to some man." She signed the documents. "There. The end of Susan Karp. Free at last, free at last, great God almighty, free at last."

"Is that how you feel?"

"Oh, not really. I don't feel anything much. Like cashing a check: You're glad there's money in the bank, but otherwise no big thing."

Karp put the documents in his jacket pocket. "I don't know. I feel kind of sad. We had some good times. I *thought* we had some good times."

She reached over and patted his hand. "We did, Butch, we were fine. It's just . . ."

"Yeah, I know." He paused, to change the subject. "Seeing as how we're friends, I have a favor to ask."

"What is it?"

"Well . . . it's a little complex, but I'm in some trouble right now."

"You? In trouble? What did you get, a parking ticket?"

"No. It's that guy in the car. His name's Frank Impellatti. He's a witness to a murder in New

York. Guys are looking for him, for us, and I need a place we can lie low for a little while until I can figure a way to get him back. I thought if it wouldn't be too much trouble . . ."

He stopped, because Susan was staring at him with an expression of mingled horror and disgust.

"What's wrong, Susan?" he said.

"You have to be out of your mind," she said in a tight thin voice, jumping to her feet and backing away. "I can't believe this! Too much trouble! My God! You brought a fucking Mafioso to my home? You brought your filth to my home? With children here? You bastard!"

Karp stood up, too. "Susan, what are you talking about! Calm down, for chrissakes! You're not in danger. Nobody knows we're here. Nobody's gonna know."

"Yeah? So twenty-one women and ten children are going to enter a little conspiracy to protect your witness? Look over their shoulders all the time and teach the kids to lie in school, so you can make your case? So you can win your little macho game? Let's be friends, you said? You don't know the meaning of the word. Maybe with your asshole buddies in the courthouse. Not with a woman. You manipulative son of a bitch!"

"Susan, there's no reason to pick a goddamn fight . . ." Karp shouted back. He recalled that it had been one of his most familiar lines during his marriage.

"Get out of here!" she screamed. Her face was reddening and splashed with tears. "Get out of here now, and get out of my life, and take your goddamn mobster with you!"

She ran out of the room. Karp considered following her and trying to make her see reason, but after a moment's thought he realized it would do no good. It had seemed like such a great idea, too. He wondered what he could have done differently. It was like his marriage, that little conversation, a ten-second digest of five years of misunderstanding, and at the end, the familiar feelings of puzzlement and vague shame. He *wasn't* a manipulative son-of-a-bitch. Marlene would have understood. He suddenly missed her with an intensity that churned his stomach.

"So? What's happening?" asked Impellatti when Karp returned to the car. "It's fuckin' boiling out here. Where are we staying?"

"We're not. She wants us out of here."

"What, your wife?"

"My ex-wife. She thinks we'd be a bad influence on the kids."

"Fuck her! Whyn't you rap her in the chops a couple?"

"Because I'm not a chop-rapper, first of all, and I don't think it would be a good idea, seeing as how we're trying to avoid notice and trouble with the law."

"She'd turn you in?"

"In a second."

"Shit! See, that's what I told you, why I don't believe in divorce."

"You made your point, Noodles. The question is, where do we go from here? You like getting a plane out of San Jose?"

"Forget it! No fuckin' planes. Not with Tona out looking. We got to drive it."

"Drive? Where to, drive?"

"The City. Two and a half days, tops." He started the car and reversed violently, then headed down the farm road, the Buick bouncing like a yo-yo and throwing a high wake of gravel.

"You mean drive straight through. The two of us?"

"No, just me. I don't passenger."

"Noodles, that's crazy. You can't drive for sixty hours straight."

"Yeah, I can," said Little Noodles confidently. "I done it before. It ain't no problem. I got whites."

Anna did not go back to bed after the cops took Felix away. She sat at the kitchen table and smoked cigarettes and tried to remember who she was. It was like waking up from a dream.

She looked around the ruined kitchen and thought briefly about picking up the smashed china and fixing the broken shelves. There seemed no point. Instead, she got some white wine from the refrigerator and drank a glass. She poured another, but refrained from drinking it down. She didn't want to get drunk. She *had* been drunk, since the night four months and seven days ago when Felix Tighe had sat down at the bar stool next to hers at Kevin O'Rourke's on Second Avenue, had looked into her eyes and said, "I've been waiting for you." It was like the songs, like TV.

But as she thought of those early days, she began (and this both horrified and beguiled her) to experience the draining of romance. Was it really over? Would she never have a man do those crazy things to her again? Maybe *she* was really to blame. Felix was under a lot of stress. If only she had . . . and so on, until dawn broke into the kitchen and the sound of the door buzzer snatched her out of her reveries.

It must be Felix, was her instant thought. She froze in her chair, scarcely breathing, all romantic thoughts of regret quite blown from her head by cold terror. A minute passed. The buzzer went off again and a voice called, "Anna? Anna, are you there? It's me."

Anna got shakily to her feet and opened the door's two deadbolts. Stephanie Mullen walked in, shaking her head and making sympathetic noises. At the sight of Stephanie's tough, pleasant face, Anna collapsed in weeping. Stephanie gathered her up and hugged her, making small soothing noises for quite some time.

Later, in Stephanie's messy kitchen, with a cup of strong tea in her and an ice bag held against her aching and swelling face, Anna began to realize that life would continue. Life was going on at that moment. Stephanie's kitchen, though none too clean, was bright with kids' drawings and pinned-up posters and Mexican pottery and houseplants. Stephanie was bustling about, getting her two boys off to school, cooking breakfast, finding homework and socks, while the boys cast shy looks in Anna's direction. When they were at last out the door, Stephanie plopped down in the chair across the wooden table from Anna and grinned. Anna returned the smile.

"Back from the dead, hey?" said Stephanie offering Anna a Kent.

Anna lit it carefully, avoiding the cut in her lip. "I feel punctured," she said.

Stephanie nodded. "Yeah, it'll do that. Funny, there must be a million women living alone in New York—they walk, they shop, they take the subway, they *jog in the park*, for chrissake, and sure, they're careful, because they watch TV and all, but until it happens, they think they've, like, got some kind of armor on, it only happens to other people, you know? Like soldiers in a war. But after, it's like it was an eggshell, the armor. They're all naked. They can't do anything. They're scared all the time, all the time."

Anna nodded. "Yeah, that's right. You sound like you know what you're talking about."

"Huh! Don't I, baby!" She turned her face in profile to Anna. "See that nose? The bump? He busted it once. Talk about pain! And people know, you know? They don't want to look at you. And you know what they're thinking? What did she do to make him do that, to rap her around?"

"Who was it? Your husband?"

"Yeah. Willie Mullen, the world-famous shithead."

"What did you do? I mean, when he . . ."

"Beat me up? Well, the first half-dozen or so times, I cried, I begged—what the fuck did I know? I was a twenty-year-old kid with two kids of my own. Then the group started to make some serious bread, do some major gigs. We opened for the Stones once. So he couldn't pop me in the face anymore, you know. He did other stuff, you don't want to know about it. We were famous for it, in our little circles.

"Then, one fine day, it was in Tahoe, I remember, I found him in the rack with a groupie. The boys, his *sons*, were watching TV in the next room. I blew up, he went out of control, and busted my nose.

"And then," Stephanie went on, leaning her head back and smiling, like a gourmet recalling some exquisite dish, "I went out, and asked around, and found this guy, and I paid him two hundred bucks to smash my dear husband into pulp."

"God, Stephanie! That's awful!"

Stephanie laughed. "Yeah, a real shame. Funny thing is, I never told Willie I hired the guy, but he knew—I'm sure of it. He never touched me again. And we broke up three weeks after he got out of the hospital. He's in the City now, you know? I see him from time to time, because of the kids, but it's like strangers. There's a lesson in that, I guess, but I'm damned if I know what it is. Want some more tea?"

"No, thanks. I've got to get ready for work— God knows how I'll get through the day, but I need the money. Especially since I'm going to lose some of my security because of that damn kitchen."

"You're leaving, huh?"

"I guess. I could never do that, what you did, you know? Hurt Felix. I just want to let it cool off, you know? And if I stay here he'll hang around and bother me, and be all nice, and I know after a while, I'll go back with him. I just feel it."

"I can dig that. So what will you do?"

"Stay with my sister, I guess. For a while, until I can save up for a new deposit. Or maybe I can sublet this place to my cousin Linda and her boyfriend. Something." Anna stood up and brought her teacup and the icebag to the sink. There was a matted photograph of Stephanie's two boys pinned to the wall, the kind taken at schools or by department store photographers for the grandparent trade. It had grease spots on it. Anna studied the picture for a moment, wondering how these two handsome and winning children had been marked by the violence and disorder of their early lives. It must go in deep, she thought. It doesn't show on the surface.

"Nice kids," she said. "It's a neat picture."

"Yeah," Stephanie agreed. "There's Jordie out front, hogging the scene, charming the hell out of the world. Just like his daddy as a matter of fact. And Josh there, pretending to smile, taking everything in. Calculating. Trying to figure it out."

"Like you?"

"Shit, no! Damned if I know where he gets it. I never figured anything out in my whole life, except dumping Willie. I just live it as it comes, baby. But I tell you one thing. I don't think you're going to see much of the boyfriend anymore."

"You mean Felix? Why not?"

"Because he's a con man. I saw it the minute I met him. A con man don't hang around when you've blown his grift. Why should he? No offense, kid, but he could make one cruise up Third and down Second and pull a sweetie he hadn't beat up yet out of every damn singles bar up there. You understand what I'm telling you? A boilermaker, a strong arm guy, hey, even a musician or an artist, he'll hang in and hang in 'til hell freezes and he'll make your life hell, too. But not Felix. He's a control freak. He loses control, he's got nothing left, dig? He won't bother you, believe me."

And all through her Saturday half-day behind a Macy's cosmetic counter, Anna tried hard to believe her friend. Stephanie seemed so wise in the ways of men, especially the more unsavory types. She had said Felix would not bother her, but Anna thought to herself that even if Stephanie was right about con men—and Anna agreed that Felix was one—Stephanie had not seen the look on Felix's face while he was beating her. Maybe, she thought, Felix was different.

By the end of the day, as it turned out, Anna knew that Stephanie was wrong.

\* \* \*

Karp finally called Marlene on Sunday evening, a little before ten. She was watching Masterpiece Theater and sucking on a jug of red Mondavi and feeling slightly annoyed at being interrupted. She let the phone ring eight times.

"Hi. It's me," Karp said.

"Who?"

"It's me, Butch."

"Butch? Oh, Butch *Karp*. Gosh, it's nice of you to call. It's only been six days, Mr. Considerate."

"Marlene, please don't cop an attitude on me here. I'm being fucking pursued by mobsters. I called as soon as I could. How's things?"

"At the office? Great. We've defeated crime and they're converting the building into a mental hospital. Little change of personnel required. How about you? Did you, uh, get it?"

"El divorce-o? Signed and sealed. I'm a free man."

"Congratulations! But with my luck they'll probably shoot you before I can get my claws into your fine young body. Listen, when they close in, tell them you have a Sicilian girlfriend. It could make a difference."

"You're not taking this very seriously, Marlene."

"I am, I am! You know I get silly when I'm nervous."

"What are you nervous about?"

"Two things. The possibility of you never coming back is one. Shit, it'd take *hours* to find another boyfriend as good as you. And the possibility of you *coming* back is the other. I mean we have to start getting serious about the big M."

"Right. I'll see if Noodles here can get me a deal on a nice ring. We might as well keep it in the family."

"So to speak. Where are you, by the way? Still in California?"

"Actually, somewhere in Ohio. Noodles is having a pee. Oops! Here he comes. This guy is amazing—Mr. Cruise Control. When they make cars that drive by robots, in the future, they're going to use him as a model. Look, what I called you about, besides expressing my undying love and all, is that we'll be back in the city by tomorrow evening. I want to go straight to the place we'll be stashing Noodles. Call Devlin and get it set up. We'll question him right away. I can't believe this—he's honking his horn, for chrissake! See you."

"Karp, wait! What are you doing in Ohio? You're supposed to be in California."

"No shit? That's why there aren't any palm trees or Mexicans. What a ripoff! See you tomorrow, cutie."

Marlene hung up the phone, relieved, but also unsatisfied in an all-too-familiar way. A lot of her interaction with Karp was on the "see you tomorrow, cutie" level. Breezy dismissal. But of course, he respected her mind and her legal skills. He said so often. And he usually did what she asked him to do, like this divorce. So what was going on, what was the problem?

Seeking the answer, she drank rather more of her jug than she had planned, and not only failed to find the answer, but overslept, and had to hustle to make her first court the next morning. Still running behind schedule, she was racing out of her office with her nose buried in a file and a dozen more clamped beneath her arm, when she ran into Jim Raney.

She hit him so hard that his shoes lost their grip

on Monday's fresh wax and the two of them crashed together on the floor, with Marlene on top. Raney was covered with her papers like a corpse in a shroud.

"Oh, shit, I'm sorry," said Marlene, struggling to regain her feet and collect her papers at the same time.

"I'm not," said Raney blissfully. "This has made my month."

"Raney! What are you doing here?" asked Marlene, flustered and blushing as she picked papers off the detective's recumbent form. He was grinning like a maniac.

"I'm lying on my back, enjoying the sensation of tiny fingers plucking at my clothes," Raney sighed.

Marlene got to her feet and straightened her skirt. "Knock it off, Raney, and help me get this crap together. Jesus, I'm going to be late again!"

Raney got to his knees, still grinning, and began gathering papers. "That was a nice hit there, Marlene. You play much hockey?"

"As a matter of fact, wise-ass, I used to play a lot of roller hockey."

"Marlene, girls in Queens don't play roller-skate hockey."

"Except for me, they don't. I was on the Hundred and twelfth Street Rangers for three years and we cleaned every clock in Ozone Park, if it's any of your business, Mr. Wise-ass. But really, were you looking for me? What's going on?"

Raney's face looked bemused as he digested yet another bit of odd information about Ciampi, and then became grave. "I thought you'd want to know. They found another dumpster kid last night, over in Queens. An old lady was pawing through it looking for aluminum."

175

Marlene went rigid. "The same guy?"

Raney shrugged. "A possible. Puncture wounds like Segura and a finger off."

"Possible! Raney, it's him! Have you identified the child yet?"

"Not yet. Uh, actually, I just heard about this unofficially, Marlene. It's not our case."

"What are you talking about? Of course it's our case. It's the guy, the Bogeyman!"

"Maybe, but the case is in Queens Homicide and Queens D.A. I talked to the guy there, Lt. Shaw. He's glad to get any info we got, but he's going to run the case out of Queens. I bet Shaughnessy is gonna say the same . . ."

"Fuck them! It's our case. They can't *do* that!"

"Yes, they can, because it turns out that this is not the first time they found one of these in Queens. They had one in April and one at the beginning of March."

"What! Why didn't we know about it? How come they haven't put a task force or something together? Jesus, Raney . . ."

"Yeah, I know. But they laid them on child abuse, just like we did. Anyway, it's a Queens squeal now. We're out."

Marlene's shoulders slumped and she sighed, her excitement gone. New York City has one government and one police department, but because each of its five boroughs is a separate county, it has five District Attorneys, and each is the prince of an independent criminal justice domain. With the exception of Richmond, on bucolic Staten Island, all of them were stressed to the limit, and the possibility that the New York District Attorney would pressure his colleague of Queens for more work, especially work on a serial killer case that would have the media clawing at his flesh for months, was remote on a galactic scale.

Karp, maybe, could kick the old fart into it, she thought glumly; he knew how to pull the levers that could make Bloom act like a real D.A. on occasion. But *she* couldn't. And Karp was not here. And if he had been here, she realized, she might not have asked him, because worse than the feeling of losing a case she felt belonged to her was the prospect of going to Karp and asking him for a favor, like a little girl asking for a doll.

A thought stirred in the back of her mind. She focused on what Raney was saying. ". . . and so anyway, I pulled together all our notes from the case and got them typed up. I was gonna take them over this afternoon. But then Pete reminded me that he gave you the list of the people with the dolls. It's a dead end, maybe, but they ought to have it."

Marlene gave a yelp and, clutching her ragged mass of paper, fled back down the hall into her office. When Raney followed her in, he found her rummaging through files and drawers and cursing herself for an idiot and a fool.

Raney said soothingly, "Hey, Marlene, calm down, it's no big deal. I don't need it today. It probably don't mean shit, anyhow."

She stopped and stared at him. "I know where he lives. I just figured it out. It has to be." She shuffled through the stacks of paper on her desk and with a cry brought forth her folder on the Segura case. In a moment she had Balducci's list of doll owners in her hand. "I was right. She's here. Irma Dean. I knew that place was too good to be true."

"Slow down, Marlene," said Raney. "You know where who lives? Who's Irma Dean?"

She showed him the list. "Irma Dean was one of the people listed as having an expensive doll collection. She runs a fancy day-care center, which I happened to visit last week because one of our secretaries has a kid in it and—are you ready for this?—she thinks the kid is being sexually abused."

"So?"

"So! What do you mean, 'so'? You don't think it's significant that one of the people who could have owned the Segura doll, also could be involved with sexual abuse of children? Maybe one of their games went wrong? Maybe one of them isn't content to just diddle them anymore, he wants a bigger thrill."

"Wait a second, Marlene. I don't like all those could'ves. It could also be coincidence."

"Yeah, it could. Did I say I was going to try this shit this afternoon? But it could also be a beginning. Aren't you curious to see if maybe Mrs. Dean knows a big blond guy in a black suit?"

"I guess it's worth a check-out. I'll put it in the file for Shaw in Queens."

"Fuck Queens, Raney! We're going up there right now and heat things up."

"Hold it a sec, boss. It ain't our case. They could fry my ass on this."

"Bullshit, man! When did you get to be such an old lady? Besides, if anybody asks, I have a legitimate complaint to investigate. Sexual abuse of a minor is still a felony rap. Let me get somebody to take my afternoon calendar and we can go."

Raney shrugged and grinned his crazy grin. "Blow in my ear and I'll follow you anywhere," he said, but under his breath.

"I remember this place from the doll hunt," said Raney as he pulled into a no-parking zone in front of St. Michael's childcare center.

"You remember the boss lady?"

"Yeah. Not a lot of laughs. Like a nun from school, a ruler artist."

Marlene laughed. "God, Raney, that's exactly what I thought! She was ready to give me three across the hand for talking in line."

They smiled at each other. It was a Moment, and Marlene couldn't help thinking briefly that it wasn't one she could have shared with Karp.

Mrs. Dean, according to her secretary, was down in the basement, where some duct work was being done. They waited in the panelled office for her. When she entered, wearing a suit in pale green silk, her dark hair in an elegant chignon, and looking as unduct-work as could be, she did not make any pretense of being happy to see them.

"Miss Ciampi," she said in recognition, seating herself behind the writing desk. "And this is . . . ?"

"Detective James Raney, of the New York City police," said Marlene. She looked at Mrs. Dean again and was startled. The woman had undergone some sort of change. Her brows seemed even heavier, and they curved upward menacingly, like those of Snow White's stepmother. Her eyes were more glittering and animated and there was more color in her cheeks. It could have been a change of lipstick, but her mouth, which had been an almost prim, pink line was now full, dark, carnivorous. She exuded energy like heat from a stove, and part of it was erotic. Raney felt it, and Marlene could feel him feel it.

Mrs. Dean did not look like Sister Marie Augustine any more, or like a nun at all, except perhaps one of the very naughty ones in Boccaccio. Her manner had changed, too. She was abrupt, as if her new energy could not be contained, but was about to spill over into violence.

"What do you want, Miss Ciampi? I'm extremely busy today."

"This won't take long. A couple of things. First, are you familiar with a large man, over six-three and over two hundred fifty pounds, between twenty and twenty-five years old, round face, very short blond hair?"

"No, I'm not. What is going on, Miss Ciampi? Why did you come here under what now seems false pretenses and why are you here now with the police?"

Mrs. Dean seemed genuinely affronted. A quiver of doubt roiled Marlene's mind, but she locked eyes staunchly with the older woman and plunged into it. "We're here because we're investigating the murders of two young girls, perhaps more than two, that have been associated with the man I just described. The man and one of the girls was associated with a fancy doll, the kind of doll you have in your collection. We believe it to be, in fact, one of your dolls."

"I have already told you there is nothing missing from my collection."

"Yes, but there's something else, too. The girls were sexually mutilated and assaulted. We have received allegations of sexual assault against one of your children."

Mrs. Dean stood up. "Both of you leave, this minute!" she ordered.

Raney stood up, too. He applied a charming smile to his mouth and said, "Hold on, Mrs. Dean, nobody's accusing you of anything."

Mrs. Dean picked up her phone. As she dialed she said, "I don't know why you have chosen to harass me or this center, but I assure you I am not without friends. If you feel you have cause for a formal complaint, I will be ready with my lawyers. But let me tell you this. If one word of this filthy slander is published before then I will sue you personally and the city and the state for more money than you have ever-seen. Now get out!"

Outside on the pavement Marlene felt the first twinges of what was sure to be a monumental depression. She had screwed things up badly and pulled Raney into the trouble with her. Against his better judgment, she recalled, to her shame. For his part, Raney seemed blithe about the fiasco.

"Well, didn't we get our asses kicked?" he said. "Old Mrs. Dean is a bitch on wheels."

"I wish I had a warrant to stuff down her throat," replied Marlene bitterly.

"Yeah, well, not much chance of that, unless we make some connection with the big guy and her. I mean what are we looking for? A doll-shaped empty space? Whips? Dirty films?"

"I know, I know, don't remind me! We may be back to zero, but I know that woman is bent. I can feel it!"

Raney laughed, "Yeah, and she sure looked like she just had a bowl of Wheaties, didn't she? Or a piece of ass, one."

"Right, like a different person. But there's something else that's funny, too. You run a day-care center, a D.A. and a cop come in, say there's some kind of hanky-panky going on, I figure you might get all concerned, try to find out who squealed, maybe even ask for help in catching the bad guys, huh? But no, she says zip and kicks us out. Which she has every right to do, but still . . ."

"It stinks," said Raney. "Look, I'll come up here, hang around, see what I can find out. Maybe the big guy's the super, or a repairman. If he was ever around here, somebody'd have to have seen him."

"Oh, great! Would you do that? That'd be terrific." Marlene's smile was like an arc lamp, and Raney basked in its glow. He reached out and squeezed her upper arm. He felt a tingle like electricity run through him. Then her smile faded.

"Shit, you can't do that," she said with a sigh. "You're off the case. You'll get in trouble."

Raney snorted a laugh. "Hey, what am I, an old lady? But if I was you, I'd worry about my own self. Did you catch what number our friend in there was dialing?"

"No, did you?"

"Yeah, I watched her fingers: 638-4300."

Marlene groaned and spat out a string of curses. It was the number of Sanford Bloom, the District Attorney.

# CHAPTER
# 9

Driving over the Queensboro Bridge, blinking in the flickering bars of light the bright afternoon made as it shone through the structure, Felix felt he was in pretty good shape as far as Anna was concerned. It had gone pretty good, he thought, all things considered. He had seen it in her eyes. She was a little scared, but also fascinated. He knew the fascination would win out; it always did, and besides he knew that, secretly, they all liked to be batted around a little. It made them feel secure.

It would have worked out OK that night, too, he thought, if that bitch hadn't butted in. He made himself stop thinking about that, the shame of being led off by the police, and the other feelings.

He thought about his car instead. A Ford Falcon, nothing special, not like he was going to have, like a red Corvette, but better than riding the fucking subway with the scum of the earth. The company made him turn the keys in when he was finished with his shift, but of course he had made dupes and they kept the cars in an open lot, so it was pretty easy to borrow a car. The only thing, it was a pain in the ass to roll the speedo back.

With such thoughts in mind, Felix arrived at the apartment house in Jackson Heights. He walked whistling up the stairs to apartment 302 and put his key in the lock. It would not turn. Kneeling down, he saw that a new lock had been installed. He cursed and shook the door, then pounded and kicked on it until his toes and knuckles ached and it was clear that the apartment was empty.

By that time several of the doors along the hallway had been opened, on their chains, and anxious or angry faces had appeared in the gaps. There were mutterings and threats to call the cops.

Felix fled down the stairway in a black haze of rage. The cunt had escaped. He must not have tied her up right after the last time. That was impossible, though. He never made mistakes. It was just that he was so screwed up with all the pressure, not having a place of his own, and that bullshit that went down at the *dojo*, and of course, what had happened at Anna's. He went to his car and sat in it with the windows rolled down. He gripped the steering wheel and shook it until his arms trembled from the strain.

After a few minutes his breathing was under control again. He opened his attaché case, took out a neatly folded white handkerchief and wiped the sweat from his face. From a plastic bottle he removed two yellow Valiums and gulped them down. Then he reached for his diary. He read through the recent notations and made neat checks next to the ones he had accomplished.

What he had wanted to do in the apartment here could, of course, not be done, and so he used his fountain pen to obliterate it in a precise black rectangle. It didn't exist any more and he forgot it. The next appointment, scheduled for that evening, was quite clear, however. He started the car and drove back to Manhattan to keep it.

"So what do we do now?" Marlene asked, slumping against the low fender of Raney's Ghia. "I'm clear for the afternoon. I guess we could sit here on the sidewalk and drink Mad-Dog until we black out."

Raney grinned and said, "I'll have to take a rain check on that. I got stuff to do, but I could drop you somewhere."

"Doing some detecting?"

"As a matter of fact, I was going to go to the Academy range and shoot. I tell you what—come along with me to the range and after I'll buy you a couple of snorts and a steak." He saw the expression that crossed her face and added, "What's the matter, don't like steak?"

"Guns."

"Oh. Bleeding heart liberal, huh?"

"Yeah. No, not really. It's *liking* them—the gun-nut mentality. It freaks me out."

"I'm a gun nut?"

"Well, you know—cops. And 'Pistol Jim' . . ."

Raney's face darkened. "Oh, that. Well, shit, Marlene, I was just trying to be nice, you had a bad day and all. I didn't want to, like, *disgust* you or nothing." He yanked open the door on the driver's side. "You want a lift, or what?"

Marlene slid into the car and Raney tore away from the curb. After a couple of blocks, she said, "Raney, I didn't mean to piss you off. I'm sorry."

He glanced at her sideways, to see whether her remark was mere convention, or whether there was something else; finding in her face some genuine concern for his feelings, he went on.

"Yeah, OK. It's just . . . you say gun-nuts freak you out? What freaks me out is that Pistol Jim bullshit, like I'm supposed to be happy about it, I killed four guys. It's almost a year now, I still got dreams, you know? Like maybe I'd a played it different, it could've gone down another way. I still get fan mail too. Some people, I'm a murderer. People think real life is a fuckin' movie: I could've shot the guns out of their hands, I could've wounded them, for chrissake."

"And . . . ?"

"And? You want the truth? The bottom line? It happened so fuckin' fast, I got no fuckin' *idea* whether it could've gone different."

"What happened?"

"What, you want to hear this shit? OK, it's around eleven at night. I'm walking back to my place. I just been to this convenience store for some milk and smokes, and I'm walking past the Schmitkin Bakery on Northern Boulevard. You know it? Yeah, a big place.

"I see there's a car in the lot there, with the two front doors and one rear open and the lights on and the motor going. OK. I don't think much about it, maybe some guys on the night shift stopping to pick up their check. Then I hear this pop, pop noise.

"They asked me, at the after-firing review if I knew they were shots. Fuck no, I didn't! I'm telling *you* this, understand; them I said, 'Yes sir, definitely shots.' But I didn't. I would've walked right by, if it wasn't for the car, you know? I put that together with the noise, and I figure, it's worth a look.

"So I walk in the office there. It's empty, but right away I smell gunpowder. So I take out my pistol and I walk into the back office and there they are. Three guys in leather jackets and stocking masks. The night bookkeeper, the night manager, and this other poor bastard they just shot, to show they were serious dudes and the manager should crack the safe and give them the payroll."

Raney paused. They were stopped at a light, and Raney was studying the red disk as if it were a cue card. Marlene said, "And then?"

"Then I killed them. One, two, three. Another guy came running from the back carrying a goddamn portable TV. I yelled 'Police, freeze,' but he drops the set and reaches for his belt. I shot him too. In the face.

"I said at the review I ordered them, the three guys, to drop their guns, but I didn't. One guy had a sawed-off twelve gauge and I saw it coming up, so I shot him in the head. He started to go down and the other two brought up their guns too. Big automatics. I just tracked across and gave them each one through the nose. That was it. It took less time than I just took to say it. One of them got a couple of shots off, probably after he was dead. Good thing, too, cause that was one of the two things that saved my ass, afterwards."

"What was the other?"

"They were all four of them white. Harps in fact, from the neighborhood, local hard boys. Honest to Jesus that was the first thing through my mind after they hit the floor. Mother of God, make these mutts not brothers or PR's!"

"Are you serious?"

"Baby, those guys'd been black, I'd be holding down a security guard job right now."

"That's bullshit, Raney."

"Yeah? I'm glad I didn't have to find out. Come to think of it, I probably would of had other opportunities if they'd of canned me. I got other kinds of fan mail too. Nice people, congratulating me for killing scum, wanting to meet me, you know? Job offers. And women. Funny how some chicks get turned on by that shit. Incredible offers I got."

"If you took up any, I don't want to hear about it."

"I could've guessed. That's also the movies, you know. That Dirty Harry crap—he's eating a hot dog and kills a guy and finishes the hot dog. Afterward, when the blue-and-whites and the cameras got there, the big hero here was out in the parking lot puking his guts and crying like a baby. Petey was there too. He had to hold my head out of it. Little do they know."

"Little indeed," said Marlene. She lit a cigarette and Raney did too. They were silent for a few minutes as Raney cruised down Seventy-ninth Street and turned south on Central Park West. "What I think is," she said, "is that that was a good story, and you're a good guy."

Raney flashed his old grin at her. "No kidding? You mean there's hope for me yet?"

"That depends on what you're hoping for," said Marlene lightly.

"Maybe I'm hoping that if I came on to you, you wouldn't laugh in my face."

"Get out of here, Raney!" Marlene said, coughing on her smoke. "Give me a break! I'm practically a married woman."

"True, and what could be better than one last fling?"

"Change the subject, Raney," said Marlene, with a curtness she did not really feel. She glanced out the window. "Hey, where are we?"

"The Police Academy. The thing of it is, Marlene, I got a slot reserved on the range and I got to qualify this month. I haven't qualified indoor since the bakery, so you can come in and watch, or split, or wait. It's up to you." He went around to the front of the Ghia, unlocked the trunk and took out an aluminum case. He looked at Marlene expectantly.

"If I come in, will you promise no gun bore talk? No hollow-point muzzle velocity crap?" she asked.

"You got it, counselor," said Raney, his eyes throwing blue sparks.

The ranges were in the basement of the Academy building. Through a thick glass window Marlene could see that all the lanes were full of men firing pistols at man-shaped silhouettes. Raney shook hands with a fat uniformed sergeant with a large red nose and long, unfashionable sideburns.

"Marlene," said Raney, "I want you to meet Sergeant Frank McLaughlin, runs things around here. Frank, this here's Marlene Ciampi. She's the head coach at Sacred Heart. I brought her along 'cause they're thinking of starting a pistol team for the girls."

"No kidding?" said McLaughlin. "Sacred Heart, huh?"

"Yes," said Marlene. "We think it would be very beneficial, with the City like it is nowadays. We think it might be a good idea if all the girls started carrying too. Like Sister Marie Augustine says, 'Trust in God, but pack a rod.' "

"Is she serious?" asked McLaughlin with an uncertain smile.

189

"Could be," said Raney. "Strange times we got now." He winked at Marlene, and led her by the arm into the range proper. The noise was a continuous harsh crackling, an immense popping of corn. Like most people in the City, Marlene had never heard a pistol fired at close range before and she was surprised at how different—punier and less dramatic—the sound was than its simulacrum in the movies. The air was unnaturally cool and stank of burnt powder.

She adjusted her ear protectors and watched Raney as he set up to shoot. He opened his aluminum case at the shooter's table, revealing a foam bed neatly cut out to hold three pistols and their associated ammunition and equipment. Raney removed a large blue revolver and began loading it with fat, shiny cartridges.

As he did, Marlene noticed some of the uniformed officers waiting to fire nudge one another and look at him. Olivier drops in at the summer stock theater, she thought. He's famous in the pistol world.

McLaughlin shouted at Raney over the din, "You still using that old piece of shit?"

"It's a good gun," said Raney flatly.

"Yeah, thirty years ago it was. Whyn't you get a Cobra? Or something with a little stopping power there."

Raney didn't answer. He bellied up to the lane barrier, clipped a silhouette target to the traveller and sent it twenty-five yards down the lane. Assuming a rigid two-handed stance, he fired six spaced shots. Then he brought the target back and scored his hits. Marlene came forward to look.

"Did you get him?" she asked.

"You could say that," said McLaughlin. He put

out a hand and covered all six of the holes that Raney had put in the chest of the target."Six in the five. Nice pattern, Jim. OK, do your rapid."

Raney qualified easily on rapid fire and at longer ranges. McLaughlin signed the qual sheet and went off to observe the other shooters. Raney popped the cylinder of his revolver open and dropped the spent shells into his hand.

Marlene said, "Nice gun, but no stopping power."

"You heard that?" Raney said, smiling. "Yeah, this is the classic police .38 revolver. Smith and Wesson Model 10. They started making them back in the twenties and must have sold a zillion of them. Now out of fashion among the young gunslingers on the job. They all want fucking cannons, like Clint. This particular one belonged to my dad, and I humped it when I was in the blue bag. Pretty touching, huh?"

"I'm dabbing my eyes—it's like the Waltons."

"Just. Thirty-four years on the hip and never fired a shot in anger. Typical."

He put the revolver away in its hollow and brought a Browning Hi-Power nine millimeter automatic out of his shoulder holster. He set up another target and shot it into rags.

"Very impressive," said Marlene. "Is that it?"

"That's it. Unless you want to try."

"What, shoot?"

"Yeah."

"Am I allowed?"

"No, but go ahead. I'll say you overpowered me and tore the gun from my hand." He reloaded the Browning and held it out to her, butt first.

She took it from him and her hand sagged with the weight of it. "It's heavy," she said, as a peculiar and unwelcome thrill began to rise through her middle. I can kill people now, she thought inanely, and then suppressed the thought, as one suppresses the unbidden thoughts of horrible death that afflict one on the subway platform or on a high roof.

Raney clipped a fresh target to the traveller and sent it out to the twenty-five yard mark. Then he came back and stood close to Marlene.

"OK, tiger," he said, "let me show you how this works. Push the little button there and hold your left hand under the butt. That's the magazine. It holds fourteen shots. Nine millimeter Parabellum rounds, hollowpoints, so I got the feed ramp throated out so it won't hang up and jam. It's got a four and a half pound pull—"

"Snore," said Marlene. "You promised. Where does the bullet come out? This little hole here?"

"Yeah, OK, I'll skip the gun-nut talk. But the fact is it's a lot easier to hit something with an automatic than with a revolver. OK, slam the magazine back in hard so it clicks. Now hold it in your left hand and pull the slide all the way back until it locks."

Marlene did so and the gun's snout emerged from the cover of the slide. "It looks like an excited Doberman," said Marlene, with a nervous giggle. *What is this* thing *doing in* my *hand*? she thought. Her breath was coming shorter and she was suddenly conscious of her heart.

Raney was standing behind her now, with his arms around hers guiding her hands over the pistol. He was warm and smelled of gunpowder. Marlene's uncomfortable feelings intensified. Her stomach rolled and the backs of her hands prickled with sweat. She saw her hands under Raney's push the slide forward. He said into her ear, "Pushing the slide home strips the top round off the magazine and chambers it. This is a single action gun, so you're already cocked and ready to fire. It'll fire the same way every time you squeeze the trigger." He continued to talk softly about the stance and the trigger pull and other gun stuff. It was like a seduction, and she didn't want to hear it.

Abruptly, Marlene stepped away from Raney, faced down range, looked down the barrel with her good eye, pointed it at the target and emptied the pistol as fast as she could pull the trigger. She dropped the weapon on the shooter's table with a clunk and turned away, feeling giddy and slightly sick, like a kid after the first fumbling experiment with sex.

Raney touched her arm. "Hey, are you all right?"

She swallowed hard and said, "Sure. Fine . . . but, I don't know, it had an effect on me I didn't expect."

"Death in my hand," Raney said quietly.

"What?"

"The feeling. That you could really kill a bunch of real live human beings right now, no more trouble than ringing up an elevator. Plus yourself. Some people have it, some don't. I never had it." He reloaded the automatic, put it back in his holster and shut his aluminum case. Then he brought Marlene's target back to the rail. Marlene sagged against the wall. "Raney, I could use a drink. Let's get out of here."

"Sure, right away, Marlene," said Raney, examining the target. He whistled softly through his teeth. "Hey, don't you want to see how you did?"

She walked over to him. "I missed every shot, right?"

193

"No. You hit fourteen times and all on the money." Marlene saw that the head and trunk of the silhouette were riddled with holes. She felt sick again. "How could that be," she asked weakly, "I wasn't even aiming."

"That's why. You didn't worry or get nervous about your score. Just pointed and shot. It's the latest training theory anyway. You ever shoot before? A pistol, I mean."

"No, and never again'll be too soon."

"Too bad—it's a major talent down the tubes. I think you're what us gun nuts call a natural shot."

Marlene laughed heartily and started singing "You Cain't Get a Man with a Gun," at high volume, attracting many odd looks until Raney hustled her unceremoniously out of the range.

He took her to an Irish place on Second Avenue in the Seventies, a place with dark wood but no ferns, where the bartenders were middle-aged and had slicked-down hair and the customers were mostly serious men who drank neat whiskeys with beer on the side.

They each tossed down a Jameson's and ordered another. Raney lit a cigarette and lit Marlene's. She relaxed and smiled at him, reflecting on how long it had been since she had come to a decent saloon. That tune came into her head again:

Broken hearted I'll wander
Broken hearted I'll remain
For my bonny light horseman
Will n'er come again.

Karp did not take her to saloons, she reflected, not without a momentary twinge of shame for this disloyal thought. Karp's idea of a good time was a pizza and a movie, or a long walk across the lower East Side to Yoineh Schimmel's for a knish. Marlene had nothing against the knish, but she liked bar-hopping and she didn't like Karp's unspoken disapproval when she drank and smoked. She glanced at Raney, who was deep in his second drink. He must have lots of bad points, too, and they were probably nasty and macho ones.

"Raney," she said abruptly, "that gun I shot . . . was that the one that you used in the bakery?"

"The murder weapon? No, I didn't bring that to the range. I usually wear the Browning if I got a jacket on, like now, but if I'm in a T-shirt, or I'm just running out for a couple of minutes I got this little Astra Constable automatic I throw in a pocket. It's a .38 double-action, so you can keep a round in the chamber and the safety off. I had it in my raincoat that night. It's not what McLaughlin would call a man-stopper, unless you shoot the man in the head. Then it stops them pretty good." He threw back the rest of his drink and studied the baseball game playing on the TV above the bar.

Marlene tried to imagine what it would be like never to go out in the street without the ability to deliver instant death to other people. Although she had worked with cops for years, and had been on good terms with quite a few, the issue had never come up. She wondered why it was coming up now.

They watched the Yankees play for a couple of innings in companionable silence and then went into the restaurant part of the saloon. They had steaks and salads and finished up with coffee and Hennessey. It was not a cheap dinner. When it was over, Marlene started to take out money, but Raney insisted on paying.

Marlene shrugged and put her wallet away. "You throw money around like that, Raney, people are gonna think you're on the wire."

"Hey, I don't do this all the time. You can't take a Sacred Heart girl to Nedicks."

She looked at him sharply. "That's like the fourth time you've dragged that out, son. Are we playing out some boyhood fantasy here? Do we see some wistful Irish lad of humble means on some Queens street corner gazing raptly at the unobtainably classy girls trooping toward the IND line and the Mesdames? Learning how to become yet more unobtainable? OK, Raney, you got my attention. What is it now, a dance at the Legion on Queens Boulevard? Are you blushing, Raney?"

Raney laughed and said, "Nah, let's skip the dance. How about we go out to Kennedy and park somewhere along Race Track Road and watch the jets come in. We could get into the vibrations when the big ones come over at thirty feet."

"You don't have a back seat, Raney."

"I got a blanket in the trunk," he shot back, and then added archly, "And what does a nice Italian girl like you know about back seats out by Kennedy?"

"Raney, don't kid yourself. I spent so much time out at the runways, I had reviews in the in-flight magazines. It's true. The pilots used to point me out: 'Folks, passengers on the left side of the aircraft will be able to see Marlene Ciampi getting her rocks off while remaining technically a virgin in that green '57 Mercury.'"

Raney cracked up at that, and Marlene laughed with him, but she was thinking, *I'm flirting my ass off with this guy, and why am I doing it? And he's not just being jolly company either. He's been giving me lingering looks all through dinner. And I'm leading him on. Because I want to see if the Champ can still reel them in, with the one eye and all? Because now that I can get serious about marrying Karp, I want to screw it up by having a flinger with this cop?*

*This cop, who by the way has terrific blue-green eyes and is trying as hard as he can not to be overbearing and is treating me like spun sugar, and who would be just the person to do something completely crazy and irresponsible with without having to practically twist his arm, and drinks and smokes and is a Catholic and.* She shut that down and stood up, her face flushed.

"Time to go, Raney. Can I get a lift?"

He rose as well and clasped her arm. It was the first time he had touched her since the firing range and she felt herself stiffen. He said, "No problem. Your place or mine?"

Her response to this sally was to keep her face hard and turn away, and she kept the chill on for the drive downtown. As they pulled up in front of her loft on Crosby Street, Raney asked, "Hey, what did I do? I thought we were having a good time."

"Yeah, we were," she said, her face softening a little. "But do me a favor, Raney. Don't hit on me, all right? I'm going through all kinds of shit right now and I can't handle it. Just compadres and fellow gun nuts, OK?"

Raney nodded and said, "Sure, Marlene. Whatever," as blithely as he could manage, which was not all that blithe, because for his forty-two fifty-five plus tip he had been expecting a little clinch at least, and maybe even a shot at the Main Event. He glanced down at his watch. It was still early enough to zip by and see if a waitress he knew in Maspeth was interested in fooling around. She was Italian too.

The Ghia roared away, the sound of its engine echoing in the empty narrow streets. Marlene climbed the four flights to her loft. Outside the door, as she groped for her keys, she heard the sound of her TV going. She felt that odd mixture of irritation and anticipation that had become familiar since the day, not many months before, when she had at last offered Karp a key to her place.

He was stretched out on her green velvet sofa, in chinos and sweatshirt, watching two men in blazers talk about baseball. His enormous sneakers were lying on the floor next to him like beached whaleboats. A hanging Tiffany lamp, one of her few real treasures, cast a warm light over the loft's living and dining regions; beyond, the remainder of the huge single room, an area the size of a couple of basketball courts, lay swathed in darkness.

"The Yanks took it six to four. Munson hit two homers," said Karp.

Marlene said, "Hello Marlene darling, it seems like years, I've missed you so much."

Karp looked up and said, deadpan, "Hello Marlene darling, it seems like years, I've missed you so much."

"Not as much as you'd miss Thurman Munson," she said sourly. "How long have you been lurking here?"

"I wasn't lurking. I came here after I got finished pumping Noodles. They said you were out with the cops, but I figured you'd be back soon, so I picked up a pizza and some Cokes. I guess you ate already, huh?"

"Yeah, I did," Marlene said, and then added quickly, to change the subject, "How did it go with Noodles?"

"Great," said Karp, giving her an odd look. "We got the whole story of the Ferro hit, for starters. Joey Bottles was the trigger, like we thought, but Piaccere gave the go-ahead, and Sallie Bollano, the capo's kid, was in on it too. Also Charlie Tonnatti. So we could possibly get the bunch on criminal conspiracy, if we can get corroboration on the killing."

"A big if, no?"

"Yeah. The cops are beating the bushes. Meanwhile he gave us a half dozen bodies stashed under cement in parking garages the Bollanos own. We're going to go after them starting tomorrow. If we score, it's more pressure we can put on them. Plus other stuff."

"Like what?"

"Like how come I'm sitting here talking to you and you're standing over there by the door like you think you came in the wrong place? Is something wrong? I got spinach on my teeth?"

She walked over and sat down on the couch about a yard away from him, but he reached out a long arm and pulled her closer. He kissed her hair, then sniffed loudly several times. "What's that funny smell?" he asked. "Like a chemical or something burning."

She sat up and sniffed at a strand of her hair. "It must be gunpowder. I was at the police range this afternoon. Raney was showing me how to shoot."

"Out with Pistol Jim, hey? You hit anything?"

"Everything, as a matter of fact. I'm a natural shot, according to Raney, another of my little girl's ambitions fulfilled. God, now that you mention it, I really stink. I'm going to take a bath."

With that she rose and went behind a painted

Japanese screen, where rested the five-hundred gallon black rubber former electroplating tank, a souvenir of the loft's previous occupants, that Marlene had refitted for domestic use. Karp turned off the TV. The loft was silent but for the delicious slithery sounds of a woman undressing. When he heard the soft splash of Marlene's descent into the deep tank, Karp went around the screen, pulled up a wooden kitchen stool, and sat down next to the tank.

The only light was a faint glow from the street through the distant windows and the jewel-like reflection of the Tiffany shade on the white tin ceiling above the bath. Of Marlene, only a white neck was visible as it rose above the black lip of the tank. Her head was lost against the black water.

"You want me to do your hair?" asked Karp.

"Oh, would you? I'd love it." She ducked her head and came up dripping rubies and amethysts. Karp squirted a glob of herbal shampoo on her head and rubbed it into her thick hair. She sighed and leaned back against the side of the tank.

"You're nice to me and I was so mean to you," she said after a few moments. "You come back from a trip and you're going to put like the entire Mob in jail and I don't even give you a kiss."

"You can correct that. It's never too late."

"Oh, I will, when the time is right." She leaned back and gave herself over to the curiously intimate business of having her hair cleaned. Karp had strong, sensitive hands, she reflected—odd when you thought about it, because in so many ways Karp was not sensitive, to art, for example, or food or music or literature. Even Raney liked

Chopin, or pretended to. She would have to ask him about that.

"Rinse," said Karp into her ear. "I'll soap you up again."

She took a deep breath and slid down into the water, wagging her head from side to side to clear the suds from her hair. Her limbs floated loosely in the warm water and they were starting to tingle with sex.

Nature's own heroin, she thought, and Karp was her pusher. Whatever differences they had, in some unexplainable fashion he held the key to her body and its pleasures. She sat up abruptly and tried to shake these feelings off. That was the problem—there was stuff they had to talk about, but rarely did because when things got spiky it was too easy to slip into flesh. Or storm out, with a loving reconciliation to follow.

So, to Karp's disappointment, when the shampoo was over, instead of rising like Aphrodite from the waves and leaping into his arms, she dried herself off properly, put on a red silk robe, lit a cigarette and sat down in a bentwood rocker in the living area. Karp clumped down again on the couch.

"Now," she said briskly, "tell all. How was California?"

"Like always. Hot and crazy."

"And Susan?"

"Looks good. Didn't give me any trouble about the papers, the divorce. We were getting along good, very civilized, until I asked her if me and Noodles could hole up on her farm for a while, just 'til Guma could figure some way to extract us with security. Then she blew her top. Ran us off as a matter of fact. That's how I came to drive home."

"What about Guma's arrangements?"

"Oh, yeah. It turned out that the day after I spoke to him he won a pile on a ball game. Took a week's leave and went to Saratoga with a bimbo to play the ponies. I slipped his mind. You know what he said when I laid into him about it this afternoon? 'I had faith in you, Butch.' Then he wanted to hear spicy lesbian commune stories."

"Have you got any?"

"If you consider being glared at by a bunch of average-looking women spicy."

"Yeah, it's funny the way some men are fascinated by lesbian sex," said Marlene thoughtfully. "You see it a lot in pornography. I've always wondered why. You would think it would repel the male libertine."

"Well it doesn't fascinate me; in fact, it gives me the creeps."

"Does it? I don't know. I went to girls' schools for eight years, and there's always a low buzz from that corner in girls' schools. Of course, at Smith in the sixties the buzz got to be more of a rattle. Long kisses in the common rooms, gasps through the walls at night and everyone being terribly sophisticated. Kind of attractive in a way, I always thought."

Karp felt a deadly chill starting in his middle. "Uh, Marlene, did you ever . . . you know, ever . . ."

Something in his tone made her look directly at him. "Me? Oh, I see. You're worrying whether you picked another joker. No, I never did, not that there weren't offers. I guess I got real close a couple of times because I had a sneaking admiration for women who were totally free of something I felt was going to drag me down. Marriage. Kids. My mom's life. As Ti-Grace used to say, 'Lesbians are the shock troops of women's lib.' So I guess I honor them for that. And for guts.

"On the other hand, you are or you aren't. I'm not. And now?—I'm not as freaked out by domesticity as I was when I was twenty. My mom sure has gotten a lot smarter in the last ten years or so.

"And I like men. I like them *because* of the difference, as irritating as that is sometimes. Not the cheap joke difference either, but the mysterious part, something to do with understanding the way the world's put together, what being human is all about. Shit, I'm drifting into metaphysics. Typical, when I just made one of the worst boners of my undistinguished career—another proof I'm in the wrong business, I guess."

"What boner?" asked Karp.

"I'm too embarrassed to tell you now," said Marlene, which wasn't strictly true, but she did not want to get into the Mrs. Dean story just now, when the feelings she had partially suppressed in the bath were now releasing themselves unmistakably in her body.

"Besides," she continued, cocking her leg and letting her gown slip away from her middle, "I think the time is right."

After coming up for air from a kiss worth a week of waiting or more, she added, "It just occurred to me that I love you because we have nothing in common. It explains a lot."

"Oh, yeah?" replied Karp. "I thought we had a lot in common."

He had managed to pry one of Marlene's perfect little breasts from its nest of red silk and was contemplating it like a jewel thief would the Hope

Diamond. He was lying on his side and his free hand was cupping the thick mat of black hair between her thighs.

"No, not that office shit. I mean real difference. Family, ideas, what's important. It's like a guarantee against submerging myself, losing it . . ." She broke off the thought in a series of gasps. Marlene in this mood had a trigger pull a good deal lighter than that of a Browning Hi-Power automatic.

"Butch, take off your clothes! Quick, quick!" she cried, throwing off her gown. "Now, do it slow. I want to watch it. Oh, my! It's so . . ." Then a period of inarticulate gasps and cries. "Oh, Butchie, this is so . . . ah, why, why can't we talk and come at the same time?"

"Because God is kind," said Karp.

From his perch behind the roof parapet of the building opposite Marlene's the Bogeyman could not see what was going on in the loft. He had an expensive pair of $10 \times 20$ binoculars that his Mommy had given him, so he could watch people better, but the screen hid the green couch from his view. He had seen the bad witch get into her bath, though, and in front of the tall man too. That was bad, he knew. Ladies with no clothes was bad. Except in church.

He kept watching. He was comfortably situated; the night was warm and he had a container of milk and some chocolate chip cookies. And he had nothing else to do. Mommy had said follow the bad witch and say everything she did. After a while, the tall man and the bad witch came out from behind the screen and climbed up on a sleeping platform and went to bed. The bed was right under the windows that faced the street and there were no curtains or shades, so he had a good view. They both had no clothes on. The man was very big, almost as big as the Bogeyman himself. He wondered if he could beat him up. He wondered if they would do dirty in the bed, but they just went to sleep. He watched for a while, dreamily, and finished his milk and cookies.

A movement in his coat pocket aroused him. He reached in carefully and removed a black pigeon. He stroked it absently for a few minutes, then replaced it in his pocket and went down the fire escape to the street.

He crossed the street to the outer door of Marlene's building. Taking out the pigeon, he stroked it a few times to calm it down and then smashed its head against the door. In its fresh blood he drew an upside down cross on the door and let the corpse drop onto the doorstep. Then he went a block down the street and sat in a doorway to wait for the dawn.

# CHAPTER
# 10

"My mom's bleeding," said the little boy's voice on the phone. The 911 operator was a skilled listener to people in trouble and caught the note of barely controlled panic in the high voice. She quickly extracted the child's name and address and dispatched a patrol car to the address given, while encouraging the boy to remain on the line. Obviously something awful had happened in his home and she wanted to keep in contact should whoever did it return.

Patrolman Martin Dienst, working the four to twelve shift out of the Ninth Precinct, caught the 911 call and was at the door of 217 Avenue A within ten minutes. He left his partner in the blue-and-white and climbed the three flights to apartment 3F North. Dienst had eleven years on the job and a year in Danang with the Marines before that, but what he saw when he reached the top of the landing was rich even for his system.

A woman lay on her side in the hallway, with her feet in the open doorway of apartment 3FN. Her blond hair was matted and dark with blood, and the blue robe she wore was slashed and stained almost black with it. There were thick ropes of congealed blood on the floor, and Dienst stepped carefully to avoid these as he approached the body. It was certainly a body. The throat had been slashed so deeply as to almost entirely sever the head.

Swallowing hard, Dienst stepped over the woman's corpse and entered the living room of the apartment. The place was a shambles, in the literal sense, being as thickly sprayed with blood as the floor of a slaughterhouse. Furniture had been overturned and the remains of glassware crunched under the patrolman's shoes. A child's stuffed toy in the shape of a small white goat lay beside an overturned chair. It too was stained with blood, and seemed to Dienst to be the most pathetic object in the entire dreadful scene.

Nearby lay the crumpled shape of the goat's probable owner, a boy of about seven, blond like his mother, dressed in shorty pajamas with little clowns on them. He was lying on his back, his limbs spraddled like those of an abandoned doll. His chest had been split nearly in two by a tremendous blow from some great blade. Blood was splashed high up the wall near where he lay. Dienst hurried by this door to the next room, which was the kitchen-dinette.

There at the kitchen table sat a dark-haired boy of about nine holding a telephone receiver to his ear. Dienst quickly checked the apartment's two bedrooms and, finding them empty, returned to the kitchen, where he gently took the telephone from the boy and identified himself to the 911 operator. Then he hung up the phone and knelt to face the boy.

"What's your name, sonny?" he asked.

"Josh Mullen. Is my mom OK?"

"We'll have to see. We have to call an ambulance. But first we both have to get out of here. I'm going to carry you, OK?"

"I can walk."

"Sure, but the police rules say I have to carry you. And also you have to keep your eyes closed."

"Why?"

"Regulations," said Dienst, and, scooping the child up and holding his head tight against his broad chest, he ran out of the apartment.

"You can't possibly want more after last night," said Marlene Ciampi sleepily, as she felt the suggestive probing of Karp's big hands. The morning sun was just blasting through the grime of the two large windows that stood behind Marlene's little white bed. This was why she had no curtains: any prospective peeper in the building opposite would be dazzled by the glare on the glass, and besides, that particular building was used as a warehouse and its windows were covered with thick green paint.

"Just a quickie to wake up on," said Karp. He lay on his back and lifted her easily so that she dropped on top of him in the right position, with many a squishing noise.

"No, wait," said Marlene, not with much conviction. "I have to tell you what I did."

"Can't it wait for ten minutes?" groaned Karp.

"How do you make it last ten minutes, as the schoolgirl said to the nun. No, really, I need to tell you." And with that Marlene spun out the whole story of the second trash-bin victim, and the transfer of the case to Queens, and what had transpired with Mrs. Dean at St. Michael's.

To Karp's credit, he did not make soothing noises and continue in the direction his body had until lately been leading him. Instead he put his hands behind his head, knotted his brow and scrooched up his chin, as was his habit when thinking hard about unpleasant things.

"You think I fucked up?" said Marlene.

"Yeah, I do. I'm trying to figure out what came over you. What did you expect to gain by it? A spontaneous confession?"

Marlene rolled away from him onto her stomach and propped her chin up on her hands and elbows. "No, of course not," she replied with heat. "I guess I thought if we told her about the bogeyman, she might—I don't know—*do* something. I just couldn't sit there while they took the case away from me."

"Well, you're sure as shit not going to get it back now. Bloom'll skin you. And as much as I hate to say it, with justification."

"What the hell do you mean, 'justification!'"

"I mean that on the basis of no fucking evidence whatever you've seized on this woman as being some kind of sexual monster, who may be connected with a couple of nasty homicides. And you've been harassing her in a way that compromises you, the Office, and maybe even the case, if there ever is one."

Marlene's jaw dropped. "No . . . what? No evidence! You don't call the doll evidence?"

"It's crap, Marlene."

"Yeah? Raney thought it was pretty good," she said angrily.

"Who gives a shit what Raney thinks! Raney's not going to the Grand Jury with this garbage, *you* are. God damn, Marlene! What the fuck's wrong with you? Since when do D.A.'s get involved in this level of an investigation? If Raney wants to go over to St. Michael's and blow smoke, let him! Cops do shit like that all the time. But it's not your job."

"Yessir, boss," she snapped, turning away on the bed. He sat up quickly then and grabbed her by the shoulders, forcing her to look at him.

"Marlene, listen to me," he said, his face serious. "I love you. But this is really aberrant behavior and it worries me. I want to make some sense out of this, and I can't if you snarl at me. OK?" She nodded glumly. He was going to lecture her and it made her stomach churn with resentment.

"Now let's look at this like lawyers," he resumed. "One. You got an accusation that is not only hearsay, but attributed to a child of six. Have you interviewed the child? No. Have you determined by a medical examination that the child has been sexually abused? No. Have you obtained a formal complaint from the mother? No. Did you interview any of the other kids at the center or their parents? No. No hits, no runs, the side is retired. That's the sexual-abuse-of-a-minor part.

"On the murder part—forgetting for a minute that you knew it was a Queens D.A. case, and that you might have fucked up *their* investigation by dicking around like you did—we have, *again* the unsupported testimony of a child, plus a police report that some miscellaneous witnesses maybe saw a man of a certain description accompanying a child who might have been the deceased.

"Do we have that man? No. More to the point, do we have a shred of evidence that this maybe-man is connected with Mrs. Dean or her center? Sure we do. We have the statement of a three-year-old child that her deceased sister was given an expensive doll by the bogeyman, and a statement by a doll expert that a doll *like* that one *might* have been in Mrs. Dean's collection or in any of a dozen other collections in the city.

"Was it Mrs. Dean's doll? We don't know. Can we find out? No. Why? Because not only is this horseshit not a case, it's not even probable cause for a search warrant. And yet on the strength of it one of the smartest lawyers in the damn Bureau— that's you, dummy—goes off and plays Nancy fucking Drew. And I'd love to know why."

Marlene tightened her jaw and tried to stare Karp down. "I know she's mixed up in it."

To her surprise Karp nodded. "Right. I believe you. You're a great investigator, Marlene. It's the truth. You got brains and energy and you got the nose for a fishy pattern. So Mrs. Dean is selling chicken out of her day-care center. So what! That's not the point.

"Christ, Marlene! I could stand on top of the courthouse and hit fifty people with a rock who I know—*I know*—did stuff that would make Dean look like Mother Theresa. And I can't touch them. Why? Because I don't have a case against them that'll stand up in court. That's what we *do*, baby— remember? We develop and prosecute cases. We don't ride out and chase the bad guys."

Marlene dropped her gaze and let out a long, silent breath. As usual, Karp had brought forth a great summation. It was a technique Karp had learned from the tough old lawyers in the Homicide Bureau and he had every right to use it on her. She was guilty, no question: aggravated fuck-upery and dumbness in the first degree. She could handle that. She understood that getting beat up was part of being one of the guys.

But what made her shudder and bite her lip

was that Karp didn't understand, had never made the effort to understand, and probably never would understand her feelings. Who did he love anyway? The perfect investigator? The great fuck? Why didn't he say, "I understand what seeing children hurt does to you, and I understand why it clouded your judgment, and I'll find some way to fix it, and I'll support you, and together we'll catch those fiends and make them stop." That's what she wanted and at some level she despised herself for wanting it.

She stood up and said in as calm a voice as she could manage, "I'm going to take a bath." Karp watched her climb down from the sleeping platform and walk naked across the floor to the great tub. He felt a pang of tenderness, mixed with remorse. She looked so vulnerable from the back— you could count her ribs and the bumps in her graceful spine and she had angel wings like a ten-year-old. With her shoulders slumped and her dragging pace she seemed like a whipped child.

He knew himself to be the whipper, and was agile in his retreat from acknowledging his own mean streak, the faint sadistic tincture in his relations with Marlene. Instead he blamed her and affected puzzlement. He knew she was smart, brilliant even. But she would get on these nutty one-track toots and everything she knew would go out the window. And he would have to yank her back, and then she would get all depressed, like now. Why did she do this to him?

They washed and dressed in silence. Karp went to the door and said, "I got an early meeting and then I'm taking a calendar for one of the guys. You coming? We could get breakfast at Sam's."

"I'll be along later," she said. "I need to make some calls from here first."

"OK, see you later." He kissed her on the cheek and she patted his arm absently. He turned to go and then he stopped himself and said, "Hey, we should meet later this week and go up to the jewelry district."

"Jewelry district? What for?" she said, blank-faced.

"To get a ring. Earth calling Marlene. Your big rock? Engagement ring? You. Me."

"Oh, yeah. Sure, that'd be great. Fine," she said, smiling with a sad eye.

When he was gone, Marlene called Dana Woodley at home and told her not to take Carol Anne to St. Michael's. "But, Marlene," Dana wailed, "what'll I do with her? I don't know ary a soul in my buildin' and I cain't miss no more work. An' I cain't afford the reg'lar day care . . ."

"Bring her to work, Dana."

"Can I do that?"

"Sure. We'll find some little things for her to do. She'll be fine and besides, it's just temporary for the summer and then she'll start school full-time in the fall. Anybody gives you any heat, tell them to see me."

That's that, thought Marlene when she had hung up. That concludes my personal obligation in re: St. Michael's Child Development Center and Whorehouse. She meant it too. Marlene had substantial reserves of stony self-control, little used of late, but available at need. She would be good from now on. She would forget about ruined children. She would take her medicine like a man. She would do the job. She would get married. She would stay out of trouble.

When Marlene saw the dead pigeon on her door step, she barely noticed it. You see dead pigeons (and cats and dogs and rats) in that neighborhood all the time. If it was still there in the evening she would boot it into the roadway. As she locked the tan steel door to the loft building she saw the reversed cross scrawled on it in what looked like red primer paint. That didn't impress her either: another graffito. They had to paint over the door every couple of months. New York is as hard on witchcraft as it is on dry cleaning.

As Marlene walked south toward the subway at Broadway and Canal, the Bogeyman stirred out of his shallow doze and started toward the subway too. He had plenty of tokens in his little change purse, and he didn't have to follow her. He knew where she was going.

Getting chewed out is never pleasant, but getting chewed out by a nasty little empty suit like Sanford Bloom, the District Attorney, is very bad. When he is right it is the worst of all. Bloom didn't even do it himself. Everybody had to love Bloom, so of course he could never yell at anyone. But he watched with a sad smile while Conrad Wharton, his administrative chief, a Kewpie doll with the soul of a toad, did the deed. Marlene took it, for what else could she do? She promised she would never even say Irma Dean's name again. She promised that she would stay away from the trash-bag killer case, the *Queens* trash-bag killer case, for the rest of her natural life. She meant it, too, at the time.

After her chew-out Marlene went to the ladies on the ninth floor and had a good weep among the gurgling pipes. Then she fixed her face and made her nine-thirty court like a good soldier. As she labored, she reflected on how right Karp was. You couldn't stop crime. You couldn't even slow it down. You couldn't save the babies. What you could do was crank the system and put asses in jail. Maybe it did some good. Karp was right, but she found herself blaming him for the way things were, for her own barely contained misery, for the collapse of civilization.

She avoided Karp at lunch. She did not go back to her office, but picked up a yogurt from the snack bar on the first floor and hid out in an empty office. She took off her shoes, leaned back in a swivel chair and began reading a Barbara Cartland romance, one of her secret vices. After a few minutes the silence of the lunchtime office was broken by the sound of footsteps and a whistled tune, the andante from the Second Brandenburg.

"Marlene!" said V.T. Newbury. "What are you doing skulking back here? I see you're improving both mind and body." Newbury was a small, elegant, handsome man with dark blond hair worn long and combed back. He had the chiseled features that Gilbert Stuart had painted into portraits of eighteenth century gentlemen, many of which were, in fact, of his ancestors.

"I'm not skulking," Marlene said, stashing the novel in her bag. "Actually, I am. I'm a little blue today."

"Anything I can do?"

"No thanks, V.T. It's just a surfeit of life. New York disease."

"Yes, I see. Well, crawling into this hole and gnawing on yogurt won't help. You need a good

uptown lunch and half a bottle of decent wine.
I'm buying. Slip into your shoes and let's travel."

"Thanks, V.T., but I have court at one-thirty."

"Don't we all? Lucky for us we're lunching with
a judge. He'll give us a note."

The judge was Herbert C. Rice, a large jolly
man in his early sixties, with a round dark pink
face, fitted with glittering teeth. His hair was curiously baby-like, pale and silken, and he wore it
swept back in the old Senatorial style. He was a
friend of V.T.'s father.

The restaurant, one of the several hundred scattered through the east side of midtown, was dark
and cozy. It had that expensive restaurant smell,
too, and after Marlene had ordered the sole and
had gone through a glass of the Montrachet that
V.T. bought to go with it, she felt better than she
had in a while.

Good food and light talk—could it be that simple? *Why do I feel like a country mouse in the big
town*, she asked herself. *I'm not a country mouse; I
was born here and I used to do this all the time. When I
was single. V.T. and the judge here still do it all the
time. Partake of civilization. Why else do people live in
cities? Because they* like *muggings and filth?*

It was not socially demanding either. Judge Rice
had a wealth of amusing anecdotes, mostly at the
expense of his colleagues on the bench and other
courthouse denizens, and Marlene and V.T. were
expected to chuckle appreciatively and not interrupt the flow.

A friendly and urbane fellow, Marlene thought,
if a little too full of himself. This pleasant mien
belied his reputation on the bench, where he was
a severe and impatient tyrant. Not-Nice Rice he

was called by the D.A. staff and the court officers. The defendant side called him Hangman Herb. Strange, Marlene thought; but judges were.

Rice was holding forth on the current deficiencies of defense counsel. He had been one, and a brilliant one by all accounts, before his translation to the bench. "It's simply amazing," he said, "how some of these nincompoops carry on in court. If you want to see true love, you ought to take a look at the affair between these people and the sound of their own voices. Look, what's the first law of questioning?"

He snapped this question at Marlene, who shot back with hardly a thought, "Never ask a question to which you don't know the answer."

"Of course," said Rice professorially. "And what is what we might call the first corollary to that rule?"

This required some thinking. She glanced at V.T., who allowed his jaw to drop slightly and a blankness to come into his eyes, in his famous impersonation of an upper class twit. After a moment, Marlene ventured, "How about, 'Never ask the same question more than once unless you want a different answer?'"

"Excellent! So this pipsqueak the other day is elaborately establishing that his defendant has never seen this other thug involved in the robbery. 'Did you ever see him before?' No. 'Did you ever meet him?' No. 'Are you sure you don't recognize him?' Absolutely. But the idiot can't stop. He says, 'So this man is a complete stranger to you?' And the witness says, 'Yeah, and he better stay a stranger, because if he comes around my house again I'm gonna break his face.'"

Marlene laughed at this, although she had heard

the story before, starring another judge and another lawyer. V.T. contributed a similar story and Marlene told the one about the client who complained to the judge about incompetent counsel and when the judge asked the lawyer what he had to say about it, the lawyer said, "I'm sorry, Your Honor, what did he say? I wasn't listening."

"OK," Marlene continued, "we've established our superiority over all these dumb lawyers. But when you look at the mess the criminal justice system is in now, I tend to doubt that the quality of legal education has much to do with it."

"But surely you'll agree that standards generally have fallen," said Rice. "Education, respect for the law, civility. My God, it used to be possible to walk in this city. I mean on the streets, and at night too."

"Yes, but I don't agree that standards have much to do with the fall of New York. People were the same in the old days, and if anything they're probably better educated now than they were then. I remember what the city was like—I'm not that young. We used to leave the house unlocked and we never got ripped off."

Rice was now looking at her as something more than a decorative and passive audience. "Yes, and you wouldn't dare do that today. To what would you attribute that change, except to a complete collapse of respect for the authority of the law?"

"Too abstract," answered Marlene, who noticed that she had miraculously stopped feeling like a cretin. "Look—take me: one New Yorker. I was born in the middle of Queens in nineteen forty-eight. Total prosperity, New York the world's greatest port, one of the biggest manufacturing cities. My dad, who barely finished high school, was able to buy a house and raise six kids, paying for parochial school for all of them, on a skilled worker's salary.

"Where I lived, I was surrounded by maybe a hundred square miles of houses and apartments in which nearly every man had a job, in which nearly every woman was home all day, taking care of kids and watching the street. Now the schools and the cops are supposed to do both of those two things, with about a thousandth of a percent of the workforce."

"Surely you're not blaming women's lib," Judge Rice said, cocking an eyebrow.

"Women's lib is a symptom, not a cause," Marlene shot back. "Women *have* to work, and they don't want to work in crappy jobs for shit wages."

"Then what would the cause be?"

"Stupidity and greed, like always. And lack of imagination. Look, they industrialized agriculture in Mississippi and Puerto Rico. Where did they expect the people they kicked off the land to go? They came here, a lot of them, just in time to watch the industries leave for the 'burbs on the big highways we were building around then. And then our captains of industry, they let the factories rot, because why invest in making stuff when you can get rich a lot faster in real estate?"

"But surely, there have been hard times before," said Rice. "The Depression, after all . . ."

"Yeah, and there was plenty of crime during the Depression, but we had a big country with only a hundred-fifty million people in it—a lot of escape valves there. And remember we hardly had any kids back in the thirties, so we got less of the casual street crime.

"And also—we always forget this—the poorest

section of the population and all the blacks, was suppressed by what amounted to state terror. You know what cops used to do to people they thought were bad guys? The kind of bad guys who didn't pay them off? And not even bad guys—*any* guy who didn't look like he belonged in a white middle-class neighborhood. Judge, jury, sentencing, and punishment in thirty seconds.

"So, then we became enlightened—no more nightsticks, no more third degree, we got Miranda, we got Escobedo—fine. I approve. But we have a courthouse and prison system that was built for that middle-class city in which the cops kept most of the crime jammed into the poverty pockets, and handled a lot of it informally. Because, God knows, the people who run this city, who ripped off this city, didn't want to pay for a criminal justice system. More cops, yes, but no place for the cops to put the mutts they catch. Hence the revolving door we have now.

"And there's no way out for the poor bastards who feed it either. That's changed too. My father paid six-thousand dollars for his house, in 1946, and he could afford it on a take-home of ninety a week. He's been offered nearly two hundred grand for it. I make six times what he made when he was my age and I'll never be able to afford that house.

"And I want to know—where did all the money go? To Japan? Bullshit! Something a lot closer to home sucked the marrow out of this country, and this city. What you were talking about, the joke of a system down at Centre Street—that's just embalming the corpse. And I'll tell you something else. You know who really pays the bill? Children. They always do, because they're the weak-

est and there's no one they can pass the pain on
to."

Marlene had not wanted to get started on this
particular hobby horse, knowing it could lead up
dangerous paths, but her argument had naturally
led to this pass, and she could not stop herself.
She thrust on.

"We're murdering our children, and we don't
know why, and we can't seem to stop. We have
this Disney myth of childhood that we all pretend
to believe in, and meanwhile we're raping and
beating and stabbing and burning the actual kids,
and even if we don't get around to the physical
stuff we're grinding their little spirits into powder. The half dozen or so kids who actually end
up in dumpsters are symbolic—the whole society
is one big dumpster for children."

She stopped and took a big swallow of Montrachet. V.T. said, "Gosh, Marlene, what a toot!
And here I thought you were just another pretty
face."

Rice's expression had turned grim. "Now that's
something that really concerns me. I couldn't agree
with you more, Marlene. It's a scandal. I'm far
from being a bleeding heart, as I'm sure you know,
but my heart bleeds when I see what people do to
their own children. I don't know, though—I still
find it hard to credit these sociological or economic explanations you give. Surely there's some
spiritual deficit involved."

"You mean the decline of organized religion?"

"No, although I do think they've failed past all
argument. I mean a rebirth of spiritual power,
something grounded more in the real nature of
the world, and the real needs of men and women."

As Rice said this, Marlene noticed that for an

instant his face took on an expression of terrible longing, one that was at odds with the image of assured authority he presented to the world. It was this revelation, even more than the four glasses of wine, that loosened Marlene's tongue. Before she had clearly thought through the consequences, she found that she had steered the conversation from child abuse in general to a particular example, and had blurted out the entire story of the St. Michael's affair, including the fiasco with Raney and Mrs. Dean, and ending with the tongue lashing from Wharton.

"That's quite a tale, Champ," said V.T. when she had finished. "What are you going to do?"

Marlene shrugged, "Do? I don't know—forget the whole thing, I guess." V.T. sniffed unbelievingly at this and rolled his eyes heavenward. But Rice cleared his throat heavily and spoke as if delivering a judgment. "Yes, from a purely legal point of view, the District Attorney is correct. There is no case, and any further intrusion on your Mrs. Dean might be construed as harassment, especially since a child-care operation is so vulnerable to charges of this type.

"But I have to tell you that what you have said is deeply disturbing to me. It's disturbing first because of what we were talking about earlier— about the ills of our society being taken out on the children. Surely we have a special obligation to the reputed victims when the victims are young children, and this may tend to counterbalance our traditional concern for the accused. And second, as you may know, I am myself associated in a small way with the center."

"You?" said Marlene, startled. "With St. Michael's? How?"

"Well, we have been associated with the church itself for many years—my family that is. And when the center started up, I think it was three years ago, Reverend Pinder asked me to be on the board. So I know your Mrs. Dean—and I agree with your reading of her: a formidable lady indeed."

"And so what are you saying, Judge? I shouldn't forget it?"

"Not exactly. Let's say instead that an investigation should proceed under less formal auspices. Let me poke around and see what I can find out; as a board member I have a certain license. Similarly, if you should happen across any additional evidence—and naturally, I am not suggesting you violate the D.A.'s orders—if you should, then perhaps you could see that it finds its way to me. In time a clearer picture may emerge."

"I felt like kissing him when he said that," Marlene confided to V.T. later that afternoon, when Rice had dropped them off at the Courthouse and they were walking together toward their afternoon tasks.

"Did you? He might have enjoyed it if you had. His wife's been dead for years. Never married again as far as I know. A good guy, I think. Dandled me on his knee when a babe, and so on."

"He can dandle *me* if he wants. What a terrific man, especially for a judge! God, I feel like an incredible load has been taken off my head. I've been carrying this shit all by myself and now another player is taking it seriously."

"You're going to keep poking?"

"Umm . . . let's say I'll be open to anything that drifts by. I think it'd be prudent to keep a low pro

223

for the next couple of weeks, until we see what Rice comes up with. But it would be good if . . . nah, forget it!"

"No, what? Forget what?"

"Oh, just thinking about Mrs. Dean. I don't know anything about her, really. Her background, her finances . . . somebody could probably pick that up without alerting her that an investigation was still going on."

"Somebody, huh?" said V.T. "Was that loud noise I just heard a hint dropping? Just because I know a few bankers."

"I didn't hear any noise, V.T. But if you decide to do anything in that line, I'd appreciate it if you didn't advertise it."

"Yeah, Bloom would have a fit."

"Fuck Bloom," said Marlene fervently. "I don't mean Bloom—*Karp* would have a fit."

Back in her office, after court finished that afternoon, Marlene called Raney. She felt that maybe she was on a roll, maybe she could needle Raney into putting a little undercover freelance investigative time into Mrs. Dean's affairs. Nothing fancy—just enough to keep the pot boiling. But when she got through to his office, they told her he was out on an investigation.

This was the truth. Jim Raney was at that moment looking around Stephanie Mullen's bloodstained apartment. Tapes on the floor showed where Mullen and her son Jordie had recently lain in their blood. The photographers and the forensic people had come and gone. Raney and his partner, Peter Balducci, were alone in the apartment.

Balducci looked at his note pad. "Three A North

isn't home. Three A South didn't know the deceased, didn't hear nothing, don't know nothing. The B's and C's are out too. Three D North is an old lady, Mrs. Banda. She said the deceased had visits from men, and that they stayed the night."

"She a pross?"

"No, a singer. Wrote some songs too. According to the guy in Three E North. Dolan, a plasterer on disability. Had a beer or two with the deceased. Said Mullen was married to a rock musician named Willie Mullen, also the father of the two kids. They were not on good terms, he says. Also, there's a boyfriend, another musician named Staley or something close, he wasn't sure. He's a brother. He also said the victim was close to a woman named Anna Rivas, lived in 3F South. But the super said Rivas moved out about a week ago, in a big hurry. Everybody else was out. What'd you get?"

Raney looked around the living room in disgust. "Not much the forensic guys missed. There's a big thumb print on the outside doorway. You don't even need dust to see it. You think this scumbag is maybe not a mental giant?

"Anyhow, I checked out the stuff in her desk. The hubby's behind on payments. There's some letters and shit from a lawyer. Also, I talked to the mother, Mullen's mother. She said she'd been expecting something like this—she seemed more busted up about the little kid than about her own daughter. I gather Stephanie was a disappointment to Mom. Anyway, she likes the ex for it. Apparently, he was a hitter—beat her up for years. And I found this."

He held up a framed glossy standard publicity

photograph of a good-looking black man with long corkscrew curls. He was shown singing and pounding on a bass guitar. The message "Love you babe—always, Dodo" was written across the front of it.

"The name is Dodo Styles," said Raney. "Quite the stud. He's first on my list to talk to."

"Him rather than the ex?" asked Balducci. "Why?"

"It's a knife job, ain't it? That always makes me think a jig. Or a PR."

"Good thinking, Jimmy, I like the way your mind works. Of course, it could be one of us wops. We're pretty good with knives."

"Nah, wops have graduated to guns. It's the jig, you'll see, Petey."

"Yeah, well let's close up here and see if we can get to see these guys. My thinking is, though, it ain't either one of them."

"Yeah? How's that? Who, then?"

"I don't know, but I figure it went down this way. The perp comes in. He kills the mother right in the doorway. The kid comes down the hallway from the kids' bedroom, or he's already standing where the hall meets the living room. He sees his mother get it, the perp sees him, and he stabs the kid right there. The question is now, why didn't he kill the other kid?"

"But the other kid didn't see nothing. He was sleeping."

"Yeah, but the killer didn't know that. One kid was up, the other kid coulda been up, too, he coulda seen the whole act from down the hall. It's a straight shot. What I'm saying is, anybody who knew there were two kids in the house woulda taken out the other kid. So . . ."

"It was a stranger. I get your point. The chain is ripped off the wall there, too, which also says stranger. He had to break in."

"Definitely a stranger," Balducci agreed and grimaced. "That means it's gonna be a pain in the ass."

"Maybe, but if we find Dodo carrying out a bag of bloody clothes, and his prints match, I'm gonna laugh in your face."

# CHAPTER
# 11

"Is this guy shining us on, or what?" said Roland Hrcany.

"No, he's telling the truth," said Ray Guma. "Why should he lie, for chrissake?"

"Yeah, why should I?" added the object of their discussion, Little Noodles Impellatti.

Butch Karp regarded without enthusiasm the five men sitting around the conference table in his office. Besides Hrcany, Guma, and Noodles, there were young Tony Harris and Art Devlin, the cop. Devlin and the two senior A.D.A.s had been bickering without significant advancement of the cause of justice for the better part of an hour. Karp, whose interest in the Ferro killings had started out slight, had recently become enthusiastic about the prospect of making a major anti-Mafia coup. Now it was all coming apart, and he found to his disgust that he resented losing what he had begun by not wanting at all.

"Guys, guys, settle down!" Karp said, rapping with his heavy knuckles on the table. They all stopped talking and looked at him.

"OK, let me review the bidding. Noodles, you have supplied us with details of three assassinations in which you were involved between nineteen sixty-six, when you got out of prison, and the present. All these murders were ordered by Umberto Piaccere in your presence. You identified the final resting place of the victims, which were all parking garages owned by the Bollano family. We had people go out to these places, we pried up two steel plates you told us about, and what did we find?"

"We found zilch," said Devlin.

"Yes," said Karp. "The concrete in which the bodies were supposed to be encased had been dug up. So we got three holes. Three holes is not good enough, Noodles."

Noodles shrugged, "Whaddya want, Karp? They must of took them."

"They must have," Karp agreed.

"This is crap, Butch," snarled Hrcany, wrinkling his golden brow. "We oughta throw his ass out on the street."

"Roland, be real for once," Guma said in a tired voice. "The guy's a corpse already. He's got no angle for not spilling what he knows. Not that he knows much."

Hrcany opened his mouth to respond, since to him everybody was lying all the time about everything, and to bother to explain why a mutt like Noodles might not be lying seemed an exercise in frivolity. But Karp cut him off with a gesture and turned his full attention to Impellatti.

The man seemed to have shrunk during the days of interrogation, as if the rich juice of Mafia status had kept him pumped up beyond his normal dimensions. That juice had nearly drained away and he had begun to seem slight and weasely. Karp looked him carefully in the eye and said,

"Noodles, we want to help you, but we can't unless you give us something to make a case, you understand? Right now, we got nothing.

"Sure, you're a witness, but we need someone to corroborate your story, which we haven't got yet. Right now, Harry's going around cleaning up the loose ends that he knows you know about. But he can't clean up everything, can he? So what I want you to do is to try to think of something that you know about that Harry *doesn't* know you know about. Can you do that now?"

Impellatti made an eloquent gesture of helplessness with his hands. "Hey, man, I'm just a driver, you know? What the fuck you expect, I'm gonna know something he don't know? You think I'm hanging around in the castle with the big shots? They tell me, I drive—that's the whole ball of wax."

But then he sat and thought through the length of three chain-smoked cigarettes, while the others waited silently. At last he spoke.

"Carmine DiBello."

"Who's he?" asked Karp.

"Just a guy. He used to hang around Bleeker Street, waited tables sometimes at Formaggio's and other joints and ran a little numbers back when. Not too bright of a guy, you know? I ain't seen him around much lately, but I heard he was working for the Ferros in Brooklyn."

"He means what about him, Noodles," snapped Hrcany, "his connection—what the fuck we care about his biography?"

Impellatti looked offended, but continued. "I'm getting to it. So when we hit Jimmy Scorsi, like I told you, Joey Bottles was the trigger. We got him when he was goin' into his car. He was keeping some bitch in this fancy place on First, and Joey nailed him with two in the head and then we put him in the trunk and drove him to the garage on Tenth just like I told you."

"Yeah," said Karp, "one of the famous missing bodies. So what's the connection with this DiBello?"

"He saw the whole thing. He was across the street in his car."

"Uh-huh. What was he doing there?"

Impellatti smiled vaguely. "That's the funny part. Jimmy'd hired him to watch his girl's place. He thought she was givin' him the horns. What a laugh, huh?"

"Hilarious. So you spotted him there."

"Yeah. I recognized his car."

"And you didn't tell Joey about it? Or Harry?"

"Shit, no, man! I'd a done that, Joey woulda whacked him out right there. I mean there was a big trunk in Jimmy's car. It was a '71 Caddie Coupe de Ville."

"Why didn't you tell them?"

"I dunno. Carmine done me a couple a favors. And it was, you know, none of my business. I'm the fuckin' driver, you understan'? I figured there was no percentage in it for me. I had a couple of words with him after, and I figured there wasn't gonna be no trouble or nothin'. If you wanna know, I never thought about why until you ast me just now."

Karp turned to Guma. "Goom, you ever hear about this DiBello?"

"No, but that don't mean much. I could ask around."

"Do that. And Art? If you could follow up on this too—see if you can get a line on him."

"Well, it's a start," agreed Devlin and left to

231

begin making his calls. That seemed to be the end of the meeting. Hrcany spoke with Karp briefly about a monster sting he was setting up on an uptown fencing operation, and then left for another appointment. Karp stood up and stretched his long frame. A couple of detectives came in and removed Impellatti.

"So what do you think, Goom?" asked Karp. "About what he just gave us? It could be what we need."

Guma toyed with the cellophane on his next White Owl and looked doubtful. "Yeah, could be. If we can find him. There's a lot of ginzos in Brooklyn. And even if we find him, there's no guarantee he's gonna roll, and go up against Umberto." He made a short overhand stabbing motion with his hand. "They don't call him Harry Pick for nothing."

Tony Harris, who had remained silent during the questioning, spoke up now, and in the tone of one who has had secrets kept from him. "Guma, I've been hearing that for weeks, and I haven't said anything, but I can't stand it any more. OK, I'm the new kid on the block—tell me, why do they call him Harry Pick, if they don't call him Harry Pick for nothing?"

"No big thing, kid," said Guma with a magisterial air. "They call him Harry Pick, because in the old days he used to work over people he didn't like with an ice pick. There's a story that he got Philly Joe Lombroso down in a warehouse across from Pier 46 and stuck holes in him for three whole days. There was even a book on how many holes he could rack up before he croaked him. I forget the exact number, but it was a lot higher than you woulda thought. A skillful guy, Harry.

Anyway, after that nobody fucked with him much. Except Vinnie Red." He unpeeled his cigar and stuck it in his mouth unlit. Leaning back in his chair, he continued.

"I also heard he hung a guy up by his pecker once. Used the ice pick too. The way he did it, I heard—"

"Thanks, Guma," said Harris quickly. "I get the picture. Great story. What about this castle, now?"

"What castle?" asked Guma.

"What Noodles said, when he said he didn't know anything about what the big guys did. He said he never hung around the castle."

"I honestly don't know, Tony. It could be . . . hey, Butch, where're you goin'?"

Karp had shoved a chair aside with a clatter and was out of the office at a run. Minutes later he was back with the detectives and Little Noodles in tow.

"It's a place the Bollanos got," Noodles explained after Harris's question had been put to him. "It's up in Nyack. What's the big deal?"

"You mean the apartment in Nyack?" asked Karp.

"Nah, nah—this is a big place, a real castle, like in the movies. Sally B. lets a guy live there—a square guy, not a family guy. It's free to him, but he's got to clear out when the bosses want to meet."

"You ever been there?"

"Nah, I told you—only the big fish go: Sally B., Little Sally, Harry, the *capo regimes*. Sometimes guys from other families or union guys. They drive themselves. But I heard about it—you know, around."

Noodles was able to give the approximate location of the place he had described, and then he was led out for the second time.

"Guys," said Karp with a grin, "I think we hit pay dirt."

"You think so?" said Guma. "I dunno—what could they be talking about? The price of olive oil? Who does the best murals of Capri for pizzerias?"

"We'll never know unless we get in there. Tony, get busy with setting up a connection with the cops upstate. Devlin knows what to do. Find the place. Then make out a petition for a wire tap and bugs."

"You think you can get something on the Ferro hit out of this place?" asked Harris, as he scribbled notes.

"Ferro for starters, baby. But this could be the biggest score since Valachi. Since Appalachin. I think it's just started to be worth the trip to California."

Raney said, "I can't believe this! *Neither* of these guys fit the thumb print?"

Peter Balducci sat on the edge of the desk in the tiny cubicle he shared with Raney in the offices of the D.A. and leafed through the report from forensic. "Neither Dodo Styles nor Willie Mullen gives a positive match on the bloody thumb print found at the scene. That's that, unless we're talking two guys and there's no evidence for that."

"Shit! Styles looked so good for it, too. What's the D.A. say? Who is it, by the way?"

"Kid named Kirsch. He says no case on either of them—keep looking."

"So where do we look?"

Balducci flipped pages in his notebook and grunted softly. "We could go back to the apartment building tonight and talk to the people we missed. We could try to find Anna Rivas."

"Who's she?"

"The woman who used to live in 3F South. The one who moved out . . ."

"Crap! I knew I heard that name. She called me!" He riffled through a pile of pink message slips until he found the one he wanted, and then dialed a number. There was a long wait and then he started to talk to someone on the other end. He motioned to Balducci, who picked up the other extension.

The two detectives spoke with Anna Rivas for twenty minutes. After they had hung up, Raney said, "What do you think? Sounds legit, no?"

"Yeah, it looks pretty good. The fucker said he was going to do Mullen and he did." Balducci got up off the desk. "But it'll look a lot better if this domestic call she talked about checks out. I'll do that now."

Balducci left the little cubicle and Raney turned again to the phone. In ten minutes Balducci returned and said, "It checks. Couple of guys on the swing shift out of the Ninth took the call. I also ran the phone number she gave us through the reverse directory. It's funny, she's the girlfriend, don't know where he lives. Anyway, she called him there. I also checked out the number she got off the business card she found. Elegante Credit Furnishings, on Thirtieth and Second. We could go over there . . . what are you laughing about?"

"Nothing—" said Raney, still chuckling. "I just got off the phone with Eddie Garcia. You remember Eddie."

"Yeah. Eddie Droop. He had that funny eye. I thought he was dead."

"Nope. Alive and well and still pushing nickel bags to the schoolchildren of the upper West Side. A great snitch."

"So what did Eddie say that was so funny?"

"Oh, well, you know Eddie owes me a couple of favors. So I suggested he keep an eye on that day-care center."

"What day care—oh, shit, Jimmy! Are you still fucking with that?"

"Hey, it's worth another look. We could get lucky and find the big guy."

"Jimmy, it ain't our case. You know what'll happen if you get caught using a dope pusher to harass a citizen? What is it—you still got the hots for that D.A.?"

"Yeah, that's still cooking. But it's mostly that bitch in there, treating me like a turd. Nobody treats me like a turd, Pete, I don't give a rat's ass who the fuck they are. That fucking nun! Only she ain't no nun. That's the funny part. I told Eddie to follow her if she went out. I figured, if she's connected to the big guy, there could be a meet."

Balducci wrinkled his nose in irritation. "Jimmy, that's the most half-assed thing I ever heard. There's not gonna be no meet."

"Wait—yeah, I know it's half-assed, but it's no big deal either. I'm just noodling around here. Anyway, he follows her to this no-tell hotel on the East Side. She checks in. Ten minutes later this real nervous-looking young dude walks in, goes into the room. Two hours later they both come out. What d'you think, Petey? Catechism class?"

"You're crazy, Jimmy, you know that? You're a fuckin' disgrace. It's a good thing I'm retired in a couple of months, I don't want to be around when the shit comes down on you, man." He glowered at Raney for a moment, but his partner had endured many a glower and was unimpressed. Then the older man said, "I'm wasting my breath on you, ain't I? OK, let's go pick up this what's his-face, the boyfriend, Felix Tighe."

Felix parked his company car in the lot and stepped out. He had a new leather blazer. He wore it with a white turtleneck shirt, black slacks, and white almost-Gucci loafers. He looked and felt good. Last night an irresistible opportunity had overcome his resolve to stay clear of burglary. He had made a good score, some nice gold and eight vials of miscellaneous downers and diet pills. He would move most of the latter at Larry's this evening. In the meantime, he had tried some of the downers already and he was feeling mellow.

In that mood, he didn't even mind coming into the office, which was what he was doing right now. He would try to get in touch with Anna again, using the office phone. She looked good and scared the last time he saw her; he figured that she'd be softened up by now. He'd put the heavy make on her, say he was sorry, and bullshit like that and she'd come around. He'd have to find out where she lived now; he already knew where she worked.

"That's him," said Balducci. "The dark guy in the leather jacket with the case, crossing the street. Give him a few minutes and ring the number."

Raney nodded and got out of the unmarked Ford from which the two of them had been observing the premises of Elegante Credit Furnishings. There was a phone booth nearby. He went in and dialed.

"Mr. Tighe?"

"Yes, this is Mr. Tighe, how can I help you?"

"Well, my name's Jim Raney. I think we have some mutual friends. I have a business proposition for you and I'd like to meet with you today—buy you a lunch."

Felix did not get asked out to lunch all that often, and he didn't ask what mutual friends. "Give me an hour," he said. "There's a chinks across the street from where I work, at Thirtieth and Second. Upstairs, the Peking Gardens. How will I know you?"

"I'll know you," said Raney, and hung up.

The restaurant proved to be a long, narrow room with a lunch counter and a small collection of tables, at the top of a steep flight of stairs. The lunch rush was in full spate and the place was jammed. Raney and Balducci stood on the landing at the top of the stairs and looked through the glass door. They could see Felix sitting at the counter with his back to them.

"It's too jammed," said Raney. "Let me go in there and get him out." Balducci nodded assent and Raney went through the crowd to where Felix was sitting. He said, "Felix Tighe? I'm Jim Raney."

Felix stood up and the two men shook hands. Raney smiled and said, "Look, it's too crowded in here. Can we go somewheres else?"

"Sure," said Felix, picking up his attaché case. "So, tell me, Jim, what line of business are you in?"

"Security," said Raney as they passed through the door. Then he added, "Actually, Felix, I'm a New York City police officer, Detective James

Raney. The guy behind you is Detective Peter Balducci. We're placing you under arrest."

Felix's eyes went wide and he whirled around to find himself looking into the barrel of Balducci's .38 Chief's Special. Raney took out his handcuffs and grabbed Felix's left arm.

Felix uttered a shrill yell, deafening in that narrow space, threw his attaché case at Balducci's head and grabbed the detective's revolver.

It's my last couple of months on the job and I'm going to kill a guy, was Balducci's thought as he squeezed the trigger. Nothing happened. Like most policemen, Balducci kept an empty chamber under the hammer of his revolver, and Felix's hand gripping the cylinder was preventing it from rotating. He saw Felix's other hand flying like a knife blade toward his face and he ducked. The edge of the hand struck him across the forehead. It was like being hit with a board and it stunned him, but not enough to make him release his grip on the handle of his pistol.

At that moment, Raney leaped on Felix's back and tried to apply a choke hold from the rear. Felix bucked forward to prevent this, seized the lapel of Balducci's jacket and executed a leg sweep that was reasonably effective under the circumstances. Balducci felt himself going over, with the long stairway yawning below him. The pistol was wrenched from his grasp. In a last despairing effort he reached out and sank his fingers into the leather of Felix's jacket.

The grip was strong enough to yank Felix off the landing, with Raney still clinging to his back. The three of them went down the stairs together, Felix in the middle and the two detectives on either side, a suspect sandwich on cop.

Felix was on top of Balducci when they reached the bottom. He managed to brace a leg and heave himself to his feet, with Raney still hanging on his head. Raney saw the Chief's Special in Felix's hand, still gripped by its barrel and cylinder. He made a wild try for its handle, which was a mistake, because Felix was then able to grab his wrist with his other hand, bend slightly, twist his body, pull on the arm, and flip Raney over his head into the street.

Raney landed with a jolt that brought blood to his mouth. He shook his head and staggered to his feet. Felix had the gun right way around now. He pointed it at Raney and squeezed the trigger. It wouldn't pull. Felix cursed and tried to clear the jam by pulling back on the hammer. He heard it click as the cylinder finally revolved.

He pointed the cocked pistol at Raney, whose Browning was just clearing his shoulder holster. Raney could see the tiny hole in the barrel of the revolver, as large, it appeared, as the sun at noon. His own pistol was coming up like the slow motion in a nightmare and he knew it would be too late.

The Chief's Special exploded and the bullet went whining off against the side of a building. Balducci had dragged himself off the bottom of the stairway, his twisted back shrieking agony, and had flung his arms around Felix from behind, lifting him off his feet and spoiling his shot.

"Throw him down, Pete, I got him!" Raney yelled waving his Browning. But Balducci did not release his grip, because he realized that as long as he kept the suspect's arms pinioned, he would be unable to aim, and unable to commit homicide *with Balducci's own gun*. This was his only thought, that and the pain. So the two of them did a little waltz on the sidewalk, with Raney as their satellite, circling around in a crouch with his gun waving, trying to avoid the sweep of the captured weapon, and trying to think of a way out of this idiotic stand-off without death intervening.

In the end, none of the heroic schemes that were running through the minds of the two detectives proved necessary. A patrolman named Donald Olson, who happened to know Raney slightly, came around the corner onto Second, on his way to the Peking Gardens for a bite to eat. He saw Raney, saw the guy with the gun, made the situation in a flash and, setting himself in his usual fast-pitch softball league stance on the side away from the waving revolver, swung from the hips with his long, black nightstick.

Felix saw the nightstick coming and wriggled desperately. He fired off two more shots and tried to get some purchase with his feet, but Balducci's grip held. The stick made the same sound against Felix's skull that a bat makes when you foul one off. Balducci relaxed his arms when he felt his captive slump, and Felix hit the pavement, spraying blood.

"Shame on you!" said a middle-aged woman who had observed the whole fray from the shelter of a doorway. "Shame on you! Three against one!"

"You look like shit, Petey," said Raney solicitously. "Why don't you take the rest of the day off and go lie down?"

Balducci grimaced and massaged his sacroiliac region. After they had booked Felix and stashed him in the prison ward at Bellevue a friendly nurse had slipped him some Darvon. It helped the pain but not the dull exhaustion. "I'm getting too old for this shit, Jimmy," he sighed.

"It's only another couple a months, Petey," said Raney with the cheerfulness of relative youth. "You can coast. I'll pound the mutts, hey? By the way, what's in the scumbag's case there?"

"Well, we got a set of keys. Some pills in prescription vials, under different names. Some order books and business papers. And this." He tossed Raney a small black book. Raney thumbed briefly through it.

"A diary and address book. Find anything interesting?"

"Yeah. For one thing, the day before Mullen and her kid were butchered there's an entry that says, 'take care of *Big Mouth*.'"

Raney flipped to July 9, the day before the murder, nodded, and then examined the surrounding pages more closely. "Lots of appointments with Anna R. last few months. Here's one says 'move in with A.,' right before that domestic call. So that checks out too. He sees a Denise about once a week too. Quite the stud, Felix."

"Yeah. Here's a matchbook cover with the name 'Mimi' and a phone number. The asshole never sleeps. I found out where he lives, too. Place down on Ludlow. Lives with a guy named Lutz. I called him, said we'd be over in about half an hour."

"OK, let's go," said Raney. He looked down at his partner, who was still seated in his swivel chair. "You coming?"

"Yeah," said Balducci, with a sad grimace. "Help me up, Jimmy. I'm like an old lady here."

One-thirty Ludlow was a New Law tenement, which meant that every apartment had to have a toilet and every room required a window. Besides that, its amenities were few. At apartment 203 Steve Lutz answered sleepily to Raney's knock. He was dressed in a dirty T-shirt and boxer shorts.

"Steven Lutz?" said Balducci. "I'm Detective Balducci and this is Detective Raney. I called and you said we could look around."

"Yeah," said Lutz backing away from the door. "Hey what's this about?" he asked.

"Just checking up on a lead," said Balducci aimiably. "Where does Felix sleep?"

Lutz led them into the smaller of the two bedrooms in the apartment. It had a window, as required by law, and was a lot cleaner than the rest of the apartment. The furnishings comprised a neatly made bed, a cheap pine chest of drawers, and several cardboard cartons. The walls were decorated with a pinned-up Bruce Lee poster and a framed certificate attesting that Felix Tighe had been awarded the rank of *shodan* in karate. Balducci caught sight of it, glanced at Raney and shook his head ruefully.

"Say, Steve—you mind if we look around through his stuff?" asked Raney. Lutz didn't mind. The chest contained clothes, all clean and neatly folded. The cartons held an orderly collection of martial arts and business magazines, as well as several ninja-style instruments of destruction—nunchuks and throwing stars and oddly shaped axes in chromed metal.

There was a rack of hooks in the closet. On one of them hung a pair of black slacks. Balducci looked at them, looked again, fingered the material, and took them down.

"These Felix's pants, Steve?" he asked.

"Yeah, they're his."

"What've you got, Pete?" asked Raney, who was reaching under the bed.

"These pants—they're stiff with something."

"Blood?"

"Could be." Balducci took a laundry marker out of his pocket and marked "P.B." and his shield number on the pocket lining of the black slacks.

Raney pulled a small brown gym bag from under the bed. Its zipper was locked with a miniature padlock. They opened it with one of the keys they had found in the attaché case.

"Well, well," said Raney, after looking inside. He dumped the contents of the bag out on the bed. A passport made out to Felix M. Tighe. A checkbook, ditto. Three clippings from metropolitan papers describing the murder of Stephanie Mullen and her son. A small kitchen knife. And a huge bowie knife in a leather sheath.

"That's some hell of a knife," said Balducci. "Cut somebody's head off with that mother."

Marlene was walking north on Broadway, when she heard the shout: "Hey, good-lookin' " followed by the loud kissing noises used by many men on the streets of New York in order to make themselves attractive to strange women. Marlene trudged steadily on, her face assuming the forbidding grimace of the accosted city woman, an amalgam of fright and helpless rage. Another shout. Ordinarily, she would have spun around and given the asshole the finger, but today she didn't need the aggravation. She had awakened feeling queasy and depressed and a day of plea-bargaining had improved neither her stomach nor her spirits.

"Hey, Marlene!"

Hearing her name called in the accents of her

childhood, Marlene at last stopped and turned. She saw the green Ghia with the primered fender and walked toward it, smiling her relief.

"Oh, it's you," she said. "You should be ashamed of yourself. How are you?"

"Pretty good as a matter of fact," said Raney. "We just caught the mutt who killed that woman and her kid over in the East Village."

"Way to go! Good case?"

"Not bad. No witnesses, but we got prints, bloodstains, the murder weapon, motive, means and opportunity. It'll fly unless you guys fuck it up. How about yourself?"

She shrugged. "The usual bullshit."

"Anything new on St. Michael's? Or the trash-bag killer?"

At this her face fell. "How should I know? That's over."

"What kind of 'over'? I thought this was a big deal to you."

"*Was* is the word. Let somebody else get kicked in the ass on that one. I had my share." She caught the disappointed expression on his face and added, in a tone that revealed her own interest, "Why do you ask? You're not still screwing around with that?"

"Yeah," he said, caution creeping into his voice. "I guess I still am."

"You ever get a case there, you could let me know."

"I'll do that," said Raney sourly, looking at her with a look she didn't care for at all.

Marlene twitched at her hair in a nervous gesture. "Well, nice talking to you, Raney, but I got to go. I have to get my hair cut."

"Get in, I'll drive you."

"No, don't bother," she protested vaguely, "it's right by the Fourth Street IND."

Raney reached across and flung the curbside door open. "Marline," he growled, "get the fuck in this car!" Surprising herself, she entered, and they shot away from the curb.

"Look, Marlene," Raney began, when they had driven a few blocks in stiff silence, "you started this shit with Dean, you got me all wound up on it, and now you're leaving me hang. What's going on?"

"Nothing. Raney, it just didn't work out. There's no case. It happens."

"No case my ass! Marlene, don't bullshit a bullshitter. You knew damn well something was going down there, something real big. They yelled at you? Fuck, they yelled at me too. Fuck 'em! I can't believe you're that hot for a pension or. . . ." He stopped suddenly, arrested by a thought. "It's Karp, right? Karp gave you the zinger on this, and you caved right in."

It was true enough and it still hurt. Marlene felt the blood rush to her face. "That's off the wall, Raney," she snarled. "Karp had nothing to do with it."

"Yes, he did. A little pillow talk, a little spankie, and you can the case. I guess I don't have that problem, counselor, because I'm not fucking my boss."

"Oh, go to hell, Raney!" Marlene shouted, and opened her door to leave. But Raney downshifted and tromped on the gas, swinging out into the traffic with such force that Marlene fell back in her seat and the partly opened door swung shut.

"What're you, crazy? Let me the fuck out of this car!" she shouted. Raney increased his speed instead, weaving through the traffic, leaving a wake of curses, horns, and rude gestures.

"You're not getting out of here until we talk," said Raney grimly. He swung around a bus and shoved a tape into the cassette player. Chopin's A minor mazurka blasted from the speakers. After a moment, Marlene leaned back in her seat and took out a cigarette. This was starting to get interesting. She had never been kidnapped by a heavily armed Chopin freak before. And she had to admit he drove like a god. And he was, of course, right about Karp, and she did feel rotten about her lie and about the case.

Raney skidded the car around the left turn at West Fourth Street and pulled into a small parking lot. He parked the Ghia with its passenger side three inches from a blank wall, turned off the engine, and lit a cigarette. The mazurka ended and the nocturne in G minor came on, slow and infinitely sad.

"OK, Raney, let's talk," said Marlene at length. "You scared the shit out of me, you soothed me with music, I'm jelly. Yes, you're right—Karp convinced me there was no case. There being no case, it's agony for me to keep thinking about the damn thing. I'm not proud of it, but there it is. Now, can I get my haircut? Raney? Hello?"

Raney didn't answer. When the nocturne was finished he sighed and switched off the deck. He slumped despondently in his seat, ignoring his captive and smoking.

"You like classical music?" asked Marlene inanely, for want of something to break the silence.

"No," he said. "Just this tape. I used to play it in 'Nam. It belonged to a guy I knew. I mean not this particular tape—this is the fourth one I bought.

I wear them out. The guy stepped on a mine made out of a one-oh-five shell. There was nothing left of him but a damp spot on the ground. And this tape. I picked it up. The tape played perfect, it was amazing. And I kept it.

"You know, I drew on a guy today—that East Village killer. I had a couple of clear shots, but I didn't, you know, pop him. I thought about you, while I was chasing this asshole around, your face was in my mind. This sounds crazy, doesn't it? You think I'm a real nut case."

Marlene thought nothing of the kind. She was filled with an enormous tenderness for him, for his suffering, for the suffering of her brother Dom, who had also, as it happened, stepped on a mine in Vietnam, for the inarticulate grief of the men of her caste and class, from whom she was irrevocably cut off.

"No," she said, and put her hand on his. He reached out then and put his hand behind her neck and pulled her towards him and kissed her hard on the mouth.

It was a good kiss, thought Marlene, delicate tongue action and no clacking teeth. She felt herself kissing back, felt the insistent tingle in the groin and the warm flutters. She imagined herself going somewhere with Raney, a room somewhere, taking off her clothes, lying on a bed, imagined what his body would be like, imagined spreading her thighs. . . .

And then, almost before she was aware of it, a powerful nausea convulsed her belly. She wrenched away from him, gasped, and was violently sick out the window of the car.

"Jesus," said Raney, in a stunned voice. "What was that all about?"

"Oh, God, I'm sorry. Oh, this is awful!" Marlene cried, tears of shame springing from her eyes. Raney reached into the glove compartment and pulled out a package of tissues. Marlene dabbed at her mouth and face.

"That's a pretty strong reaction, Ciampi," he said. "I been turned down before, but . . ."

"Oh, shit, Raney, I wasn't, it isn't you. I've been nauseous all day. I must have picked up the flu or some food poisoning. I'm sorry, but, oh shit! I don't know what to say—let's forget it, huh?"

He smiled and started the car. "We should call it the world's shortest romance. OK, where's this beauty parlor you're going to?"

Raney duly deposited her at Vittorio's on Sixth off Fourth Street and drove off. Normally, a hairdo was a relaxing experience for Marlene. She liked being cosseted and admired and immersed in trivia and amusing gossip. Today, however, she could not shake her irritability. She was short with her favorite hairdresser, who soon gave up his attempts to engage her, and snipped away morosely in silence. While he was blow-drying, she felt sick again and had to rush to the bathroom.

"Darling, you look wasted," said the cutter sympathetically, when she returned. "Are you OK?"

"Yeah, fine," said Marlene. "Hey, what's everybody looking at?" The cashier and several waiting patrons were clustered in the doorway, looking out to the street and talking excitedly.

"Oh, the funniest thing. As soon as you left for the powder room, this absolutely enormous man came trundling in and grabbed up some hair off the floor. Yours, as a matter of fact, and then raced out."

"What did he look like?" asked Marlene, her heart thumping.

"Oh, huge! Six-five, maybe two-ninety. Dressed in a black suit. Sort of a round head, like that guy in the Charles Addams cartoons . . . say, where are you going—you're not dry yet!"

Marlene had scooped a handful of bills from her purse and flung them at the cashier and then dashed out the door and into the street. She looked up and down Sixth and then raced around the corner and checked West Fourth, but of the big man there was no sign.

Karp knew something was wrong the minute he walked into Marlene's loft. It was just past nine and Karp had spent the last four hours arguing with the members of six different law enforcement agencies with whom he would have to coordinate his projected raid on the Bollano family's secret castle. Then he had been soaked during his walk home by the rain that had started in the evening. He was not in a good mood, and he now suspected, as he looked around, that he was not about to be greeted in a way that might improve it.

The immense room was dark except for an eerie red glow emanating from the sleeping platform end. A sour odor hung in the still, warm air. "Marlene?" he called. No answer. He dropped his briefcase, shrugged out of his dripping suit jacket, kicked off his wet shoes and climbed the ladder to the sleeping platform.

The windows over the bed had been covered with sheets and blankets roughly tacked up. At the foot of the bed was a large stainless steel bowl, the source of the sour odor. The only light came from two small candles in red glass holders on Marlene's vanity table. Marlene's boudoir suite was the very one she had used during her girlhood in fifties Queens—white with flower decals. The vanity had an oval mirror and a crinoline skirt. It usually held Marlene's large collection of Dolls of Other Lands—weird enough, Karp had always thought—but these had been displaced by the candles and an array of religious items: a small statue of Our Lady of Lourdes in luminescent white plastic, two rosaries, one black and the other amber, a pewter crucifix, and an array of scapulars, holy medals, and the colored cards bearing pictures of saints that are given to young ladies in convent schools when they have been particularly diligent.

"Hey, Marlene, what's up? What's wrong—are you sick, or what?" Karp addressed these questions to a lump curled up under the bedclothes. Receiving no answer he gently tugged back the covers, revealing his own cutie lying on her side with a wad of pink Kleenex as large as a cantaloupe clutched to her tear-damp face.

"Marlene, what's wrong?" he demanded again, touching her face, which was cold and clammy.

"Nothing," she mumbled.

"Don't tell me 'nothing'! You're crying under the covers, the windows are covered up like *Great Expectations*, and this religious stuff—what, the Pope is coming to lunch?" Karp spoke lightly, but he was fighting against his worst and most secret fear: that Marlene's porch light had finally flickered out, that she had gone from merely nutty, to nuts.

She sat up suddenly and clutched at him like a

drowning child. "I just got scared being alone," she said into his shirt.

Since Marlene had always seemed to him utterly fearless, Karp couldn't help laughing. "You? Scared of what, for chrissake?"

"No, really, Butch! Look at this!" She rummaged under the blankets and pulled out a damp 5 by 7 photograph, which she handed to Karp. It was not a very good photograph, being pale and grainy, with a blurred cross in one corner that showed it had been taken through a small-paned window, but it was clear enough to preserve the identity of its subject, which was Marlene. She had been shot wearing her plaid flannel bathrobe and sitting in this very bed.

Karp glanced up at the covered windows, and Marlene followed his glance. "Yeah, right," she said. "He took it through that window at night, from the roof of the building across the street."

"Where did you get it?"

"I found it down on the street. It was wired under the drainpipe on the corner."

"Wired . . . ?"

"Yeah, the water washes away the image, and the person gets sick and dies. It's witchcraft."

Karp snorted. "What're you talking, witchcraft?"

"It's true. God, Butch, I feel better now that you're here! I was paralyzed." She stood up and got a cigarette and then sat down next to him on the bed. She was still in the clothes she had worn to the office that day. "This afternoon a guy came into Vittorio's and picked up a swatch of my hair, a guy, by the way, who matches the description we got of Lucy Segura's boyfriend. The bogeyman."

"Did you see him?"

"No, but the people in the place did. It's the guy, Butch."

Karp took a long breath. "Ah, Marlene . . . aren't you getting a little carried away here . . . ?"

"I'm being hexed," she said bluntly.

"You're kidding!" said Karp, with a smile he didn't feel.

"Do I look like I'm kidding? It's working, too. Look, I haven't been sick a day since I had chicken pox when I was ten. Now I feel like death warmed over. I've been vomiting continuously since I got up this morning."

"So you're sick—it's the flu, or maybe food poisoning. Have you seen a doc?"

"I went to Larry downstairs. He doesn't think it's the flu. And how could it be food poisoning? I already puked up everything I've eaten for the last two weeks. Then he asked if I was maybe pregnant." She let out a short rough laugh.

"Are you?" Karp asked casually.

"Of course not, dopey! I'm late, but I'm always a little screwed up that way. Also I got a loop in, as you know very well."

"Yeah, but . . . look, Marlene, Larry downstairs is a nice guy, but he's not a doctor."

"He's a nurse."

"My point—you need to see a real doctor."

"And what if nothing's wrong with me—physically?"

Karp sighed and said gravely, "If nothing's wrong physically, then I think you should, you know . . . see somebody."

"Somebody? You mean a shrink? You think I'm crazy?"

"No, I think you're upset. I think you're still obsessing about this damn day-care center and the trash-bag killings, for reasons I can't understand. And it's sent you off on a toot, and now it's affecting your body. Witchcraft! For crying out loud, Marlene . . . !"

"What about that photo? I made that up?"

"A crazy, a peeper. We'll get shades."

Marlene sagged back against the pillows at the head of the bed. "OK, you got all the answers, as usual. Thank you, Dr. Karp, for the diagnosis. I knew I could count on your warm support. . . ."

"Don't be like that, babe. I'm really worried about you. I want to help . . ."

Her one eye, reddened with weeping, regarded him balefully. "You want to help? Then bring me that fucking bowl. I got to puke again."

# CHAPTER
# 12

"**V**.T.," said Marlene, "did you ever dig up anything on Irma Dean?" She had found Newbury in his office, where she had gone right after finishing her court work for the day. It was the day after the stolen hair, the day after the dripping photograph.

Newbury looked up curiously. "Yes I did, but I thought you weren't interested any more. Say, Champ, are you OK?"

"Everybody keeps asking me that. No, I'm not. I'm sick, and I'm scared."

"What's wrong?"

"I'll tell you later. What did you find on Dean?"

Newbury went to his file drawer and pulled out a slim folder. He gave it to Marlene, who was curled up in his side chair like a wounded bird. She tried to read through the sheets of notes and printouts in the folder, but found it impossible to concentrate.

"What's the story here, V.T.? Briefly, I mean," she asked.

"Deposits in two accounts, monthly. She's taking in ten to twelve K a month, in cash, besides the monthly check for $12,550 she gets from the

St. Michael's Foundation. The expenses for running the school are paid out of that—see, that's out of the Citibank account itemized on the next sheet. This other account picks up her monthly check from St. Michael's she gets as director—for $1518—as well as the cash deposits, always in small amounts. What's the source, is the question. There's nothing in the St. Michael's financial statement that reflects those deposits. I mean, it's a charity. The parents don't pay anything, or at least not much.

"She owns the building the school is in outright, and she's got a mortgage on the adjoining one. The third building, the one on West End Avenue, is income property, but it still doesn't add up to—"

"Wait a minute, she owns a third building?"

"Yeah, it backs on the day-care center, with the front on West End. Is it important?"

"Could be. My head is screwed on wrong today. Look, V.T., can I take this and study it some?"

"It's yours. I have a copy. So, tell me, what's wrong? Early menopause?"

"I only wish. Listen, V.T., if I ask you a question, promise not to laugh, all right?"

"Promise, unless you tell me you're having a sex change operation."

"No, seriously. Umm, do you, ah, believe in witchcraft?"

V.T. did not laugh. On the contrary, he seemed to observe Marlene with new interest. After a moment, he said, "That depends on what you mean. I think quite a lot of what we could call witchcraft gets practiced today, and not just in places like Haiti. In New York, too, not to mention Miami and New Orleans. Immigrants from

the Caribbean and South America and the Orient
bring occult practices from home, for one thing.
New York probably has as many practicing witches,
brujos, curanderos and so on as it does obstetricians.

"Then there are the mainstream weirdos, usually middle-class kids who got off on acid and
never came down—all these little shops selling
tarot cards and theosophy books."

"I don't mean that," said Marlene. "I mean
summoning the devil, and black masses, and cursing people."

"Oh, *that*," said V.T., leaning back in his chair
and staring up at the ceiling. "Charles Manson
and beyond. Yeah, we got that too. People who
want to get kicks and don't care who gets hurt
usually can come up with a justifying structure.
But what you're really asking me is, does it work?
Does the devil really come? You're asking is the
supernatural real?"

"Yeah, I guess."

"Then I'd have to ask you what you mean by
'real.' We know that symbols have real power.
People die for symbolic reasons all the time. We
know that people will give their wills over to
other people and do things they would never do
otherwise, so that it seems like magic. Hitler, and
on a tiny scale, Manson, are examples. We know
that psychological states have physical consequences, everything from hives to hysterical pa-
ralysis to voodoo death. And we know that people
see and hear what they want to or what they
think they ought to see and hear. Probably most
of what passes for the supernatural comes from
that kind of psychological stuff.

"For the rest . . . as a skeptic who doesn't understand how a color TV works, I reserve judg-

ment. Somebody once said that magic is science that we haven't formulated laws for yet. . . . I'm sorry, I'm not being helpful, am I?" He had observed her sinking lower and lower into herself as he talked.

"No. I wanted you to say that it was all bullshit," Marlene answered, her voice barely audible. "I can't believe I'm saying this to anybody, but I think I'm being hexed, and I think it's working." Marlene related the story of the big man in black at Vittorio's, and the connection with the trash-bag killings, and her current malaise. V.T. considered this for a long moment, and then said, "But you said you started to feel bad yesterday morning, before the big guy got the hair."

"Yeah, but who knows what else they got? Do I track every Kleenex I toss? How do I know how long they've been doing this? Why are you shaking your head?"

"Because it won't wash, Marlene. Maybe you've uncovered a band of demon worshippers, and maybe they're out to get you. I'll believe that. And you got sick. I believe that. But that doesn't mean there's a connection, that the forces of darkness are working you over. I don't think your head is going to start turning backwards and shit is going to start flying around. And your demon worshippers are going to turn out to be a version of the old scam—some sordid combination of kicks and money. Remember those deposits in Dean's account?

"Listen to your Uncle V. The first thing you should do is see a doctor. If there's nothing wrong with you physically, then go see a shrink. Or a priest. But I totally reject the notion that Lucifer is dropping in on Riverside Drive and giving Irma Dean the power to bind and loose."

"How can you be so sure? I mean I believe you, and all, but . . ."

V.T. laughed. "Because this is New York, Champ. The devil doesn't need any help."

Marlene left without saying anything about what she thought was happening to her. It was really too stupid. She called Raney and gave him a sketch of what V.T. had discovered. He was short with her and seemed uninterested. So, that was that. Grimly, she went back to her chores. It was better than going home.

Freddie Kirsch sighed and threw down his pencil. Perfection was hard. He looked at the typed sheets of the three hours of Q and A he had done on Felix Tighe. He thought it was the best one he had ever done, but still. . . . The problem was that Tighe was such an incredible liar. All mutts lied, of course, but Tighe was so plausible, so charming. And shameless. When caught in a lie, he just smiled and admitted his lie, "but now he was telling the truth." The Q and A was a mass of contradictions, backtracks, misdirection, explanations.

The alibi, for example. Felix had told him that he was with a girl at the time of the murder. What girl? He couldn't remember her name. He had written it down on a matchbook. Balducci had produced the matchbook with "Mimi" on it. Felix had brightened up like a lantern, like Balducci had saved his life.

So they found Mimi. Yes, she had been with him, but not, it turned out, on the night in question. Oh, no, Felix had meant another girl, Josie,

Jackie, or something. And then there was the waitress at the place he was at—Larry's. She would recognize him. Should he take a statement from the waitress? Or forget it? The pages swam and he rubbed his eyes. He looked at his watch. Seven-fifteen. His wife would be pissed off and get on him again about why couldn't he get a job with decent hours?

Why not indeed? He was working on it. Meanwhile, *People v. Tighe* would have to wait until tomorrow. He stood up and switched off his desk lamp. The funny thing about it, when he thought of Tighe, he couldn't help sort of liking him. The guy was amusing, anyway, which was more than could be said for the surly toughs that featured in most of his cases.

He put on his jacket and stacked his Q and A transcript neatly. He had a strong case, anyway. He should be able to get a tough plea with no trouble.

Felix Tighe's new lawyer was a barrel-shaped little man who favored rumpled glen plaid suits and bow ties. He wore his thin dark hair stretched across his scalp like electrical cable, but his eyebrows, ears, and nose were luxuriantly supplied with the growth that had deserted the more conventional locations. His complexion was coarse and sallow. He had a little stump nose like a parakeet's beak and—his only remarkable feature—large, luminous eyes, which could blaze out or withdraw into dark, hooded sockets according to his purpose. Despite his unprepossessing appearance, he had a reputation as a bon vivant and ladies' man and as one of the dozen or so best criminal lawyers in Manhattan. His name was Henry Klopper and Felix was terrified of him.

They had met the day after his arrest, when Felix was still recovering from the pounding administered by Patrolman Olson. His head still throbbed and he was dulled out from the analgesics they had given him. He had sought yet more dullness, but his charm had drawn a blank; Bellevue locked-ward nurses are very hard charmees and stingy with dope.

Thus he had been in no cordial mood when the small man strode briskly into the curtained enclosure around his bed, sat down in a straight chair, and pulled a yellow legal pad from a worn briefcase.

"Who the fuck are you?" Felix snarled.

The man took a pair of gold-rimmed glasses from his breast pocket and hooked them on before answering. "I'm Henry Klopper. Your mother has retained me as your attorney."

"Yeah? Well, when am I getting out of here?"

"Probably tomorrow, if the doctors OK it. They'll move you to Riker's Island Jail and then—"

"No, asshole! I mean *out*—like on the street."

Klopper regarded Felix with an expression that mixed pity and contempt, heavy on the latter. He said quietly, "Mr. Klopper, Felix."

"What!"

"You call me 'Mr. Klopper,' Felix, and in a respectful tone of voice."

"Fuck you, jerk! I want my mother in here—now!"

Klopper ignored this outburst and continued in the same quiet tone, like a doctor explaining the tumor shadows on the X-ray film. "The reason for that, Felix, is that you are a vicious little shitheel and you are about to go up for at least twenty years. To Attica. Think about that for a minute,

Felix. You believe you're a tough guy, but you're not, Felix, not compared to the boys up there. Compared to some of those bucks up there, you're just a momma's boy, but you haven't got the sense to lie low and play the game. They will break you like a stick the first week.

"So don't ask for your mommy, Felix. She can't help you and she knows it, which is why she hired me, and you can't help yourself because you're a complete and utter fuck-up, without the brains God gave an ant. The only person who can help you is me. Now if you want me to help you, you will be respectful, as I said, and speak when spoken to. I am not interested in your plans or opinions. You have only one thing to think about, Felix, and that is to do exactly, precisely what I tell you to do, and nothing else."

He paused to let what he had said sink in. It hadn't. Felix did not admit negative comments on his personality or behavior into his consciousness. At that moment he was running through his options. Smashing Klopper's face in was the preferred one, but he couldn't do that because his right hand was cuffed to the bed frame. Escaping was always a possibility—get away somewhere, maybe the Caribbean. He could get free on bail and skip . . .

"What about getting me out on bail?" Felix asked.

Klopper stood up, removed his glasses, put his pad in his briefcase, and locked it. "Felix, you're thinking," he said, wagging his finger. "And when you start thinking is when I start leaving. Bail, my Aunt Fanny!"

Felix did not see Klopper again until he was arraigned on the criminal complaint, at which time the lawyer made a perfunctory request for bail, which was perfunctorily denied. Because of his attempt to escape custody, and the nature of his crime, Felix was no longer a good bail risk, despite his job and his ties to the community. After that Klopper had let him stew in Riker's for the better part of a week. This was a good place to think about spending twenty in Attica and at their next meeting Felix had adjusted his tone to meet Klopper's expectations. The lawyer was not impressed.

"Very nice, Felix," he said. "You're playing the good boy now. 'Mr. Klopper, this, Mr. Klopper that'—very respectful. I know it's bullshit, Felix. You still don't seem to understand: I *know* you. All psychopaths are the same person. Right now you're thinking, 'Let this little dork ramble on until I can find some edge I can use to manipulate him, find what phony line I can use to make him happy, so I can game him.' Right? But it won't work, Felix. You're not going to play me—I'm going to play you."

Felix felt a spasm of fear, akin in an odd way to what he felt when Denise called him, a violation of his hollow and steel-hard center. What Klopper had described was exactly what he had been thinking. He tried to meet Klopper's eyes and stare him down, but found it impossible. He swallowed in a dry mouth as the lawyer continued.

"OK, Felix, this is your first little doggie trick. You're going to tell me the truth. I know that's going to be hard for you, Felix, but I insist. You see, if you don't tell me the truth, I might make a mistake, and we might lose, and you would go upstate. Not that I give a crap about you, but losing is bad for my business. See? That's the truth—a little demonstration.

"Now *you're* going to try. And to make it easy for you, since you probably don't have any experience at it, we'll do it like baseball. You get three strikes. Three lies I catch you in and you get a new lawyer, and believe me, Felix, *I* dump you and you're going to wind up with an ambulance chaser that'll fuck it up so bad they'll reinstate the electric chair just for you.

"So here's the first question. When did you decide to kill this Mullen woman?"

"I didn't kill anybody!" said Felix sulkily, looking down at the table.

Klopper smiled unpleasantly. "Strike one," he said.

"What did the doctor say?" asked Karp anxiously. Marlene had been sick every day for over a month. Previously slim, she now approached the unnatural dimensions of a fashion model or a Dachau alumna. During that time Karp had been nagging at her in increasing desperation to see a doctor, and that morning she had finally agreed to see a local M.D.

She let out a bitter laugh. "He gave me a scrip for Valium."

"There was nothing wrong with you?"

"Only with my head, according to Dr. Herman Myers. Another hysterical broad—I could see him thinking it. Give her some dope and get rid of her. Maybe I'll fill it. I could take the whole bottle—"

"Oh, shut up! I can't stand it when you talk like that."

"Sorry," she said and laughed again, without much humor. "This is wearing me down. I can't work. I can hardly watch TV. Maybe I *should* see a shrink—or an exorcist, one."

The two of them were standing near the circular information desk in the first floor lobby of Centre Street, in the area reserved for people with official business. From this vantage one could see the main entrance doors as well as the lobbies where the elevators let out. If you stayed there long enough, you would see pass by (a depressing thought) virtually everyone connected with the criminal justice system in New York County.

"Who're you waiting for?" asked Karp, to change the subject.

"Judge Rice. His office said he'd be coming in about now, and I hate to make an appointment to see him in chambers just for a couple of minutes."

"You've been spending a lot of time with him. What are you seeing him about now?"

"Wouldn't *you* like to know? A girl could have her little secrets," she said with a spark of her old spirit.

"He's too old for you."

"*You're* too old for me, if it comes to that. I'm obviously going to retch my way to an early grave. Maybe I should just immerse myself in young flesh for the little time that remains to me. That one's about right."

"Who, that little kid?" asked Karp, following her pointing finger with his eyes.

"Yeah, isn't he gorgeous? Why should the male perverts have all the fun?"

Marlene had indicated what appeared to be a boy of about eight or ten, walking deep in conversation with a coffee-colored man of extraordinary appearance. They were an odd couple even for this milieu. The smaller figure was dressed in a blue suit, as if for an elementary school assembly. He had that finely chiseled, preternatural beauty often obtained when the inheritance of all the human races are combined: curled fine chestnut hair, high cheekbones, large dark, almond eyes, and a flawless complexion in a permanent sun tan shade. He was slender and stood somewhat under five feet in height.

His companion, by contrast, was chocolate brown and a giant, taller than Karp by half a foot, and dressed in the panoply of the successful street dude: a suit of some rich, pale nubby material over a peacock blue silk shirt open halfway down his chest. Apartheid was obviously not one of his big causes, for he wore enough gold rings, bracelets, and chains to support the Republic of South Africa for the better part of a year.

"I know that guy," announced Karp, as the mismatched pair approached.

"Who, the kid?"

"No, the big one."

And, in fact, as the two passed by the information desk, the giant glanced at Karp, made to go by, stopped, looked Karp up and down, scowled, and then pointed at him with a finger like a center punch.

"Hey, I know you, man," he said in a deep rumble of a voice. "I played Rucker ball with you."

"Yeah," agreed Karp, "a million years ago. Matt Boudreau, isn't it?"

The big man broke a grin, showing yet more gold. "Yeah! Matt the Cat. Well, how about that! And you're, don't tell me—Butch, something . . ."

"Karp," said Karp sticking out his hand, which the other shook enthusiastically. "Man!" exclaimed

Boudreau, "we played some ball, didn't we?" To his companion he said, "Junior, this guy used to play ball with me in the Rucker League. Best white bread ball player I ever saw. Hey, Karp, this my partner, Junior Gibbs." Karp shook the tiny hand, then introduced Marlene.

Marlene looked closely at the beautiful boy when she shook hands, and realized with a start that he was not a little boy at all, but a miniature man in his late teens or early twenties.

"You still play ball, Karp?" Boudreau was asking.

"No, I got hurt in school. My knee. You?"

"Yeah, still the king of the playground. I played three years at Kentucky. I woulda gone pro, I mean, I had the moves, you know? But I had a couple of problems at school . . ." He smiled and shrugged, and Karp vaguely recalled a gambling scandal a decade past. Matt the Cat didn't seem inclined to pursue it. He said, "So what you doin' here? You a lawyer, or what?"

"A D.A."

"No shit? I'm in wholesale myself." They chattered a while about games past and what had happened to what schoolboy player. Marlene searched the crowd for Rice, while Junior Gibbs shot blazing smiles at her whenever he happened to catch her eye.

After about ten minutes of this Karp began to look pointedly at his watch. Boudreau seemed to have no pressing engagements. Karp excused himself at last, saying it was his morning for sitting in calendar courts. He did this as often as he could, to keep his subordinates honest, or rather, to keep the necessary crookedness within decent limits.

"I'm going to watch Kirsch," he said. "God help us."

"He still a problem?" asked Marlene.

"Yeah, but not for long. I hear the private sector beckons—he's getting out soon."

With that, Karp waved and stomped off, followed soon after by Matt Boudreau. Gibbs did not appear anxious to leave, in fact, seemed delighted to have Marlene all to himself.

"So you're a D.A. too, huh?" he said.

"Yes. And what do you do, Mr. Gibbs?"

"Hey, call me Junior. Oh, a little of this, a little of that. Hey, you like to dance? You ever go to clubs?"

"No, I have a wooden leg," said Marlene, looking around desperately for someone to rescue her from what experience had told her was going to be an embarrassing proposition. She found it in a slouching bearish man lugging a bulky cardboard carton toward the main doors—Peter Balducci. Marlene waved him over with enthusiasm. He rested his carton on the edge of the information counter and sighed, massaging the small of his back.

"Long time no see, Peter. You must be getting short."

"Yeah, I hand in the potsy in a few weeks."

"Good for you. What's in the box? Bribes?"

"I wish. No, it's the stuff from the trash-bag case. I left a message for you—we're transferring out of here now that the action's in Queens." He saw her expression change and he said kindly, "Don't worry, kid—we'll catch the mutt. And maybe the doll and the stuff we collected here'll do some good."

"Yeah, maybe," said Marlene doubtfully. "You got the doll in there?"

"Uh-huh." Balducci lifted the lid of the carton and hoisted up the top of Lucy Segura's Belgian doll, wrapped in a plastic bag. He chuckled. "It still knocks me out—ten, twelve grand for a doll!"

"That doll's worth twelve grand?" exclaimed Junior Gibbs, standing on tip-toe to get a better look. Balducci seemed to notice him for the first time. He frowned and said, "Hello, Junior."

"You two know each other?" asked Marlene.

"Yeah, Junior and I go back a couple of years. Still going through the transom, Junior?"

"Nah, I'm clean now, Balducci. Ask my parole officer."

"Yeah, right. You're hanging around the courthouse for old times' sake," said the detective, picking up his carton. "Marlene, don't tell this mutt where you live—he goes through keyholes. See you around." He headed for the doors.

"You're a burglar?" asked Marlene, fascinated.

"I done some," admitted Gibbs, flashing his boyish grin. "But I was younger then, you know . . ."

"How old are you now?"

"Old enough, baby, old enough. How old are *you*?"

"Too old to be standing around jiving with crooks. See you in court, Junior." She turned to go, having spotted Judge Rice coming through the main revolving door, but Gibbs tugged at her sleeve and asked, "Hey, lady, is it true about that doll being worth twelve large?"

Marlene nodded. "True. It's a collector's item. Some folks have dozens of them, and some worth more than that. It's an unfair world, Junior."

Gibbs registered innocent amazement. "No kidding. Like what folks is that?"

And now, as she looked into his greedy, perfect little face, Marlene did something she would regret profoundly later on, something she knew was wrong and stupid at the time, but which, as sick and angry and frustrated as she was then, she found irresistible.

"Folks like Mrs. Irma Dean," she said, and gave him the address.

As that afternoon wore on, Karp was sitting, with a newspaper and a miscellany of overdue paperwork, in the back of an unused jury box watching the unstately progress of Part 45 of the Supreme Court of the State of New York. The jury box was empty because Part 45 was a calendar court, today operating in Karp's favorite courtroom, the one with the mural behind the presidium —a faded allegory featuring a robed 1930's-style woman who stood, amid groves, in some uncertain relationship to two small children, a boy with a sword and a girl. It was untitled, and what it represented no one knew, although V.T. had once remarked that it ought to be called the "Spirit of Mopery." Karp thought it was a good symbol for the business transacted beneath it: obscurely comforting but essentially void of meaning.

Above the mural was another of Karp's delights, the motto that read, because of an apt crumbling of old paint, "In Go We Trust." This, in fact, captured perfectly the spirit of the calendar courts, where alacrity of process had usurped all other legal considerations.

In the cockpit of this contraption sat Judge Herbert Rice, driving it well, Karp had to admit. It was a matter of tone, Karp decided. A judge sitting in a calendar court could influence the process in a number of ways that had little to do with what was in the statute books. By being serious, by *pretending* seriously that the people had a right to justice, a judge could lend some gravity to the plea-bargaining game.

This was what Rice did; Karp could see why Marlene liked him. Right now a defense attorney was arguing that the felony charge of first-degree burglary against his client should be dropped to the misdemeanor of trespassing.

The A.D.A., who happened to be Tony Harris, was hanging tough. He pointed out that Mr. Ortiz had fourteen prior arrests, and two convictions, for which he had served a total of nine months in prison; he had been captured by the police when an alert officer had noticed during a routine traffic stop that Ortiz had an unusual amount of electronic equipment in his car, including a mammoth projection TV that occupied the entire back seat. It was a good, clean pinch and Harris was asking for three to five.

Defense counsel asked to approach the bench. Karp leaned back and turned to his newspaper. He knew what was going on off the record. The defense would argue the guy was a pillar of the community, steady job, family, and Harris would say the obvious, that he was also a pro burglar. The defense would say he hadn't hurt anyone, and Harris would come back with since when is burglary a victimless crime. With a hard-ass like Rice on the bench, the defense would offer a bullet, a guilty plea in return for a sentence to one year upstate. Karp hoped Harris would hang tough for three to five.

He did. Rice rumbled ominously and said to the defense attorney, ''Mr. Lowry, I'm the judge of what's fair in this courtroom. That's why they call me the judge. You've heard what the people have

271

offered—I'm prepared to set a trial date right away."

The defense went for the trial. Next case, although Karp knew it still might not go to trial, and the mutt might still get off with a light sentence. But it was better to be ahead in the bottom of the eighth than behind. Harris spotted Karp, waved, and came over. "How'd I do?" he asked, grinning.

"Not bad for a punk kid. You get that bug order for Nyack set up yet?"

"Yeah, it's all set up. The affidavit and the court order are on your desk. You have an appointment to see a Judge William Armand in New City tomorrow at eleven-thirty. That OK?"

Karp said it was, Harris scooted off to his next appearance, and Karp settled back for a peaceful afternoon. As he watched the parade he made notes when it was one of his staff in the A.D.A. slot, notes about personal appearance, demeanor, preparation, and whether he thought the People had been rooked.

Here was Freddie Kirsch: no problem with appearance, nice clear voice, pure class. Freddie had a string of cases in this court: hit-and-run, a manslaughter, a homicide, another homicide. It was getting late and Karp was getting dull and he might have missed it except for the defense attorney. He sat up. Henry Klopper was always fun to watch and he wondered how Freddie would do up against the legendary Chopper Hank.

Klopper was being quiet, Karp observed, which was always a sign that he was pulling a fast one. He mumbled, too. Karp caught the words "summary dismissal." He saw Rice nodding. He saw *Freddie* nodding! Something was seriously wrong.

Karp went over the rail of the jury box and was at Kirsch's side in an instant.

"What's going on here, Freddie?" he demanded.

Kirsch seemed surprised to see him and not pleasantly so. "Oh, hi, Butch. Just running through some routine calendar junk."

Judge Rice spoke up, "Mr. Kirsch, did you hear what I just said?"

"No, Your Honor, I'm sorry," said Kirsch.

"Who is this guy, Freddie?" asked Karp irritably, using the heavy whisper that counsel used in the well of the court. "Who'd he kill?"

"This is the guy they picked up for the Mullen thing in the East Village. Tighe his name is."

Karp ran through the files in his brain. A connection with Marlene, with that cop she hung around with—Lacey? Raney? He remembered it now, and when he looked down at Kirsch his eyes were angry. "This is *that* guy? Freddie, he killed a woman and a child with a fuckin' sword? What're you talking dismissals for?"

Rice tapped his gavel. "Mr. Kirsch, could we proceed? Or is Mr. Karp representing the People now?"

Karp looked up when he heard his name, and said, "I ask the court's indulgence for one moment, Your Honor. We're at cross-purposes on what the People's position is in this case."

"That's just his openers, Butch," Kirsch explained. "He'll plead to manslaughter second."

"Man two! Are you nuts? He won't do fourteen months on that shit. This guy goes for the top count if we got any case at all. Do we have a case?"

Kirsch looked down at the floor. "Yeah, I guess.

A circumstantial case. Good prints. Motive, means, opportunity."

"Then why are we throwing it?"

"Uh . . . I was just clearing my decks. You know, getting rid of the cases I had."

"Because you're leaving?"

"Yeah, I got a week to go. I figured it would be easier, more convenient, if I didn't have to explain my cases to the new guys. So I'm trying to get through them all this week."

"Give me the case file!"

Freddie handed him the heavy folder. "Freddie, you can't do this," Karp said. "This guy killed two people and you're gonna let him out on the street because it's *convenient*? You're a fucking disgrace! Be in my office first thing tomorrow with all your cases up to date. This is your last court appearance. Now get the fuck out of here!"

Kirsch turned scarlet and started packing his briefcase to go. The Judge said "Mr. Kirsch? Are the People ready at long last? Mr. Kirsch, where are you going?" Judge Rice was growing annoyed.

Karp moved toward the presidium. "Your Honor, Mr. Kirsch is no longer associated with this case. I will be taking it over as of this moment, and I'd just like to say that the People are ready to begin trial on the top count of the indictment immediately. Unless Mr. Klopper would like to plead his client to intentional murder."

"Judge, this is preposterous," began Klopper in his typical ranting tone. "I had an agreement with Mr. Kirsch . . ."

"Which is void, Your Honor, assuming it existed," said Karp pleasantly.

And there was nothing to be done, of course, and Klopper knew it, although he made a major show, for the record. Karp thought the judge seemed unduly tolerant for Not-Nice Rice, but he didn't mind because it gave him time to read the salient points of the file. The indictment was good, there were no grounds for dismissal. Rice set a trial date two weeks hence and banged his gavel with more slam than usual.

In the back of the courtroom, Jim Raney observed all this with satisfaction. Karp was good; he could see what Marlene saw in him on that end—a serious player, for sure. But a bit of a stiff, no? Not a party kind of guy. Maybe she would get bored, start looking for a piece of strange. With this relaxing thought in mind, Raney let his glance swing idly from Karp to the others at the front of the courtroom. A trim, well-dressed woman stood up and began walking up the aisle. Raney stared in surprise. What, he wondered, was Mrs. Irma Dean doing in this court?

# CHAPTER
# 13

Judge William Armand had been a judge for a long time and, if the framed and signed photographs on the walls of his office were any evidence, had spent most of his career sucking up to every politician who had ever ventured within the borders of Rockland County, New York. Karp had a lot of time to study them because Armand was fifteen minutes late, and his secretary had stashed Karp in the judge's chambers.

When Armand arrived, still in his black robes, he made no apology, but sat down in his high-backed chair and lit a cigar. He had a horse face, longish silver sideburns and an affable manner, which last he exercised on small talk for a number of minutes. After an interval, Karp brought up the subject of their meeting and the judge obligingly asked to see the affidavit setting out the underlying probable cause for the placement of a wiretap and eavesdropping devices in a certain premises in the County of Rockland.

Armand glanced at it and flicked it into a drawer in his desk. "I'll take care of it after lunch," he said genially. "Let's you and me have a bite. I always like hearing what's going on in the big town."

They ate at one of those smoky, clanking places that attract the legal establishment in county seats throughout the nation. Armand seemed to know everybody. A remarkable number of people seemed to want to say a few words into the judge's ear and shake his hand, and although no envelopes were passed, it was fairly clear to Karp what sort of judge William Armand was. Karp ate his cheeseburger moodily and wondered whether he was wasting his time.

But Armand signed the order as soon as they returned from lunch. He signed it without reading it, which didn't make Karp feel much better.

"Who's doing the job for you?" the judge asked, handing Karp the order.

"Lieutenant Corcoran's in charge of the stakeout," answered Karp uneasily, wondering why a Nyack judge wanted to learn the name of a New York City police officer. Armand nodded, smiled, they shook hands, and that was it.

Driving back to the city, Karp ignored the early fall beauty of the lower Hudson Valley, and gave short answers to the sports talk of his driver, Detective Doug Brenner. He had the feeling he was being played with. As they crossed the Spuyten Duyvil into Manhattan, Brenner said, "You want me to shut up, I'll shut up. I don't care."

"Huh?"

"I'm just saying I been talking to the steering wheel for the last half hour. What happened, you didn't get the tap order?"

"No, I got it all right," said Karp and shook his head as if to clear it. "I'm sorry—I've been thinking. This whole operation is starting to stink." He told Brenner what had happened in the judge's office.

"You think Armand is bent?" Brenner asked.

"It's a possible." Karp also had his doubts about the cops involved but he didn't mention them to Brenner. The crookedness of cops was a subject Karp avoided around Brenner. It made the time they had to spend together more pleasant.

"What are you going to do?" Brenner asked.

"I don't know," said Karp. "I'll think of something."

When Karp stepped into his office, Connie Trask waved him down and thrust a message slip at him.

"Harris wants you to call him. He said it was urgent."

"What's it about?"

"I don't know and I didn't ask. I got enough urgent today. That Woodley girl quit on us with no notice and I'm covering two jobs."

"Woodley? The skinny one with the little girl?"

"Yeah. Went back to Skunk Hollow—guess she couldn't handle the big city. I'm about to follow her." She turned away to answer a ringing phone and Karp went into his office to make his call.

The number rang a precinct in Brooklyn. Harris's voice on the phone was excited.

"They found DiBello."

"Alive, I trust."

"Alive and kicking, but not talking yet."

"OK, bring him in," Karp said. He hung up the phone and buzzed Connie on the intercom. "Get Guma," he said. "Tell him it's urgent."

An hour later, they had Carmine DiBello in an interrogation room. He proved to be a short, heavy man with a big nose and a dull expression. He sat at the table like a fire hydrant. Karp sat in a chair off to the side and doodled on a yellow pad. Guma was seated across from DiBello, asking questions, drawing blanks and getting pissed. He tried again. "Carmine, we know you saw the Scorsi hit. Noodles told us. We don't wanna get you in no trouble, understand, but we need you to talk on this. Noodles is a friend of yours, right?"

"Never heard of him."

"Yeah, right. You never worked for Jimmy Scorsi, neither. What do you do for a living, Carmine?"

"I'm in the meat business."

"Does that mean you unload reefers after they hijack them?"

Shrug.

"OK, let's try this. You heard of Vinnie Ferro, right?"

A considered pause. "Yeah, I heard of him."

"Hey, we got a 'yeah' out of this guy! Finally! Very good, Carmine. And you heard he got shot, right?"

Nod.

"And you worked, you still work, for Vinnie, right? And his brothers?"

Nod.

"So don't you think Billy Ferro and Charlie Chan would want you to put the finger on the guy who aced their brother? I'm talkin' about Joey Bottles here."

Pause. Shrug. "Nobody said nothin' to me about that."

"You know that withholding evidence in a felony is a crime?"

Shrug.

"Yeah, you know but you don't give a shit." He turned to Karp and motioned him to go outside.

In the hallway, Guma re-lit his cigar and said,

"This sucks, Butch." He tapped his temple. "First of all, we got ourselves a *scemo* in there—the guy's a couple of quarts low. There's room in his head for one idea at a time and right now it's 'keep your mouth shut.' No petty shit we can nail him on is gonna change his mind, if I can use that term.

"Second . . ." he made a short stabbing gesture. "This is not the kind of guy who goes up against Harry Pick and Joey B. alone. Harry don't like rats."

"So what do we do?"

"I said 'alone.' If the Ferros tell him to, he'll sing cantatas. Why don't we feel them out? I could set it up easy. I could. . . . You're rolling your eyes—you don't like it?"

"I hate it. Guma, we don't deal with the mob to make cases. No way."

"What're you talkin, 'deal'? It's no deal—we're just giving the Ferros a chance to be good citizens and help bring a vicious killer to justice."

"Still no. They're the bad guys, Goom. I don't buy this Godfather horseshit."

Guma seemed about to launch a new argument, but stopped himself and said, "OK, OK—if we don't do that, how about this? We keep our rocket scientist here on ice for a coupla days, get the word out he's corroborating the Noodle. That should stir things up. Maybe something'll shake out."

"Maybe. Maybe we can get the Ferro hit on the agenda the next time the Bollanos visit the castle. Of course, if it doesn't shake and we let DiBello out on the street carrying that rep, the Prudential isn't going to sell him much of a policy."

"Fuck I care! Am I his godfather?" answered Guma indignantly.

"You're a sweetheart, Goom," said Karp, grinning and shaking his head. "OK, do that, but no Ferros, Guma—I mean it."

"Got it. No Ferros," Guma replied, looking as sincere as Guma ever looked.

Karp left him at the interrogation room and walked back to his office. He put his feet on the desk, loosened his tie, and picked up the telephone. While he waited for the man he had called to come on the line, he studied the picture over his desk. It was a framed blowup of a famous World War II photograph, the charge of the white-gloved Pomorske Cavalry Brigade against German panzers in 1939. He had received it as a present from his friends when he made the Homicide Squad, back in the days when there was a Homicide Squad. It was supposed to symbolize insane courage.

Karp looked around his office and sighed. When they gave him that picture he had an office the size of an apartment bathroom. Now he had drapes and an American flag. He was a bureau chief. Authority. Responsibility. On the side of the panzers. He felt like a dull old criminal justice bureaucrat nowadays, like the man who had just answered on the other end of the line.

"Pillman, this is Karp."

A longish pause. "What do you want, Karp?" said Elmer Pillman, the Special Agent in charge of, among other things, liaison between the criminal justice agencies in the New York City area and the local apparatus of the Federal Bureau of Investigation. Pillman did not like Karp, but he owed him a big one, which was the sort of relationship

Karp liked to have with the gentlemen of the Bureau.

"Pillman, I got a deal for you."

"Just a minute, Karp, I got to lock up my wallet. What kind of deal."

"Bollano. The big guy."

"I'm listening," said Pillman.

Karp sketched out the deal, and Pillman grunted assent, then hung up without saying good-bye. Karp said, "I love you, too, Elmer," into the dead phone, and felt better than he had since he had seen Judge Armand slip the Bollano wiretap affidavit unread into his desk drawer.

Marlene normally ran in and out of the Criminal Courts Bureau office half a dozen times a day. In general, she was focused narrowly on some particular mission, so it was not surprising that she failed to notice that Dana Woodley's desk had been cleaned of personal effects: the little framed picture of her parents, and the large one of Carol Anne, and the plastic doll and the religious motto on the tiny easel were gone.

"Hey, Connie," Marlene called across the office, "what happened to Dana?"

The secretary grimaced in annoyance. "She split—no notice, no warning. Just a note on my desk. She went back to Dogpatch. Oh, yeah—she left a note for you, too." Connie rummaged in her desk drawer and handed Marlene an envelope.

Marlene opened it with a feeling of apprehension and guilt. In the past weeks she had managed to forget what had triggered her ill-fated involvement in St. Michael's. Dana hadn't said another word to her about it. The little girl had spent a couple of weeks hanging around the office, playing quietly at the foot of her mother's desk and then had started public kindergarten without incident when school opened. Marlene realized that she had been unconsciously avoiding the typist, as one avoids someone with whom one has engaged in an exploit both embarrassing and dumb.

The envelope contained a single sheet of yellow legal. The handwriting was in a round grade-school hand of surpassing neatness, saying:

> Dear Marlene:
> I am going back home I am so misable here. You have been good to me but not others. And I miss my kin. My cousin Louise wrote me they are hiring at towle plant for good pay I will try and get work there. I didnt tell you I was so shamed but Carol Anne said nothing bad happened at that place like I told you that time. She said she made up scare storys with the other little ons for play. And you went to all that troubel. I am sorry you was put out any I give her a good whiping for it. You are a fine woman and care about folks. Well thats all Im going now. Lord bless you and keep you.
>
> > Your Freind,
> > Dana P. Woodley

Marlene read this twice with mounting irritation, cursed sharply, and stamped her foot. Connie Trask looked up at her curiously. "Anything wrong?"

"No," Marlene replied bitterly, "I'm just a fine woman who cares about folks and the prize asshole of the Western World."

She called Raney first, and then Balducci, but both of them were out. She then called Judge Rice's chambers. The Judge was in and would see her in half an hour.

Marlene felt sweaty and faint. She went to the rest room, washed her face, reapplied make-up and sat down on the worn blue vinyl couch. She lit a cigarette, took two drags and crushed it out. Her hand was trembling. *I'm too nervous to smoke,* she thought—*that's a laugh.* The outer door opened and Marlene got up to go, but stopped when she saw who it was.

"Hi, Suzie."

Suzie Loser smiled at Marlene and then did a little double-take, peering intently over pink, sparkly cat's-eye glasses.

"Well, hello you," she said. "What's the matter?"

"With me? Nothing, just a little tired is all."

"Darling, don't tell Suzie nothing. You look like *dreck.* You're eating? You're killing yourself with some crazy diet?"

Marlene forced a weak smile. "I wish. I've been nauseous for a month. I can't keep anything down."

Suzie nodded and sat down on the couch next to Marlene. "You seen a doctor yet?"

"Yeah, today. He said it was nervous exhaustion. He gave me tranks."

"Which doctor, might I ask?"

"Myers, over on Pearl."

The social worker made a disgusted sound deep in her throat. "Him? They should have pulled his ticket twenty years ago. A pill hustler, you're lucky he noticed you're a girl." She looked narrowly at Marlene and asked, "He do a pelvic on you?"

Marlene caught the look. "No, he didn't. Why should he? I'm not pregnant. It's just some damn bug that won't go away."

Suzie raised an eyebrow. "You got your period?"

"Yes, I did! I mean, as sick as I am it's bound to be off. It's happened before. I missed whole months in school. I got a coil in, Suzie. I'm not pregnant."

"Darling," said Suzie gently, patting Marlene on the arm, "listen to me—see a real doctor. Come by later, I'll give you some names. And we'll talk."

Marlene was not willing for this conversation to continue to what she knew would be its natural conclusion—her blubbering her guts out on the most sympathetic shoulder in the Greater Metropolitan Area. She shot to her feet, glanced at her watch, took her leave, and trudged grimly toward Judge Rice's chambers, like a convict to the gallows. I'm going to have to resign, she thought, and the notion increased in attractiveness the nearer she got to Rice's door. The embarrassment of what she had been caught up in for the last five months made her stomach churn even more than usual.

Her stomach! *Oh, God*, she wailed inwardly, *I'm ruined! I get some kind of fucking psychosomatic nervous stomach and I holler witchcraft! What a nincompoop. I'll never be able to look V.T. in the face again, not to mention* . . . but she couldn't bear to even think about Butch, the contempt he must feel. The wedding was definitely off, until she could get her head back on an even keel and put her life in order again.

With these thoughts rattling through her brain she entered Rice's chambers and was gratified to find that his secretary had stepped out. She walked to the closed door to the inner office and listened. Hearing nothing, she knocked, heard a muffled response, and walked in.

Rice was behind his big walnut desk in shirt sleeves. He smiled when he saw her.

"Marlene! Come in! We've been talking about you."

"You have?" she said, startled, then thought "we?" and looked, and saw that in one of the two leather wing chairs before Rice's desk there sat a thin, distinguished man in black clerical garb.

"Yes, about this unfortunate business at St. Michael's you turned up," Rice went on. "Ah, I see you haven't met. Marlene Ciampi, Reverend Andrew Pinder, Pastor of St. Michael Archangel."

Marlene said, "Christ!" and then threw her hand up to her lips, as a ferocious blush rose to her cheeks.

"No," said Pinder, "but I do try." He stood and held out his hand, a good-natured smile appearing on his boyish face. He was about forty, slim, with thick sandy hair in a stylish cut and intelligent dark blue eyes.

She made herself join their laughter at this sally, and sat in the other chair when Rice invited her to. Rice said casually, "I've been wanting to get you two together for some time. This is a dreadful thing for the center—"

"That's what I came to talk to you about," Marlene broke in. "It's really embarrassing . . . but I think it all may be about nothing." She fingered Dana's note while the two men stared at her in surprise. "That woman I told you about, Judge. Woodley? She just quit her job—went back home and left me this note. It seems her kid made it all up. Or so she says." Marlene met their eyes with effort and swallowed hard. "I'm just incredibly sorry—I don't know what else to say."

The two men exchanged a quick glance and Marlene prepared herself for a tirade; instead, Rice said, "But there *was* something going on, Marlene. That's what we were just talking about. Both Andrew here and Mrs. Dean are terribly upset."

It was Marlene's turn to stare. "What do you mean?" she said, her mouth drying.

Pinder cleared his throat. "Mrs. Dean called me this morning. She said she had found evidence that suggested that one of the janitors had been abusive with some of the children on late care."

"Who is he and what's the evidence?"

"That she didn't say. She was very disturbed, as Herb said. But she did mention your name as somebody who . . . knew about the case. I thought she was rather mortified at having rejected your accusation out of hand, but you have to understand —for something like this to happen at St. Michael's —it's like finding a cockroach in your soup at Lutece."

Marlene sighed and said, "I wouldn't know, Mr. Pinder, I usually eat in the office. I guess I'm getting tired of hearing how impeccable St. Michael's is and how we have to protect its rep."

Judge Rice said reasonably, "I can see how you might feel that way, Marlene. This has put you through some kind of hell. But the thing is now to act professionally and continue the investigation. What we want is to stop this man, whoever he is, from harming more children, without destroying the best day-care center in the city and, incidentally, dragging those poor children through the courts."

"You want me to cover St. Michael's?"

Rice smiled sadly and spread his hands open on his desk.

"Just be careful, Marlene. And clever. I don't want to see you hurt either."

Was that a veiled threat? Marlene looked closely at Rice, and then over at Pinder. Their faces showed genuine concern, although whether for her personally or their own reputations she couldn't tell. She stood up, and realized she was still holding Dana Woodley's note. "What about this?" she asked, waving it. "It seems to say the opposite of what you've just found out."

Pinder shook his head sadly. "It's quite common, I'm afraid. Abused children often go into deep denial. If we could get her into some good therapy . . ."

"It's probably too late for that," Marlene said. "They've apparently gone back to the hills. Anyway —I guess the next step is to contact Mrs. Dean and get her evidence, get a line on this guy, maybe, and take it from there. That sound right?"

They both beamed. Rice said, "That sounds perfect. In fact, I know Mrs. Dean is waiting for your call." He wrote briefly on a scratch pad and handed Marlene an address and a telephone number. "You can get back to her here. It's not the Center—best to keep this whole thing isolated from there until we know more."

Marlene took the paper and after some desultory conversation, left the chambers. Returning to her own office, she called the number Rice had given her. Mrs. Dean answered herself on the second ring. She sounded anxious and made a nice apology to Marlene and hoped that she hadn't gotten in trouble. Marlene said it was all right.

Mrs. Dean asked if Marlene could come by that afternoon to the address Judge Rice had supplied. They wanted to keep this very confidential, and since she was known as an Assistant D.A. at the center. . . . Marlene resisted the temptation to say that she was coming to the Center door in a blue-and-white with sirens and a paddy wagon, said that was all right, too. End of conversation.

Marlene felt at this point that she was no longer in control of events, and was more than willing to be carried along by the preferences of others, anything to bring this miserable affair to a close. She felt almost giddy with relief and, as she gathered up her tattered brown legal envelopes and went out, she realized that for the first time in almost two months she was not nauseous. In fact, she was ravenously hungry.

Gingerly she tested her revived appetite. She thought of hot grease and spices, fried onions, pepperoni pizza, sour pickles, hot sausage sandwiches. Her stomach contracted at these imaginings, but not with revulsion. Clearing up her afternoon's work with dispatch, she repaired to Sam's Luncheonette, off Foley Square, where she ordered a double cheeseburger, fries, extra pickle, and a black-and-white ice cream soda. She ate slowly, savoring the simple, strong flavors, waiting to see if the dreaded heaves would appear.

But there was only the usual feeling of faintly guilty repletion one got after consuming a large meal of New York peasant fare. Marlene sat back in her leatherette booth and lit a cigarette and considered her most recent megrim. She seemed to be emerging from some kind of waking nightmare, in which she had believed herself to be the victim of witchcraft, a belief in which her body had concurred. There was nothing wrong with her physically, so she must have been crazy.

On the other hand, she had known something was going on at St. Michael's and that was now confirmed. That wasn't crazy, although, of course, no one had mentioned the tie-in with the trash-bag killings, and she had been too bowled over by Rice's information to bring it up. She wished Raney was available.

Or Karp. Funny how she pulled back from him in her mind when she thought she was really going nuts. Karp and the Job: a connection, and a negative one. She could finally admit it: she couldn't stand working for him. It screwed up both her love life and her work life without any compensating benefit. OK, that had to change. Transfer to another bureau or resign completely? Too big a decision to make just yet, and what would she do if she quit? Practice criminal law? It was to vomit.

She got up, paid her bill, and walked back to the Criminal Courts building. It was shaping up to be a fine autumn afternoon, the air miraculously clear and slightly damp, a reminder to the huddled masses that their grim city was still located by the sea. Marlene's head was clearing up too. She skipped back to her office. She began to look for the files she had kept on the St. Michael's and trash-bag killings case.

Filing was not Marlene's major strength. Despite her lack of storage space, she could never bear to throw anything away. She had high ceilings, however, and had used this space to build a ziggurat of cardboard boxes on top of her sole bookcase. She put a straight chair on her desk, arranged several thick law books on its seat, and clambered up on this makeshift ladder.

As she rummaged through the papers in the cartons she became aware of another presence in the small room. Looking down, she saw Guma standing by her desk, positioned for the best view up her dress.

"Guma! What are you doing here?"

"Just passing through. The word is you don't wear any pants on Tuesdays. I thought I'd check it out."

"It's Wednesdays," said Marlene. "Here, you can help. Catch this!" She tossed a heavy carton down to him and then climbed down herself. She pawed through the papers in the box and pulled the one she wanted out with a yell of triumph.

"What'd you find?" asked Guma.

"The stuff on St. Michael's and the trash-bag murders."

"I thought that was dead."

"Not any more it ain't. The lady who runs the place has summoned the kid here for a discreet confession. Which I have a feeling is a prelude to a whitewash. The janitor, my ass!"

"What are you talking about, Champ?"

Marlene briefly explained the events of the last half hour and what she made of them.

Guma said, "So you still think they're running a kiddy whorehouse?"

"I know it. Shit, I wish I could reach Raney—anyway, I got to go now. I'll take this with me or it'll get lost again. Wish me luck!"

"*In bocca 'l lupo, paisan*," said Guma cheerfully, at which, to his great surprise she grabbed his head, kissed him soundly on the mouth, and ran out.

"Hey, Marlene," he called after her. "More tongue action next time."

Her excitement building, Marlene ran to the Bureau office to look for Karp. She was seized by the need to talk to him, to get close to him again. But Karp was out, somewhere with the cops. Did she want to reach him? She declined—she didn't want to talk to him by phone, or worse, over the police radio. She scribbled a note—"Off to St. Michael's—don't worry, all coming up roses. See you tonite." She left it on his desk and departed for the appointment with Mrs. Dean.

I'll cook a meal, she thought, as she rode uptown on the IRT. I haven't cooked for us in months. I'll make minestrone soup from scratch, and a big lasagna with four kinds of cheese and sweet sausages. And a good bottle of something. And I'll stop off at Zabar's while I'm uptown and get bagels and lox and smoked whitefish. We'll have a balanced ethnic weekend, and talk about being married and what I'm going to do with my life. Our life. And then I'll see if I can sweet-talk my way into getting laid.

The address Mrs. Dean had given her was on West End Avenue off Seventy-eighth Street. It was a reddish townhouse with large bay windows stuck between two condo-ized towers, the kind of building that was usually broken up into apartments in this neighborhood. It had the usual broad stone stairway leading to the front door, but Dean had told her to ring at the wrought iron gate under these stairs. She did, received an answering buzz that released the gate's lock, and rang the bell belonging to the door of the ground floor apartment.

Mrs. Dean herself opened the door for her. *She*

*looks older*, was Marlene's first thought as she shook hands with the woman. Mrs. Dean was dressed in a wide-skirted black dress with a small white collar: the return of the nun. She gave Marlene a cold, formal smile and ushered her through a long ocher-painted hallway dimly lit by sconces made to resemble candelabra and into the living room.

This proved to be a large dark room furnished in the style of the high-bourgeois West Side—good Duncan Phyfe sofa and wing chairs in pale striped silk, flanking a mahogany coffee table, heavy brocade drapes on the windows, oriental rugs over beige carpets and, on spindly dark side tables, large ceramic statuary lamps with pale silk shades, the lamps in the shape of classical lovers or funerary urns. There were tea things on the coffee table.

"Please sit down, Miss Ciampi," said Mrs. Dean, motioning to a love seat in pale green silk, and seating herself in a wing chair on the other side of the low table. "I thought we could have some tea while we talk." She poured for herself and Marlene and then sat back and looked steadily at her, as if waiting for her to begin something. The apartment was very quiet; the heavy drapes muffled the street sounds. Somewhere a mechanical clock ticked.

Mrs. Dean seemed to be making an effort to be pleasant. It was a lovely day. This was a nice room. Marlene drank her tea and waited for the older woman to get to the point. When this failed to happen, Marlene took a yellow pad and a pen out of her briefcase and said, "Mrs. Dean, why don't we start with this man you've identified. What's his name?"

Mrs. Dean seemed not to hear this question.

Instead she glanced around the room, and said, "I've always meant to redecorate this place. It was my late husband's apartment before we were married. My second husband. But we never seem to have time—my work keeps me so occupied."

She looked back at Marlene, who felt obliged to say conversationally, "Yes, running the center must be a big responsibility."

"Oh, not the center. My real work. As you very well understand."

Marlene shook her head slightly in confusion and smiled. "I'm sorry . . . ?"

Mrs. Dean went on, oblivious: "You're very subtle, but very powerful. That's what put me off; I ought to trust my vibrations always. I couldn't imagine you would strike directly at *Him*."

"Mrs. Dean, I'm getting lost here. What are you *talking* about?"

"Of course, when you sent your agents against me I had to act. You'll be saddened to learn that the little fool got the wrong doll."

Marlene felt a flush start across her face. She had forgotten about Junior Gibbs. Was it possible that he had burgled the Dean place, been caught, and ratted her out? She gave herself some good legal advice and kept her mouth shut. Mrs. Dean stood up abruptly and began pacing back and forth in an agitated manner. "No," she continued, "you were clever, but not clever enough, my dear. One of the few advantages of age, I think, in our profession."

She's flipped out, thought Marlene. Completely loony tunes. This was certainly a new wrinkle on the case, and Marlene was content to sit back and let the lady rave on. In fact, except that her feet were quite cold, she felt remarkably comfortable just sitting and listening and drinking tea, as at a childhood visit to an aging aunt not quite right in the head, but harmless.

What was she talking about now? Something about her marriage to the Prince of Darkness and the Son of the Dark Union. Actually, her feet were *very* cold, almost numb. There must be air conditioning on, which was crazy, it was such a nice fall day outside.

"All for Him," Mrs. Dean was saying, "as was foretold—first the rituals, then the blood, then He shall come into His power and rule in the name of Lucifer all the kingdoms. And woe to any servant of the powers of earth who does not bend her knee in homage."

"I'm going, Mrs. Dean," said Marlene, reaching for her briefcase. "I hate to say this, but you need psyo . . . phys . . . psychological help." That was odd—she seemed to have trouble talking. Her briefcase was impossibly far away, Marlene thought. Why did I put it way over there? She had to get out of this cold, too. It had crept up to her thighs; her calves and feet felt like frozen meat. Mrs. Dean kept talking and her voice seemed to be getting louder, even though she seemed much farther away.

"Yes, I knew that he was one of the Powers of the Earth the minute I laid eyes on him. And he in turn knew me for an adept. I was seventeen, and he took me away from that stifling little town that very night, and we rode through the stars together. There was never such a love. He blazed with an immortal fury and we did things that had not been thought of since Egypt was new.

"He crushed our enemies with his power and then . . . until . . . he said I must leave you for a while, leave this sphere, I am called by our Father below, but I leave you a babe who shall be greater than I, the greatest the ages have known. I shall live again in him, and you shall live forever with me in him.

"In Him. Who you have profaned, and chained. But great workings are under way, never fear. I know your power and I know how to stop it. Now listen to your fate. In ten days it will be the full moon. I will take you out and place you on naked earth, and pierce your heart with a sword of iron. I will eat your heart on a table made of a sacrifice, a child without blemish. In ten days, your power will flow into me and He will be released."

I've been drugged, Marlene was thinking as this went on. One part of her mind accepted this while another part was screaming in terror like a rat in a slowly contracting cage. Mrs. Dean sat down across from her and patted her on the cheek. Marlene's face felt enormous under her touch, as it did at the dentist's.

"That's right, relax," said Mrs. Dean. "We find it works so well with the children. Of course, we give them a lower dose, so that they'll wiggle a little for the uncles. Money for the cause, money for the cause.

"Yes, it was my second husband who taught me about that. His tastes ran that way. Not that I minded. After all, I was wedded for eternity to my Francis. No mere earthly bond could interfere with that. And he was so rich. Francis would not have wanted me and the boy to be degraded by poverty.

"Of course, he wanted a son of his own. I told him that my womb had been enobled by carrying the Son of the Son of the Morning, but he would not listen, being a crass man of money and a creature of no spirit.

"In the end, I bore him a son, of a kind, one that would be but a foot-stool to Him, the firstborn one. And then he died for his impertinence. Mr. Dean, I mean. And the son never grew; I had to keep him at home with me, although I said that he was in an institution. But he is useful for some of our work. Very useful. Our services make a nice exhibition for the children. They never tell." Mrs. Dean giggled.

Marlene heard the door open, but she couldn't turn her head to see who it was. She heard heavy steps approaching. Mrs. Dean said, "I don't believe you've met my younger son. This is Alonso."

"Pleased to meet you," said the Bogeyman, sweeping Marlene up off the sofa and into his thick arms, like a child.

# CHAPTER
# 14

**K**arp burst into the Bureau office, moving fast,
slamming the door, the wind of his passage lifting
papers from nearby desks. People moved to get
out of his way. They expected no recognition nor
did they receive any. While he did not actually
run anybody down, he would have. Passing by
Connie Trask's desk, he said, "Anything?" She
shook her head sadly and he cursed under his
breath and plunged toward his private office. This
had been going on for three days.

Ray Guma and Tony Harris were waiting for
him within, sitting at the scarred oak conference
table. The table was littered with newspapers,
tabloid and respectable, all turned to the same
story, which was, as one of the tabloids had
unfelicitously headlined it: LADY D.A. IN MOB
SNATCH.

Guma picked up the tabloid and tossed it contemptuously down again. "This is such bullshit,
Butch. Mob snatch, my ass!"

"Not now, Ray" said Karp.

"Kidnapping a D.A. is not a wise-guy trick,
Butch. *You* know that! The call we got is a scam,
Butch. 'Lay off the Bollanos or else!' It's from the

movies, for cryin' out loud! These aren't crazy Colombians, Jamaicans, who knows what—we're talking respectable middle-class gangsters here."

"They're still gangsters. I'm not saying Bollano ordered it. It could be some punk out to make a rep. It could be some asshole off the boat from Palermo. They shoot *judges* in Sicily—maybe he figures a D.A. is fair game."

"Butch, I talked to Marlene before she left. I was probably one of the last people in the office to see her. She was talking about a break on this child abuse thing she's been hot on, the one she says is hooked into the trash-bag killer. Isn't it more reasonable—"

"There's nothing there, Ray. I've been over it with Marlene. And it's not our case."

"Our case, horseshit! Did you check it out?"

"Yeah, as a matter of fact, I did. I got a judge and a minister saying she was en route to the child-care center to look into what appeared to be a minor case of kiddie diddling. She never got there."

"How do you know that?"

"Because it turns out that Jimmy Raney has had this mutt watching the center on and off for weeks under the obviously mistaken impression that the center is tied in with these trash-bag murders, and the mutt says she never showed up on the afternoon we're talking about. What the fuck is this, Guma? You cross-examining me to see if I'm trying hard enough to find Marlene? Fuck you!"

The color had risen to Karp's face, an unusual and threatening sign. Guma flung out his hand in a gesture connoting extreme frustration and looked pointedly up at the ceiling, but said nothing more.

After a moment, Tony Harris entered the uncomfortable silence. "Butch, on this Ferro killing thing for the grand jury: I'm missing something. You're calling all the guys Noodles said were in Nyack the morning after, right?"

"That's right," said Karp. "They were all at the castle too."

"But the castle was a bust. We got nothing," Harris complained.

"So it appears."

"Then why are we going ahead with these?" asked Harris, irritably smacking the sheaf of subpoenas down on the table. "In fact, why did we stage that raid anyway? You had Armand spotted for a crook weeks ago. So he tipped Bollano, we know that. The bugs were all disconnected, nobody said anything on the phone. They have a meeting anyway, the cops are there snapping away, and it turns out the cops can't quite get anything that's in focus enough to identify anybody, nor are any of them willing to swear they recognized any of the participants. Maybe they're all on the wire, too."

"It's possible," said Karp abstractedly.

"So what I want to know is, what are you gonna ask them that's gonna do us any good?" Harris asked, observing his boss with dismay. He's losing it, thought Harris, as he observed Karp's slumped affect: exhaustion and boredom mixed. This thing with Marlene has taken the edge right off him. For his part, Harris felt abandoned and resentful, especially after what had happened with the great raid on the Mafia castle. Karp regarded the younger man wearily and said, "We're just going to ask them if they were there, what they talked about, like that."

"But what good will *that* do. It's no crime to

have a meeting, especially if we have no evidence there was conspiracy taking place."

"It's a crime if they lie about it," answered Karp. "All grand jury witnesses have transactional immunity. If they lie we can get them on perjury."

Harris's irritation grew and his voice got louder. "But Butch—they don't have to lie! They *know* we got nothing."

"They'll lie," said Karp with assurance. He looked sharply at Guma. "They'll lie because they're mutts and they think they can get away with it."

"Relax, kid," said Guma, "he's got a ringer."

Harris stared. "What do you mean 'ringer'? What's he talking about, Butch?"

Karp said neutrally, "I did a deal with the Feds. There were two FBI agents planted as electrical linemen on the road outside the castle. They had cameras and a parabolic mike set up. They can ID everybody there and testify about a lot of the conversation at the meeting."

"No kidding!" said Harris, hurt feelings and admiration warring in his tone. "That's great, Butch, but it would have been nice to tell me about it, considering I'm putting together all this grand jury stuff."

"Sorry, Tony," Karp said in a mollifying tone. "I'm devious. It comes with the job."

Harris stood and gathered his papers. "Yeah, well, I guess I should contact the Bureau and set up their testimony. Oh, by the way, any word on Marlene?"

"No, not yet," Karp said quickly. "Go direct to Pillman on that, Tony. We're keeping the whole thing kind of close."

Harris left and Guma started chuckling as soon as the door had closed. Karp snapped, "What's so funny, Guma?"

"You. Him. 'Devious.' I love the way you come on like somebody who's totally out front, and all the time the wheels and deals are turning around. I'm glad you finally admitted it. It's good training for the kid there and an inspiration to your loyal staff. Personally, I intend to take it to heart."

Karp shot him a lowering glance. "Don't be cute, Guma."

"Who, me?" said Guma, goggling his eyes like Little Orphan Annie. "Never happens. And by the way, not to change the subject, but how did it go in court today? The Mullen murders."

"Not bad. The general can still use a bayonet. Klopper is a pain in the ass, of course: His way of insinuating that his client and him are being crushed by the awesome power of the state. And the bastard wears you down with a shitload of objections he knows are going to be overruled. It's exhausting, it confuses the witnesses and the jury. . . . I don't know though, I got a feeling it's going to backfire with Montana."

"Yeah, I always thought Judge Montana was a stand-up, no bullshit guy."

"I'm counting on it. Anyway, today I had the engineer in, Shannon, to establish the shape of the apartments and the whole crime scene. That's critical, because we're going to be talking about two incidents in the same hallway—the murder itself and the business with Tighe beating his girlfriend—also the thumbprint that ties our guy to the scene is out in the hall, on the doorway. And Tighe threatens the victim in the hearing of two cops out in the hall. So I want the jury to be as comfortable in that hallway as they are in their own hallway.

"Then the first cop on the scene, Dienst. Big

guy, good witness. Describes the horror scene, the little boy in the bloody apartment."

"You gonna call the kid?"

"I could, but he's out of town with the dad. I got some scruples about dragging him through it again, you'll probably be surprised to know. *I* was surprised. No, I'll deliver a statement, which the defense will stipulate to. If not, I will call the kid and after he testifies they'll lynch the fucker right there in the courtroom. Which Klopper knows, of course."

"And the girlfriend . . . ?"

"The girlfriend, yeah—great witness," Karp said enthusiastically. Guma noticed with satisfaction that the worn look he had seen on Karp's face earlier was fading in the enthusiasm of retelling the events and strategy concerning the trial of Felix Tighe.

"Rivas, her name is. We established he beat her and she screamed and the deceased called the cops. He broke her place up too, the girlfriend's, with karate blows, suggesting he was not averse to busting things up, like breaking down the door to the victim's place. We established that the chain lock was ripped out of the wall by great force.

"She also testified that the day of the murder, this scumbag meets her after work and tells her that he's going to quote take care of the victim, that she'll read about it in the papers—that's a quote too—and that he's got an alibi, so she quote shouldn't worry about him.

"Also, he forces her, by threat of violence, to accompany him down to the building where the murder took place. He tells her he has quote unfinished business in the building. In the cab, they're jostled toward one another by a pothole, and she reaches out and touches something hard stuck in his belt."

"What, this is the day of the murder?"

"Yeah."

"And he shows her the knife?"

"Not that good, but almost. He tells her quote he's got something, he's carrying something. She didn't see the blade but we can show he's a knife artist."

"What, from priors?"

"Yeah, a good one. A year ago in Queens he got stopped on a burglary and he ripped the cop up pretty bad with a big knife."

"Last year? You mean he walked on the attempted murder?"

"Skipped. Convicted *in absentia* and they lost the damn wanted card."

Guma whistled and shook his head. "Sonofabitch! So how're you gonna bring it out?"

"Cross on the accused."

"Klopper's gonna *call* this sweetheart?" asked Guma in amazement.

"He's got to, to try and impeach the girl's testimony and explain the thumbprint. Also, this fucker is not a shaved head with five o'clock shadow and a mean scar—the guy looks like a prince, a movie star. He'll be a good witness—articulate, clever. Confusing. I used all my challenges to get an all male jury."

"So you think you got it locked?"

"I never think that until the guy stands up and says 'guilty, Your Honor.' But yeah, it looks good unless they fuck with my evidence. The girl and the print you could explain away: woman scorned, she's a slut anyway, the accused hung around the place, his prints are here and there.

"But we go to his room and find a knife that could be the murder weapon *and* a diary that says 'fix big mouth,' *and* a pair of pants soaked in blood, the same type as the victims', *and* newspaper clippings of the crime . . . and now it looks a helluva lot better. And I got to say, little Freddie Kirsch did a good job on the Q and A and the Grand Jury testimony. Everything we need was brought out there."

"How could they fuck with it, Butch?"

"A million ways," said Karp grimly. "And Klopper knows them all. I don't like this guy Lutz, Tighe's roomie, for one thing. He testified on the evidence before the Grand Jury, but who knows? He's sort of a skell himself."

Guma smiled as Karp continued his comment on the case: What he would do if they did *that*, what if they did *this*, how he would sum it up, together with commentary on law and precedents. Nothing juiced Karp up like a trial, and winning it would put him in as good a mood as he could achieve while his loved one was in the evil clutches of whomever. And Guma needed Karp in a good mood, since he was about to do something that, had Karp known of it, would have put Karp in a very bad mood indeed.

An hour later Guma was in his car, a black '57 Mercury junker, its paint iridescent with age, tooling along the Belt Parkway in Brooklyn. He drove to Cropsey Avenue and Bay 14th Street in Bath Beach and parked behind an immaculate white stretch Cadillac with dark glass windows.

A young man with sunglasses and a good tan, dressed in clothes a little too tropical for the season in New York, stood at the rear door. He nodded at Guma and threw open the door of the white limo for him. Guma climbed in and sank back into cream leather soft as thighs.

"Guma! *Cosa dic'*?" said the man in the back seat, a broad and gold-glittering smile splitting his deeply tanned face.

"*Lo squal' incula il pe'c'*," replied Guma. "You're looking well, Anthony." The two men shook hands with warmth and enthusiasm.

"Drive," said the tan man softly. The engine purred into life, the young man in the tropical clothes leaped into the front seat and Guma and his friend Anthony Buonofacci cruised out into the littered streets of their shared boyhood.

"You should get some more sun, Goom," said Buonofacci. "You look like a mozzarella. When you gonna come down to Miami, anyway, huh? I told you, I'll set you up good—plenty for a legal eagle to do down there. What d'you say?"

This was a ritual. For almost twenty years Tony Bones had been trying to get Ray Guma to work for him, and Guma had always refused. Guma was comfortable with Tony as a friend; he would not have lasted five minutes as his lawyer.

They chatted about old times for half an hour, as the big limo went past the landmarks of their misspent youth—the parochial school, the canals, the warehouses, the bars, the grungy shoreline of Bath Beach. Tony poured a couple of scotches from the built-in bar.

"What a shithole, when you get right down to it," he said gesturing toward the streets. "The old neighborhood! My mother won't move, can you believe it? I got a condo for her, on the beach— she won't move." He struck himself on the head with the heel of his hand. "*Testard*'! Like a rock, huh?" He sipped his drink, put it down, slapped his knee and said, "So, tell me, you said you had to talk to me, so talk. What can I do for you?"

Guma pulled from his pocket a newspaper article roughly torn from the *Daily News* and gave it to his companion. It showed a small picture of Marlene Ciampi and the story of her disappearance.

"She's a friend of mine, a D.A. Somebody grabbed her a couple of days ago and we got a call from somebody who said he was from the families. My *padrone*, Karp, this is his girlfriend. He's got a squeeze going on Sallie Bollano, Harry, all of that outfit. He figures they snatched Marlene to get him to lay off."

"That's horseshit," said Tony Bones.

"You think I didn't tell him? He don't listen, he gets an idea in his head, all he wants to do is run right up the middle. Like your Mama. But the main thing is to find the girl."

"Yeah. A cute little thing, by the way. Who grabbed her, you think?"

"She was on to somebody she thinks was selling hairless pussy on a major scale out of a fancy day-care operation. She was on her way to talk to the boss of the place when she disappeared."

"And the cops . . . ?"

"The cops think what Karp thinks—it was a family thing. Also, this bitch who runs this joint—she's got some kind of heavy juice downtown. Nobody's going to roust her unless we can get some edge on the whole business."

Tony Bones chewed his lip for a moment and studied the traffic. Then he said, "So, what do you want me to do? I got no organization up here, but if it was a pro job, I could ask around . . ."

"No—I need you to set up a meet."

"Yeah? With who, Big Sallie and them?"

"Right, with them, and another with the Ferros."

"The Ferros? Well, well. You know, I used to be pretty tight with Charlie Chan."

"I remember. That's why I thought of you, and when I heard you were in town again. . . ."

"This squeeze that your guy got on Sally—it have something to do with Vinnie Red?"

"Yeah, we got them, the whole family, the don, the kid, Charlie Tuna, Joey. We have the wheelman and a corroborating witness. We got a conspiracy charge, too—tapes, pictures. The Bollanos are finished."

The other man whistled softly through his teeth. "Very interesting. So what's the deal—if you got 'em, why meet?"

"I want them to help us find Ciampi."

"Uh-huh. Also interesting. So tell me: one, what makes you think they can help; two, what you gonna give them if they do?"

Guma took a deep breath. "They can help because nobody sells ass in New York, of any kind, without some kind of cover from the families. So we need names, a feel for who's buying, who's selling—the whole setup. If I get some help from the Bollanos, I can probably swing it the don doesn't have to go up. He's over seventy, it must be—he doesn't want to spend his golden years in Attica."

"And where do the Ferros come in?"

"They're interested in fucking the Bollanos because of Vinnie, but they don't have the muscle for a serious war, not to mention that with Vinnie gone they lost half their brains and ninety per cent of their balls."

"Yeah, yeah, but where do they come in . . . ?"

"The corroborating witness is one of their guys."

Tony Bones thought about this for a few seconds, and then his face broke into a wide grin, and he began to laugh, an almost soundless aspiration that could, Guma thought, be terrifying under the right conditions. The spasm over, Tony wiped his eyes with a handkerchief and said, "What a pisser you are, *paisan*! Are you ever on the wrong side—what a waste!"

"So you gonna set it up?"

"Are you kidding? I wouldn't miss it. You're gonna get the Ferros to set up your case on the Bollanos, and then you're gonna walk the don. How about Harry? He gonna walk, too?"

"Come on, Tony, you gotta leave me some room here."

"OK, kid—I'll set it up. But I tell you—like my Mama says, *'Non fa' il passo lungo della gamb.'* "

"Thanks, Tony," said Guma, surreptitiously wiping the accumulated sweat from his upper lip. Later, in his own car on his way back to Manhattan, he reviewed the bidding. He had told Tony he had a corroborative witness to the Ferro killing. That was a lie. They had DiBello, who could corroborate Noodles's testimony and tie Joey Bottles to another killing, which they didn't have a body for. But if the Bollanos and Harry believed they were nailed they would move heaven and earth to find Marlene. And they *would* believe it if they found the Ferros were allowing one of their people to rat. Which they would find out, if Guma had anything to do with it.

Getting the Bollanos off on the murder rap for doing this service was easy, since without a real corroborative witness there *was* no case. The problem was getting the don off on the perjury charge Karp had set up. He had told Tony Bones that the don would walk. As far as the fabrication about the witness was concerned, no big thing: Tony wouldn't mind a little lie from an old friend, and Guma could always plead a misunderstanding.

And Tony would certainly make out handsomely from the information about the incipient fall of the Bollano family; he was probably making calls and selling the information at this moment. But if old Salvatore Bollano went to jail, his reputation as a dealer and a don in his own right would be hopelessly compromised, and this he would not forgive even an old friend. *Lo squal' incula il pe'c'.* Guma knew who the shark was and who was the sardine and who would get fucked if this didn't fly.

Guma got off the highway at Third Avenue and swung left through the streets of South Brooklyn and into Red Hook. He found a saloon rotting in the shadow of the Brooklyn-Queens Expressway, went in and ordered a scotch up and a beer. This was deep Ferro country. Vinnie Red had shot his first man, the first that Guma knew of anyway, within three blocks of this place, up on President Street.

While he waited for the booze to supply him with ideas, he wondered idly why he was risking his skin to save a woman who had never given him the time of day, except for that last conversation before she vanished. It had to do with Karp. Karp was barely human to begin with, in Guma's opinion, but at least if he got enough nooky he was willing to make an effort. Guma thought about the Karp of the last three days being projected into the indefinite future and shuddered.

No, he was doing the right thing. Somehow he had to extricate Big Sally from the net that Karp was tightening, which meant that, like a search and destroy mission in Vietnam, he had to shaft Karp in order to save him. He finished his drink. Yes, he thought, it could be done, although Mrs. Buonofacci would probably have bet that he had indeed stepped longer than his leg.

Steve Lutz awoke with a start and the knowledge that there was somebody else in his bedroom, somebody who didn't belong there, somebody silent and very large. This person sat in a straight chair by the window that gave on the street. Lutz could estimate his size from the silhouette made by the street light, and he could also see that there was something wrong with the man's head, some subtle misshapenness that added immeasurably to the horror of the moment.

Lutz lay frozen with fear, sweating, his heart thumping loud enough to be audible in the room. He hoped the man was a bum who had wandered in looking for a crash. But how had he penetrated the locks on the front door? He was just about to see if he could make a dash for the bedroom door when the phone rang.

Lutz let it ring three times. When the figure at the window remained still, he grabbed it from where it lay on the floor next to his bed and held it to his ear.

"Steve Lutz?" asked a soft voice.

Lutz croaked an affirmative. His throat felt full of chalk.

"You're going to be a witness tomorrow at the trial of Felix Tighe, aren't you?"

"Yeah. Who is this?"

"A friend. Listen. The police are trying to frame Felix for that murder. They invented all that evidence they found in your place."

"Yeah? How did they get it in there, in Felix's bag then? And them pants with the blood is Felix's pants—I seen them on him lots a times."

"They are very clever. But it is all a fabric of lies. This is why you must tell them, tomorrow, that the knives and the pants they will show you are not the knives and the pants that you saw in the apartment when the police were there."

"Wait a minute, who *is* this? What is this shit, you want me to lie to the D.A., in court? I already told them a million times it was the same stuff—they'll break my chops."

Lutz was aware of a movement by the window. The figure had risen and had taken a step toward the bed. The voice on the phone continued. "Steve, don't be foolish. There are things involved here, great events, that you cannot understand. The order of the universe requires that Felix Tighe walk free. If you help, you will be rewarded; if you refuse . . . do you see the person in your room?"

"Yeah," said Lutz, caught between wishing there was some light on the creature's face and being glad of the dark. "Yeah, I see him."

"He came into your room tonight. Locks cannot stop him. Walls cannot stop him. He is very powerful. And very skillful. Did you ever have a broken leg, or a broken finger? He could break all your fingers and your arms and your legs, with his hands. Can you imagine what that would feel like?"

Lutz said nothing, his exiguous mental powers being entirely occupied with the suggested image. The voice on the phone told him to hand the receiver to the man in the room. The huge shape lifted the instrument to its head for an instant, then threw it to the bed, turned, and walked out of the room, making remarkably little noise for one so large. Lutz heard the outer door close. After a breathless minute, he ran to it, to lock it again, and was astounded to find it already locked.

The worst thing for Marlene was that she had stopped being able to tell dreams from reality. There were moments when she opened her eyes and seemed to see clearly where she was. There was a concrete ceiling a few feet above her head, some chemical stink in the air, the scrape of rough canvas against her back. Her arms and legs were immobilized and there was tape across her mouth. She was naked, covered with a wool blanket. And she remembered who had put her there.

But then that clear vision would switch off, as if someone had changed the channel on her interior Sony, and the scene would be replaced by phantasmagoria. Candles, the smell of burning wax, the smell of blood, she was floating through the air, many hands were stroking her, thick substances were being smeared on her face, on her breasts, first hot then chilled and sticky. There were chants and colored vapors. A beast with horns was standing over her. She could feel his hot breath. His tongue shot out, impossibly long, and licked her face. He had blue eyes like steel knives.

The Bogeyman was there too. The moon-shaped face was her one constant, in the nightmare, in the stone room, hovering over hers, a gentle smile on the too-small budlike pink mouth, the hair, almost white, soft as candy-floss against her body as he lifted her, the mild eyes blinking behind thick yellow caterpillar lashes. He helped her go to the toilet, he fed her soup and juice. And she ate, knowing there were drugs in the food, but unable to formulate even the thought of resisting.

And he talked to her. He told her long, rambling stories in a soft voice, with the inflection and vocabulary of a six-year-old. What did he talk about? Dreams. The petty injustices and triumphs of childhood, the kind of babble told to a stuffed animal in the night. And she would listen, saying nothing, because if you're dreaming, what's the point? It will all be explained in the dream, or else it won't and you wake up with that curious feeling of having mislaid something important but nameless.

Until one time, when the drugs had reached the low point of their cycle in her body, when he had removed the tape across her mouth, and had propped her up with pillows, and had held a plastic cup of apple juice to her lips, his motions so practiced, he so obviously kind and willing to oblige, an idea had penetrated at last through the fog.

He's done this before, she thought. This is how he did the trash-bag children. Suddenly she remembered Lucy Segura and from somewhere there flooded into her a fierce will to live, to not end her being in a trash bag in a green dumpster. Segura— there was something else, something Raney had said about Lucy and the Bogeyman. She twisted her mouth away from the cup. "I don't want that any more," she said petulantly, keeping her voice high. "I want a cheeseburger and french fries and a Coke."

He smiled tentatively, then shook his head firmly. "I'm not spose to. I'm spose to give you kitchen stuff, from the kitchen. Mommy said."

"Yes you can," said Marlene. "You did for Lucy. You got *her* a cheeseburger and a Coke. It's not fair."

He thought about this for a minute, chewing his lip. "OK, I guess. I could get a cheeseburger too."

"Yes, you could," said Marlene, tears of relief burning in her eyes. "We could eat our cheeseburgers together and, and if you leave my mouth open I could tell you a nice story."

"Like on TV?"

"Better. Why don't you go now? I'm really hungry."

He rose and he seemed to fill the whole space of the alcove in which she lay. He turned to go and then suddenly whirled on her, his fists clenched and his face crumpled into a dreadful scowl. Marlene's heart jammed itself into her gullet.

"But, but," he stammered, "no dolls!"

Marlene let out her breath. "That's fine," she said weakly. "I have plenty of dolls."

# CHAPTER
# 15

Groggy and stupid from lack of sleep, Karp staggered into his shower and let the scalding water beat against his head. He emerged cleaner but hardly refreshed, brushed his teeth, ate the last two Extra-Strength Excedrin in the bottle on the sink, and flung the empty, rattling, into the tin wastebasket. Two points.

Karp had spent the night in his own apartment, a one-bedroom unit in an old building on Sixth in the Village, as he had since Marlene had disappeared. At Marlene's loft he had arranged with neighbors to feed the cats and water the plants. He was not going to stay there, surrounded by her things and the memory of her.

In his own place there was nothing but a bed, an antique rowing machine, a black-and-white portable TV and Karp. The rest of the space was occupied by dust bunnies and Karp's immense misery.

He let a guilty glance fall on the rowing machine. There did not seem any point in exercising any more. Or eating. Or sleeping. Work still had a point, but even that was going. Karp had heard of sea captains' wives in the old days of sail who had been visited by a dire premonition of death at what later had proven to be the very moment that their spouses' vessels had gone under. He felt that way about Marlene. There was in his head and body an empty space that had been filled with the hum of her being. He had scarcely noticed it then (more guilt!) but now it was a felt void, as when the electric power goes off in the daytime and all the little forgotten motors stop.

He dressed in one of his three identical blue pin-striped suits. One of the trio was at the cleaners, the other on the closet floor waiting to be dropped off. For murder trials Karp always appeared in a freshly pressed suit each day.

Karp usually walked the mile or so to the criminal courts. He liked the exercise, while the filth and disorder of the subways depressed him. Today he found he lacked the energy and doubted that the subway could drive him any lower than he now was. He took the D train and arrived in time to spend an hour and a half re-reading the case file on *People v. Tighe*.

It was a good case, a classic circumstantial web, motive, means, and opportunity woven together by that colossal criminal arrogance, that sense of invulnerability without which the forces of justice would be in even worse shape than they are. He kept the *knife*! He wrote it down in his *appointment book*!

Yes, a good case, *People v. Tighe*, except that to Karp, as always, it was *Karp v. Tighe*. It was his dirty secret. You weren't supposed to get your personal feelings mixed up in the austere and objective majesty of the judicial process. Karp had said that himself to babies out of law school, without a blush, but to Karp, in a trial, it was *all* personal, every time.

There was a knock on his door and Peter Balducci stuck his head in. Karp was struck by another pang of guilt as he remembered Marlene, and realized that he had been able to entirely forget her when immersed in the trial. But of course, Balducci was part of the trial, too, as well as being involved in the kidnapping investigation.

"Anything new?" Karp asked.

"Not yet, that I heard of. It could be somebody's got something, though. Shaughnessy's got me inside cleaning ashtrays. It's my last week. He figures I won't have my mind on my work. So maybe . . ."

"Yeah."

"We'll find her."

"Yeah," said Karp again, without conviction. He picked up a sheaf of notes on yellow legal and an arrest report form. "OK, Pete, you're finishing up today. The defense is going to have you on cross and they're going to push on this alibi."

Balducci frowned. "They are? But we already showed it was bullshit! Plus, the guy ran when we tried to pinch him. We got the bloody pants, the motive, the girlfriend. You really think they'll bring it up?"

"Trust me. Look, any evidence can be impeached in the eyes of a jury, and anything that can't, they can say the cops planted it. Will the jury believe it? If the defendant shows as Mr. Truth, they have a chance, which they have to take, since they got *bupkes* otherwise. I got five black men and two Spanish on the jury. No offense, Peter, but what's the odds that that bunch thinks the NYPD is straight arrow? That the cops never, never picked up and railroaded the wrong guy?"

Balducci grunted noncommittally.

"So the thing is, we got to show him as Mr. Lie when they try it. He's a crook, right? We know it, but we got to show it, is the game."

Balducci nodded, and Karp laid out the line of questioning he thought the defense would bring up in the cross-examination and what he would pursue on the redirect. "He's going to attack your credibility, but he's got to do it backhanded, understand? Because the fact is that you're telling the truth. Especially about the fake alibi."

"That girl, Mimi."

"Yeah. Tighe told you and Freddie Kirsch he was with a girl named Mimi Vasquez in Larry's Bar at the time of the murder."

"Then he changed his story."

"Right. Because you found Vasquez and she said she'd never been near the place with him on the night. Klopper's game will be to confuse the identity of Mimi Vasquez with another girl that Tighe pulled out of a hat when you braced him on the lie—what was it?—Joseline?"

"Yeah. But why don't you just call her up there, Mimi, and get her to tell them he was blowing smoke?"

"Can't do it. It's *his* alibi. I can't do anything with the alibi or her unless he brings it up, which he knows, which is why he's going to hint at it, play with it, but never really bring it out. All he's doing is building a reasonable doubt, which is all he needs. I'll object like crazy and hope that Montana backs me up on it. By the way, just checking: Did you ever find this Denise in the appointment book?"

"Nope. And he won't talk about it either. Funny, the guy talked like blue blazes about every other piece of ass he got. Is it important?"

"Not really. Just funny. A missing piece."

Balducci nodded. He got up to leave and then stopped. "Oh, did I tell you? Speaking of ladies— the mutt's wife showed up."

"Who, Tighe's? I didn't know he was married."

"Yeah, and made in heaven too. He kept her tied to the bed and whipped her with a coat hanger. Had a shotgun rigged to blow away anybody trying to rescue her. You want her name and address?"

"Not really. I can't call her, and with a story like that I doubt they'll use her as a character witness."

Balducci rolled his eyes and walked out. Karp ran down the list of his other witnesses. Balducci had almost finished his direct testimony the previous day. He had been good in describing the pursuit and near escape of Tighe—the guy was a desperado, right?—and having him there would help carry the memory for another day.

Then the cross and the redirect. If Klopper tried to tease with the alibi, he would refute it like crazy, and then whip over to the forensic technician, a solid guy named Dugan, who had lifted the thumbprint from the scene, and then the fingerprint tech, Cibera, also convincing. Juries loved fingerprints. And although Klopper would do his best to cloud that evidence, he would fail, because fingerprints were sacred. They were on TV cop shows. A good close for the day.

*How can I be dicking around with this shit?*, Karp asked himself as he gathered up his papers. *Marlene may be dead or being tortured by some maniac. I'm dying, but I'm still up for this trial*, he thought as he took the elevator up to the twelfth floor. As he took his place at the prosecution table, however, these thoughts faded, his stomach muscles tautened, his palms got wet, and he began to breathe consciously, big deep breaths, as he had done at those points in a tight game when he knew his coach was going to send him in.

The jury filed in and the clerk called their names. The judge came in, all rose. Judge Thomas Montana, a diminutive and swarthy man with shoe-button eyes and wearing thick, paper-white side-burns under a thatch of black hair, sat down. All sat. Peter Balducci took the witness stand and the trial resumed.

For an unconcerned spectator in search of entertainment, a criminal trial is ordinarily a good place to avoid. The law radiates tedium the way a ballet does grace or an orchestra harmony. Despite this, the courtroom was packed, a fact attributable to the semi-sensational nature of the case (EX ROCK STAR KNIFED!), to the inclement weather, and to Karp himself. There was a small, ever-changing claque of trial connoisseurs (mostly young A.D.A.s) in the back of the room, who drifted in during their spare time and spent half an hour watching, as it were, Arcaro up on Native Dancer.

Karp rose and asked Balducci about the torn piece of matchbook he had found in the bag in Felix Tighe's room, establishing that the "Mimi" whose name was written there was in fact Mimi Vasquez, the non-alibi lady, and no one else.

Karp sat down and the judge asked for cross-examination, but Klopper chose this moment to protest once again the admissibility of the evidence in the brown bag. "At this time," he said, "if the court pleases, since there was no knowledge on my part of the evidence seized in the apartment at 130 Ludlow Street, I therefore ask for a hearing at this time in the absence of the jury for a determination by the court of whether the search and seizure is valid and not a violation of the constitutional rights of the defendant."

This was such an obvious lie that Karp was for a moment stunned. Then he got up and pointed out all the places in the official transcript, in the pre-trial records where Klopper had been so informed. Montana, looking disgusted, disposed of the motion and the trial proper resumed with the cross-examination of Balducci.

Karp looked over at the jury and saw knotted brows. That, and not any real hope of getting the evidence tossed, had been the reason for the motion. Enough objections, however often overruled, might add up to a reasonable doubt in the minds of certain jurors. Sometimes the big lie worked.

Klopper was good on cross. He flickered from point to point of evidence and testimony, always trying to elicit a weak or indecisive answer. How tall was Mimi Vasquez? Didn't know. What was in the defendant's wallet when arrested? Didn't know. Did you personally identify yourself as a police officer at the time of the arrest? No. Did you question him about the appointment book? No. Did the district attorney question him about it? I don't recall. Karp could feel the jury thinking, what *does* this guy know?

Then Klopper asked, "Who is Mimi Vasquez?"

Karp objected instantly. He was overruled.

"Is she involved with the case in any way?" asked Klopper. Balducci looked worried. *For God's sake, don't start looking shifty on me now, Peter,* prayed Karp silently. He rose and said, "I object to the form of the question, Judge."

But Montana's curiosity had been piqued. He asked Balducci, "Who is she?"

Balducci said, "She's a female that the defendant said that he was with at the time of the homicide."

*Two points for the bad guys,* thought Karp. There's the alibi floating now, and from a judge's question! That could stick.

So on the redirect, Karp leaped directly into the attack on the phony alibi. Karp established that because Tighe had claimed that on the night of the murder he was at Larry's Bar with a woman he had met at a bus stop, a woman named Mimi, Balducci had tracked down a woman with that name, using the phone number written on the matchbook stub.

*OK, Klopper, here goes,* thought Karp, as he asked, "What, if anything, did she say about visiting Larry's Bar with the defendant on the night in question?"

Klopper leaped up. "That's objected to! Hearsay!"

Karp shot back, "Counsel brought up this woman in the first place, Your Honor. I think it's only fair and proper that the detective explain it. The woman is available for counsel to call."

"It's available to him too!" snapped Klopper, the silver mask slipping just a little.

Karp replied coolly, "Your Honor, counsel knows very well I can't call her until counsel does."

"That's not so! That's not so at all!" Klopper's voice went up, and Montana banged his gavel. "Stop arguing, Mr. Klopper! Objection is sustained."

Karp tried a couple more times to get Balducci

to convey the burden of what Mimi Vasquez had said, but was blocked by sustained objections. Then he suddenly changed his line:

"Did you ever determine whether the defendant was in Larry's that night?"

"Objection!"

"Overruled."

"Yes, I did," said Balducci.

"What was the result of that enquiry?"

"That the defendant was never in Larry's on July tenth at the time in question."

"No further questions," said Karp, and took his seat, feeling reasonably satisfied. It was a good strong statement by Balducci. The defense would try to confuse the issue again by suggesting that there were two women and that the cops had found the wrong one, but we had the matchbook and they didn't have the other woman. The jury would see it for the horseshit it was. Karp was definitely ahead at the half.

The remainder of the afternoon went as planned. Karp called Dugan, the crime scene technician who had lifted the thumbprint in the hallway outside the murder apartment. Then he called the fingerprint technician, who said that the prints matched Tighe's, and finally he called Raney, briefly, to establish that Tighe was in fact fingerprinted on the day of the arrest. In the testimony, Karp brought out the fact that the print was shiny and wet at the time it was taken—in other words, fresh, and not to be confused with the others that Felix Tighe might have left around during his visits to the building.

They broke for the day around four. Judges like to get a jump on the traffic. As Karp stuffed his briefcase, Klopper came over to the prosecution table, with a pleased expression on his face.

"I need to talk to you," he said.

"I'm listening, Mr. Klopper."

"Your star witness, Steven Lutz, called me last night. It turns out he doesn't want to be your witness any more. He wants to testify for the defense."

"Oh?" said Karp blandly, "lucky you. Here's a tip: Try to get him to stop shifting his eyes and licking his lips. He does it even when he's telling the truth. God knows what he'll do when he's lying through his teeth."

With that, he nodded politely to Klopper and walked up the aisle, casually, with his face set in a pleasant, neutral mask. He had almost expected this, but it was a blow anyway. Friends of the defendant often rolled when the time came for them to betray their buddies in open court, but Lutz had not seemed to be much in love with Felix Tighe during the one interview Karp had done with him. In fact, he had seemed fairly hostile. Karp wondered briefly what had caused the flip, and then turned his mind to the line of questioning he would use to impeach Lutz's testimony tomorrow. He was halfway to the subway when he realized that he had not given Marlene Ciampi a single thought for five and a half hours.

Jim Raney, waiting outside the courtroom, observed Karp's passing without interest. He was looking for someone else. He buttonholed a court officer. "Hey, Frank," he said, "that lady walking down there—in the black outfit—you got any idea who she is?"

The officer nodded and told him. Raney's mouth opened in amazement. He thanked the court officer, and then leaned against the wall and thought for five minutes, oblivious to the flow of traffic around him. Then he walked out of the courthouse to his car, and headed for the Queensboro Bridge. He would have to check some things, but he now thought he had a good idea who was responsible for the trash-bag murders, and by extension, who had really kidnapped Marlene Ciampi.

"Your Honor, this concludes the People's case," said Karp and sat down. He thought the People had a pretty good shot at Felix Tighe, all things considered. The stipulated testimony from the surviving son had been a good thing to close on. (He sees his mother with her head nearly cut off and brings her a glass of water!) Before that, the medical examiner's people had testified, for the record, that the stains on Felix's pants were human blood, that Felix's knife could have made the wounds on the deceased, and that the wounds caused the death of the deceased.

Simple stuff, but not much good if the jury thought that the knife and pants they had seen in the courtroom did not belong to the defendant, a thought Mr. Klopper was about to try and insert in their collective mind.

First, though, a little shimmy. Klopper moved to have the case thrown out for lack of evidence associating the defendant with the crime. Montana denied it promptly. Then Klopper called his first witness, and Steve Lutz, wearing a cheap, but new, blue suit shambled up to the stand.

Karp rubbed his face and struggled to bring his senses into the required sharp focus. Another night with little sleep, ground glass under the eyelids. Lutz, he thought, did not look much better. That was interesting: Lutz had the basic rat look at all times, but now he seemed a trapped rat. What was he looking around the courtroom for? Who was he looking for?

Klopper took Lutz through the basics: who he was, the fact that he was letting Felix Tighe stay in his apartment on Ludlow Street; then he asked him about the day that Balducci and Raney had come to look at Felix's room.

"And these officers came to your door?"

"Yeah, they said could they take a look at Felix's room."

"And you let them in?"

"Yeah."

"Did they show you a warrant?"

"No. But, you know, it was the cops. I didn't want to get in no trouble." Karp thought, that's cute, a little suggestion of forced entry without a warrant. And no grounds for objection.

"And what happened then?" Klopper continued, and extracted from Lutz the story of how the brown bag and the dark, bloodstained pants had been found.

"This was the brown bag that was presented in evidence?"

"Yeah. It was closed and it had some stuff in it, so they said, 'could we open it?' And I, like, said, 'OK.' So they did. They found some clothes inside. And two knives, one big, one little."

"Did they find anything else?"

"Yeah. A couple of papers, newspapers. A little book, like an appointment book. And then they looked around the room. There was some clothes hanging in the closet. They took those out. There was a white jacket, a sports jacket, a black shirt, and a pair of dark blue pants, on a hanger, in a cleaner's bag."

"Are you sure about the color of those pants?"

"Yeah, I'm sure. Blue."

Klopper went over to the table where the trial exhibits were kept and picked up the bowie knife Karp had introduced earlier.

"Now these knives," he said, "did you look at the knives the officers found?"

"Yeah, they showed me the knives three times down at the D.A.'s office . . ."

Klopper interrupted, "Excuse me, I show you this knife, marked People's Exhibit Fourteen. Was this one of the knives the police removed from the brown bag at your apartment that day?"

Lutz shook his head and hunched forward as if preparing to avoid an invisible blow. "Uh-uh, no. That's the one they showed me in the D.A.'s office."

"But not in the apartment?"

"No. That was a different knife. It was like, wavy, the blade, like a what-do-you-call-it, a bread knife."

"Now when you were in the D.A.'s office, did you tell them that this wasn't the knife in the bag?"

"Yeah, I told them it wasn't. I was down there three times. No, two times in the office, and one time, it was like this, like a trial. But with no judge."

"The grand jury?"

"Yeah, that."

Klopper put the knife down on the table and picked up the pair of pants in their clear plastic bag. He said, "Now I show you this pair of black pants. Are these the pants that they took from your apartment in your presence?"

"No, those weren't them. Those pants were blue, and real clean. It was on a hanger in a cleaner's bag."

"And at the grand jury, was this the pair of pants that they showed you?"

"Well, they took some pants out of a bag and said, 'Is this the pants,' but it was like a big room and they were far away. I couldn't tell."

"But you said they were?"

Lutz looked pained. "Yeah, but it was so fast—in, out. Then I started thinking it maybe wasn't the same pants."

"Now, on the two occasions you were at the D.A.'s office, talking to Mr. Kirsch—did you tell him on both occasions that this was not the knife and these were not the pants?"

"Yeah, I told him and told him—wrong color pants, wrong kind of knife."

Klopper put down the pants and picked up the newspaper clippings about the murder that the police had found in the brown bag. He approached Lutz.

"I show you these newspaper clippings. Do you see your signature on them?"

"My initials, yeah. They got me to sign at my place."

"Yes, and did they have you sign anything else? The knives, or the pants?"

"No, nothing. I asked them why they was taking the clean clothes, and all, and they said, for the testimony."

"And your memory is absolutely clear about this?"

"Yeah."

"It was not the same knife and it was not the same pair of pants?" Klopper was smiling, his voice unctuous. Lutz had visibly relaxed.

"No, not the same, right."

"And you do have a good memory, correct? You remember, for example, what officer Balducci was wearing when he came to your apartment?"

Lutz raised his eyes to the ceiling and let his mouth go slack, in a parody of deep thought. "Yeah . . . he had a blue jacket, gray pants, black shoes. No hat and a red-striped tie. The other guy had a leather jacket on, no tie, but one of them high, turtlenecks, dark blue."

"That's all. Thank you."

Karp got up and stood in front of the witness, his expression mild. "Mr. Lutz, you have a good memory, do you not?" he asked.

"Yeah."

"So you remember a conversation you had with an Assistant District Attorney named Frederick Kirsch on July seventeenth of this year?"

"I dunno, I was down there a couple of times."

"This was the day the detectives came to your apartment and found the brown bag. You remember?"

"Oh, yeah, that time."

"Yes, that time. Now do you remember a time when Mr. Kirsch showed you those black blood-stained pants and asked you to identify them as the pants removed from your apartment that very day?"

"That wasn't the same pants, I told him."

"I see. Now, there was a stenographer present, who took down the conversation between you and Mr. Kirsch. Let me read a portion of this conversation to you and ask you if you remember giving these answers." Karp swooped over to the prosecution table and grabbed the transcript of the Q and A that Freddie Kirsch had done.

"Mr. Lutz, it says here on page eight that Mr. Kirsch asked you, 'Did you observe Detective Balducci remove a white jacket and a pair of black pants from your apartment?' And you answered, 'Yes.' And then you were asked, 'Did you have any objection to the detective removing this white jacket and black pants?' And you said 'No.' And then Mr. Kirsch showed you these black pants and asked you, 'Are these the black pants that Detective Balducci removed from your apartment on July seventeenth of this year?' And you answered, 'Yeah, that's them.' Do you recall making those answers?"

"I don't remember," said Lutz, beginning once again to stare wildly around the courtroom.

"But you have such a good memory, Mr. Lutz. I show you the page of transcript. Isn't that your signature on it?"

Lutz took the transcript gingerly. "Yeah, but I never said it was black pants," he said lamely.

"Let's try again, Mr. Lutz. Starting on page fourteen. Mr. Kirsch asks you, 'And did you see what, if anything, Detective Balducci removed from the brown bag?' And you answer, 'Some papers, newspapers, and a big knife.'"

"Two knives!" said Lutz. "A bread knife and a little one."

Judge Montana broke in, "That's what you said. It's written there."

"I never saw that knife. It ain't that knife!"

"Please continue, Mr. Karp," said Montana, a crinkle of disgust beginning to show on his neat, brown face.

Karp nodded to the bench and resumed. "As I was saying, page fourteen. Mr. Kirsch said, 'I show you this knife. Written on the blade just under the hilt are the word, *Vindicator*, the letters capital *EM*, the numbers 2176, and the word, *Korea*. Do you see that?' Answer, 'Yes.' Question, 'Were you present today when Detective Balducci removed this knife?' Your answer, 'Yeah. It was in Felix's bag.' Do you recall giving those answers to Mr. Kirsch?"

"Yeah, but we were talking about the other knives. I told you, I never seen that knife."

Karp went over to the clerk's table, picked up the bowie knife, and held it in front of Lutz's face. Lutz seemed to cower away from it, like a goblin shying from an enchanted sword.

Karp said, "I ask you to read what is written, engraved, on the blade of that knife."

"I never seen that knife," said Lutz, like a broken record.

"He didn't ask you that," said the judge. "Read what he told you to!"

"I can't read," said Lutz, his voice rising.

"Did you sign the stenographic transcript of the question and answer session you had with Mr. Kirsch as being true?"

"Yeah, yeah, but they told me . . ."

"And here, on page sixteen, where you are asked, 'Has everything you have said today been the truth to the best of your knowledge,' did you answer yes?"

"Yeah, but . . . it was different, they pulled a switch."

Karp walked to the presidium and handed the knife to the judge.

"Your Honor, would you please read the inscription?"

Montana read from the blade the same inscription Karp had just read from the Q and A. Now the disgust was patent on his face.

Karp returned to the questioning, going through the grand jury minutes and demonstrating that Lutz had on a separate occasion, and under oath, identified the black pants and the knife as being the items removed from his apartment. But it was anti-climax; from the moment the judge read the words written on the knife, Steven Lutz was utterly impeached as a witness. Karp settled back and thought nice thoughts about little Freddie Kirsch and his unexpected gift: a perfect Q & A.

The remainder of the trial consisted of the defendant's testimony. This was anticlimax, too, at least to Karp. Had Felix Tighe lived an exemplary life, had he been a pillar of the community, it might have been remotely possible that against the net of circumstantial evidence that tied him to the murders a clever lawyer like Chopper Hank Klopper might have inserted a reasonable doubt wide enough to spread the meshes.

But Felix was a mutt. He lied with every breath, and about things that could be easily verified, too, and that was what destroyed, at every turn, Klopper's efforts to insert that doubt.

The pants weren't his because, he went on, they weren't his style, because he had to dress well, *because he was a sales manager*. The knife wasn't his, and *he had never owned a knife like that*. He couldn't have done the murders because he had an alibi for the night: He had gone to Larry's Bar, *and he had been served by a waitress named Marge, whom he proceeded to describe in detail*.

Karp could see it in Klopper's face and in his manner. He knew he was being lied to, and on the stand. There is nothing more obvious, or pathetic, than a defense attorney with a defendant witness who is out of control. Klopper began subtly to withdraw from his client. Once or twice, he even snapped at him, "Just answer the question, please." But Felix loved to talk, especially about himself, and with all these people watching, hanging on his words, he gladly hung himself.

Karp was practically salivating when his turn came to cross-examine. Not only had Felix owned a big bowie knife before, but he had used it to stab a policeman during the course of a burglary, wasn't that so? It wasn't like that. Didn't you stab him? I can explain that. *Didn't you stab him and weren't you convicted of stabbing him?* Yes, but. . . . Next question.

Karp went over the initial Q and A that Felix had recorded with Freddie Kirsch. Here he had lied about everything. He didn't know Stephanie Mullen. He didn't know Anna Rivas. He had never been in the apartment on Avenue A.

He was confronted with his address book, with sworn statements from witnesses. Oh, *that* Anna Rivas. Yeah, I know her, but I never beat her up. Well, maybe we had a little argument. Oh, *that* Stephanie Mullen. Yeah, I knew her, but I never killed her. I was in a bar with a girl. Oh, not *that* girl, I remember now, *another* girl.

Karp brought all this out, letting Felix tangle himself. Finally, under Karp's relentless pressure, Felix admitted he had lied, because he was afraid Kirsch was trying to frame him. He hadn't trusted Kirsch.

"And did there come a time when you trusted

Mr. Kirsch and at last told him the truth?" asked Karp.

"Yes. I thought we had, you know, a rapport. I finally told him, you know, I knew Anna, and we had some words, and that woman called the cops. That happened. I told him."

"You mean, you lied until you were caught at it?"

"That's not what I would say. I would say, I didn't trust Fred Kirsch, because I didn't think he was, that he had my interests in mind at the time. I would say . . ."

Here the judge interrupted. "Just answer the question, don't make a speech."

"Well a lie, that's not what I would call it."

But Karp could see, from a quick inspection of the jury, that the jurymen knew what a lie was. Frowns. Rolling eyes. Terrific.

A good close, too, on the cross, Karp thought. Always leave them laughing: "Mr. Tighe, did you ever meet the murdered boy, Jordan Mullen?"

"Yes, he was around. I think I met him once."

"You were introduced to him?"

"Not actually introduced, no . . ."

"But he knew you, he would have recognized you?"

"Yeah, I guess."

"Is that why you stabbed him to death after you had killed his mother?" asked Karp blandly.

"No."

"No further questions," said Karp.

On redirect, Klopper could do little to repair the damage. He tried to show Felix as a man who gave facetious answers under pressure, the kind of spunky guy who might appear to lie when pushed around by the bullies of the law. It was weak and brief. That ended the defense case.

On his rebuttal, Karp focused on the alibi. Karp had elicited from Felix a detailed description of the cocktail waitress. He even had him point her out where she sat in the courtroom. Then he called her to the stand, where she testified that on the night of the murder, she had been off duty. Murmurs in the courtroom.

On cross, Klopper could hardly attack the woman's memory. She had never said that she recognized Felix—he had said he recognized her. He walked back to the defense table and broke a pencil.

The rest of the rebuttal witnesses were Felix's supervisors, from his current job and previous ones. He was not a sales manager, nor had he hope of becoming one. There had been complaints from clients. He had been fired repeatedly for skimming, for abusive behavior. The People rested. The defense rested. Final arguments were scheduled for the following day.

As Karp left the courtroom, he saw Felix speaking urgently in Klopper's ear. Klopper didn't seem to be listening.

# CHAPTER
# 16

*This must be what sensory deprivation is like*, thought Marlene. Since she had conspired with Alonso to bring her undrugged food she had been left in the dark and unmolested, except for mealtimes. There had been three of these, or four, she was not sure. Kid food, and she was glad to get it: pizza, hot dogs, burgers, candy bars, milkshakes. In between she was left tied up on her cot, in total darkness. Ten days, Mrs. Dean had said, until the full moon. Marlene wondered how many of them were left.

As the unmarked hours passed, deprived of vision, hearing little but her own breathing and the creak of her cot, her sense of smell had become preternaturally sharp. She had become aware of a universe of subtle odors: the damp smell of old stone, the sharp odor of the canvas, the oily smell of the wool blanket, a musty rotting odor she couldn't quite identify—perhaps some food that had been forgotten and had gone bad. Pervading all these was the stink of her own unwashed body, and the spicy-sulfur smell she remembered from childhood, before her house was converted to oil heat. She was in a coal cellar.

This discovery gave her some pleasure, as indicating that her brain was still working and that she was not entirely helpless. She thought about coal cellars for a while, about the excitement when, as children, she and her older sisters would hang around the coal truck on delivery day to see and hear the black lumps rattle and roar down the tin chute.

More excitement—coal cellars had chutes! That meant there was a way out of this place, or had been. Maybe it was still open and she could slip through. From this moment Marlene began to think actively about escape. All she had to do now was to free herself from her bonds and overpower or evade a monster the size of a Mack truck.

Pending that, she occupied herself with thought. What else could she do? And some action, even mental action, was better than dissolution into sobbing terror. Marlene had no difficulty admitting her fear, but she had long practice in suppressing it through an act of will, which is the only way a person with a vivid imagination can achieve courage.

She thought a lot about Karp. Karp would not be afraid, she thought, and thought half-enviously that his bravery had nothing to do with controlling imagination. Karp had, she knew, no more imagination than a manhole cover. Despite all the proof to the contrary, despite all the destruction that fate had visited on his body, he retained a belief in his own indestructibility.

Yes, Karp was brave. He was also ferociously honest, about deeds, if not feelings, trustworthy, intelligent, a great piece of ass, good-looking, neat. He washed dishes; he picked up dirty clothes: in short, he was a storehouse of all the manly virtues, beneath which noble edifice Marlene had detected an impacted zone of tender sensitivity, to whose excavation she intended to devote a good portion of her energies after marriage. If she didn't die here in this hole.

She also thought about escape. She had given up on rescue. Judge Rice knew that she was going to visit St. Michael's, but that was no help, because Mrs. Dean had only to say, "Yes I was expecting her, but the dear girl never showed up." Why shouldn't the cops believe her? Even *Karp* would believe her.

The key to escape was also the greatest barrier: the Bogeyman, Alonso. She had already won a concession from him, in the form of undrugged food, and where one concession had been given, others might follow. In an odd way, he seemed anxious to please her, almost as much as she (exhibiting, as she realized, florescent Stockholm Syndrome) was anxious to please him.

He seemed to enjoy feeding her and tucking her in and tending to her physical needs. After he fed her, he would sit at what looked like a child's desk near the doorway, a desk that came barely to his knees, and play with little toys, which he would set out on the surface of the desk and converse with. Marlene could not see them clearly enough to make them out, but they appeared to be tiny Kewpie dolls, dressed in bright colors.

But Alonso was not mentally retarded. Somebody (and Marlene thought she knew who) had through some hideous warping of the processes of nurturance frozen him emotionally at about the age of five. His two governing emotions seemed to be a terror of his mother and a bottomless loneliness. Marlene sensed that he was making her into a little friend. Marlene understood that she had to extract from this friendship enough concessions to enable her to break free before he did to her what she suspected he had done to his other little friends.

She began to sing, to keep her spirits up and to pass the time; and to sass anyone who might be listening she sang prison songs. She sang "Parchman Farm," "Morton Bay," "No More Cane on This Brazos," "The Peat Bog Soldiers," in English and again in German, and Dylan's "I Shall Be Released." In between prison songs she sang "My Bonny Light Horseman," and thought about Karp and about Raney, or rather about some unlikely blend of their best features.

As she sang, she heard the rattle of a heavy lock being opened and the squeak of hinges. In a minute, she gradually became aware of a presence hovering near her, a soft breathing, a change in the pressure of the air currents on her cheek, and the smell of frying. She stopped singing. Silence and then a chair scraped and Alonso turned on the light.

The overhead light was dim but it dazzled her. When her vision cleared she saw that he was carrying a brown bag. He said, "I brought lunch."

"Oh, is it lunchtime already? What did you get?"

"Cheeseburgers and french fries and chocolate milk," he replied, unwrapping these things.

He pulled his chair closer and made as if to lift her head up and bring the cheeseburger to her mouth, but she whined and turned her head away.

"What's the matter? I thought you liked cheeseburgers."

"I love cheeseburgers, Alonso, but I want to eat

them myself, with my own hands. Couldn't you untie me? Just my hands?"

He looked doubtful. "I'm not sposed to."

"Come on," Marlene urged. "What am I gonna do, beat you up and escape? You're a great big boy and I'm just a girl."

He considered this for a while, chewing his puffy pink lips. Then he said, "OK. But don't tell, all right?"

She smiled at this and nodded for all she was worth and he reached over her and untied the ropes that held her hands to the cot. He smelled faintly of some light and distressingly familiar perfume. Baby powder, she realized with a shock, and something sweeter and not as wholesome underneath it.

Then he handed her the food and watched her as she tore into it. "Mmmm, chocolate milk," she said through a full mouth. "I used to love this when I was a kid. St. John Bosco was my favorite saint because I thought he invented chocolate milk."

Blank look.

"Because of Bosco—you know, chocolate syrup."

"What's saints?" he asked.

"Saints? You know, *saints*—people who were very holy and had special grace of God, and intercede for us in Heaven."

Alonso frowned. "We don't like that," he said, with a dull finality she decided not to challenge. Catechism class could wait.

"No, I guess not," said Marlene quietly. The giant continued to watch her as she finished her meal. She licked the grease from her fingers and then said, "Well, Marlene needs to go potty now. Could you untie my feet?" Be polite and others will be polite to you. Sister Marie Augustine, she thought, I hope you knew what you were doing.

He loosened her ropes and led her, wrapped in her blanket and grasped tightly by the arm, out of the coal cellar through what appeared to be a furnace room, past a heavy door with a big outside hasp and padlock, and down a dim corridor.

Off this corridor was the toilet. Marlene had shameful drug-dimmed memories of being carried to this room and placed on the toilet while her captor watched. Now when she started to close the door, Alonso stepped forward and stood dumbly on the threshold.

"Can't I have some privacy?"

"I want to watch."

"You can't! It's naughty. Don't you know that? Didn't your Mommy tell you that it's naughty for girls and boys to go to the bathroom together?" *This is the right play*, Marlene thought. *This is the weak place. He's never had a real adult to deal with before, except her.* She had understood, almost instinctively, that the key to controlling Alonso was using the same tone she had used with her little brothers and their friends when she was eleven. It worked. He pulled back, his face worried and confused, and she slammed the door shut.

Later, back in the coal cellar, Marlene sat on the cot while Alonso played with his dolls. He seemed restless and irritable. The little dolls fought one another and conversed, through the man, in high-pitched angry squeaks. He broke off the game after a few minutes and placed the dolls between layers of tissue in a gold candy box.

He rose and came toward her. "I have to tie you up now," he said.

"Alonso, please. I can't escape. You have that

big door with a lock. . . ." She made her voice high and trembly. "And I'm scared of the dark."

He looked confused. "You can't be scared. You're a bad witch. My Mommy said." He said this with absolute finality and Marlene was not about to contradict him. Something flashed into her mind.

"Yeah, right, but, if you don't tie me up, I'll give you my evil eye. Then I won't be able to do anything magic to you, or escape."

Marlene saw his huge round face light with interest at this suggestion. "Really?" he asked.

"Sure. But only if you don't tie me."

He held out an immense hand and she removed her glass eye from its socket and solemnly handed it to him.

He examined it closely, openmouthed in amazement, and then carefully placed it in the inside pocket of his black suit jacket. He turned to go, then spun around on her with a fearsome scowl. "You, you better not try to run away, all right? If you run away, I'll be in big trouble. I'll have to squoosh you, just like him."

"Like who, Alonso?"

"The little man. He stole a doll and it was my fault. Mommy said. And I got a licking and I had to squoosh him. I squooshed him with my feet."

Marlene felt a rush of guilt. Junior Gibbs had taken her hint and died for it. She swallowed hard and said, "You're really a good squoosher, aren't you, Alonso. Did you squoosh a lot of people?"

The great head shook vigorously from side to side. "No. Only him."

"Not Lucy."

He looked hurt. "No! Lucy was my friend. But she got broken. I put them in the garbage when they get broken." He smiled and said proudly, "That's my big-boy job."

She stared at him, and felt the smile curdling on her face. He gave her a little wave. "I hope you don't get broken for a long time. I like you," he said and walked out.

Marlene waited until she heard the sounds of the furnace room door shutting and the lock scraping against its hasp as he locked her in. She stood up and began to explore her prison.

She quickly determined that there was no longer any chute from the old coal cellar to the outside. There was a patch of relatively new brick to show where one had been in the past. The doorway from the coal cellar led to a room measuring about three yards by five yards, containing the dusty hulk of an old coal burning furnace that had long since been converted to oil. Next to it was a shiny new forced-air oil burner feeding into three wide galvanized sheet metal ducts.

The work looked brand new. There were still chips of glittering sheet metal lying on the floor. Marlene felt a thrill of hope. She recalled that on one of her early visits to the day-care center, Mrs. Dean had been supervising duct work. It must have been part of this furnace installation, which meant that she was still in Manhattan, probably in the basement of St. Michael's.

She went over to the door and pushed on it without much expectation. It was firmly padlocked from the outside. No chute, the door locked—come on, Marlene, use your noodle! She paced back and forth waiting for something to enter her mind. It was warm in the furnace room and she had dropped the blanket. She looked down at her nude body. She appeared to be putting on some weight from all that junk food. Still, she remained pretty skinny. If there was a window, even a small one, she might be able to . . . suddenly she stopped pacing and struck herself on the forehead.

The ducts! She pulled Alonso's little desk across the floor to the new furnace and stood on it with her ear against the warm metal. Nothing but the gush of the blowers. That was surprising. If these ducts led to the school she should be hearing voices or at least some indication of an active building. Alonso had said that the meal she had just eaten was lunch, but that could mean anything. But if there was no one in the school, it was probably late at night. She stood listening until her legs grew tired, and then jumped down.

She decided to move at once. Alonso had just left, which meant he might not be back for several hours, which would give her enough time to open a duct, crawl through, and run. She examined the duct joints, and found that they were held together by four sheet-metal screws. A screwdriver, she thought, there's always an old screwdriver in a furnace room, sometimes two, along with the babyfood jar of assorted screws.

She searched with growing frustration, running her hands along the base of the walls, peering behind both furnaces, but nothing like a screwdriver turned up. There was a fuse box, but no cabinets to search. The only drawer in the place was in the little desk. She yanked it open. Some marbles. A comic book. A gold candy box. The sweetish odor that she had detected on Alonso seemed stronger here. She opened the box.

It was Alonso's doll collection. He had five of them, each one dressed carefully in a different color, in clothes made from little scraps of bright cloth. They were not, however, as she had thought, miniature celluloid dolls. When she saw what they actually were, she dropped the box and staggered backwards, biting her lip to keep from shrieking in horror.

Little fingers.

Guma had never actually met Giancarlo Ferro, but he had heard plenty about him, little of it complimentary. If Vinnie Ferro had been the brains and guts of the clan, Giancarlo had been in charge of cruelty. He was a heavyset, almost squat man with a face as round and yellow and cratered as the moon, a face to which his narrow pouched eyes gave a decidedly Oriental cast. He affected double-breasted suits in pale colors and sported a thin mustache, which explained his nom-de-street.

He really does look like Charlie Chan, Guma thought. They were sitting in the back room of a restaurant the Ferros owned off President Street in Brooklyn: Guma, Tony Bones, Charlie Chan Ferro, and Billy Ferro, an otherwise colorless thug, present only because family matters were being discussed.

Charlie and Tony did most of the talking, which largely concerned violence, chicanery, and sex in the Brooklyn streets of twenty years past. Guma was familiar with many of the names and knew some of the individuals personally. He had been part of that life. He found himself (uncharacteristically) wondering what had kept him in school and sent him to college and law school while all the referenced fucking, shooting, and stealing had been going on. Bad luck, was what he guessed.

The talk drifted on: The two mobsters seemed to have no urgent appointments. Guma grew bored and, since liquor was apparently on the house, he drank two Teachers' on the rocks, and a Schaeffer. He tore little holes in a napkin. Suddenly he became aware that the hum of talk had ceased; the three men were looking at him expectantly. It was his cue.

"We know who did Vinnie," Guma said. "And we're gonna take him in."

Charlie Chan looked sideways at Tony and a sneer twisted across his wide face. "Is he fuckin' serious? Forty people saw Joey Bottles do Vinnie." He glared at Guma. "You gonna bring him in? Go ahead and try. You gonna find forty people was tying their shoelace."

Guma stared back at him. "Wrong. We got him already, plus Harry and the Bollanos. Joey's wheelman ratted him out."

"I heard," said Charlie. "So what the fuck does that do for me?"

"We need another witness. Your guy DiBello saw it too. We want him to talk."

Charlie snorted in contempt. "DiBello? That lame? He saw shit!"

"He saw it. We're holding him as a material witness. All you got to do is call him and tell him to spill the whole story on Joey B."

Charlie Chan came up out of his chair violently, shaking the table and spilling drinks. "What the fuck makes you think I'm gonna do that, asshole? Who the fuck you think you're talkin' to? You think I can't take out Joey?" He turned to his other guest, his features now writhing with anger.

"Tony, what the fuck you doin' to me here? You think I can't handle the Bollanos. You think I need fuckin' help from the fuckin' D.A.?"

Tony smiled icily and said, "Guma, why don't you wait in the car?"

Half an hour later, the door to the white limo opened and Tony Bones climbed in. Guma had been watching *Dialing for Dollars* on the little TV and making free with the bar. He switched off the set and said, "That's some tough guy in there. I was worried about you there for a while, Tony."

After a sharp look to make sure Guma was joking, Tony laughed. "Yeah, he's hard as nails. Fuckin' guy! I'm trying to break it to him gently, if he doesn't go along with this, put the Bollanos out of action, he's dead. In a oil drum with an ice pick up his nose. No, he's gonna get them. Fuckin' ludicrous, right? Him going against Harry Pick? But he don't listen, does he? The Ferros! The fuckin' family hasn't shown any sense in twenty years. At least Vinnie had brains. This one—*un' scimmia, un scicco!*"

"So he won't?"

"He will, he will—what d'you think, I can't roll a scumbag like Charlie? Yeah, he'll do it. You know what I told him? He'd have a better chance to put it to Joey, if Joey was in the slams. He figures, if there's no Bollanos left outside, Joey won't have no cover inside. Like Joey needs cover."

"He doesn't know Big Sally's going to walk?" asked Guma with a nervous laugh.

"Hey—that's our little secret," Tony answered, grinning.

"Right," said Guma. "We going to see Bollano now?"

"Yeah, it's all set up. I got to get this shit over with and get back down south. The fuckin' spics'll be all over me as it is." Tony spoke to the driver and the big car moved smoothly away from the curb.

Guma finished his drink, and said, "Tony, one

last thing . . . I need a couple of minutes alone with the old man."

"Alone?" Tony frowned. "How come you want to see him alone?"

"Let's say if he wants to stay out of jail, I got to put something in his ear. Otherwise the whole deal falls apart."

"You just tell this to me now? I'm hanging out all over the street on this." Guma was startled by how quickly the pleasantness had drained out of Tony's face. He did not like looking at what was left.

"I know, Tony. There's no problem. We're under control here. But you understand, unless I can tell Big Sally a couple of things, he's gonna go up with the rest of them."

Tony calculated briefly and then slipped back into a cool smile. "OK, *paisan*, for you, I'll see what I can do."

Guma relaxed. The tiger had jumped through the hoop and was back on its little stand. Now all Guma had to do was to convince Salvatore Bollano to use Guma's plan to escape the clutches of the grand jury, while allowing his own son and several of his most trusted associates to go to jail. No problem, thought Guma. A chair in the face, a few blank shots, he'd go through the hoops like Tony. Gangsters he could handle. His real problem was keeping all of this from Karp.

Karp buttoned his suit coat and stood up and walked to his favorite spot in front of the jury. Klopper had just finished his summation and Karp was about to enjoy one of the few advantages the prosecution retained in criminal cases: the right to have the last word.

Karp's last word, of course, had to contain a convincing rebuttal of what Klopper had said. This he had composed in his head as Klopper spoke. Mentally, he slotted this rebuttal into the structure of logic he had composed, then outlined and all but memorized the previous night. He took a long, deep breath and began.

The crime was murder. Karp explained what murder was, what he had to prove: That the deceaseds were dead, and dead as a result of the criminal acts of the accused. The Mullens were dead, all right. He had shown that. He reminded the jury of the gory circumstances.

Then he reconstructed the web of circumstantial evidence that tied Felix Tighe to the crime. Anna Rivas's testimony. Felix beat Anna, the victim called the cops. "I'll remember that." He had a knife on the night of the murder. He had the black pants on.

Then the evidence from the Lutz apartment: the knife, the black pants, tying in and confirming the testimony. And the diary—the notation "Big Mouth—9:30," the day, the approximate time of the killings, confirmed by Josh Mullen's call to 911. The vacuity of the defense—the exploded alibi, Lutz's fabrications. Finally the fingerprint on the door frame of the victim's apartment, a fresh, sweaty fingerprint, laid down on the night of the murder.

That was the evidence. But he now had to deal with the twist that Klopper, in his summation, had put on all those facts in order to lay a reasonable doubt: It was *too* pat. The cops were framing a convenient bad boy. Could you really believe that an intelligent man like Felix Tighe would have made so many incriminating mistakes?

"Gentlemen of the jury," Karp said, looking at each member in turn, "I ask you now to consider the character of the accused. That too is part of the evidence. It has been suggested by Mr. Klopper, in his able summation, that the very weight of the circumstantial evidence against the defendant should give you pause. You have seen that the defendant is a clever and articulate man. How could such a clever man have made so many mistakes? Boasting! Keeping the knife! The black pants! Writing down his appointment for murder!

"I will tell you how. Our legal rules require that the People prove their case beyond a reasonable doubt, to a moral certainty. I'm sure Judge Montana will explain to you in his charge what a reasonable doubt is. But let's look closer at that interesting term, moral certainty.

"It means that when you make a decision as a member of a jury you are not striving for scientific or mathematical certainty, but for a kind of decision that engages your full conscience. That's why the term 'moral' is used. It's not merely a rational calculation: you're men, not machines. And you bring your moral history as human beings with you to the courtroom: your understanding of good and evil, your experiences with crime and punishment—you've all had these—everything that makes you fit to sit in judgment on your fellow man, that enables you to make a judgment 'to a moral certainty.'

"But we have seen here in these past days another kind of judgment, the judgment of a man who knew that he was above any moral law. He *knew* it! It may be hard for you to believe this, but we know from his history and his actions that the defendant could not conceive of ever having to pay for his crimes, however dreadful.

"Didn't he nearly kill a policeman and calmly walk away from his trial? Didn't he nearly kill the detectives who were trying to bring him to your justice? Didn't he lie and lie when confronted with the overwhelming evidence against him? And change his lies to suit as each old lie was proven false?

"That is a kind of certainty that you may not have much experience with, gentlemen, but I have. It is immoral certainty. It is the feeling of invincibility that the hardened criminal has, the sure knowledge that he will never be brought to book for his crimes, and well you know from the papers and TV how justified that feeling is in today's world.

"That is the explanation of why the defendant did not cover his tracks better, why he made so many of what now appear to be mistakes. It was the immoral certainty, the brazen arrogance, of the criminal mind.

"And so, gentlemen, it is for you this afternoon to bring your common sense to bear on the facts of this case, and your moral certainty to bear on the character of the defendant and his deeds. If you do that, you will find that the defendant, Felix Tighe, did indeed go to apartment 3FN at 217 Avenue A on the night of July tenth, and stab to death Stephanie Mullen and her little son Jordan Mullen.

"In this case, good conscience commands, common sense dictates, and justice cries out that you find this defendant guilty, guilty of the murder of Stephanie Mullen, and guilty of the murder of Jordan Mullen."

Karp sat down. Judge Montana charged the jury. A good charge, Karp thought. You always knew when the judge thought the defendant was guilty, however much they reached for impartiality. Judge Montana did not like naked perjury in his courtroom. The re-run of the evidence helped, too, since the great bulk of it was, by the nature of the case, People's evidence.

The jury deliberated for an hour and ten minutes, came back, and found Felix Tighe guilty of both murders.

Karp had never freebased cocaine, but he doubted that the fabled rush had much on what he felt in the few seconds after the foreman of the jury said the magic word. He felt powerful, relaxed, expansive. Sexy. That's why Victory is a goddess.

There was a disturbance. Felix was screaming obscenities at his lawyer, who was paying no attention, apparently glad to be done with the case, maybe even a little glad that he'd lost.

Karp ignored them. You had to figure Felix Tighe would have no dignity, would be a sore loser. He packed his papers into his cardboard folder. The problem with a rush, he realized, is that after it's over you have to either get another hit of dope or face the world. Karp had no other convictions pending and Marlene was still gone. He walked up the aisle, his face grim, toward a world empty of hope.

# CHAPTER
# 17

The first thing that Raney did when he got back downtown from Queens was to go into Marlene's office and search through her files. Given the state and scope of Marlene's files, this took him the better part of Friday afternoon. The file on St. Michael's and the trash-bag killings was, of course, missing, since Marlene had taken it with her when she had left for her fateful appointment with Mrs. Dean.

Raney sat in the littered office and rubbed his face, as if that would make his memory work. He pulled out his notebook and read through the notes he had taken at his interview with Mary Tighe. It takes a tale of quite extraordinary depravity to sicken a New York City police detective, and Raney felt an echo of the queasiness he had experienced as the woman had related the details of her married life with Felix Tighe.

That was not what interested him now. What had impelled him back to Queens was the information he had from the court clerk that the woman he knew as Irma Dean was Felix Tighe's mother. His first notion was that Felix was associated in some way with the child murders. As he had traveled to his appointment with Mary Tighe, he had come to realize that it wasn't possible. Felix had been in custody during at least one of the trash-bag killings, and besides, he hardly matched the description of the person Raney knew as the Bogeyman.

Mary Tighe had cleared that up: two marriages and two children, and two different names. Mary Tighe had only seen her brother-in-law once; her impression was that he was institutionalized up-state somewhere. But the description she gave him was unmistakable: a blond, goofy-looking giant.

This was why Raney was searching for Marlene's file. It was inconceivable that such a creature could have completely avoided the surveillance Raney had placed on the street in front of St. Michael's. Townhouses don't have back doors onto the street, which meant that the Bogeyman had to be working out of another base.

He vaguely remembered that Marlene had made some mention of another property owned by Mrs. Dean—Marlene had gotten some guy in the D.A.'s office to run a check on her—but he could remember neither where it was, nor the name of the guy, if she had even mentioned it. He recalled, with guilt, that at that period of their professional relationship he had been mainly concerned with getting into her pants.

He was aware of the passage of time. It was getting late, and the rumble of business noise from the hallway was growing fainter. He was also aware that what he should do was to call the lieutenant in charge of the kidnapping investigation, turn over his notes and his speculations, and go back to his current assignment, which was investigating one of the seventeen homicides he was currently responsible for out of Manhattan South.

But that particular lieutenant was a famous dork, who was convinced that the kidnapping was a Mafia operation, and would not appreciate contradictory evidence from a woman with a story that even Raney thought might be half-crazy, a woman who had every reason for a heavy grudge against her old man and his mom.

Ordinarily, he would have discussed the problem with Pete Balducci, but Balducci was set to retire this week, besides being busy with marrying off his daughter, and Raney knew he would not take kindly to any suggestion that they freelance on a case as messy as this one. That meant he had to go to see Karp, something that, for reasons he did not like thinking about, he had been avoiding since the beginning of his involvement with Marlene Ciampi.

In the hallway outside Marlene's office, Raney paused and looked out the tall window. The sky over Baxter Street was bruised purple with rain and the streets were already shiny with the prelude to the autumn's first serious storm. He smiled. Cops like anything that keeps the people off the streets.

Karp, he soon found, was not in. Karp was in court, waiting for the jury to convict Felix Tighe. Raney wandered into Karp's office. No one stopped him; people wandered into Karp's office all the time, dropping papers on his chair and leaving notes. Raney looked around, examined the desk, looked at the framed diplomas and photographs on the walls.

One caught his eye, a war picture it looked like,

a picture of mounted soldiers charging at tanks. There was an inscription on it in French, and it was signed, "Marlene, the Goom, and V.T." A memory popped up into Raney's consciousness: the name of the guy who had done the workup on Dean for her. He spun and was out of the office in an instant, off to find V.T. Newbury.

Snarled in the kind of rush-hour traffic that only five o'clock and a rainy Friday can produce in Brooklyn, Ray Guma had been pulling over whenever he spotted a phone booth and trying to reach Karp. He had been unsuccessful for the same reason that Raney had: Karp was in court. The Bollanos had been very helpful with information about the child pornography and prostitution business. They knew who Mrs. Dean was, and they knew who some of her customers were.

Guma thought Karp would be very interested in several of these names, and perhaps even grateful enough for receiving them to forgive Guma for what Guma had just pulled off. Or maybe not: Guma did not intend to find out if he could help it. He shoved a quarter into the slot of his current phone booth. It clicked down the chute, but produced no dial tone. This was not a good neighborhood for public phones. He slammed the instrument with his fist, screamed a curse, and ran back to his car.

The traffic was no better on Broadway. Raney crept uptown, peering through a small clear space in his fogged windshield. The defroster on the Ghia had long since packed it in. He was soaking wet, too, having left his raincoat in the back seat of the unmarked NYPD car he shared with Balducci.

It was dark by the time he arrived at the address on West End Avenue. There were no lights on in any of the windows, and the building had a deserted look. Raney glanced around and saw that the driving rain had cleared the streets of pedestrians. He walked up the stone stairs, pulled a set of picks from his pocket and went to work on the front door lock.

It took him three minutes to break in. The front door gave on an entry hall. Raney took out a pencil-beam flashlight and shone it around. Peeling brown paint, wall sconces without bulbs, gritty dust: It was obvious that this floor at least was unoccupied. A wide stairway with wooden banisters and tattered red carpeting led upward. Raney passed this by and explored the rest of the hallway. Someone was redecorating. Walls had been torn apart and the floors were littered with the detritus of heavy plumbing and electrical work.

There was a door at the end of the hall leading to the back stairway, a relic of the age of servants. Raney descended. You search a building from the bottom up.

The lowest floor was set up as an apartment: an expensively furnished parlor, a modern kitchen, a bath, and two small bedrooms, one furnished for a child with cartoon character sheets and a Popeye lamp, and the other spare. Like most ground-floor rooms in Manhattan, these had their windows covered with grilles.

As he inspected these rooms, he became aware of a hollow booming noise, as if someone were beating on a metallic tank. It seemed to come from below him. He crouched and put his ear to a heat register. Bong. Bong-bong. And a voice, indistinct and angry.

Raney took his Browning from its shoulder holster, jacked a shell into the chamber, and replaced it in the holster. Then he returned to the stairway he had just left. From the landing there a hallway ran to a glassed and wire-meshed door that led to some kind of yard. In the other direction, a short flight of stairs led down to a steel fire door. Following his ears, Raney went to the fire door, and pressed his face to the cool metal. The shouts and banging were louder. He opened the door.

A gust of oily warmth flowed past his face as he advanced down a short corridor. It was lit by an overhead bulb, and Raney put away his flashlight. To the right a red door, locked and bolted; ahead a stout wooden door equipped with a padlock and a hasp hung half open. Raney stepped past the door in a fast crouching movement, pistol out.

Moving deeper into the room, he saw the cot and the ropes hanging from it, and his stomach thrummed with tension. He turned and saw the furnaces. Someone had removed the filter panel from one of the sheet-metal ducts leading up from the new oil furnace. From this space, as from a stereo speaker, came the banging noise. Raney could make out what the voice was saying now. He ran out of the furnace room, through the corridor and the door and up the service stairs.

Marlene lay in a heat duct two feet square, her head filled with Alonso's bellowing and banging. "You come outa there! You're in real trouble! I'm not your friend any more! Come outa there! COME OUTA THERE!" Over and over again. And banging with some hard object. Her head was splitting. She could see him by the light coming through the vent he had removed, see his arm and shoulder and part of his head, and the tool he was using to bang with.

He could not, of course, come in and get her, but neither could she escape. The vent was just wide enough to allow her shoulders to fit snugly in the diagonal dimension. She had ascended from the furnace room by pushing with the sides of her bare feet against the sides of the duct. In this way she had made a slow progress to the second floor, where Alonso had found her.

When she had entered the ductway, Marlene had counted on there being an unscreened heat vent from which she could escape. In fact, there were none open on the path she had chosen. In her horror and her blind rush to escape, she had not stopped to consider that, nor had she considered what the rough screws and edges of sheet metal that projected into the duct would do to her flesh and to the soles of her feet. Every time she pushed down against the metal it felt as if she was walking on fish hooks.

Beyond her head lay the blackness of a vertical duct, but she no longer possessed the energy to climb it, nor could her bleeding feet bear the agony of a descent. She was stuck here until Alonso figured out how to tear the wall and the duct apart to winkle her out. That shouldn't be hard; he was smart and clearly strong enough. Before he got her, she decided, she would go down the duct head first. Let him have the finger. Then the banging stopped suddenly and she heard Alonso's voice raised in furious reproach. And there was another voice.

Raney slid off the safety on his pistol and held it high in both hands as he moved forward. The banging and shouting was coming from one of the rooms on the second floor. He approached the doorway slowly over the litter of construction debris that lay all around. The room was lit by a single dim bulb hanging from wires from the ceiling. By its light he saw a huge man in black kneeling at the wall, yelling and banging something metallic within the wall. It did not occur to Raney to question why his quarry should be doing ductwork at this hour. He came up softly behind him and said "Hey, you!"

The man looked over his shoulder. His mouth dropped open in surprise. Then a furious scowl came over his face and he rose with astonishing swiftness and waved a fourteen-inch pipe wrench at Raney.

"You better get outa here! Nobody's allowed in here but me," he shouted.

Raney kept the gun trained one-handed and flashed his shield. "Police officer. Put that wrench down and put your hands against the wall! Move it!"

"You better get outa here," said the giant again, as if he hadn't heard. He moved a step closer. Raney looked in the pale jerking eyes. The Bogeyman was maddened with fear, but Raney had the odd feeling that it was not fear of Raney's gun.

Raney clicked the Browning's hammer back and pointed the weapon at the man's face. Looking down at the muzzle of a cocked 9 millimeter pistol usually had a sobering effect on bad guys, but the giant seemed not to notice it. He seemed, in fact, to be working himself into a tantrum. His face was crumpled and red, and to Raney's amazement he had started to cry. "You're in real trouble if you don't get outa here," he bellowed. "I mean it!"

The detective worked to control his own growing anger. He understood that it was something of a standoff. This monster probably knew where Marlene was, might be the only person who knew, which precluded blowing his brains out.

As he thought of this it flashed briefly through Raney's mind that he might have permanently lost his taste for shooting people in the head. He could shoot him in the knee, but one, he might miss; and two, there was no guarantee that this jerk couldn't take him apart standing on one leg; and three, he might pop an artery in the guy and have him bleed to death, and then he would have to explain why he went into this with no backup, telling no one where he had gone.

No, the important thing was to find the woman. In a reasonable tone he began, "Look, fella, this is a gun. I'm a cop. Just keep quiet, back off and tell me where you have her and I'll get out of your hair."

At that moment there was sound behind the Bogeyman, a scrape of metal, a little cry, and Marlene Ciampi staggered, naked and bleeding, into the room.

Time seemed to slow down. The sight of Marlene's nude body caught Raney's attention, as evolution had designed. His pistol wavered. Alonso moved like a snake, faster than anyone that large had a right to move. The pipe wrench flashed out, breaking Raney's thumb and sending the pistol skittering away. It went off when it landed, the shot reverberating through the room and sending up a cloud of dust. Marlene screamed. Raney yelled, "Marlene! Run!" and launched himself at

Alonso, his left fist clenched in what he expected
would be his last punch in this life.

"V.T., you seen Butch?" asked Guma, eyes
wildly searching V.T.'s little office as if his chief
might be hiding behind the furniture. V.T. looked
up from his work. "Have you been swimming,
Raymond?"

"No, it's raining like a sonofabitch outside. Where
is he? I gotta see him right away."

"I think he's in court."

"Which one?"

"Beats me. It's *People v. Tighe*. Look it up on the
calendar."

Guma made for the door, and V.T. called after
him, "What's the crisis this time?"

"I got a lead on Marlene," he said, and told
V.T. what he had learned at the meeting with the
Bollanos.

V.T. whistled softly. "That's really interesting,
Raymond. I just had a cop named Raney in here a
half hour ago, desperate to have a look at the
material I'd pulled together on Mrs. Irma Dean.
Wanted the address of a building she owned. So
it looks like our girl was really on to something.
The only problem was, why would Dean want to
kidnap Marlene? She hasn't been active in that
case for months now."

"Maybe she found out something new."

"Maybe. But Raney came in here with this idea
that Irma Dean is also the mother of the guy that
Karp is now trying for a double murder, and I
looked, and sure enough, Irma Tighe was married
for seven years back in the fifties to a man named
Francis Tighe. Issue, one son. She called herself
Denise Brody, in those days."

"Holy shit! That's weird! How come Marlene didn't realize this a long time ago?"

"Beats me, but now that I recall it, when I gave her the file she seemed really distracted, like she didn't even want it any more. I just touched on the high points with her—money, mostly. I'm sure I didn't mention the connection. Not that there was any connection to make, because that was before Karp got involved with Tighe.

"Another thing: you say, 'weird.' It's weirder than you think. The original Mr. Tighe was something of a sinister figure: He had a police record from upstate. Ran some kind of spiritualist racket with violent overtones. Black masses, orgies, grave robbing—the whole nine yards. Accused of statutory rape, no conviction, but they got him on an extortion charge in Plattsburg and he served nine months."

He tapped a folder on his desk. "It's all here. After Daddy Tighe died in 'fifty-nine, Mom and son moved to the City, where she took up with and married a businessman named Horace Dean. A son from that marriage, too, but he's institutionalized, according to my info. Anyway, Mr. Dean died after a couple of years, in 'sixty-six, that was, and left her with three buildings on the West Side, but no money. He had a family from a previous marriage, who fought the will. She got a loan on one of the buildings for ready cash, but she needed an income. That's when she hooked up with Andrew Pinder and started this day-care operation."

"They let this lulu run a day-care center?"

"Why not? She had no record. She was the widow of a respectable businessman, with property. She was vouched for by pillars of the community. Just to make sure, she started using her middle name, Irma, but that's no crime."

"So if Marlene wasn't on to her racket," said Guma, "why the snatch?"

"The son, Felix. To protect him."

"What, to blackmail Karp? But why the call about the Mafia?"

"According to Raney, a diversion—and it worked." V.T. leaned back in his chair and pursed his lips thoughtfully. "But, I'll tell you—I could kick myself for not making the connection at the time, but Marlene thought she was being hexed, that somebody was using witchcraft against her.

"So maybe it wasn't blackmail at all. If Marlene was right about Dean, if she was kidnapping children and using them ritually, as—I don't know—human sacrifices to get the dark powers on her side, then who better to use than the consort of her son's chief tormentor?"

Guma rolled his eyes. "V.T., do you realize how fucking crazy that is? This is the twentieth century in New York, for chrissake!"

V.T. folded his arms. "I rest my case," he said.

As Karp left the courtroom after the verdict in *Tighe* he realized that he had no idea of where he was going or of what he was going to do with the remainder of the day. He would drop his briefcase back in his office and get something to eat. Then there was the evening. And the weekend. And then the rest of the month. And his life. Even his workaholism had failed him; he had no spirit left for putting more asses in jail. Several people passed him and congratulated him on the conviction. He nodded and mumbled conventions.

Then Roland Hrcany was standing in front of him, a sardonic smile on his lips.

"The winner and still champeen," Hrcany said. "You wouldn't believe the points the books are getting on you. You want to shave it a little one time, we could make a fortune."

"Sounds good. What's another shit-canned felony more or less?"

"Right," said Hrcany, falling into step beside Karp. "Listen, I came up here to get you. We pulled off that sting operation on the fencing ring. Got about a million in stolen goods and most of their mid-level management. There's a black dude we picked up. He's down in the pens. Says he knows you personally and needs to talk to you."

"Yeah, they all know somebody. Not tonight, Roland. I'm whipped."

Hrcany said, "Yeah. A wacky story, anyway. About one of his burglars went into a house after some antique dolls and got, I don't know, captured by some demon worshippers. Some shit like that."

Karp stopped walking. His stomach churned. "Let's see this guy, Roland," he said. "Now."


Before she knew it, before the pain from her bleeding feet could even register in her brain, Marlene was out of the room and running down the hallway. She did not know where she was going, except that she was not ever going back to that furnace room. She heard thumps and cries behind her, but she did not spare a thought for what was happening to Jim Raney.

The hallway appeared to end in a blank wall. The thumping stopped. Her teeth chattering with terror, Marlene threw open what appeared to be a closet door and went in, shutting the door quietly behind her. Blackness. Marlene stumbled forward. Now she could feel her feet again and was nauseated by the pain. She stepped again and her foot came down on air and she fell into the dark, stifling a cry. She was on a stairway.

Gingerly, she rose to her feet and, walking on the uninjured outsides of her soles, she descended a winding series of short flights. There was a light ahead, coming from a slit under a door. Opening this, she found herself in a dimly lit corridor. A metal fire door stood open to one side, and looking through it she saw her former prison. She went the other way, through a safety-glassed door that, to her delight, led out of the building.

She was in the open air: night, clouds above, lit by the eternal glow of the City, and the smell of recent rain. Her heart lifted as she scented freedom and she limped on. To either side high wooden fences walled off a narrow yard-like space between the building she had just left and the dark loom of one ahead. She tripped over something that clattered and spun away on the concrete. It was a plastic riding horse with wheels, suitable for ages three to five. She was in a play area for small children. Toys and wooden blocks were scattered around a grassy patch and the lumpy surface of a large sandbox. Marlene at last knew exactly where she was.

The back door into St. Michael's day-care center was locked. Marlene went to the sandbox and picked up a child's building block, a foot-long slab of solid maple. As she looked back along the concrete path she had traveled she gave a cry of dismay. A perfect line of dark, crescent-shaped bloody footprints led from where she now stood back into the darkness whence she had come. Alonso would be along shortly and he would know precisely where she had gone. She smashed a pane of glass in a small window near the door, twisted the window catch, and climbed in.

It was a utility room. By the gray glow coming from the yard she could make out large sinks, mop buckets, an automatic washer and dryer. She opened the dryer, found a T-shirt, ripped it into strips and bound her feet. She heard a door slam. It was some distance away, but it revealed that someone else was in the building. Maybe Raney had brought some back-up.

Then she heard a familiar bellow and the sweat broke out anew on her face. A glance around the little room showed nothing that could help her; she was not going to hold Alonso off with mops and brooms. Then the glint of dim light on the glass of an electric meter gave her an idea, something from an old movie. She went to the fuse box attached to the meter, yanked out all the fat cylindrical Buss fuses and threw them to the corners of the room. Then she hobbled out.

Outside the utility room door lay the glistening floor of the center's great ballroom of a main play area. It glowed in the light of the red emergency lamps like an anteroom to hell. As she started across the floor, she saw a huge shape appear at the entrance to the playroom. Clever Alonso! He had seen where she was going and had run around the corner and come into the child-care center from the front. Now he was between her and the only door out; she knew she could never make it back the long way she had come. He would catch her climbing out of the utility room or in the yard, among the children's toys.

Looking down, she saw to her horror that her feet were bleeding through their bindings, not footprints any more, but quarter-sized blotches. Even in the dimness they were visible against the pale linoleum. Alonso was clicking a light switch on the other side of the room. He was calling her, shouting threats. Suddenly, Marlene remembered the last time she was in the center, a century ago. A nice young woman was showing her the play equipment in a little room. There were windows in that room, windows that had shown the color of green trees on the street.

She moved cautiously through the door to the equipment room and closed it silently behind her. The room was filled with cold blue light from a streetlamp and Marlene felt an involuntary sob of frustration burst from her throat. There were windows but, this being New York, they were barred by heavy ornamental iron grilles. She heard heavy footsteps on the linoleum. They were slow and deliberate. Alonso was moving in the darkness from stain to stain, tracking her by her own blood. She looked desperately around the shelves, and all at once she saw her only, thin chance.

"I hear you got something to tell me, Matt," said Karp when the guards brought Matt Boudreau into the interrogation room.

"You mind if I sit down first? I had a hell of a day."

"Suit yourself," said Karp. The tall man slumped into a chair and arranged his ankle-length leather coat around his legs.

"About the doll . . ." Karp suggested.

"Yeah. Hey look, man, I was just there with a friend. Dude say, you know, pick yourself up a color TV, a VCR. I thought it was gonna be like some kinda flea market."

"I'll do what I can, Matt. No promises, but you give us some help on this other thing, I'll personally talk to the judge, all right?"

Boudreau flashed a gold and ivory smile. "Yeah, talk to the judge. OK, you know Junior Gibbs? No? Real little fella. OK, Junior and me been tight for a long time, you know? Hey, we walk down the street together, big an' little, it's a trip, dig? The ladies dig it, you understand?

"OK, so Junior brings me stuff from time to time, see if I can get a price for it. So, about two weeks ago, he comes to my apartment. He don't look so good—nervous, and all. And he shows me this, like, fancy doll. Like it was an antique, dig?

"Now, you understand, I do not deal in this kinda shit, no way. Stereo stuff, fur, jewelry is my main line. Silver. But no antiques. So I tell this to Junior, and he says, no, this doll is worth like ten, twelve grand. And he says, it's true, because this lady D.A. *told* him.

"So I told him, 'Shit, man, you tellin' me a fuckin' *D.A.* told you to rob this doll? They gonna put you *under* the jail, man.' Then he starts tellin' me 'bout all this devil shit. . . . I din listen no more man. I got no time for that, you know? They's enough shit goin' down on the street, I don' need to worry 'bout no devils, you understand?

"Anyway, he on me an' he on me, and finally I tell him, I give him two hundred an' a half for the doll. Maybe I could sell it somewhere, give it to some fox, whatever, and, like, him and me are tight, like I said. Then the crazy motherfucker say, he goin' back for more. He say they got a bunch of dolls, man, and it's a easy take off, because while they're doin' this devil jive, voodoo or some shit, there ain't nobody watchin' the house.

"Oh, yeah, the other funny thing was, it's like some kinda care center for kids, this place. They got all these kids in there watchin' the voodoo. They got this other kid tied down on this table and all these weird dudes jumpin' around and pouring shit on her, and cuttin' her and jackin' off on her. An' this old bitch runnin' the show, like a preacher in front of the church, you know? That's what he said, man. I din believe half of that shit myself.

"And Junior, he ain't no bigger than some damn kid hisself, so he could slip in easy. Anyway, the thing of it is, I saw where somebody kidnapped this lady D.A. and then when Junior din show up. . . ."

"When didn't he show up?" asked Karp.

"He was spose to come over my place last Wednesday. But he din show. I akst around, but nobody seen him. And that's like unusual, 'cause Junior, he don't travel much, you unnerstand? A homeboy. He ain't been to Jersey his whole life. So I figure somebody grabbed him, too. Maybe the same folks who grabbed the D.A. So I figure, you know, I'd like tell you."

But not until you were in trouble yourself, thought Karp uncharitably. He turned to Hrcany, who had come into the room during Boudreau's tale, and said, "Roland, call Balducci. He's probably home now, but get him! Ask him if he still has that fancy doll he picked up in that trash-bag case. If he's got it, get him to bring it here. If he hasn't, ask him if it was marked in any way, any kind of identifying mark. Matt, where's the doll you got off Junior?"

"In my place, if I ain't been ripped off yet."

"OK, Roland, get the address and the key and send Brenner along with Matt here to get it."

Hrcany looked bemused. He squinted at Karp and said, "You *believe* this horseshit?"

"I don't know what I believe any more, Roland," said Karp. "But I want to see both those dolls."

Alonso, bent almost double, followed the bloody smears across the floor of the playroom. That was another thing he would have to clean up. He had so much to do, he couldn't hold it in his head all at once. He had to get the witch tied up again; that was the first thing. His Mommy said. Tonight she had to go away. Then Brother would be OK. The witch was hurting Brother. That made Alonso feel bad, as if it was somehow his fault. Maybe it was. Everything was Alonso's fault. No matter how hard he tried, it never was enough. That's because he was bad. And stupid. Not like Brother. Felix was perfect.

Then he had to wrap up the policeman and take him away to the garbage. The policeman wasn't supposed to be there, so it was *his* fault. What else? Fix the window. And the lights. Alonso didn't think he knew how to do that. His Mommy would be mad. So many things to think about. He could never do it all. He would get a spanking. Hot tears came into his eyes and splashed down on the floor. Another thing: clean the floor.

He straightened up and cocked his head. That was a funny sound: a clicking, buzzing sound, like some kind of machinery, but irregular. The sound grew louder. He saw a white shape in the shadows coming toward him. The witch. Running? No, not running, faster than running, impossibly fast, with a noise of wheels.

Karp stared at the two dolls on the table in front of him as if waiting for them to confess. They were as silent as the three men in the interrogation room with him: Hrcany, amused, Brenner, carefully neutral, and Balducci, irritated and inclined to show it.

"Can I go now?" Balducci said. "I got dragged away from a wedding rehearsal for this bullshit. My daughter's getting married tomorrow, I don't need to be working nights."

The doll that Boudreau had told them he got from Junior Gibbs was a bride, wrapped in a white confection of satin and Alençon lace. At the mention of weddings, looking at the doll, Karp experienced a flash of pain so intense that it clouded his vision and choked his throat.

Idly, nervously, he fingered the fabric of the bridal doll, pulled at the ribbons that held its veil. The veil came loose in his hands. He turned the doll over. The high-necked gown was closed with a row of miniscule buttons down the back. He flicked at these with his fingers and they came open, revealing a white porcelain neck.

"Balducci, you ever look under your doll's clothes?" he asked.

The men laughed, and Balducci, flushing, said, "No, I never did. It's a doll, for cryin' out loud. And I told you—it don't lead anywhere."

"There's a number on this one," Karp said quietly. "Maybe there's a number on the other one." The three men rushed to look where Karp was pointing. On the nape of the bride's neck, where the porcelain met the fabric of the body, a six digit number in black ink was inscribed. In a moment they had unclothed the Lucy Segura doll enough to see a similar number in the same place.

"Well, look at that!" said Hrcany.

"It don't prove anything," Balducci snapped. "It don't prove she owned the doll. It could be like an antique dealer's number."

"It could," agreed Karp.

"I'll tell you what," said Balducci. "First thing tomorrow, I'll take both of these down to that doll guy and get them checked out. Maybe there's records, from auctions or something."

Brenner said, "You gonna skip the wedding?"

Balducci clapped his hand to his forehead. "Oh, shit! Yeah, well Raney'll do it. I'll call him tonight. That OK, Butch?"

"Sure. Fine," said Karp absently. He was recalling a conversation he had had with Marlene in her loft. He had been right about Marlene's case, hadn't he? The evidence wasn't there to connect Lucy Segura to Mrs. Dean. It was a fantasy, ludicrous in comparison with the evidence he had just used to convict Felix Tighe. He had been right; why then did he feel so massive a sense of despair?

These thoughts were interrupted by the entrance of Guma, who threw open the door to the interrogation room and announced his presence with a loud sneeze.

"Christ! I'm catching a cold!" said Guma, rubbing his eyes. When he saw Karp he brightened. "Butch! Damn it, man, I been looking all over for you. I missed you after court and I been sitting in your office for a couple of hours. A cop came by

looking for Roland and said you and him was
doing something up here. What's going on?"

"Not much, Goom. Playing with dolls. What'd
you want to see me about?"

"Nothing much. I just figured out what happened to Marlene. It wasn't the wise guys who
got her. It was that bitch with the day-care center."

Karp felt his face break out with cold sweat. He
cleared his throat heavily and asked, "What'd you
find out Guma?"

"She never went to the day-care center the night
she disappeared."

"What do you mean? Where did she go?"

"That I don't know yet. What I do know is that
Dean is definitely running a kid sex racket out of
that place."

Karp frowned. "How do you know that, Guma?"

"Informants," said Guma, too quickly.

Karp's eyes grew steely. "What kind of informants, Guma? What is the bullshit, anyway? I got
a judge and a minister who say that Marlene left
for the center. She never got there."

"Yeah. But it turns out that both the judge and
the minister are well known baby-fuckers themselves. Maybe they're Dean's customers too—"

"Are you crazy!" shouted Karp. "Rice and
Pinder? That's impossible!" But even as he said it,
Karp knew that it wasn't impossible at all. Marlene had sensed it at some level, the existence of a
criminal conspiracy involving people with creden-
tials so lofty that even to suspect them would be
to bring down the wrath of the establishment.
Which meant that they could do virtually anything
—exploit children, murder children, kidnap an
assistant district attorney—with no fear of getting
caught. Immoral certainty. And Karp had played

his role as part of the establishment, of the conspiracy of ignorance that made it possible.

"The other thing is," Guma went on, "V.T. and Raney think that Irma Dean is Felix Tighe's mother. V.T. thinks she could have been snatched because of her connection with you and the murder trial."

Karp gaped. "V.T.? What the fuck does *V.T.* have to do with this? Dean is Tighe's moth . . . ?" Then he stopped. Events were obviously out of his control. Instinct took over. When the game plan broke down, when all else failed, go for the basket. Karp stood up. "Fuck all this! Brenner, Balducci—get the dolls! We're going to see Mrs. Dean."

# CHAPTER

# 18

It was true, Marlene thought insanely: Once you learned to roller-skate, you never forgot. She had found neat rows of shoe-style neoprene-wheeled roller skates in the equipment room, most of them in kids' sizes but some for the teachers too. A pair of these was on her feet, not quite a fit, but far better than hobbling on bloody rags.

She snapped a look over her shoulder. Alonso was a dark shape panting and stamping like a water buffalo. He was getting closer. Marlene pumped her legs and pressed her stinging feet against the wheels. The shape and the sounds receded. She veered to the left and heard the footsteps accelerate as he moved to compensate. Marlene understood what he was doing. He couldn't catch her on the flat so he was staying far enough behind her and shifting direction, so as to herd her into one of the corners of the room.

It might have worked; the man was stronger and faster and Marlene was exhausted. But Alonso was not, as Marlene was, a child of the streets. He had not had four seasons of roller hockey, a ferocious game played with steel skates and home-made sticks on asphalt side streets strewn with broken glass, lined with cars, and peppered with speeding traffic. He was not maneuvering Marlene; she was maneuvering him, getting him away from the only available door to the street.

Marlene sensed the corner of the room approaching. She braked. He was two steps away. He reached for her. She accelerated briefly, faked right, cut left, dug her toe in, spun on it into a tight 180 degree turn, ducked double and whipped by him, missing the wall by inches and leaving him standing flat-footed, staring at the empty corner.

Then she was away, speeding across the room. The open door to the hallway loomed ahead. There were two shallow steps; Marlene bent her knees and took them in a single jump. Her wheels raced over the hardwood floor of the hallway. Yes! He had left the door unlatched. She braced, turned, flicked the door aside with elbow and hip and was again in the open, drizzly air, clattering down the front steps, free.

They took Balducci's car, which was conveniently double parked on Leonard Street. On the drive uptown, Balducci put the flasher on the hood, and they screamed up the West Side Highway at eighty, Karp silent and brooding in the back seat, Brenner and Balducci in front, talking cop talk and communicating with back-up forces over the crackling radio.

They turned off the highway at Seventy-ninth, onto Riverside Drive. Balducci took the flasher off the roof. They headed south, crossed Seventy-eighth Street. Suddenly, Balducci slammed on the brakes and the car skidded wildly on the wet street. "Jesus Christ! Did you see that?" Balducci shouted.

Karp had been thrown hard into the back of the front seat. He shook himself and sat up. "What was it?"

"A damn woman with no clothes on. Christ, I almost hit her!"

Karp rubbed the mist off the rear window and peered out. What he saw was impossible, yet achingly familiar. He knew that naked rear as well as he knew anything. "It's Marlene!" he yelled. "Go back!"

Balducci shifted into reverse for half a block. Karp grabbed a raincoat that lay crumpled on the back seat and leaped from the car while it was still moving. "Marlene!" he shouted, his heart in his throat. "It's me, Butch!"

Ten feet ahead of him, she shot him a wild look over her shoulder. He saw her face, a white mask of terror, the black hair plastered down with rain and sweat. She stumbled, slowed.

Then he had her, wrapping the raincoat around her, hugging her, kissing her face. She was shaking and sobbing. "The Buh-buh . . . the Bogey-man. . . ."

"There, there," said Karp inanely.

Balducci and Brenner were standing by the open doors of the unmarked car looking back at this scene in amazement. They heard heavy steps on the street, slowing to a stop. They looked up the street, where the headlights shone.

"Who the hell is that?" said Brenner.

"That's him! That's the guy!" yelled Balducci. Both detectives drew their pistols and moved away from the car.

"Hey, asshole—you!" Balducci shouted. "Get over here and get your hands up!"

Alonso stood stupidly in the headlights for a

moment, then darted out of the light, between two parked cars. The detectives took off in pursuit.

Karp led Marlene back to the car. He looked at her closely for the first time and cursed. "God! Baby, what did they do to you?"

"Shit! Don't ask. I don't know." She stiffened suddenly. "Butch! Raney tried to rescue me. He's hurt! We've got to find him."

"Marlene, the cops'll do that. I want you in a hospital right now."

She pulled away from him. Now that she was safe, energy was flooding through her body from some inner source, making her tremble with excitement. "No, it's a fucking maze in there—all her buildings are connected. They'll never find him. Come on!"

With that, to his amazement, she skated away from him, putting her arms through the sleeves of the raincoat as she rolled. Something heavy in the raincoat pocket banged against her leg.

She soon caught up with Balducci and Brenner, who were standing in front of the locked door of the day-care center, pounding on it and ringing the bell. Marlene skidded to a halt next to them and staggered. She grabbed Brenner by the sleeve, as much to support herself as to attract his attention. Her brain was working, but her body was fading rapidly. A black ring closed briefly around her vision. She shook her head and said urgently, "Doug. Jim Raney's in a second floor room at Two fifty-six West End Avenue. He's hurt and—"

"Marlene, OK—we'll get the back-up on it, but we got this big guy loose. . . ."

"No! That's the point—the buildings are connected! One of you has to go around there and block the entrance or he'll escape."

Brenner exchanged a quick glance with Balducci, who nodded, and Brenner took off at a run for the car. Karp came thumping up to the doorway, shouting, "What the hell's going on! Where did Doug go with the car? I got to get her to a hospital. . . ."

At that moment the door opened. Mrs. Dean stood there, in basic black, looking tired, but otherwise perfectly composed. "Yes? What is it?" she asked calmly.

For a moment the three of them stared at her. Then Balducci, who still had his pistol out, waved his shield and said, "Ma'am, we're in pursuit of a suspect. We think he might be highly dangerous. Please get out of the way and let us in."

Mrs. Dean didn't move. "What suspect?" she said contemptuously. "There's no one here but me." She glared and pointed a thin finger at Marlene. She said, "This woman has been persecuting me for months, and if you think—"

Marlene let out a bellow of rage and thrust forward. "You fucking bitch! Cut the shit! Your fucking fat son kidnapped me and you know it!" She leaped forward, thrusting Mrs. Dean aside with a roller-derby-style hip slam and made off at speed down the hallway. After a stunned instant, Karp and Balducci chased after her.

Down the hall and across the playroom again, Marlene retraced her escape, this time energized by fury. Now the door to the play area was open. She could feel the night air blowing in. The weight in the raincoat's pocket kept banging painfully against her thigh as she skated. She took it out. It was Raney's Astra Constable. She held it tight in her hand as she rolled through the courtyard.

Entering the house, she could hear Balducci

puffing close behind her. Karp must be in the rear. Cold wet weather always made his bad knee painful to walk on, she recalled, thinking also, *Poor Karp! I put him through so much trouble. And Raney. . . .*

Balducci caught up with her on the back stairs. He grabbed her by the arm. "Marlene! Jesus, wait up! Did you see him?" His eyes were frightened and wide in the dim light.

"No, but if he hasn't got past Brenner out front, he's either in the furnace room,"—she pointed toward it—"or upstairs. Raney's on the second floor unless he moved him."

The mention of his partner's name seemed to lend the man determination. He dashed down to the furnace room and came back.

"It's empty. What's the layout here?"

"There's a complete apartment on the first floor. The second floor is gutted. I don't know what's above that. There's a front stairway and a backstairs. That's these here." She indicated the stairwell that twisted up into darkness.

Balducci stared grimly up at it. "What the fuck am I doing here?" he said softly, as if to himself. "My daughter's getting married tomorrow." There was a sound of sirens in the street. "That's the back-up," he said to Marlene. "I'm going up. You wait here, understand!"

Marlene nodded weakly and slid down the wall. She put the little pistol back in the raincoat pocket. When Karp caught up, wincing, she was mechanically untying the roller skates.

Karp knelt beside her. "You nut!" he scolded. "Why the hell did you run off like that!"

Marlene tossed the skates away with a clank and the soft sound of wheels spinning. A driblet of blood ran from the top of each one. Karp looked at her feet in horror. "Good God!"

Marlene wiggled her bloody toes. "Yeah. It looks worse than it feels. I think I can walk all right. Help me up."

"The hell with that!" exclaimed Karp. "I'm going to carry you." He picked her up and rose to his feet. Her body felt like a bag of styrofoam.

Then the shots began from the floor above.

There were two, then two more and finally, in a few seconds, a fifth. Karp was too stunned to hold her and by the fourth shot she had wriggled from his grasp and gone up the stairs at a fast hobble. Karp made a clumsy grab to restrain her, slipped on the first step, landed wrong on his bad leg and with a pang like a lance of fire shooting up through his groin and spine, his knee locked up. Biting his lip, he began to crawl up the stairs on his hands and his good knee, the bad leg sticking out behind him like the tail of a petrified lizard. In the dark stairway, he heard another shot, and screamed, "Marlene!"

The first thing Marlene saw when she emerged from the staircase was Balducci lying unconscious on the floor, groaning softly. Then she saw Alonso leaning against the wall. He was wearing a blue flannel bathrobe with red piping, and blue terrycloth slippers. It was obvious that he had been getting ready for bed when Balducci burst in on him, making a desperate escape to nowhere but the land of dreams. In his hand, looking as harmless as a toy gun in that great mass of meat, was Raney's Browning Hi-Power.

Alonso was leaning against the wall. He was crying, and the front of his robe was darkened and wet. Little drops of red fell on his blue slippers as Marlene watched. He was bleeding.

He saw Marlene. "I'm hurt," he said. "I want my Mommy."

"Yes, she's coming, Alonso," said Marlene, her voice shaking. "But you have to give me the gun. It's not yours."

"Is too mine," he replied weakly.

"No, it's a policeman gun. Only policemen can have it. Now, give it here." Marlene took a step closer to him. There was a clatter and a thump behind her and Karp clambered into the hallway.

Alonso's face contorted with fear and terror and he raised the pistol toward the ceiling, then snapped it down and aimed it at Karp. He was shooting as little boys shoot with their fingers, as if he were throwing the bullets out by snapping his arm. He jerked on the trigger and the slug tore a chunk of plaster out of the wall two feet from Karp's head. His hand pointed high for another shot, but before he could bring it down again, Marlene took Raney's pistol from the raincoat pocket and put a bullet through the center of his upper lip. He fell crashing to the floor and, after the briefest interval, so did she.

Marlene awoke in a hospital bed, crying and struggling against the tapes that held her left arm to the bed frame. There was a tube running into her arm and a large, dark-faced woman in white was holding her shoulders. "Stop that shaking, honey, you'll pull your IV out," she said. Marlene tried to say something, but found her throat too parched to do more than croak.

The nurse saw her problem and gave her some

water. "Where am I?" Marlene asked. "Was I shot?"

The nurse said, "Roosevelt Hospital, and you're not shot that I know of. You came in for a checkup and exhaustion and dehydration and being generally beat up. Then you picked up a secondary staph infection and started spiking fevers. You been in and out for about a week. The folks're gonna be pretty glad to see you. You're a pretty famous person, you know that?"

Marlene looked around the small room. Every surface was crowded with floral arrangements. She started to remember what she was famous for and shook her head from side to side, as if willing the unwanted memories back into the dark. "I shot somebody," she said weakly.

"Yeah. You sure did. We got the papers and the TV waiting to talk to you. Your husband's been keeping them off. He's been here almost all the time you been under. Would you like to see him now?"

*Husband*? thought Marlene. *How long have I been sleeping?* She nodded and the nurse turned to go. "Oh, and you'll probably be glad to hear: The baby's fine."

Marlene cleared her throat. "Umm, what baby would that be?"

The nurse smiled. "Your baby, honey. You're close to eight weeks gone." Her eyes narrowed. "You don't mean you didn't know?"

"I can't be pregnant," said Marlene, flushing. "I have a coil in."

"Not any more you don't. They did a complete pelvic on you while you were out. It's routine in any, ah, case where there might have been, ah . . ."

"Sexual assault?"

"Uh-huh. Anyway, I've seen it before. When they tell you those things are ninety-eight percent effective, they mean it. Ninety-eight ain't a hundred."

Marlene felt sweat break out over her body, and a feeling of lightness, as if she were about to faint again.

A concerned look appeared on the nurse's face. "Are you feeling OK, dear?"

"Yeah. Yeah, I'm fine. A little shaky is all."

"I can understand that. Should I go get him for you?"

"Yeah, as long as he's here," said Marlene.

Karp came in, looking haggard and drawn. He sat down on a straight chair next to the bed and patted her hand tentatively. "Hi. You're back," he said. "How do you feel?"

"Physically, not bad. But I feel like I'm going to start crying and won't be able to stop." Silent tears were already starting, running down her cheeks and soaking the gauze pad over her missing eye. She forced a laugh. "Karp, we have to stop meeting like this."

"Yeah. In the whole history of the New York D.A.'s office, only two Assistant D.A.'s have ever been kidnapped in the line of duty, and both of them are in this room. We must be doing something wrong."

"I did everything wrong."

"No, we all let ourselves get isolated. You were right about the center and the child killings. I should have followed up on it, but I didn't. I wasn't paying attention. A common failing of mine. I'm sorry."

"Me too. How about a kiss, cutie? Pardon the leaky plumbing."

"Very nice," said Karp, after many a minute. "I really missed you, Marlene. I thought you were dead. Shit, I'm going to start crying too." He blew his nose into a tissue.

"You were here all the time?" she asked. "When I was out?"

"When I could get away. Your folks were here a lot. In fact they just left. And V.T., and Guma, and Raney came by a couple of times."

"Raney! God, I thought he was dead!"

"No, he's got some broken bones, but he's all right besides that. What he told me was, when the big guy knocked him down, he just played dead, like you're supposed to do when you get attacked by a bear. He got pounded a couple of times but basically he didn't think Alonso was all that interested in killing him. He just wanted people to leave him alone so he could run errands for his mother."

"Yeah. His big-boy job. And Balducci?"

"Also survived, but not by much. He took one in the gut. Apparently, he'll pull through. That guy wasn't much of a shot, thank God. I talked to Balducci this morning. He says to tell you thanks."

Marlene was silent for a minute, not wanting to ask but knowing she had to.

"I killed him, didn't I?"

"Yep."

Marlene felt something enormous rising out of her vitals, an impossible balloon filled with toxins. She threw back her head and howled, a beast noise, a sound that was pure pain. Karp jumped up on the bed next to her and tried to hold her, but she threw him off, thrashing her arms and legs and her head spastically, like an animal dying on a highway. The nurse stuck her head in the door, alarmed, but Karp waved her away.

After several minutes she collapsed into racking sobs, and then Karp was able to hug her, and say all the comfortless things that were all he had to offer: that it was in self-defense, that he was a murderer, that she saved both his life and her own life and Balducci's life. . . .

"It doesn't help," she replied through sobs. "I know all that. But . . . what he did, he didn't really do it. He didn't understand. He was like a baby. God in heaven, what she did to him, what his life must have been like! And almost his last words were, 'I want my Mommy.' " She mopped her damp face with a towel.

"If there's any evil in the world, that's evil," she said. "It's like that line from St. John—the sin against the Holy Ghost, for which there is no forgiveness in this world, or the next. I never really understood what that meant until now."

"You can't blame yourself, Marlene. You did what you had to do."

"Yeah? Maybe Irma felt she had to massacre little children and murder the soul of her own kid. No, you're right, but, oh hell! Life is such a shit pie!" She sat up on the bed. "Christ, I need a cigarette, and I know they won't let me smoke in here. So tell me, where is the old bitch now? In jail, I hope."

"She's dead."

"Dead? What happened?"

"She took poison."

"Couldn't handle being arrested, or what?"

"We never arrested her."

"What! Why not?"

Karp sighed. "It's a long story, Marlene. Are you sure you're up to it now?"

"Am I ever! You know me. Everything on the surface. I don't bury things in a dark Jewish soul like some people I could mention. I had my cry. It'll always hurt someplace, but I know where it is, and why it is, and, fuck it, life goes on. So tell me, what happened?"

"Well, Raney noticed Mrs. Dean at Felix Tighe's trial, and started wondering about that, and when he found out she was his mother—"

"What! Dean was Tighe's mother? Alonso's brother?"

"Half-brother. Yeah, she was his sweet mom—anyway, when Raney found that out, he realized that there was another connection between you and her, the fact I was putting her son on trial. So he went out to see Mary Tighe, Felix's wife."

"That shit was married?"

"Yeah. She turned up in the original murder investigation but Freddie didn't bother talking to her. I didn't even know she existed until Balducci told me. So Raney runs out and has a really interesting conversation. According to her, for about six months before he did the murder, Tighe kept her chained to the bed in a booby-trapped apartment, and came home every day or so to feed her and potty her and occasionally whip her with a coat hanger.

"She says he's doing this because she found out his big secret. One day, she overheard Felix making a date with a girl named Denise. So she follows him to the love nest and finds . . . are you ready for this? . . . Denise is Mom."

Marlene gasped in astonishment. "Mrs. Dean was getting it from her own kid?"

"So it seems. Also Felix was so fucked up behind it mentally that he totally denied it. He was in another zone completely. When the wife tried to get him to break it off, he went batshit and creamed her. After that, whenever he was with Mrs. Dean in her Denise mode, he would come home and whale her. Or beat up on other women, she thinks."

Marlene shook her head in wonder. "My God, what a family!"

"Yeah, to quote Guma, 'I heard of bad motherfuckers in my day, but I always thought it was a figure of speech.' Anyway, one day he forgot to chain her up and she escaped. Felix had to look for other prey. That may be why he slammed into Anna Rivas and why he killed the Mullens. Whatever—I got a conviction and I'm going to ask for the max, two consecutive twenty-five to life terms. And I'll get it, too."

"Good. So that's why Raney came after me."

"Right. He looked up V.T., who, I understand, ran some traces on Dean for you a while back, and V.T. told him about the third building. Since he knew you weren't in the other two, he figured you were there."

"And he told you?"

"And he didn't tell me. I probably wouldn't have believed him if he had."

"So how come you showed up with Balducci?"

Karp related the story of Matt Boudreau, Junior Gibbs, and the dolls. "But," he added, "even that might not have convinced me by itself."

"Why not?"

"Because you talked to Judge Rice before you left, and he swore that you were traveling to an innocent interview with Mrs. Dean about some janitor, and we thought we knew that you never got to the day-care center."

"But he *knew* I was going to the West End Avenue address. He *gave* me the address . . . Oh, my God! Not him!"

"Yeah, him. That's what tipped it for me. Guma came in with some information, which I don't want to know where he got it, that Rice and that minister, Pinder, were pedophiles. They were in with her deep."

"I'm nauseous," said Marlene weakly, covering her face with her hands. "I told him everything. I spilled my guts to that man, and he was *so* kind and *so* understanding. . . ."

"Yeah. Not-Nice Rice. Well named as it turns out. Not a judge anymore, needless to relate."

Suddenly, she straightened up. "Wait a minute! Why didn't you arrest Dean?"

Karp took a deep breath. "I'm coming to that. The fact was, we didn't have much of a case."

"Get outa here! No case, my ass! You had me, didn't you?"

"Yeah, but what did that prove? Alonso was dead. After she recovered, Dean expressed shock and horror that her dear departed son was this kidnapper and trash-bag killer. What a scandal, and so on, but *she*, of course knew nothing about it."

"But I *saw* her. She gave me all this devil crap. She drugged me!"

"Sure, but, once again, try to prove it. It's basically your word against hers. You have a long history of trying to persecute her, you were out of your mind, you're a D.A., for chrissake! And we'd be fighting some of the most respected names in the community. It'd look like a witch hunt. So to speak. And who's going to run the prosecution? Me? With my connection to you? Bloom? Give me a break!"

"But what about all the kids?"

"Yeah, also a great case," Karp said facetiously. "You know how easy it is to tear apart a kid's testimony on the stand? Kids under seven? And yeah, even if we're successful, not only do we put a couple of dozen kids and their parents through incredible torture, but we get her on some pissy little procuring charge. What would she get? Eighteen months? Somebody who has connections with the kind of people she knows? Maybe."

"So what'd you do?"

"I got Felix to rat her out."

"He ratted his *mother*?"

"Of course he ratted his mother. Felix Tighe? The prince?"

"But Butch, you did a deal with that scumbag?"

"Never! He's going for the max."

"So how. . . ."

"Freddie Kirsch."

"But Freddie doesn't work for us any more," said Marlene, confused.

"No. But Felix didn't know that when Freddie went to see him."

"You set it up? How come Freddie went along with it?"

"Actually, I didn't exactly set it up. I mean, how could I? Any representation made by Freddie acting as my agent could be construed as a deal."

"So?"

"It was the Queens burglary. He had to be sentenced for that, in court, in Queens. An opportunity. So I called the firm where Freddie works now and found out when he was going to be in court. Even lawyers like Freddie have to go to court once in a while. And I went up to him and congratulated him on the great job he did on preparing the case on Tighe. That was true at least. And he was knocked over.

"And then he congratulated me on winning the case. We shake, we laugh, we're buddies. Then I say, 'Hey, Freddie, Felix wants to see you, how about that?' 'What does he want to see me about?' says Freddie. 'I don't know, but do me a favor. Be in Queens County Court on such and such a day and just wave at him. See what he does. It could be important.'

"Now Freddie knows he was a fuck-up here. He's making a lot of money now, but still . . . he knows he crapped out in the majors. He could've had a big conviction, too, but he didn't have the balls for it. So here I am, his old Bureau chief asking him a favor, just wave at the guy. Of course he's going to do it."

"But wait a minute—how did you know Felix was going to go for it? He didn't really ask to see Kirsch, did he?"

"No, but I figured when he saw Freddie he'd remember that Freddie almost let him go once. Maybe he would do it again. And it worked. He called Freddie over, they had a nice chat, and Freddie saw him in Riker's the next day."

"But didn't Freddie tell him he wasn't with the office any more?"

"Of course. He said he was a private citizen. Felix just laughed, and said he knew a lot about a lot of things the D.A. would like to know about, and would Freddie do a deal. Freddie says, hey you want to do your duty and reveal crimes, that's OK by me, but I can't deal. Felix laughs.

You understand—he's *reading between the lines. He's clever!*

"And then God reached down from heaven and touched Kirsch with inspiration. Freddie looks Tighe in the eye and says, 'You know, Felix, if it was up to me, you'd be out of here.' Which was brilliant because, of course, it's perfectly true. And then Felix gave it to us."

"What? Come on, I'm dying here!"

"A safe deposit box, full of records of all her clients, names, dates, what they paid for, the kids involved. And pictures. Mrs. Dean was obviously preparing to cover herself if anything happened. She had shots of some fairly prominent citizens in the act with kids. And worse stuff, too. Snuff films of their rituals. She used to gloat over them with Felix, and he used to run them to the bank, which is how he knew about the box."

"And when you showed her the evidence, she killed herself?"

"I don't think it was the evidence, or the fear of going to jail. I think it was Felix. Her whole life was based on a fantasy about him being this noble son of the dark forces. When he turned her in, she collapsed. The air just went out of her."

"You were there?"

"Yeah. We showed her the stuff and told her how we got it. She didn't say anything. After a while she asked for a glass of water and took out a regular drugstore vial. She took a pill, right there in front of us, as calm as ice, and in thirty seconds she was blue and convulsing."

Marlene was silent. He went on, "Felix did not reciprocate. He didn't bat an eye when we told him his mother was dead. Just asked us if the deal was still good. He was very upset when I congratulated him on his free and public-spirited help in solving his mother's crimes. *Then* he went crazy.

"By the way, that's why she grabbed you. Pinder spilled the whole story when we braced him. He was the high priest, or whatever, by the way. She thought all of Felix's troubles came from someone working a spell on him, or some shit. She picked you as the witch. They were going to take you out to bare earth and run an iron stake through you. It's traditional. The only thing that saved you was they had to wait for the full moon."

Marlene shuddered and Karp put a protective arm around her.

"You better rest now. You have to get out of here soon—we got a bunch of conspiracy to commit murder cases to prepare off this, and you're in charge. Not that we're going to get much. A schlemiel off the street could plead them on insanity. But it'll keep them away from kids. For a while."

Karp spoke briefly about the office, politics, the mysterious collapse of his murder case against Salvatore Bollano. He stopped when he saw that Marlene was barely listening.

Marlene had flopped back on the pillows, suddenly exhausted. The mention of returning to work had brought something urgently to mind. "Uh, Butch—I have some news, too," she said nervously.

"Oh?"

"Well, you remember how I was always sick the last couple of months, and we thought it was stress and psychosomatic and all that?"

"Yeah?"

"Well, it wasn't. It was morning sickness. I'm pregnant."

She watched his face closely. First he started to smile, as if she was cracking a joke. Then, as he observed that she wasn't joking, a look of pure delighted amazement came over his face, and he looked about ten years old. "But," he protested, "how come you didn't know? I mean, periods and all. And you have one of those thingees, don't you?"

"Well, I've tried to shield you from my various female problems, my dear, but in common with many of us skinny hard-driving career girls, I'm about as regular as a rusty alarm clock. And yes I did have one, but it appears that one of your little spermatazoons laid a body check on my thingee and went in to score. It happens."

A grin spread slowly across Karp's face until it became an image of complete joy. His gray eyes, which ordinarily had the sheen of sabers, almost twinkled.

"You're happy, huh?" she asked.

"You could say that. You must be knocked out."

She nodded. "Funny isn't it? Out of all this death and misery and murdered children. *Race de Cain, ton supplice, Aura-t-il jamais une fin?* as Baudelaire asks. And the answer? The envelope please. Better kids. Easy, huh?" She saw he was staring mindlessly at her, the idiot grin still fixed to his face. "What are you thinking about?"

"Oh, this, us, a family. It just occurred to me that that's all I ever wanted in life. It's just such a gift. . . ."

"I hope that means you'll change diapers."

"Yeah, but I thought I'd mostly do the athletic training. Like, we could start this one at point guard. Then as the other four came along we could work them into the team. How does 'Magic Karp' sound? It has a certain ring to it. 'Larry Bird Karp'?"

"It's a boy, huh?"

"Of course, it's a boy. I mean, face facts, Marlene. There's no money in girls' basketball."

He rattled on, and she let him, enjoying his delight, but at a distance. She was relaxing now, tuning in to the secret messages her body was sending and enjoying it. *I'm going to plunge into this*, she thought. *I'm going to treat it as a gift, a surprise from cruel heaven. And I'm going to call her Lucy.*

# Save up to $400 on *TWA* flights with The Great Summer Getaway ∅ from Signet and Onyx! ⊗

## Look for these titles this summer!

### JUNE

**EVERLASTING**
Nancy Thayer

**EARLY GRAVES**
Thomas H. Cook

### JULY

**INTENSIVE CARE**
Francis Roe

**SILK AND SECRETS**
Mary Jo Putney

### AUGUST

**AGAINST THE WIND**
J.F. Freedman

**CEREMONY OF INNOCENCE**
Daranna Gidel

### SEPTEMBER

**LA TOYA**
La Toya Jackson

**DOUBLE DOWN**
Tom Kakonis

*SAVE* the coupons in the back of these books.
*REDEEM* them for TWA certificates
**(valued from $50 to $100 depending on airfare)**
*The more GREAT SUMMER GETAWAY coupons you collect,
the more you get.* (up to a maximum of tour)

## IT'S THE BEST DEAL UNDER THE SUN!

• Send in two 2 coupons and receive: 1 discount certificate
for $50, $75, or $100 savings on TWA flights
(amount of savings based on airfare used)

4 coupons: 2 certificates
6 coupons: 3 certificates
8 coupons: 4 certificates

---

**B O N U S**

# And to get you started, here's a BONUS COUPON!

**B O N U S**

• This bonus coupon is valid only when sent in with three
or more coupons found in the books listed above.